BECKAM

In the Company of Snipers

Book 20

Irish Winters

COPYRIGHT

Beckam; In the Company of Snipers, Book 20

Copyright ©2019 by Irish Winters
All rights reserved

First Edition

This is a work of fiction. Names, characters, dialogues, places, and incidents either are the product of the author's imagination or are used fictitiously. Any resemblance to actual events, locales, or persons, living or dead, is entirely coincidental. The publisher does not have any control over and does not assume responsibility for author or third-party websites or their content.

No part of this book may be reproduced, scanned, or distributed in any printed or electronic form without permission. Please do not participate in or encourage piracy of copyrighted materials in violation of the author's rights. Purchase only authorized editions.

Cover design: Kelli Ann Morgan, Inspire Creative Services
Cover image: Paul Henry Serres Photography, www.paulhenryserres.com
My gorgeous cover model: Francis Brunet again!
Interior book design: Bob Houston, eBook Formatting
Editor: Linda Clarkson, Black Opal Editing and Proofreading

ISBN Paperback: 978-1-942895-81-7
ISBN eBook: 978-1-942895-80-0
Library of Congress Control Number: 2019917859

In the Company of Snipers

You can find Irish Winters

On Facebook:
https://www.facebook.com/author.irishwinters

On Twitter: https://twitter.com/irishwinters1

For news on upcoming releases, sign up for Irish Winters' Newsletter at IrishWinters.com.

For more information about all my books, visit IrishWinters.com.

IN THE COMPANY OF SNIPERS

This series revolves around former Marine scout sniper, Alex Stewart, and his covert surveillance company, The TEAM, home-based out of Alexandria, Virginia. An obsessive patriot and workaholic, he created the company to give former military snipers like him, a chance at returning to civilian life with a decent job, security, and a future.

This is not a serial with each book ending at a cliffhanger. *In the Company of Snipers* is a collection of passionate love stories involving strong women and men who are tough enough to take on the world alone. Each is a stand-alone read, complete in itself.

Spoiler alert: Every story contains adult scenes including sexual situations (some explicit), language, and violence. I don't write sweet romance, so be forewarned.

Book 1, *ALEX*, reveals how The TEAM came to be, as well as how Alex met Kelsey, how they fell in love and fought all odds to stay together. Each of the following books is a complete romance in itself, where, in the course of an active TEAM operation, one agent comes face to face with his or her demons. The men and women I write about are all patriots and warriors, dealing with what they've lived through or mistakes they've made.

It's my hope that you will come to realize along with my heroes...

Love changes everything.

Prologue

"Run! Alana, run!"

Alana wanted to scratch Molina's eyes out for the hard, relentless hand shoving her along the dock. But her husband was right. Their time in Honduras was over. Their profit-making schemes ended. They had to run. Rumors of a military coup d'état ending President Manuel Estevez's reign had been brutally confirmed during the night. His closest confidants were now being rounded up and shot. Cold-blooded General Morales was in charge now, and he was not known for leniency.

Molina carried the heavy backpack filled with their precious jewels, their cash-on-hand, and the illegal documents he'd paid dearly for. Their entire life was in that bag. Their future. Alana only carried their daughters. One-year-old Camilla clung to Alana's neck like a frightened monkey. But precious, elfin Acindina slept soundly in the baby sling Alana had hurriedly fashioned from the thin scarf at her neck.

Acindina should've never been born. She certainly hadn't been planned, not with this country's government in shambles. But, oh, how desperately she'd been wanted.

While Camilla was her father's pride and joy, Acindina was Alana's fault, the dearest sin of her life. Soon the truth of her parentage would be harder to hide but for now, Molina believed she was his. Acindina was safe. But Alana had noticed the changing hue in her month-old yet still dark baby eyes. The barest hint of *his* blue was just beginning to show around the edges. Not Molina's murky brown like Camilla's when she'd been born. No, Molina's eyes were a dark, muddy brown, and Camilla's would be as well. This shade of blue belonged to the other man in Alana's life. The man she loved.

Acindina was a miracle. A blessing. After Camilla's traumatic birth, Alana had been told her body would never withstand another pregnancy. That she must never fail to use birth control. Alana had believed her doctor. He'd sent her home from the hospital with a year's supply of birth control pills, and she'd been faithfully taking them until...

Three months later, an American journalist with as Spanish a name as one could ever imagine, came along. Carlos Salas. The offspring of the single Spanish branch in a nearly all-white American family tree that had bred Harvard graduates for generations. He still starred in Alana's dreams.

Carlos was everything Molina was not. Brave. Adventurous. Tall and blonde with crisp, golden hairs on his muscular arms and long legs. Strong. His bright blue eyes seemed able to see what others had missed. The future of beleaguered Honduras. The upcoming revolution. The demise of yet another corrupt president. A young woman's broken heart.

Their affair happened soon after Camilla's birth, but Alana had been lonely long before that. When Carlos came along, she'd fallen into his arms like a star-struck fool, hungry for his hugs and kisses and—yes, his brand of brash, American love. He'd said he loved her within days of their meeting. He'd even said he'd buy her safe passage to America when, or if, the revolution started. She'd believed him. Why wouldn't she? He was the brave one in her life. Not Molina. Though now, as the soles of her shoes slapped against the narrow wooden dock leading her way out of Puerto Cortes, she wondered.

Had Carlos used her to get inside the presidential palace? She'd certainly taken him there often enough. It had been fun. Almost like a date. But had he only said what she'd desperately needed someone—anyone—to tell her? That she was still breathtakingly beautiful. That she was the woman of his dreams. Would he meet her in New York City like he'd promised? Somehow, running away with Molina negated every promise Carlos had made. That he'd keep her safe. That he loved her. If he'd loved her as he'd so ardently declared, why wasn't he here now? Carrying one of her babies? Helping her to get away from this nightmare? Watching out for her with those sharp blue eyes of his? Ready to die for her?

Molina was. For the first time in months, he'd strapped on his underarm holster. Despite the tropical heat of this awful night, his two favorite pistols were hidden beneath his leather jacket. He would kill for Alana, and she knew it. Would Carlos?

"Hurry. Hurry!" the ugly, whiskered man at the edge of the dock called out, waving for them to run faster. "We must go. Now!"

"Faster, my darlings," Molina urged.

As if she could hold onto two babies and run. Sweating and out of breath, she growled back, "These girls are heavy. I'm hurrying as fast as I can."

The moment she came within reach, the ugly man grabbed Camilla out of Alana's arms and handed her off to another uglier man on the gangplank. He, in turn, passed the frightened, screaming one-year-old to yet another smelly brute. They were like a line of beastly firemen in sloppy pants, passing her daughter like they'd pass buckets of water to quench a burning building. Next, Alana found herself lifted off her feet, swung over the rail, and handed off to yet another foul-smelling guy.

"Shut the fuck up!" The sailor—or whoever held Camilla—yelled at her.

"Mama!" she shrieked, her head tipped back and her mouth wide open.

"Give me my daughter, you slob," Alana ordered in her most imperious tone. "You're scaring her."

"Aye, she's got a mouth on her, I'll give you that. You'd better shut her up or I'll toss her overboard," he threatened, pointing Alana toward the wooden bench at the front of the foul-smelling boat. "No one said we were transporting a bunch of whining brats. Sit yer arse down and shut up. Then I'll give you the kid."

Where was Molina? Why didn't he run to her defense? Carlos would have.

Glancing back, she caught her husband in time to see him handing over the bulging leather envelope he'd carried. Stuffed with the last of their cash-on-hand, he gave it to the first smelly sailor who'd yelled at them to hurry.

"Don't!" she yelled at her idiot husband. "What have you done to us? How could you?"

He glared at her as the envelope left his fingers, his eyes hard and his chin lifted. "Perhaps I should ask you the same, wife."

Wife? She had no time to consider what he meant by that ugly tone, no time to worry what he thought he knew. The sailor holding Camilla like a bag of rotten garbage had just shoved the girl at Alana with a nasty, "Brat's all yours. Gag her yap 'fore she gets us all in trouble."

Alana caught her frantic child to her breast. But the dirty vessel rocked sideways with an incoming swell, and Alana lost her footing. She reached for the back of the bench, but because she'd worn her Sunday flats to mislead anyone who might've been watching their estate, she was now sliding across the slippery, slimy deck with a screaming daughter who would not shut up. The ends of the baby sling around Alana's neck unraveled under Camilla's frantic need to hang on. In the chaos, the sling flipped upside down, and...

No! Acindina tumbled onto the deck.

"You're choking me," Alana snapped at Camilla, reaching for the blanket still bundling Acindina. The babe hadn't made a peep when she'd fallen. All Alana needed was to grab onto one corner, and the infant could go on sleeping in her padded nest.

With another swell, the boat pitched hard against the pier, jolting everyone on board. Camilla screamed, digging her fingernails into Alana's neck, choking her. Acindina rolled out of her blanket and—

"No!" Shoving Camilla away, Alana dove for her baby. Acindina was wide awake, but precariously close to rolling off the deck. Her frightened bleat pierced Alana's heart.

Now on her hands and knees, crawling as fast as she could to get to Acindina, she shouted, "Someone help me! My baby!"

The boat's motor growled to life. The entire deck shuddered. Some oafish bastard bellowed, "We ain't got time for this shite. They're coming! We gotta git!"

"My baby!" Alana shrieked again as—*God! No!* The little girl she loved more than anything else, disappeared over the edge. "Acindina! Goddamn it, Molina! Where are you when I need you? Acindina! Baby! Mommy's coming!"

At last! Molina did something right. He raced past the stupid, stupid men he'd hired to help his family escape Honduras. With one clumsy leap, he was over the railing and diving into the murky, midnight water.

"Save her!" Alana ordered her husband as she clung to the lower part of the rail, her heart pounding as the catastrophe unfolded in the dark, murky waters below.

"Papa!" Camilla bawled.

"Will you shut up?" Alana screamed back at her, sick for the child she'd lost and so damned pissed at the idiot one-year-old bellowing as if she were the only one in the world. She wasn't. Hadn't been since her sister had arrived.

But there was no sign of Molina or Acindina in the murky depths. No sign of life. Not even a ripple of bubbles. Well past midnight, it so hard to see past the pearlescent, diesel-coated waves. Only flotsam bobbed at the surface. Not Acindina. Not Molina.

"Shite!" one of the sailors hissed as he tossed the heavy, wet rope from the dock onto the deck. "If we don't get underway now, we're finished. Load up, men. We're about to get bloody. Get that guy back in the boat. Leave the brat. Jesus Christ, this was supposed to be easy."

Still on her knees at the edge of the deck, Alana turned all her fury on the man who had to be the captain of this piece-of-shit vessel. "If you save my baby, I'll pay you another million."

His brows narrowed like a snake's would, if snakes had been born with brows. "Guys, you heard the lady—"

He never finished his order. Molina had surfaced and tossed her baby on deck. "I tried," he sputtered, clinging by his elbows to the side of the boat, his eyes dark as he squeegeed a hand over his face.

Alana scrambled to the quiet bundle he'd just treated like a fish. *Please, please, please God, let her be safe.* She grabbed Acindina to her and frantically peeled the sodden blanket away from the child's face. But, yes. Sadly, yes. Her only reason for living was drowned and cold. Not moving. Not breathing. Dead in her arms.

"You killed my baby!"

He refused to meet her gaze. Neither did he deny her accusation.

Camilla barreled into Alana's side, sobbing and frightened and—still alive. Still breathing. Still warm. Just not the daughter Alana loved. *Damn her to hell. This is her fault. She'll pay for this.*

"Get away from me," she snapped, holding a fist out to her daughter instead of an open palm. "Stay back or I'll throw you into the sea next. Let's see if Papa saves you!"

No one spoke as two sailors dragged Molina on board and the boat got underway. Yet even as the vile words had flown out of her mouth… Even when Camilla bounced off her hard fist... Alana couldn't believe she could ever be so wicked to a helpless child. But she had. And she meant it. Acindina was gone, and with her, Alana's love for Carlos. Yet Molina's favored brat still lived. Breathed. Scrambled into her worthless father's arms like the conniving little bitch she was.

Still clinging to the limp body of her precious child, Alana turned away from her husband and her firstborn. "I love you," she told the silent corpse in her arms, smothering Acindina's perfect baby lips with desperate kisses and salty tears. She cupped the back of that sweet angel's head one last time. "Oh, baby," she breathed, her heart broken but hardened at the same time. "I will always love you best. I will never forget. You are the only child of my heart, made of light and love and everything true. Only you."

She knew it then. Losing Acindina was her penance for the lies she'd told Molina. For falling in love with another man and cheating with him on her too-absent husband. Like the unrequited love for the American journalist she would never see again, this little girl wasn't meant to be. Acindina was as lost to Alana as Carlos. Karma had reached out and made certain of that.

But Alana still had Molina. That was something. He was weak, but he would forgive her. He always did. Eventually. Only now he would change his name to Luis. They would become Americans, the Lopez family. Honduras could go to hell.

Chapter One

Eight Years Later

"You fed the pigs yet?"

"No, sir. Haven't had time. Been wrangling Lucky back into his pen all morning."

"Alone?"

"No big deal." Beckam shrugged. But yeah. Alone. With his dad on blood thinners after a heart scare, Beckam wasn't about to let him take chances with the champion bull. At eighteen, he was too young to lose his father.

Ross Garner had undergone a heart procedure the week before last that included three stents, and scaring Beckam to death. Since then, he'd stepped up and taken as much load off his dad as he could. Every morning, he got his butt out of bed before the rooster crowed, fed and milked the Garners' twenty head of dairy cattle, fed the pigs, mucked the cow barn, fired up the ATV, and checked the fields to make sure none of their one hundred fifty head of Charolais beef cattle had gotten into trouble overnight.

After he'd finished his chores and gotten Lucky squared away, Beckam woke his younger sister Mary Lou. It was her job to feed the chickens, collect eggs, and milk her two goats before school. That gave her an hour to do those chores, eat breakfast, and be ready by the time the bus rolled to a screeching stop in front of their house. If she'd cared about helping her dad, that is. But Mary Lou was a spoiled fourteen-year-old diva, who hung with the popular kids at school this year and didn't have time to waste on chores.

On the days she dawdled, or whined she was too tired or too sick or too—*whatever*, Beckam did her chores for her. Like it or not, those goats she'd had to have for 4-H, needed to be fed, watered, and milked every morning. The poor things couldn't wait for her to get a *'round tuit'*. Some things plain had to get done. So again today, Beckam had done his chores and then some. And he hoped his dad lived forever because of it.

This morning was no different. After he'd done her chores, he'd told Mary Lou twice to get her butt moving. He'd showered, dressed for school in his usual uniform, jeans and button-up shirt, then finished his AP math homework before his dad came into the kitchen. Beckam had even fixed a pan of stone-cut oatmeal, hoping his dad would join him. It'd be nice to have company.

Usually, his mom Carolyn would've fixed breakfast for everyone, but she'd gone to California yesterday on some writer's convention. She'd almost changed her mind about leaving so soon after Ross's procedure, but he'd insisted. He and Beckam could take care of things.

So, Beckam took care of things. Everything.

"You use the staff on that bull like I told you?" Ross asked.

He was still dressed in a t-shirt and flannel pajama bottoms. His eyes used to be bluer than the sky, but they'd turned gray this past winter. Grayer. And he'd gotten thinner. He looked tired again today. Come to find out his heart had three blockages. He'd collapsed while cutting the first crop of grass hay this spring, ended up in the emergency room before noon, then surgery that evening. The stents saved his life, but he'd come home from the hospital feeling weak and discouraged. Said he should feel better now that his heart was fixed, and he was getting more oxygen.

But he didn't. If anything, he tired quicker, and he fell asleep if he sat in one place for too long. Said it was hard to think, that he felt old and unneeded. Doctors told him to be patient, that every heart procedure was an invasive setback for his entire body. That recovery took time. *Just take it easy. Take your meds. Rest. You'll see; you'll be back on your feet in no time.*

But Beckam worried. He'd never seen his hero looking so old nor acting so defeated. It just wasn't fair. Ross Garner was a father to be proud of. Former Army, he'd been one of the first into Baghdad, fighting Saddam Hussein and the million-man army that ultimately offered up the quickest surrender in history.

"Yeah, Dad. Hooked the staff to Lucky's nose ring and snapped a lead to his halter just like you showed me. He was pretty docile, but I was extra careful." *You can trust me. I'd never let you down.*

Some farmers scoffed that bull staffs were old-fashioned, that a sturdy halter was good enough. But they were wrong. No bull was safe, didn't matter the breed or the time of year, or if you'd hand-raised him from a calf, bottle fed him, and known him all his life. There were no two ways about it. Twelve-foot staffs kept a bull twelve feet away from his handler, whereas a leather or rope lead let you think you were in charge and that he was a pet, when he was anything but. A lead that short let a bull run over you the instant he decided you were in his way.

So, yeah. The Garners stuck with what worked. Bull handling, even a docile breed like this Charolais, was dangerous work, and Beckam had been taught to never take chances.

Ross Garner leaned across the kitchen sink to peer out the window. "Damn that rack of ribs. If Lucky keeps this up, I'll turn him into brisket. I swear I will. This time I'll barbecue him, and we'll have all the neighbors over. I can't have him tearing things up every spring."

Which Beckam knew his dad would never do. The three-year-old Charolais bull meant no harm; he was just horny. Oklahoma springs always turned Lucky into a randy dandy. Like any other red-blooded, champion male, he wanted a chance with the bovine ladies calling to him from the pasture beyond the barbed-wire fence.

Based on a two-hundred-eighty-three-day gestation period, Lucky was going to get lucky real soon. For the herd to drop their calves early next March, Beckam planned to turn Lucky out into the field with the ladies the first of June. Which meant Beckam had three long weeks to wait, and Lucky would make sure those three weeks were exciting. He was smart for a bull.

"No, Dad, I've got this. Figured I'd sink that twenty-foot steel post we've been talking about after school today. Anchor it in concrete. Let it cure for a week, then hook one end of that tow chain to his nose ring, the other to the stake. That ought to fix his wagon."

"Hope so, son," Ross breathed. "We can't have a bull roaming the county while you're in school."

Beckam liked that his dad included him in that *we*. "No, we can't. Only two weeks left. Finals are this week. If I needed to, I could miss the last week of class. It's mostly a waste of time."

"No, son. You belong in school. I'll keep him penned in the barn while you're gone, then help get that stake in the ground tonight."

Beckam was not going to argue about who helped who with that stake. His dad wasn't up to much strenuous work yet. Digging that hole and mixing concrete was no big deal. Beckam could handle tonight's chore, easy.

"You want a bowl of oatmeal?" he asked. "It's fresh, and I left some of Mom's strawberries for you."

That made Ross smile. He shook his head as he pulled up the chair at the end of the table. His chair. The one to the left of Beckam's. "Don't mind if I do. Thanks, son. You're sure growing up fast, you know? Too fast. How's end of year testing going? You going to pass?"

"Yes, sir." As if flunking were ever a problem. It was the tenth of May. Only three more weeks of school, and Beckam would be a senior, a senior with big plans. June first, he had an appointment with an Army recruiter to take the high school student version of the ASVAB, the Armed Services Vocational Aptitude Battery test. He'd had that scheduled for months, plus he'd successfully finished his junior year in JROTC, Army Junior Reserve Officer Training Corps. Things were looking up. If life didn't throw him any fastballs, he'd be in boot camp this time next year.

"What are you going to do with yourself after school's out?" Ross asked as he poured two cups of coffee, one for himself, one for his only son.

Beckam smiled. Now was his chance to share his good news with his dad. But the second he opened his mouth—

SCREECH! BANG! Moooooo...

Ross shoved his chair back. "What the hell was that?"

By then, Beckam was one foot out of the porch door, craning to see the gravel road that ran from east to west in front of their home. Looked like Mrs. Jones' Ford, and— Oh, God, she'd hit a cow. A Holstein. The dying animal lay thrashing and bellowing alongside the ruined vehicle.

"Car crash, Dad. Mrs. Jones hit a cow. Looks like one of Strickland's. Call 911," Beckam ordered as he grabbed his pistol from its holster hanging on the hook beside the door.

"You be careful, son," Ross called out, the house phone already cradled on his shoulder.

"Always," Beckam replied, his throat tight and his mouth dry as he headed toward the wreck, knowing what he had to do next. The cow was suffering, bellowing. Its back had to be broken. This couldn't wait.

"Jesus," he murmured as he crossed the ditch bank to the road, already smelling the stink and gore. Collisions with cattle were never merciful or clean, and somehow, Mrs. Jones had broadsided this poor old sister.

When a vehicle collided with a long-bodied animal, it didn't just bounce off the grille like an empty soda can, and the driver didn't just drive off dismayed at that unfortunate encounter like he might a feral cat. Physics showed up with dastardly consequences.

The force of this impact had curve-balled the Holstein's rear end around and into the driver's side, shattering the window and mashing the driver's side door. To make matters so much worse, everything in that animal's three stomachs had been horribly released through that broken window and into the entire front seat, drenching Mrs. Jones with a firehose of excrement and urine. As if that weren't bad enough, her one-year-old twins in their backseat booster seats, were equally drenched, scared, kicking their feet, and screaming bloody murder.

Mercifully, Beckam dispatched the Holstein first with one steady round to the poor thing's head, then pulled Corky and Carrie out of the car and ran them back to his father. Mary Lou was on the back porch by then, still dressed in her sleep shorts and tank top, but at least she'd put her bra on. He handed the twins to her and turned back around before she could complain she hadn't had her coffee yet.

"How bad is she?" Ross called after Beckam as he headed back to the wreck.

"She's unconscious," Beckam tossed over his shoulder as he ran, his heart pounding and very afraid Mrs. Jones would be dead by the time he returned. He ran faster. Cleared the ditch and knelt at the bashed-in driver's side door. That Holstein had hit hard. This was going to be bad.

"Ma'am, are you hurt? Can you hear me?" he asked as he grabbed the door handle and pulled. The door was concave from the force of impact, but thankfully, it wasn't stuck. The latch sprang open. Beckam jerked the door open as wide as it would go, then wedged himself between it and the front seat.

He was scared. Mrs. Jones still hadn't answered.

On a good day, she was a perky, platinum blonde with bright green eyes and a dynamite figure. She'd been friendly enough the one time she'd talked to him, the night he'd won the state wrestling match. It'd been held at his high school, Eisenhower High. His parents were there. All his friends. His coach. Yet she'd walked up to him and shook his hand like she knew exactly who he was. Like they were old friends or something. She couldn't have been more than five years older than he was, but why she'd been there, he never knew. Surely, she hadn't come just to watch a bunch of sweaty teenage boys wrestle. But he hadn't forgotten the light in her eyes or the way she'd said, "Way to go, champ. I knew you could do it."

At the time, he didn't know what she was talking about. But soon after that night, word in town was she filed for divorce from her farmer-husband, told him she was headed back to Tulsa and what she called civilization. She'd had enough of country living, smelly cows, and tornado alley. She was taking the twins, moving out and up. Word in town was she also had a boyfriend, not that Beckam cared what folks said. Gossip traveled like lightning in small towns like Horse Hollow, Oklahoma, but as much as the rumor persisted, that boyfriend was not him.

"Hey, can you hear me?" he asked again, needing her to wake up and crawl out of the car. Not like she could. He'd reached between her legs and the steering wheel, but the wheel's adjust lever wasn't working. He couldn't get the wheel out of her lap. Man, she had to have been going ninety when she'd hit that cow.

She didn't answer this time, either. Just moaned and squirmed, started to shake and shiver. No wonder. Her feet and legs, both bent at unreal angles, were covered with blood and bovine excrement. The floor of the car was not where it should've been, by quite a few inches. Neither was the firewall.

Beckam reached around her to at least undo her seatbelt. Her head lolled onto his shoulder, her hair in his face. Green apples and sage, that was the scent that filled his nose for all of two seconds. Then the coppery sweet scent of blood and the sickening sweetness of cow shit.

"Jesus, help me get her out of here. I know I can do it." But the damned seatbelt latch wouldn't give, and Beckam was running out of time. *Please don't die. Not like this. Not here on the road without someone who loves you by your side.*

His dad was somewhere behind him by then. "Pull her out."

"Can't," Beckam answered, his voice deep and low and scared. "She's stuck and her legs are both broke. Can't move the steering wheel and the seatbelt won't give." *And I don't want to hurt her more than she's already hurting.*

A knife handle landed on Beckam's shoulder, a knife that a man on blood thinners had no business carrying. At least its blade was sheathed. Beckam made quick work of the seat belt, but that worked against him. The instant she was free, Mrs. Jones sagged into his shoulder. He'd had more room to work when she'd been restrained.

His strongest oath breached his lips again. "Damn."

"This car isn't that old, son. Doesn't the seat tip back?"

Both good suggestions. But neither the seat adjustment lever nor the recline switch worked. Running on pure adrenaline now, Beckam worked one hand over her knees and down her legs. She'd have to be eased out sideways. It was the only way. Blood warm and slick ran over his fingers, but he could do this. Until he smelled fumes. The fuel line was leaking, and—

"Get out of here, Dad. Hurry! Get back!" he ordered, sweat dripping into his eyes. "If this thing blows—"

"It won't. You're doing fine. Slow and steady wins the race."

"Yeah, but—" *I can't lose you!*

"I'm not leaving, so stop arguing. Just get her out. Then we go together."

Beckam nodded, his heart hammering up his throat. Now he had two reasons to worry.

At last, he finessed her left leg out from under the wheel, then her right. She had been in white shorts and a tank top, both now covered in a brown-yellow-red mix of cow shit and blood. Only the bright red blood pooling between her legs had nothing to do with the cut on her forehead.

"Jesus! I think she's pregnant!" *Was.* "I think she's miscarrying!" There was so much blood. Which might've explained why she'd been speeding. Her car was pointed in the direction of Saint Joseph's hospital. She could've been going there in a hurry.

"Can you lift her yet? I can help carry her then."

"I think so," Beckam muttered, pressing her thighs into the seat. "Sorry ma'am," he offered contritely when he was finally able to ease her out from under the wheel.

But how do you lift a pregnant woman whose life, and whose baby's life, literally rested in your hands? Beckam had never handled a girl, much less a woman, like this. Not one so lovely nor so delicate, so obviously female, mature, and just as obviously in desperate need of a physically strong male, one who knew what to do. He tugged her head onto his shoulder, slipped one hand under her drenched backside, and without any effort, he lifted to his feet with Mrs. Jones against his chest as easily as if he were simply lifting a day-old calf.

Sheriff West had pulled up in his cruiser with Deputy Judd by then. West carried a blanket; Judd carried their first-aid suitcase. Both were in their tan uniforms, their weapons and other important stuff latched to their belts. Beckam walked past them to his dad's porch, needing to be far from the vehicle if it blew. When it blew. Between the methane and gasoline fumes, it'd only take one tiny spark.

While his dad filled the sheriff and deputy in on what had happened, Beckam dropped to one knee and gently laid Mrs. Jones on the wooden bench by the porch steps. He took care not to bump her head, but as he laid her down, her eyes popped open. She clutched the front of his shirt.

"I'm sorry," she wheezed. "I had to do something, say something. I told him it was you."

"Me, what?" he asked, not understanding.

Mary Lou stuffed a wet hand towel into his hand. "Here, Beck. Wipe the shit off her face. It's getting in her mouth."

Carefully, he smoothed the towel over Mrs. Jones' face, wiped the crap out of her eyes and away from her mouth. Off her bloody lips. She must've bitten her tongue.

They had an audience by then. His dad and Sheriff West were standing over him, while Deputy Judd tended to the wreck and the wrecker that had arrived.

Mrs. Jones' hand went to her belly. "That it was you, Beckam. That you're my baby's father."

He couldn't believe his ears. "I'm what?"

"I... I..." Mrs. Jones groaned as her hand flattened over her belly. "Oh, God. I'm losing her. It hurts."

"Ma'am, I don't know what you're talking about. I never—"

"Don't... please, don't let him... hurt... my little girl!" she sobbed brokenly. "Tell him she's yours. Please. He'll kill me, but you can protect her. I know you can. I t-t-trust you."

"No one's going to hurt you or your baby, ma'am," his dad said. "Just take a deep breath and—"

"You don't know Brent," she whined, writhing and bleeding all over the simple wooden bench that Beckam had made in woodworking shop his sophomore year.

He eased to his feet and out of her reach. Mrs. Jones was delirious. She had to be. That was the only thing that made sense. Because he and his dad knew her husband, and Brent Jones was a good guy who worked long hours on his three-hundred-acre spread. He didn't have much, and he didn't ordinarily say much. But he'd planted corn this year, and he pastured a hundred head of golden-red Limousin beef on his other fifty acres. Brent was a sunup to sundown kind of farmer, always hard at work making a good life for his wife and kids.

"Maybe not, ma'am, but Beck isn't this baby's father," Ross told her unequivocally. "I know that for certain. You got something to say, you tell it to Sheriff West. But blaming my son—"

"I had to," she murmured, her features gone scary still and her eyes unfocused. "It was the only way he'd let me go. I was running away. To something… someone… better..." She went still as the breath wheezed out of her.

The ambulance had arrived by then, and Beckam stepped farther back as the medics took over, his mouth and throat dry at what this woman he barely knew had accused him of. Thank God for his dad setting Mrs. Jones straight. Beckam didn't know Sheriff West. Didn't want to find out the hard way if he was a fair man or not. But Sheriff West had heard everything, and he was looking funny at Beckam now.

Mary Lou had gone back into the house with the twins. "Kids at school say she's been tight with Gus," she whispered through the screen door behind him.

Gus Butler, the high school quarterback, light on his feet, and Hollywood handsome. Yeah, Beckam could see Mrs. Jones going for Gus. And vice versa. Gus was a cocky rich kid who drove a bright lime-green Challenger. He'd been at that wrestling match that night. Now it made sense why Mrs. Jones was there. But why finger Beckam?

As if she'd read his mind, Mary Lou whispered, "Gus's daddy has big plans for his son. Don't think Gus being a gigolo's one of them."

"Well, I am not that baby's father," Beckam told her quietly out of the corner of his mouth, "and a paternity test will prove it."

The medics had Mrs. Jones on their gurney by then. She was covered, but Beckam had seen the way they'd packed multiple pads between her legs. He also saw the covert glances they shot him when they wheeled her away.

Yeah. They thought he was lying.

Ross turned with a grimace. "Don't worry, son. Desperate women will say anything to get what they want."

"I've never been with her, Dad." Beckam felt the need to say.

Ross nodded. "I know. You're smarter than that. Now, let's get those little ones cleaned up, so Sheriff West can take them to their daddy."

All Beckam could think was, *Poor Brent.*

Little did he know...

Chapter Two

Current Day

Camilla Brinkman knelt to give Hector one last pet. She'd been feeding the orange tabby stray for weeks now. It might be time to take him to the pound. No one had answered her ad in the lost-and-found section of the local paper. Nor her post on the neighborhood Facebook page. Not like she'd expected her stuffy neighbors to reply. They didn't know her, and she didn't know them. Didn't want to. Wouldn't think of inviting those pretentious, high-society busybodies into her house to get to know them better. Not anymore.

That day ended when Heath Brinkman moved out of this mausoleum on the Potomac River and left her in debt. That was when her troubles really started. As of this morning, her house payment was officially two months overdue. Christmas, for what it was worth, was behind her, thank God. As usual, it had been a predictable non-event. She didn't believe in the virgin birth or a baby savior who'd supposedly come to save this fucked up world any more than she believed in Santa Claus. All lies. Christmas was just another day to avoid her family, not like that was hard. Luis and Alana Lopez were the life of every holiday party in the fuckin' District. They had to be seen with everyone who was anyone. Just. Not. Her.

But the day after Christmas, an ice storm plowed over the Eastern Seaboard and the temperature dropped. In the middle of it, this fat, ratty tomcat showed up on Camilla's front step, and, well. She'd succumbed to his growly meows and let him in, but just long enough for him to get warm. Just until the bad weather passed.

She hadn't meant to do more than kneel and pet him—once. But when he'd climbed up onto her knee and rubbed his head under her chin... When he'd purred like a tiny striped tiger in her empty arms... Well, it *was* the day after the loneliest Christmas of her life.

So, she'd let him stay, but just because the weather was bitterly cold and just for one day. Then she let him stay one more day. What would it hurt? Nobody was looking for him. Now here it was, weeks later, and Camilla couldn't shove Hector's fluffy butt into the cold and lonely street again. She just couldn't.

But soon, she'd have to. They'd both be out of a place to live.

"I get paid today," she told him. "How about grilled tuna tonight?" She liked to cook for Hector. He, unlike Heath, appreciated what she did for him.

Hector blinked his golden eyes at her and meowed.

She played along. "Oh, chicken? Again? That's what you want? Well, okay then. Rotisserie or roasted?"

Her only friend in the world licked his lips, blinked those big golden eyes, and meowed like he really was answering.

Camilla nodded as she slipped into her winter coat, stepped into her heels, and prepared for another day in Hell, aka The TEAM. "Roasted, it is, my furry, little friend. Be a good boy while I'm gone. Don't scratch my curtains anymore. Or my sofa. It's leather. Promise?"

Hector stretched on the couch where he'd spent his lazy days. "Meow, mrowww, mrowww."

"No, kitty cat. I don't get any good days," she reminded him. "I know you mean well, but that's just the way it is. Life sucks and then it's over. Bye now."

With one more growly meow, he curled into himself, tucked his nose under his tail, and closed his pretty eyes. She winked at her lazy, sleeping buddy on her way out, locking him inside where he'd be safe and warm for a couple more days. Banks didn't evict people in the middle of winter, did they? And who knew, maybe Hector was right. Maybe today would be different. But what did he know? He was just a cat.

Beckam Garner watched Senior Agents Mark Houston and Harley Mortimer beeline for Alex Stewart's office. Again. This made the third time today, and it was only nine o'clock in the morning. Both senior agents had been unusually quiet, as in the deadly kind of calm-before-a tornado quiet. If that wasn't bad enough, they carried black folders with them this time, ominous precursors that meant someone was headed into the field on federal, top-secret, classified work. Two meant two separate black operations, two different operators. Just. Not. Him.

It was the second week in January. After a semi-white Christmas of ice, then slush and drizzle, winter hovered over the East Coast with more cold than snow. Most TEAM agents were still on hiatus, the extended leave Alex had granted after a particularly long and gruesome operation.

Beck had been there when it ended with the death of one nastier than nasty woman, namely Catalina Montego. The Cuban serial killer had gained her brand of evil fame by overpowering young military men, then torturing them into her twisted version of servitude. He'd worked alongside Agents Renner Graves and Seth McCray on that op, as well as with a few of Montego's previous victims who'd survived her previous foray into America. Made him feel useful to end the psychotic woman's reign of terror. Only now…

He'd come back from two weeks with his family in Horse Hollow, Oklahoma, needing more of that useful feeling. Work was what he'd been made for, and the Army had honed him into a lethal, but intelligent fighting machine. He was a leader; always had been. Wanted to be again.

As the latest newbie to join The TEAM, he still wondered at the tight brotherhood of this mostly former-USMC, civilian company. But Harley was also former Army. Alex trusted him as much as he trusted the jarheads on staff. Alex trusted Seth and Adam, too, one Army, the other Navy. So, whatever was happening behind those closed doors had nothing to do with USMC bias, or whether Beckam couldn't get those black-op jobs done. He could. He just wasn't inside the tighter-than-tight inner TEAM circle. Didn't know how to get there, either.

Still wishing he had something more important to do than correcting his last after-action report, Beckam stashed his insecurity down deep in his gut. He'd been an Army captain, had earned his Ranger tab. He was more than qualified. So, why wasn't he in the boss's office being given a chance to prove himself?

"For the last time, it's Kah-me-ah!" The TEAM's pain-in-the-ass secretary/diva/monster screeched from her desk behind the customer service counter.

Since the morning she'd darkened the office with her finely plucked, perpetually slanted brows of disdain, Miss Brinkman had brought nothing but negative energy to the office. From the moment she showed up every day until she left each afternoon, it ebbed through the office like a thick, sticky, black tsunami, smashing into everyone with her get-the-fuck-out-of-my-way attitude. Her presence made everyone else wish they were already home.

Single-handedly, she'd sucked the good-natured rivalry out of The TEAM. Most agents avoided her. Others talked behind her back. She was their own privileged, entitled witch on a broom. Hostile. Mad at the world. Taking it out on poor Fed Ex at the moment.

The guy's face turned red. "Yes, ma'am, sure sorry about—"

"And I'm not a ma'am, damn it. I'm not some old nag, and it's Kah-me-ah—not Cam-ill-a—Brinkman. How many times do I have to tell you idiots that? The Ls are silent!"

Probably as long as you spell it with those two Ls.

"Ah, umm, I was just being polite, and—"

"Kah-me-ah," she growled. "Say it with me. Kah. Me. Ah."

Fed Ex looked like a deer caught in headlights. Not answering. Probably wishing he were anywhere but here.

"Fine then. From now on, I guess I'm *ma'am*," Miss Brinkman muttered before she jumped to her feet, leaned over her counter, and yelled, "Can everyone out there hear me? If you can't say my name properly, from now on just fuckin' call me *ma'am*." She put plenty of chin-bob and head swagger into that demand. "You idiots can handle that, can't you? It's simple enough."

Normally, Beckam would let her insult roll off his back. He'd worked with plenty of asshole drill instructors before. Unfortunately, less than half the office caught her latest demand. Probably less than that, since most of the workstations ahead of her were devoid of life, those agents still on Alex's generous Christmas break or out of the office on assignment. *Lucky stiffs.*

But Beckam was directly in her line of sight, and he'd had enough. Pushing to his feet, he headed over to rescue yet another hapless victim.

"Whatcha got there?" he asked the muscular man quivering in his boots.

Mr. Fed Ex handed over his tablet, relief splashed all over his youthful, blister-red face. "Need someone to sign for a package, that's all. It's heavy, so I left it next to the elevator door like I'm supposed to."

Using the stylus swinging by a chain to the device, Beckam signed the dotted line and handed the tablet back. "No problem, buddy. I'll take care of it. You have a nice day now."

"Thanks, mister," Fed Ex breathed a quick path to the elevator.

Miss Kah-me-ah snorted through her pretty white, terrifically straight teeth. "That's my job."

"Then you need to do it without verbally assaulting every delivery person who stops by your counter," Beckam told her. "It's a *customer* service desk. Do you even know what that means?"

She glared—as usual. "Why don't you go back to your desk and mind your business?"

He glared right back. "I am. This entire place is my business. In case you haven't noticed, we're a team here. We get along. That way, everyone goes home happy at the end of the day. You ought to try it sometime."

"Go fuck a duck," she spat.

That was another thing. Kah-me-ah used ugly expletives like he used ammo on the range. "You talk to your mother with that dirty mouth? Really?"

That earned him one intensely, spiked brow. Overly-plucked, when they lifted, her brows turned into arrows that pointed toward the ceiling.

Mark appeared out of nowhere at Beckam's side. "Boss wants to talk to you. You too, Camilla."

Leave it to Mark to know how to pronounce her name correctly. But hearing his name in the same sentence as hers didn't set well with Beckam. "On my way," he told his senior agent.

"Sit," Alex said when Beck cleared his door. "Got a job for you."

Whew. He'd said *you*, not *both of you*. While Mark leaned a hip against the credenza behind Alex, Beckam took the chair closest to the desk. The boss kept a neat office. No clutter on his desk. No files, loose pencils, or pens. Just that spit-and-polished, black granite surface and the framed picture of his happy family smiling back at him.

"You too," Alex told Kah-me-ah when she walked in. "Sit."

The last bit of Beckam's good feeling slithered to the floor and crawled away.

"I prefer to stand. What'd you want?" she answered from the open door, tapping her toes like she had better things to do—like bully another delivery person—than wait on her boss. She'd worn a dress again today, one of those slimming styles, tan all over except for two black inserts that ran down her sides in an hourglass design. Matching heels, the kind with thick soles that added height to her five-foot-nothing attitude. The cut of the bodice accentuated her full breasts. Too bad it didn't accentuate her good disposition. Oh wait, she didn't have one.

"I said sit," Alex told her again, steel in his voice. "And close the door. This is private."

"There's hardly anyone else in the office," she argued. "Just spit it out."

"And I said close the damned door."

Her nostrils flared, but finally, with a huff and a mumble, Kah-me-ah did as Alex asked. Shutting the door, she took the chair beside it, sitting at the edge of her seat. Man, she reminded Beckam of his sister Mary Lou. A spoiled brat in all things. A drama queen who needed her backside paddled. Just once.

It had certainly curbed Mary Lou's teenage obnoxiousness. The day she'd sassed her dad back once too many times, Ross had turned her fifteen-year-old smart mouth over his knee and wailed on her fanny until she'd screamed bloody murder for Mom to come save her. Which Mom hadn't, because she'd probably put Ross up to it.

Beckam wouldn't have believed his mild-mannered dad had it in him, but he'd been there in the kitchen. He'd seen his dad's broad palm slap that obnoxious rump about twenty times. Hard. Like he'd put up with enough.

Beckam had just come in from finishing chores outside. He'd stood watching and grinning at every spank of long-overdue-comeuppance Mary Lou received. You can bet your bottom dollar she never talked back to Ross or Carolyn again after that. In fact, she'd turned into quite a reasonable young lady. Beckam actually liked her now. And she did her chores. Without being asked or nagged. Corporal punishment worked. Who knew?

Not Beckam, at least not by experience. He'd never pressed the envelope like Mary Lou had, never sassed his parents. Not once. Never thought of arguing with the two folks he knew loved him more than anything. His dad needed his help around the farm, so Beckam just did as he was asked, when he was told to do it. That was all there was to it. A man stepped up. Which was why he'd become an Army Ranger after he'd graduated and enlisted. Someone had to do the hard and dirty jobs. Everyone couldn't be a whining snowflake with a stick up her ass. But mostly, he adored his dad. He still wanted to be just like Ross Garner.

Sitting straight as an arrow, as usual, Alex interlocked his fingers on the desk in front of him and leaned forward. USMC to his jarhead soul, he'd served as a Marine scout sniper, a profession Beckam respected and understood. Most other agents in the office were former snipers. Now, courtesy of Alex's need to create honorable jobs and careers for men like him when they finished serving their country, Beckam, as well as a hundred-plus others, called Alexandria, Virginia, home. Alex created and stationed The TEAM there to provide covert surveillance to the country he still served. The world provided the need.

"As you know, while we were caught up tracking Catalina Montego, there've been several other murders in the District, all of them transients. Mayor Tillis has asked for our help catching the perpetrators. I told him yes."

"Good," Beckam replied, all but smacking his lips in anticipation. "It's about time."

Okay, not exactly the classified op he'd hoped for, but he'd already shot that hope down the moment Mark invited Kah-me-ah to this meeting. This op was better. It served the street people that he, and quite a few of the other agents, kept track of in the District. It was The TEAM's little side project, to reach out and protect any veterans who were unemployed or unemployable. It was a small thing, but a guy always felt good at the end of the day when he knew he'd done all he could for his brothers and sisters.

"So?" She-Whose-Name-Should-Never-Be-Misspoken hissed. "What's that got to do with me?"

"So, you've complained three times just this week that the work you're assigned isn't important. This is. I'm sending you and Agent Garner undercover to nail these sons of bitches before they strike again."

God, no, not her. Not with me. Beckam nearly closed his eyes to avoid the train wreck barreling down the track at him. Why wasn't she invited just to take notes or dictation or something? Anything but this. Alex wanted a trained Ranger to take this untrained, former, female agent from Fish and Wildlife Services—the same agent Beckam would have long ago fired—into the field? On a real operation? To sniff out a dangerous murderer when she couldn't summon the decency to say please or thank you?

Predictably, Kah-me-ah barked a less than pleasant laugh. "You've got to be kidding. Do I look like I'm dressed for undercover work? Me?" Man, if her nose twitched any farther, she'd be pointed in the wrong direction. "Why should I save anyone who's stupid enough to be homeless? They're all crazy, and you know it."

Beckam's jaw clenched at the blatant prejudice pouring out of her mouth. Why the hell was she working with a business as reputable and as known for getting the hard cases done as The TEAM? The woman plain didn't belong, and if Alex wasn't careful, she'd bring him down.

Alex leaned farther over his clenched fingers, his already icy-blue eyes now gone hard as diamonds. "What I expect you to do, Miss Brinkman," he clipped, "is either shit or get off the pot. I've had enough of your hostility, your disrespect, and your lack of restraint. It stops today. Take it or leave it, I honestly don't care. You've made everyone in this office miserable, and I'm not Dear Abby. You want professional help, find it somewhere else. The TEAM is a team. It's mine. I built it from the ground up. Either step up to the plate, join in, or…" He stuck his chin at the door to her immediate right.

Beckam focused on Alex and Mark. Those clever dogs. They were doing this on purpose. They'd set Kah-me-ah up, and he didn't blame them. She was by far the most uncooperative person he'd ever worked with. Err, make that, been around, since she'd never really worked.

Kah-me-ah glared as only Kah-me-ah could. Icy black stare. Narrowed eyes. Pursed lips. And oh, yeah, cold heart. If there was a shred of authentic human kindness in her soul, it was buried beneath a glacier of stone-cold ice.

Beckam held his breath, hoping she'd take Alex up on his offer, get pissed and storm off on one of her snits. She was a Rubik's Cube, a puzzle of all pointy corners and impossible to solve. Beckam flat didn't want to be saddled with her the rest of this meeting, much less for however long this simple assignment took. Not for one week. Not one day. Not ever.

At last, she blinked, bowed her head and stared at the floor. Not many could withstand the withering USMC stare Alex did so well. Especially not this particular woman who had to be twenty years old, twenty-one, tops. Camilla Brinkman had no social skills. Only money. And a well-connected husband whose wealthy father trolled the District like every other lobbyist. A bottom feeder.

The office stilled as Alex straightened his arms, pushed away from his desk, and tipped back in his chair. Mark folded his arms over his chest. They were waiting. Not a glimmer of anger, disgust, or elation crossed their faces. But Beckam suspected they fully expected her to say something mean before she quit and left. Oh, how he wished.

Her lips twisted as if she were fighting more nasty comments.

Do it. Get mad. Leave. Just walk out, and don't let the door hit your spoiled, entitled ass when you do.

Her fingers clenched into fists.

Hurry, hurry, hurry. Come on, leave. Before Alex fires you.

But at last—*Damn it!*—Kah-me-ah's nostrils flared, and she bit out, "Fine. I'll do it."

Damn it, no! Just no. If Beck hadn't been a Ranger, he would've cried.

"You'll need a firearm," Mark said evenly, his dark brown eyes now on Beckam. "Agent Garner will take you upstairs to the vault and equip you with the weaponry you'll need to complete this mission. But before you can work any covert op, you will spend, at minimum, one full day at the range to prove your proficienc—"

"For fuck sake, I don't have to prove anything," she shot back at her senior agent. "I know how to shoot better than anyone out in that bay."

Ouch. Embarrassed for her, Beckam winced at the brazen disrespect oozing out of her mouth. Did she have any idea how ugly she looked when she acted like this?

"Stop the language," Alex ordered sternly.

"I can say whatever I want," she came back at him, "or haven't you heard of the First Amend—?"

"My house, my rules!" he bellowed, steamrolling over her. "And just to be clear, Miss Brinkman. The First Amendment guarantees freedoms concerning religion, expression, and the right of individuals to petition. It forbids Congress from promoting one religion over others. It restricts Congress from restricting individual religious practices. It guarantees individual freedom of speech by prohibiting Congress from repressing individuals who speak freely. But Goddamn it, I'm not Congress, and The TEAM is not a democracy!"

There went Kah-me-ah's evil brows and those flared nostrils again. Man, she never backed down. Beckam wanted to throw up. Alex might not be entirely accurate, and he'd just cursed the mother of all curses in Beck's book—he tried to never use the Lord's name in vain—but this entitled brat owed Alex the respect due any employer. Especially one who'd kept her lazy ass on the payroll as long as he had. Beck would've fired her months ago.

"I could sue you," she threatened.

Beck shook his head at her, inadvertently warning her not to poke this USMC Devil Dog.

"Then do it," Alex dared her. "Have your lawyer call my lawyer. Today. Why not? I've kept good records. I know just how much work you've done, and I know every last thing you've refused to do. Trust me. You're not the first. Others have tried. For God's sake, do something!"

"Sue us for what?" Mark asked conversationally, still propped against the credenza and his arms still calmly crossed over his chest as if he had all day. "For broadening your work experience? For doing as you asked and finding something *more suitable* to your so-called talents? Those are your precise words. What *are* your talents, Kah-me-ah? You won't assist agents with research. You refuse to learn how to use a word processor. We can't even get you to answer the phone that rings on your desk and do it politely."

Her head canted as if she wasn't sure whether he was humoring her or digging at her. "Not secretarial," she replied haughtily, her chin and nose lifted. "I should be doing fieldwork like I did for FWS." FWS being the Department of Fish and Wildlife Services.

Alex nodded. "Understood. You want to be a junior agent."

She leaned forward, her neck stretched at Alex like a snake about to strike. "No, I want to be a senior agent. Like Agent Houston. I've got the education and I've got experience. You know goddamned well I can do it."

"I know no such thing," Alex said flatly, his hand raised and his fingers ticking off his reasons. "You have no experience as far as I'm concerned. You've never served. You've never been in combat. You've never led men or women into battle. I'm sorry, but FWS doesn't count. It's not Defense.

And number one on my list, you haven't earned one single person's respect in this office."

"Who cares what those ignorant grunts out there respect?" she hissed, her index finger stabbed at Alex's door and beyond. "Isn't that the word for them? Isn't that your word? Want to bet I've got more education than all of them combined? Want to compare IQs? God!" She sat back with a huff, clutching her crossed arms.

"Agent Adam Torrey is a former Navy SEAL, as well as a board-certified general practitioner," Mark said evenly. "Senior Agent Harley Mortimer is a former Army K-9 handler as well as an accredited veterinarian. David Tao is a former Marine like me and Alex. He holds masters in both Psychology and Economics. Steven holds an MFA. That's Master of Fine Arts, in case you—"

"I know what a fuckin' MFA is," she muttered, drumming her fingers on her biceps. "So what? I've got more masters than all you guys put together. Even you." She leveled that last nasty barb directly at Alex. "If you're so smart, what degree do you have? Huh? Anything? Maybe a business degree. Or wait, General Ed? I'll bet you don't even have a fuckin' GED."

Beckam licked his lips and looked down at the floor, unsure how Alex and Mark could keep their cool in the face of such blatant hostility and arrogance. She was right. Alex had no college degree. Everyone knew that. His complete life's story had been front page news when his TEAM led the assault on the meat-packing plant last month and ended one of the world's deadliest serial killers.

But God's honest truth was that Alex didn't need a degree. Years ago, after he'd come back from deployment to bury his first wife and child, he'd quit the Corps. Then he'd struggled to get what he still called his hare-brained idea, aka The TEAM, up and running. But he'd done it, by hell, on sheer American grit and know-how.

He didn't need a degree. Over and over, he'd proven to himself and the world, that he was not only a savvy businessman, but a genius at OPSEC, aka Operational Security. He had the instincts of a killer with the finesse of a master gamesman. He knew inherently how to lead, badger, and love his team into accomplishing the impossible with incredible skill and diplomacy. Beckam didn't know another man on earth more dedicated to his men or his country than Alex Stewart.

Until now, Beckam also hadn't known how deadly Alex could be. Beckam's ears actually hurt with the sound of— Absolute. Dead. Silence.

Alex only stared at the mouthy upstart on his team.

At last, Camilla broke eye contact again. Her backside shifted. She drew her feet beneath the chair, crossed her ankles, and dusted a piece of nothing off her skirt.

"You know what? Who cares what degrees you've got—if any." She couldn't seem to resist throwing one last dig. "What's the difference between you guys and the jerks at FWS anyway? I've apprehended smugglers. I've brought people to justice, and I—"

Mark cleared his throat, interrupting her. "Excuse me, but the men and women who work for Fish and Wildlife are not jerks, and you, ma'am, inflated your service record," he stated flatly. "You took credit for operations and arrests you weren't directly involved in. You built a resume on inaccurate dates, times, names, and fictitious operations. Yes," he nodded, his dark brown eyes gone nearly black this morning, "I follow up on all new employee records, job applications, and referrals. No matter how credentialed they say they are."

Her brows lifted at that. "You do background checks?"

"Thoroughly."

Duh. Beckam very much wanted to smile. Maybe laugh out loud. Why should that surprise her? The TEAM was one of the few private security businesses in the country that worked classified intel for the State Department. Alex's agents had to be above reproach to do that. She should know. She'd been excluded from enough black ops after-action briefings by now.

"I said I'd do it, didn't I?" Kah-me-ah ground out. "When can I start? Where do I go?"

"You and Beckam—"

"No." That hard, know-it-all head was shaking now. "I work alone. Don't need Boy Scout in my way."

Once again, Beckam kept his opinion to himself. But Boy Scout? Really? Him? Did she have any idea who any of the guys and gals in that outer office were? How much he or they had given for their country? What he'd survived or done?

Obviously not.

"You'll work with whom I tell you to work with and when," Alex replied, his voice threateningly full of gravel. Beckam had always heard his boss had little to no patience. The calm man he was witnessing now had to be some kind of miracle. "Agent Garner will escort you to the range, where you'll prove proficiency with any and all weapons he chooses. You've made a lot of claims since you came here. Prove them."

"Or what? You'll fire me?"

"Yes," Alex said bluntly. "I run a business, not a daycare. I don't need someone on staff who won't work."

And there it was. Her line in the sand. Either she stepped over it and spat in Alex's face, or she finally, actually, wholeheartedly joined The TEAM, and earned the abundant paycheck she didn't mind taking home every two weeks.

Beckam found himself holding his breath. Wishing she'd pull her usual bitch routine and leave, just walk out the door, and never be seen or heard from again. That'd be nice.

The woman was smart, no doubt about that. At least, she could be when she wanted. But she was emotionally immature. She'd come to The TEAM with so much nasty baggage that she'd alienated even the most levelheaded agents over the last several months. He found himself wondering why Harley hadn't been included in this meeting. Of all the agents, he'd tried the hardest to make friends with Brinkman. But it was highly possible the known recovering alcoholic, who openly admitted he suffered a TBI and dealt with PTSD, couldn't deal with the continual condescension Brinkman dished out. What did she do every morning, tell herself she was God and everyone else was scum?

"Fine," she huffed. The way she said it translated into a loud and clear *'Up yours, Boss.'*

"Good," Alex answered as if he hadn't caught her attitude. "Beckam is the Agent-in-Charge of this op. You have questions, you go through him. You need something, you—"

"Yeah, yeah." She waved Alex off dismissively. "I get it. I'm just the dumb fuck, he's the brains. If I want to breathe—"

Alex jumped to his feet, towering over his desk, those glacial blues all but spitting ice cold fire. "If you ever— EVER!—address me like that again, Miss Brinkman, I'll fire your ass so fast, you won't know what day it is. This might not be a house of God, but by God! My TEAM is a son of a bitchin' house of order. Common courtesy, *Kah. Me. Ah.*" Every syllable of her name reverberated like a rifle report against his office walls. "My TEAM operates on simple, common courtesy. Respect for all. Even our hard-working delivery people. Every last one of them. You should try it sometime. But if you can't control your mouth, clear the hell out. Now."

Alex must've heard her rant at the Fed Ex guy.

That shut her up. Her neck muscles seemed to be working extra-hard. Her tongue slid over her bottom lip as if she was having trouble swallowing. Her young face paled. Her normal Puerto Rican, overly-bronzed and blushed complexion, had now turned slightly gray around the edges.

"Yes, sir," she said, meek for the first time since she'd arrived. "Control. Got it. Listen to the Agent-in-Charge you assigned. Fine. I can do that."

I doubt it. Beck noticed she hadn't said *my* Agent-in-Charge. He blew out a quiet but desperate release of breath that did nothing to ease the sensation of desert spiders crawling up his spine. Man, this was going to be one long, tough mission.

Chapter Three

I'll show this fuckin' Boy Scout, Camilla thought as she killed yet another target, then rang the heavy steel gong five hundred feet on the berm beyond that POS piece of cardboard. Just because she could. Any day with any caliber. Chambering another round, she stared through her scope at the two-thousand-yard mark, five-hundred-feet past that simple-to-hit gong. A plate-sized piece of pounded metal, it spun like a top on its axis whenever some lucky stiff managed to hit it.

You want to see proficiency, then watch me nail that mark, you dickhead.

But damn, it was freezing cold today. Her fingers went stiff an hour ago, and her backside felt like a frozen block of fat beneath her TEAM-worthy black, but stylish, jeans.

Agent Garner had insisted she qualify at the FBI range at Marine Corps Base, Quantico, Virginia, instead of the private range The TEAM usually used. This one boasted longer firing lanes, as well as all the challenges nature provided. Like the fifteen-mile wind out of the northwest and the weak winter sun shining in her eyes. Like the bite of January cold making her nose run. She'd had to swipe the back of her hand over her nose twice now, but did Boy Scout care? Fucking ass.

Worse, this range boasted a male RSO, range safety officer, who'd physically inspected her rifle before he'd assigned lanes. Like some male chauvinist pig out of the last century, the old fart assigned her the station at Boy Scout's right, then asked if she'd wanted a stand or a chair to be more comfortable. Like she couldn't fire from a prone position? Like she was some little mouse of a housewife who needed a big strong gorilla like Boy Scout to help clear any jammed rounds while she sat on her ass and filed her nails?

Camilla had shown him, too. She was nobody's bitch.

Lucky thing she'd run home and changed into TEAM casual wear before this stupid, waste of time exercise. Boy Scout insisted on driving her, but she'd dashed into her apartment before he could do something stupid like open the car door for her. She'd rushed like a maniac, put dry cat food into an extra-large bowl for Hector, then filled the sink with water. She had no way of knowing how long she'd be away, but locating one stupid murderer couldn't take long. It wasn't a hard job. Hector would be okay until she returned.

It was also lucky that December's ice had turned into January's dirty patches of slush and glare. But damn. She'd been at this waste of time proficiency training for hours now. She was tired, cold, and hungry. Yet Boy Scout just kept firing, hitting his marks, reloading, and firing again.

She'd noticed he also kept a log and recorded every shot he made, something she wished she'd thought of doing. The more he kept writing, the more she was convinced he was also keeping track of her shots and targets. How many she fired. How many she hit. The two she'd missed. Windage. Elevation. Angle of sun. Time of day and temperature. He was obviously slow, and he seemed like the type who'd rat on her. Dimwitted. Methodical. Had to write things down, so he didn't forget them. *Men.* They all thought they were smarter than she was. *But not today, Boy Scout. Not today and not ever.*

She was not only gifted intellectually, but her eyesight was exemplary. She could see in the dark. Boy Scout probably couldn't. She wondered how many national trophies he'd won, if any. Certainly not the President's Rifle Trophy, something only available to the match winner during CMP, the Civilian Marksmanship Program, national matches. Did the United States Army even expect good marksmanship from uneducated grunts like him? Or was 'close' good enough, like with horseshoes and hand grenades?

Her right index finger itched. Camilla stilled and let muscle training take over. Her father had never liked it, but she'd won enough national competitions before she'd married to give Boy Scout here a run for his money. High-power rifle events were where she truly excelled. They were also where she found the most peace in her disappointing life. She was good at long-distance shots because she was far-sighted. A true natural. It was the one thing her parents had never been able to influence or take from her.

Her body stilled as her world narrowed down to the line between her and that plate, a good mile away. Even Mother Nature complied. The breeze ceased. A cloud skittered across the sun, shading her face. The slightest smile curled her lips and—

The target spun like a bright silver top on its post.

Shit! Some ass had just spoiled her perfect shot. Who the hell…?

Boy Scout chambered another goddamned round.

She turned on him. "You! You did that on purpose!"

Of course, he couldn't hear her, not wearing protective ear-gear like every good Boy Scout did. As he had all morning, he ignored her, aimed, focused, and… *Pew!* He hit that damn target again.

She had to squint to see through the breeze in her face now, but yes. Damn him. The plate spun like a top. Impressive. Just as it slowed, the breeze kicked up harder and cloud cover broke. The sun glared into her eyes as Boy Scout hit his mark again. Then again. Damn. He was good. Not like Camilla would ever tell him, but at least, he had skills. He was someone worth watching. So she did.

Agent Garner wore a black beanie over his bulky protective headset. He also wore one of those farmer's quilted jackets, the boxy kind with a stupid *Carhartt* label on its chest—like that was anything to be proud of. The jacket had no style, and it was definitely not tailored to fit his frame. It was a nice, bland, sandstone color instead of the bright orange jackets most rednecks wore, though. That was something.

Sherpa-lined, it looked comfortable and warm. He wasn't shivering. In fact, the cold didn't seem to bother him at all, not like it bugged the hell out of her. All morning long she'd shivered in her designer skinny jeans. Why not? She'd needed something classy to make his atrocious TEAM-wear look good. Only now, she wished she'd dressed for weather, not the runway. She wished she'd dressed like Beckam.

While he proceeded to ignore her, Camilla stole another glance. They were both on their bellies facing their individual shooting lanes, a series of berms beyond, each one higher than the previous one. Boy Scout was a good foot longer than she was. He was all broad shoulders and wide chest, his stove piped legs spread wide behind him. He'd dressed in The TEAM's prerequisite black denim jeans. Scuffed, brown leather work boots that didn't match his jeans, but at least complemented his jacket. Black fleece gloves with no fingertips. The dark glasses he'd worn on the drive south from Alexandria rested stems down on the open rifle case at his side.

Boy Scout didn't bat an eye in her direction. Didn't smile. Didn't frown. Didn't seem to care how well she did, if she were still there, or if she'd frozen solid. Just kept reloading, as if he could shoot paper targets and metal plates a mile away all day.

The guy did have a nice enough profile. Straight nose. Solid square jaw. Big chin. Nothing model-worthy, though. He wasn't pretty-boy handsome, and his smile always seemed forced. It seldom reached his eyes.

If anything, Agent-in-Charge was as ordinary as any other blue-collar worker. His features were rugged but plain. Rough. As if someone had carved him out of a chunk of leftover, dirty granite instead of fine, unblemished marble. His short hair was a dirty dishwater blond. His eyes were an interesting indigo blue that glistened with aqua when he turned at just the right angle in the bright sunlight.

But looks did not make the man. How well Camilla knew that. He'd never amount to much, not working for Stewart. Which was just as well. Guys like Garner were a dime a dozen. Just because he'd done his patriotic duty didn't qualify him for anything important in the real world. Which was why he'd ended up working for The TEAM. Stupid name. That alone proved how smart Stewart and his men were. Not very.

The barrel of Beckam's weapon didn't jerk when he fired, not even a little. Which meant he'd practiced plenty. He knew his weapon and he operated on muscle memory. That made him a tiny bit more interesting.

"What?"

Camilla blinked at him like a dumb deer caught in a hunter's crosshairs. "What, umm, what?" she asked as snarkily as she could. He didn't need to know he'd caught her looking at him. She hadn't been. Not really.

"I asked if you needed anything," he said, enunciating each word as if she didn't understand English. His earphones were hanging around his neck. How long had he been watching her watching him?

"I'm not stupid. I heard you." Which she hadn't, but why admit it? Let him think whatever he wanted.

His jaw dropped, and he blinked, but not in surprise. More as if he had something to say, but wouldn't say it. Like he was actually thinking twice before he opened his big mouth again. A gust of frosted vapor billowed out of him. "You *are* proficient with a long rifle," he said that like he was impressed. "How about we move to the indoor range, and you show me how good you are with a pistol?"

Camilla couldn't decide. Was he daring her or did he really mean what he said? Did he think she was good? Her mouth tightened. "I don't need to prove anything to you. I'm good with all firearms."

His head dipped, but there was a decided sparkle in his eyes. "You just can't take a compliment, can you?"

"Can too," she shot back at him. "If I ever heard one." Wasn't that the truth?

There went his jaw again. Agent Garner had a way of shifting it to the side when he was thinking. Which he did a lot. Complex decision-making must be difficult for him.

Interestingly, he didn't wear a ring. She'd noticed that in the office. Not like it mattered. It didn't. Not at all.

He canted his head, blocking the sun from his eyes, shifting his entire face into shadow. "You're cold," he told her quietly, his voice discernable even though the other shooters continued firing. His eyes were bluer. Deeper. The aqua sparkles deep inside his irises persisted, but Camilla was so much better than this guy in every way. If this was his attempt at a come-on, he flunked. Big time.

"I'm not cold. Don't blame me if you need to go inside and—"

"I'm not blaming anyone. You've proven yourself. Let's go in, grab some lunch and a drink. Then hit the indoor range." He said that like he meant it.

"I don't drink on the job."

The sparkle faded. "I didn't mean that kind of drink."

"Well... well, good." Could she sound more juvenile?

With a sigh, Agent Garner fingered his dark glasses up from his rifle case, angled the stems under his beanie and over his ears, then settled the bridge on top his nose. The headphones went back over his head to his ears. "Have it your way," he breathed as, once more, he snugged his rifle stock to his cheek, lined up another shot, and nailed that damned plate a mile away.

Camilla stared at the spinning disc in the distance. Shit. She'd missed her chance to get warm. Now she'd have to lay out here until he decided he'd had enough. Or until he grew cold, which might take the rest of the day. Maybe longer. This range stayed open late for night shooting. He'd called it NVG practice. 'Course, he'd also called it fun, the dumbass.

Damn, there was no way to beat this guy, and worse, he'd never be impressed by anything she did or said. Why try?

Beckam gave it his best shot. He'd been respectful. He'd been friendly. Yet nothing got through to the prickly woman at his right. He doubted even a spanking would change Camilla Brinkman into anything but an angrier woman. Not that he'd do such a thing. Ever. Women were to be handled with deference and treated with respect. Even the rowdier ones who fancied themselves as good or better than men. Beckam didn't ascribe to the battle of the sexes or to the political agenda behind the feminist movement, either. His mother had taught him young and well. There were no ifs, ands, or buts. Ladies— all ladies—were better than most men, any day of the week. They were smarter. Most of them were a sight prettier, and— the ultimate crown of glory—they were able to bear babies. No man on earth could top that.

Yet the female Rubik's Cube was angry to-the-bone, no two ways about it. Rage echoed in everything she said and did. It colored her words and it messed with her complexion. She was like a thermometer. The angrier she got, the harsher her language became and the higher that ruddy flush crept up her neck until her face turned bright red. He had yet to say anything that hadn't merited her scorn. She probably glowed like a nuclear reactor at night with all that stored aggression.

That thought, oddly, made his aim more accurate. Not that he needed a full day of rifle practice to be accurate, but the steady, repetitive drill of hitting one target after another, pausing only to adjust his scope's diopter—which he'd done once so far—was as much mental therapy as physical practice. It soothed the ocean of angst lying between him and his companion agent.

In combat, every operator depended on the other's muscle training. Heroes were never the glory seekers. Uh uh. True heroes were the men and women who threw themselves in harm's way to protect the brothers or sisters at their sides. They didn't think; they reacted. Sometimes they lived to talk about it, but most times... they came home in flag-draped boxes. Automatically, he gave a nod of silent respect to the men and women who'd given their lives defending their country. No greater love indeed.

And plink. Kah-me-ah hit that two-thousand-yard mark!

"Nice shooting," he congratulated.

Which earned him an indifferent grunt, a twist of her nose, and yet another frosty huff of disdain.

Laying his rifle on its side, Beckam turned to the woman who wouldn't lower herself to type a memo for his boss, but who insisted she was senior agent material. "Is this how it's going to be the next two weeks?"

She rotated her head and gave him an icy glare. Those perfect brows arched. "Two weeks?"

"Or longer. We'll need time to get friendly with the locals. Maybe spend a couple nights at the local soup kitchen or on the street. Make friends. You know, the usual covert stuff. It'd be nice if we at least got along."

Her nose wrinkled. "I am not making friends with you or any homeless trash. I give this job twenty-four hours, maybe forty-eight, tops."

That he wanted to hear. "How do you figure?"

Of course, she rolled those bright, sharp, beady eyes as if answering him were beneath her. "Do your homework, Agent Garner. Most transients are murdered by other transients. Occasionally, a street gang's involved, but only when some

idiot wanders onto their turf. It's basic Law of the Jungle 101."
Another grunt emphasized how much she thought she knew.

Beckam drew in a gutful of patience along with a belly full
of cold air. "Sounds like you've had experience," he said,
though he knew better. "Let's hit the clubhouse. I'd like to
hear—"

"No. Let's just go. Now. I've got better things to do than
waste time."

He closed his mouth then, and just as well. She'd narrowed
down on that far off target and plink, plink, plink. It spun with
every round she fired. Kah-me-ah the Magnificent really could
shoot. She had good form, a great eye, and excellent control.

But if she thought this operation on the cold, hard streets
of Washington, DC, would be over in two days, she was in for
one helluva surprise.

Chapter Four

"Hey, Harold. Hey, Dave," Beckam called out quietly to a couple down-on-their-luck, crusty old friends who camped near the District's busy Union Station. "I've got day-old donuts. Want some?"

The sun hadn't broken through the early morning yet, and it was cold. Bitterly cold. But it was Bruce who looked up with bleary eyes from the shabby sidewalk hovel where he and his two friends had huddled for the night. Not Harold or Dave. Their place in this corner of the sidewalk was no more than a patchwork cover of cardboard and someone's cast-off, bright blue tarp, draped together to escape the elements.

Beckam's heart hurt for these Vietnam War veterans, all too damned old to be so forgotten and so neglected. After what they'd given their ungrateful country, they deserved a free room at one of the many local hotels in the District and a lifetime of decent meals at the nearest country club. Yet here they were. Homeless. Hungry. Probably penniless and hungover.

"Why aren't you guys at Lorelei's Kitchen where you'd be warm?" he asked as he handed the extra-large box of donuts he'd purchased earlier off to Camilla. He dropped one knee to the concrete, worried what he'd find under that tarp.

Located a few blocks east of the Senate buildings, Lorelei's Kitchen served free soup and sandwiches twenty-four-seven for veterans, runaways, drug addicts, basically anyone who stopped by. All anyone had to do was show up, and, if they timed it right, they could be well-fed and stay out of the frigid weather most of the night.

Owned and operated by Lorelei Vishinski, a German immigrant, she'd named her refuge after the legendary siren who in ancient times, lured sailors on the Rhine to their deaths. Only this Lorelei's heart was pure gold. She never judged a person by the color of their skin or their choice of bad habits, and always said, in her no-nonsense way, that God didn't care as much about the sin as He did the sinner. She always made sure she had room for one more.

"I own't know," Bruce rasped even as he pulled the tarp tighter under his chin.

Gingerly, Beckam peeked under one corner of the plastic cover to find Harold and Dave curled into themselves, back to back, and both out cold. "Have they been drinking?"

"I own't know," Bruce said again, whinier this time. Like his throat hurt and he was tired of answering. "Guess so, but they din't share nuthin' with me if they were."

Which meant Bruce hadn't been with Harold and Dave last night, and somehow, one of these two old codgers had gotten lucky—or unlucky—depending on which side of the street you staggered home on. Alcohol wasn't anyone's friend on bitter cold nights, and last night had been wicked cold. Temperatures had dipped into the low thirties. Add in the humidity and wind chill factors, and the temp had most probably bottomed out in the twenties. These guys were lucky they weren't stiff as boards and frozen solid this morning.

Camilla stepped away from the men, sniffing. Yes, the aroma drifting up from under that tarp smelled bad, but

Beckam was worried. He'd patrolled this section around Union Station regularly after he'd moved to the East Coast and joined The TEAM. It's what most TEAM veterans did. They looked out for other vets down on their luck. Yet as hard as everyone tried, The TEAM, Metro Police Department, and others, these three men continually refused all offers of warm beds and showers. They were quick to say others needed those beds down at the rescue mission more than they did, that there were families with kids on the streets who deserved safe shelter, not them.

Beckam didn't know if Harold, Dave, and Bruce's problems were Agent Orange or just plain alcoholism related. He only knew they'd served together in far off 'Nam, in a forgotten place called Lam Sung. They'd been through some shit, but when the Veterans Administration let one of them down, all went down together. They were in trouble this morning.

"I know a better place," he offered quietly. "You three will be better off there."

Instead of answering, Bruce stared up at Camilla. "Hey, pretty lady. Whatcha doin' hanging 'round Beck? He banging you?"

"For Pete's sake, Bruce," Beckam scolded. "What kind of question is that to ask a lady? She's here to help you guys. Watch your mouth."

Bruce's lips twitched like he had more to say, but kept it to himself. Which was good.

Camilla's mouth had already twisted into that ugly sneer of hers, and her scorn was clearly etched on her face. And that was okay. Bruce might get suspicious if she actually said something nice or acted like she cared, which Beckam was pretty sure she didn't. Not the way she'd argued about wearing the cast-off pants, shirt, and sweater she had on today, all extra nasty because he'd dug them out of the trash behind the District's Judiciary Square, another hangout for transients and homeless. But she had to look authentic. Had to smell authentic, too.

"Come on, Bruce. This is serious. I need to get Dave and Harold to their feet." Beckam didn't dare tap his earpiece to alert Senior Agent Mark Houston that he had an uncooperative veteran down. That'd be like sending an SOS for all hands-on-deck. Every agent within spitting distance would come to the rescue.

Turned out he didn't have to. Bruce had no more than grumbled back at him when Beckam caught sight of Zack Lennox humping his way across the street, a gigantic backpack towering high on his shoulders. He waved in recognition and called out, "Hey, Beck! Hey, Cam! Brisk morning, huh?"

"You could say that," Beckam replied even as he ignored Kah-me-ah's hiss at Zack's nickname for her. Harold and Dave had yet to move, and they were infinitely more important than some snooty diva from the wealthy side of the tracks. "Harold and Dave are in trouble. Give me a hand?"

"That's why I'm here." Zack shrugged the pack to the sidewalk, pulled out a thermal, fleece-lined jacket and tossed it at Bruce. "Try not to lose this one. You think these grow on trees, big guy?"

"Is everyone back at work today?" Beck needed to know. A full crew on the streets would surely be nice.

"All except Mother. She's still MIA, somewhere on a tropical island in the South Pacific. Probably sipping a Hurricane with extra rum and basking in the sun."

Mother, aka Sasha Kennedy, was Alex's genius technical assistant and the quintessential Girl Friday. Nosy. Bossy. Currently on extended leave after the death of her daughter. And Zack was an enigma, built like a weightlifter with a heart just as big. He'd taken to the streets when he'd first joined The TEAM, searching out cast-off veterans who hadn't yet made it all the way back home. Junior Agent Jake Weylin had been one of Zack's lost souls. For years, Zack simply opened his doors to his PTSD-damaged buddies. Now the entire TEAM did the same.

Today he was dressed for work, in all black from the knit beanie on his shaved head down to his spit-and-polished work boots. Still reaching out to the men and women he'd always looked after.

Bruce grumbled, but stuck his arms into the jacket's sleeves and zipped it up to the salt-and-pepper stubble on his stubborn chin. "Don't know what you're talking about."

"Jake'll be by shortly with coffee," Zack said instead of arguing. "Can you stand?"

Jake rambled around the District in The TEAM's version of a roach coach, distributing coffee, juices, soda, sandwiches, and water to the homeless, while watching out for anyone at risk at the same time.

Bruce nodded, still seated on the cold concrete. "Yeah. Don't want to, though."

"Your back again?" Zack asked.

"My foot. Damned arthritis gots me all twisted up." Arthritis was Bruce's sanitized name for the stump where his left foot used to be. He'd left it in Vietnam, not that America cared. But those phantom pains in that missing limb were killers in cold weather.

"I've got something for that," Zack said, tapping his earpiece just once. "Hey, Mark. Our regulars need a good, hot breakfast, maybe a medic. Clean, warm beds, for sure. Yes, Bruce again, but Dave and Harold are here, too. Send the wagon. Two of the three aren't moving. Pretty sure I'm looking at alcohol poisoning."

"I ain't goin' to no shelter," Bruce declared even as Beckam helped him onto his good foot and crutch. "Neither are Dave nor Harold. You can't make us."

Which wasn't exactly correct, since Harold and Dave had yet to move or voice an opinion. Beckam knew he could carry both men and whatever was in their meager backpacks if it meant getting them to safety. He'd done it before.

Zack's hands came up, placating the argument before Bruce could drag it out. "You're right, man," he agreed easily, "but you guys are going to the free clinic over by the river, not the mission or the city shelter. You know Kelsey Stewart's place?"

Bruce nodded. "Sure. Everyone on the streets knows Miss Kelsey's place."

Wasn't that the truth? Alex's wife ran Raymond's Kids, a private home/rescue mission for runaway juveniles, derelicts, and other people at risk. The local billionaire, Jed McCormack, had recently added a new wing to the old high school building in the middle of December no less. Which had increased the staff, but also allowed for more clean, warm beds for men like these three. All Beckam had to do was convince them to stay there. Kelsey and her people would do the rest.

"Well, lucky for you Kelsey's on call this morning, and she's holding three beds for you guys once the doctor at the free clinic says you're good to go. She'll make sure you'll be in the same room with Harold and Dave. You know I don't lie. She's got your back. She'll get you settled. No police reports. No nothing. Just an open invitation to stay as long as you guys want."

Bruce grumbled. "Dave ain't gonna like that."

"Please," Beckam murmured from the sidewalk where he still knelt with Bruce's comatose buddies. "Dave's in trouble, Bruce. He's not breathing right. Let's get him and Harold some help before you lose them for good."

That got Bruce's attention. "Well, whatcha waiting for then?"

The donuts would have to wait. Beckam spent the next half-hour loading two of the three old codgers into The TEAM's suburban, both on stretchers in the back. Bruce would be riding shotgun, but for now, he lingered at the rear gate, keeping a sharp eye on his buddies. Transporting them together was the only way any of them would go. None of them trusted hospitals, ambulances, or police. But Kelsey? Her they'd trusted enough over the years to finally accept a hand-up.

Thank goodness. Agent Eric Reynolds had just returned to TEAM HQ from the Seattle office. He worked with Murphy Finnigan, Alex's friend and a damned smart senior agent unto himself. The former Marine was riding with Mark. A navy medic in his old life, Eric was one of those tall, dark, handsome types that caught women's eyes wherever he went. He had a charismatic kind of charm. Right now, he looked the part of a doctor with that stethoscope looped around his neck. In seconds, he'd swathed Dave and Harold with heated blankets.

"What are we looking at?" he asked as he checked their vitals. "Same as last time?"

Beckam nodded. "Yes, alcohol poisoning or worse. You think the free clinic can handle these three?"

Eric nodded, his lips thin and his brows extra dark while he assessed Dave first, then Harold. "Sure, but these men really belong in the ER. Do we have a choice?"

"Always got a choice. Not going to no hospital, guys," Bruce warned threateningly. He still stood at the rear gate, leaning into his crutch while he kept track of his friends. The poor guy was grizzled and his eyes rheumy, as if he hadn't slept in days. "If the free clinic can't help, then let us be. We'll take our chances out here where we belong. We been living on the streets long enough. We'll be fine."

"But you can't legally speak for Dave or Harold, can you?" Eric reminded him as he cocked his head, listening intently to Harold's chest through his stethoscope. "I know you guys are tight, but I've got to be honest, Bruce. Harold's in rough shape. Do you really want to be responsible for his death?"

Bruce snorted, his nostrils flared like he was ready to fight. He aimed the end of his crutch at Eric. "You're just saying that. You know damned well Harold and Dave ain't gonna die. They wouldn't. They're tougher than anyone." His throat worked extra-hard. "They can't."

"Yes, they can, buddy," Beckam told him gently. Like it or not, it was come-to-Jesus time. "Let Mark and Eric save your friends, then all three of you stay with Kelsey and recuperate awhile at Raymond's Kids. You know she's fond of you old farts."

"Well…" Bruce stalled.

"These men are running out of time." Eric steamrolled over him, snapping a blood pressure cuff on Dave's scrawny wrist. "Get in or stay, Bruce. First stop, emergency room, Mark. Move it."

"Wait up. I'm… I'm goin', too," Bruce grumbled as he worked his sticks around the vehicle to the passenger seat. "Goddamned pushy bastards."

Beckam let the insult slide. He helped Bruce climb in alongside Mark, then secured the crutches between the door and seat where Bruce could reach them. At last on his way, Mark pulled away from the curb. He maneuvered the van around lines of bright orange barricades marked DeWitt Construction at the confluence of Union Station Drive and Columbus Monument Drive, then headed across town for the nearest hospital.

"Thanks for staying with these three," Zack said as he loaded what few belongings the men had left behind into his backpack. "They're a handful, but they'll be better off with Kelsey."

"No problem. See you back at the office."

"Or on the streets," Zack answered cheerily. "We're all out here until this killer's behind bars."

"That's good to know. Take care."

"You know it. Hey, Cam. You're sure quiet today."

Camilla barely glanced at Zack as he headed west to connect with Jake. But Beckam breathed easier knowing this operation wasn't up to just him and his reluctant partner. The District covered a lot of land, and comprised four distinct quadrants: Northwest, Northeast, Southwest, and Southeast. Included within those quadrants were the poorer, all black neighborhoods southeast of the Anacostia River, the wealthier homes northwest, up in Cathedral Heights and Embassy Row, as well as all the neighborhoods in between. That the entire

TEAM was engaged in this effort would go a long way toward catching whoever was behind the brutal killings.

"Disgusting," Camilla muttered once Zack was out of earshot.

"Who? Zack?" Beckam had to ask. "Or the fact that these three Army veterans chose to live on the streets? Or the fact that most Americans don't care enough to help them?"

Her nose wrinkled. "Those men aren't right in the head, and you know it. They don't want help. They want drugs and alcohol. You saw them. Both those passed out guys are drunks. Both wanted to lay there and freeze to death. Even if you save their lives this time, it won't matter. They'll just go out and get drunk again. Statistics show most homeless people are crazy—"

"Statistics are just numbers, Cam, and numbers can be manipulated." Beckam cut her off. "We're dealing with real people, and if those three men go out and get drunk again, then let's hope we're here quick enough to help them the next time, too."

"My name isn't—"

His hand came up, palm in her face. "Your name is Cam, and knock off the self-righteous bullshit. You're undercover, remember? You keep spouting your real name, someone might recognize you. You ever think of that? From now on, you're Cam, just Cam, and I'm Beck. We met on the road. We're traveling together. That's all. Understood?"

Her upper lip lifted with her usual snarky disapproval. "But everyone on the street already knows you."

He nodded. "All except our murderer. Besides, what do you care? You're the one who wanted a chance to prove yourself. Like Alex said, it's time you put up and shut up, or move off The TEAM. Your choice."

"Stewart's an ass," she grumbled.

"Yes, he can be," Beckam agreed easily. *Didn't everyone already know that?* "But he's the best boss I've ever worked with, and he makes a difference every damned day. Do you?"

"Whatever. When do we actually start our *mission*?" She added a hearty dose of sarcasm to that last word.

Beckam grunted. "We already have. This is it, girlfriend. Why don't you head around the station, see if you can buddy up with any bag ladies you find back there? That's where a couple like to hang out."

"Me?" Could that snooty lip twist any tighter?

He nodded. "Yes, you. They'll warm up to another woman quicker than they will me."

Cam bared her teeth. "I am not your girlfriend, and these people stink. I thought we were supposed to stay together?" An interesting question for a woman who, until now, had made it crystal clear she didn't need anyone.

Beckam wanted to laugh. The uppity prima donna from the office didn't smell so good, either. But she was finally mingling with the real world. "If you're worried, I'll be there in a few minutes. You've got your pistol. It's loaded, right?"

"Yes, but I'm not worried. Fuck, I was just—"

His palm came up automatically again. "Stop. Cursing."

Right on cue, her nose twisted even tighter. "Jesus! Fuck's not cursing! Can't anyone even—?"

"No. You don't get to verbally abuse me just because you can't restrain yourself."

"I'm not verb—"

"Then what would you call it? Freedom of speech? Creative expression? Your inalienable right to say whatever you want at my expense? Oh, I get it. You have rights, but no one else does."

Her brows clenched into her usual pointed, angry scowl.

But Beckam wasn't finished. "See here's the thing, Cam," he said in his best captain's voice, handing out donuts to every down-and-out person he came across. "My name's Beckam or Beck, not hey you, asshole, or prick. I was Captain Garner while active duty, not Boy Scout. Your rights end where mine begin, and I have the right not to be badgered or bullied by another person, including you. Understand that and we'll get along fine."

"I don't want to get along fine with you, and I'm not your girlfriend, *Beck*." Again, with the sarcasm. He'd never known anyone could pack so much vitriol into a single syllable.

"No, you most definitely are not my friend." He handed her what was left of the donuts. "Do me a favor and go make nice with any homeless women you find. I'll skirt around the other side of the station in case someone else had too much to drink last night. See you in twenty."

He could've sworn he heard a hissed, "Whatever, Boy Scout," as she stomped away.

Chapter Five

Camilla did as her Agent-in-Charge directed, not like it was hard to shove a donut at the two obviously homeless women sitting on the edge of the concrete platform like they were waiting for the train they couldn't afford to ride. One of the old ladies had a shopping cart packed full of aluminum cans and other trash parked behind her. A dog leash with no dog. A plastic shopping bag filled with other plastic bags. Crushed, empty soda cans. The kind of worthless crap that would only net pennies on the dollar—if she were smart enough to take them to a recycling station in the first place.

Professional people who actually had somewhere to go, stepped over and around the women and their garbage-filled bags, as if they were used to dealing with riff-raff.

"You see any strangers around here?" Camilla asked, not making eye contact in case these two old nags recognized her. Which was fuckin' impossible. There was no way these crazy women had ever traveled in the same social spheres she did. They were probably drug addicts like the rest of the vagrants in this city. *Disgusting.* "Want a donut?"

"No, thank you," the gray-haired, older looking bag lady replied as she handed back the pastry that Camilla had all but tossed at her. Dressed in corduroy pants, a threadbare but warm jacket over a turtleneck sweater, she, at least looked semi-clean. Decent. "And no, I haven't seen any strangers lately, but thanks for asking."

"Just you. You're pretty strange," the old hag beside her cackled. "You walk like you got a stick up your ass. What you been drinking for breakfast, pickle juice?" She chuckled after she said that, wiping the drool off her mouth with the back of a dirty hand.

Talk about ugly. This woman was one big puffy puddle of wrinkled flesh with legs. Dirty pants. Mismatched boots. Her quilted winter jacket was stiff with grime, and her teeth were yellow and crooked. Her breath probably stunk too, not like Camilla would ever get close enough to find out that disgusting detail. And the hag was rude.

"Bitch," Camilla snapped. No one would ever make her look foolish again. Not ever. "I was just being nice. See if I bring you anything else."

"There's no need to be sharp with us," Gray Hair soothed. "Georgia doesn't mean any harm." She, at least, has clean hands and intelligent eyes. Her friend was just another grimy, crazy woman with wiry, salt-and-pepper hair that stuck out from under a dirty, red ballcap. Which she'd probably stolen. Or found on the sidewalk. And obviously slept in last night.

"Why don't you mind your business?" Camilla would've marched away if she hadn't spotted Boy Scout rounding the opposite corner of Union Station, headed along the dock in her direction. Great. He'd probably seen Gray Hair refuse the donut.

"Well, if it isn't two of my favorite ladies," he called out, waving at Gray Hair and Dumpy, a big grin on his face. "Hey, Georgia!"

"Hi, handsome!" Dumpy called out with a wide, enthusiastic wave, kicking her feet against the platform like an excited little kid. "'Bout time you showed up."

Wow. The look on Boy Scout's face at this old hag's screechy greeting changed everything. It made him—good-looking. Really good-looking. His blue eyes actually lit up. You would've thought he was reconnecting with his mom or… or someone equally important in his life, instead of a dirty old bag lady.

Unexpected jealousy rippled up Camilla's spine, lifting every last one of her hackles. Why was he wasting time on these two grubby women? *Why doesn't he smile like that at— at me? I'm smarter than they are. I'm younger and… and… and fuck! I don't care who he smiles at. I don't! He's as big an idiot as they are. Look at that dumb look on his face. Stupid ass.*

Yet that six-foot-four stupid ass had just crouched down between these two dirty old women like he actually liked them. Like he genuinely cared. Camilla understood then. He was their version of a dashing, fairytale prince on a prancing steed passing through their mixed-up, messed-up lives. They could never really have him. They knew that and they didn't really want him. They had each other to sleep with in the gutter every night. He was just eye-candy to these two aged women who'd never had much of a life to begin with.

"How're my girls this fine wintery day?" he asked, that scruffy square chin of his turning first to Georgia, then to Gray Hair. "Joslyn? How's that cold? Anything I need to know?"

Gray Hair, aka Joslyn, nodded. "Oh, you." She blushed. The old hag actually blushed! "I've been using the inhaler you gave me. Thank you again for being so thoughtful. I'm much better this morning. But Mr. Fancy Pants was by earlier. He's selling something different today. I don't know what it is. He called it bath salts, but knowing him, it's probably not."

"Ah." Boy Scout nodded knowingly, his elbows on his thighs and his long slender fingers between his knees. "Did they come in little foil or plastic packets?"

"Why, yes, they did. Tiny pretty foil envelopes." Joslyn leaned back on one hand to look up at him. "You've seen this before?"

"Unfortunately, yes. Way too often. It's the latest craze among teenagers, bath salts that can be ingested by sniffing, snorting, smoking, or injecting. Which way did he go?" he asked as his gaze tracked the crowded platform behind Camilla.

Georgia stuck her chin toward the Senate Building a few blocks south. "That way. Said he had clients waiting on him; he couldn't afford to be late. Asked us how much we wanted. Said he'd give it to us cheap."

"But we told him no," Joslyn said firmly, "like we always do. Can't figure why he keeps badgering us, Beck. We've never bought anything from him."

"Because you're beautiful," Boy Scout purred, "and Kevin's not as dumb as he looks. He knows a couple sharp ladies when he sees them. Anything else?"

Georgia turned coy, twisting a grimy finger in her dirty hair. "Another kiss'd sure be nice," she coaxed, then tapped that same disgusting finger to her chapped lips. "Only this time, give me some tongue."

Oh, my hell, she's got whiskers! A mustache! Disgusting!

Camilla's entire face wrinkled at the suggestive way the ugly woman came onto her Agent-in-Charge. But of course,

Boy Scout just tipped his head back and laughed, as if he thoroughly enjoyed the thought of kissing this old toad.

Her heart did a funny kind of acrobatic flip at the sight of his strong, tan neck. That was an unexpectedly warm but painful feeling. She'd never seen this side of Beck, nor the clean, trimmed edge of his sideburns. Not the jut of his chin nor the childish abandonment in a grown man's profile. For certain, she'd never heard anything so heartbreakingly tender as the rich baritone notes pouring out of his throat. Like honey, his voice was melting all over her. As if he truly enjoyed everything she hated. How was that even possible? What *was* there to enjoy about life?

But then…

He leaned into Georgia like he meant to fulfill that old crone's wish. He was going to kiss her.

Oh, my God! Camilla closed her eyes, then opened one. Just in case. Peeking. This she'd have to see to believe. How dumb was this idiot to kiss that old woman on the mouth? *Ewwww!*

Boy Scout cupped the back of Georgia's head, his fingers under her cap and in her hair, his smile sweet and tender—like he loved her. He leaned forward. Her ballcap fell off. Georgia closed her eyes and... he did it. He kissed her!

Only, thank God! He'd just kissed the middle of her wrinkled forehead. But then, he whispered, "I'd never take advantage of a fine, upstanding lady like you. Now behave yourself before you get me in trouble."

Camilla could've laughed out loud. *Lady?* What'd he think? That this old toad was a queen and he was a knight in shining armor in *Merry Old England*? Camilla had to look twice when Georgia's shoulders came up and she giggled like a naughty little girl instead of the ugly witch she was. For a second there... *No. Couldn't be. Just could not be.* There was no way Georgia's complexion could've changed into a younger, prettier, less wrinkled version of the girl she might have been a long—*long*—time ago. Was there? Yet for a second...

No. Just no. Camilla shook the notion off. Georgia was still as ugly, whiskered, and smelly as ever. "Donuts," she interrupted sharply, in case Boy Scout had forgotten why they were loitering out here in the cold to begin with.

He straightened to his feet, his back cracking. "Ah, duty calls. I'm off to pass out what's left of these pastries. You ladies sure you don't want one? They're fairly fresh day-olds," he said with a mischievous smile.

"No. We've already had breakfast burritos. You will come by and see us again soon?" Joslyn asked, looking up at him, the first of the morning sun in her eyes.

"Don't I always?" he asked as he leaned over and stuck his hand between the sunlight and her face, creating a shadow to protect her eyes. "Where are the winter hats I brought yesterday?"

Hats? Yesterday? Camilla frowned at that tidbit of news. He'd come here before they went to the range yesterday? Huh.

"It's right here." Joslyn tugged a knitted cap up from the pocket of her winter coat that desperately needed dry-cleaning. Hell, it needed to be tossed in the trash and replaced with something better. Newer. Something respectable. "Wool gets too warm to wear sometimes. But don't worry, Beck. I haven't lost it."

"Yet," Georgia cackled as she produced a knitted cap from her pocket and waved it at him. "Here's mine! See? I keep it in my pocket, just like Jos. Like my ballcap better. Where'd it go?"

Beckam scooped it off the ground where it had fallen during that kiss and settled it back on her fuzzy head like he was dressing a little child. "There. You look amazing, Georgia."

She smiled like she believed him, the idiot. "Don't worry 'bout us, Beck. We take care of each other. Joslyn watches out for me when I git forgetful, and I watch out for her. We're besties. Ha!"

Joslyn was the quieter of the two, definitely the smarter. Her eyes were as gray as her hair, but she seemed more... intelligent, if that descriptor could, in any way, fit a bag lady in shabby, cast-off clothes. And sad. Joslyn enjoyed Boy Scout's visits, but when she looked up at him, the sadness shining in her eyes was unmistakable.

"Do you ladies need anything else?" Camilla asked, though why she'd called them ladies, and why that odd request had popped out of her mouth, she couldn't explain. It just had. But there was this store over on Constitution Avenue that recycled clothes—better clothes—and…

Never mind. Cam didn't need to get involved with these two, and that's what would happen if she offered to take them shopping. Talk about a stupid idea.

"No, we're fine," Joslyn replied. "Thanks for asking."

"Already got what we want." Georgia grabbed Boy Scout's ankle. "This guy right here. He takes care of us. Don't need the likes of you hanging 'round."

"Sure, we do," Joslyn soothed. "We can always use more friends, Georgia. Please come visit us again, umm, I'm sorry. I don't remember your name."

Because I never gave it to you. Camilla's spine stiffened. She wasn't about to get cozy with two old hags, and it didn't matter if they knew her name or who she really was anyway. They weren't important. They were nobodies. They had no clout or money. Who'd miss them?

And yet Boy Scout had turned his shoulders toward her. Everyone was watching. Him, most intently of all. Expectantly.

And damn. Camilla had to be polite, didn't she? That was what they were waiting for, her to perform, right? As odd as it felt, even these kinds of street people deserved some level of common courtesy, didn't they? Or did they? What difference did it make if she just turned her back on them and walked away? They wouldn't miss her. No one ever did.

She let the moment stretch, and she didn't know why. But maybe she did. All her life, Camilla had been the odd duck, the girl who knew too much and had never belonged. Why was it important to even consider the tiniest relationship with these old crones? Yet she felt a weird connection with the women that she couldn't explain or understand. It'd be nice to belong just once in her fuckin' life. But where? With these old goats? God, the thought…

It was then something warm and deep inside Boy Scout's deep, blue, indigo eyes reached out and breached the turmoil churning in her mind. Must've been those here-one-moment, gone-the-next turquoise sparkles. He stood there watching, his feet spread in that alpha stance he did so well. But his gaze had softened like he trusted her not to let him down. As if he'd wait all day for her to make up her mind. As if he knew how hard it was for her to be kind.

Okay then. But just this once. Camilla licked her dry lips, then nodded one curt nod at Joslyn. The smart one. Not Georgia, the toad. "Cam. You can call me Cam."

Boy Scout cocked his head and smiled as if he were seeing her for the first time. The corners of his mouth curled, drawing her eyes to his lips. Not even chapped. Yet he licked the bottom one. Smiled wider as if he actually liked her. And that shit had to stop.

"This time," Camilla growled emphatically at the two older ladies. "You can call me Cam, but just this once."

A truly beautiful light shifted over Joslyn's face, but it wasn't a ray from the morning sun. This was a different light brightening those gray eyes, turning them blue. Light-blue like the sky after the sun broke through the storm clouds.

"It's very nice to meet you, Cam," she said politely, "and I look forward to seeing you again. Will you please come back and visit me, even when Beckam can't?"

"No." Camilla wanted to slap that sappy smirk off his face. "We're just passing through. Right, Beck?"

His upper teeth scraped over his bottom lip as if he were hiding another damned grin. The ass. He was laughing at her, and she knew it. He was just like everyone else in this stupid world.

"Speak for yourself. I pass through here nearly every day. You're always welcome to come along, but if you girls need some alone-time, you know, just to talk..." Both his broad shoulders lifted, making him look more like a little boy than the strapping man that he was. The jerk!

"No," Camilla said with authority.

That old witch Georgia cackled and kicked her feet against the dock like the bully girl she really was. Boy Scout smiled wider. Damn him. He was making her look stupid.

Camilla turned her back on him and his disgusting, old lady friends then. They meant nothing. Neither did he. Ab-so-fuckin'-lutely nothing.

Chapter Six

"You kissed them!"

Beckam nodded thoughtfully at Camilla's scorn-filled accusation. "I always kiss them, Cam. They're sweet."

"They reek! And stop calling me Cam!"

He chuckled low in his throat. "In case you haven't noticed, we don't smell so good, either."

"Yes, but I'm washing this crap off the second I get home today. They live smelling like that. Day in and day out." She shook off yet another shiver of disgust. "Did you see Georgia's teeth? Sure, you did. You were close enough to know her breath stinks. It probably doesn't bother you. I'll bet you don't shower any more than they do. But I'm not staying in these clothes until we catch whoever's killing these people. I'm not."

These people?

"Yes, you are," he said deliberately. "You're with me, remember? And we're not going home until the mission's over. Now that we've been seen together, this is where we'll be and what we'll do until these people are safe again."

"Bite me," she grumbled. But then, Kah-me-ah had been doing a lot of grumbling since they'd dressed down and dirtied up at TEAM headquarters in Alexandria earlier this morning.

Miss Perfect hadn't appreciated the wrinkled, extra-smelly clothing Beckam had acquired the night before on his self-appointed rounds through the District's homeless venues. It was an unspoken rule he'd fallen into after leaving the Army, to look out for any former military, but especially homeless, older veterans. They all needed a hand up, and when nights got too dark and booze didn't help, they often needed someone to drag them to a shelter or take them home with them. That was how Zack rescued Jake Weylin from the streets. By nothing more than constant, steady friendship. Maybe a bottle or two.

Quite a few other male TEAM members did the same. Mark, Harley, Rory, Connor, hell, almost everyone. Agent Lee Hart and his wife Tess even worked at Lorelei's Kitchen when they could.

"This is our neighborhood now," Beckam reminded her. "We need to be seen together for you to be trustworthy. The locals will tell us if they see anything odd, trust me. I've already gone over this. We stick together."

She made a sound under her breath.

"Say again? I can't hear you when you mumble."

"I'm not mumbling," she bit out. "I'm upset. Can't you tell the difference? Jesus!"

He shook his head as they made their way west and away from Union Station. January weather ensured fewer people were out and about, but the few they encountered on the sidewalk still cast suspicious glances their way. Which served Beckam's need to be nondescript and incognito. He meant to blend in with good people like Georgia and Joslyn for as long as it took.

"Why now?" he asked patiently. Training a newbie shouldn't entail this much drama, but here he was, asking Her Highness what made her mad this time.

"Because whoever we're looking for won't be out in broad daylight." He could almost hear her implied *'you idiot!'* "We need to lay low. Wait until dark. That's when the majority of murders go down."

"True," he replied evenly as they headed toward Lorelei's Kitchen. "But the last three homeless people our killer murdered were struck in the head from behind, and, as near as the ME can determine, TOD, that's medical examiner and time of death—"

"I know what TOD means," she snapped.

Beckam rolled his shoulder. "Great. Then I'll skip forward to COD. All—"

A horn blared behind them. He turned in time to see a man rag-dolling across the street. Brakes screeched. Someone yelled an obscenity. Another horn sounded and traffic halted as the guy's boots hit the curb in front of Union Station. But Beckam only had eyes for the man with his feet still in the gutter while traffic hurried past him as if he were just another piece of garbage.

"Hey, Mark. We've got a man down," he reported into his mic as he ran to the scene.

Mark came back instantly with, "One of ours?" Code for *'is this someone who needs a hand up or is this someone—a victim—who needs immediate police intervention?'*

"Call 911. Not sure who he is. I'm checking now," Beckam answered as he took a knee at the stranger's side.

Oddly, Cam hadn't spouted one of her biased, snarky opinions. Maybe because the puddle of blood beneath this guy's head just kept growing.

"Not ours," Beckam reported somberly to Mark. "Tell MPD to hurry." Then, "Hey, stay with me, man. Who did this?" he asked, needing the stranger to do more than stare at the sky.

"Shell," he breathed, his breathing ragged and shallow. Dressed in mismatched and worn boots with holes in their soles, his breath smelled of coffee and mint. Not booze. Not even tooth decay. His eyes were a scary, murky green and fixed somewhere far overhead. Two slender dirty fingers lifted out of the guy's long jacket sleeve to the center of his chest. They tapped right over his jacket zipper. Over his heart. "Shell… Shell, Shell, Shelly…"

By then, Beckam had Metro PD dispatch barking in his ear, verifying location and requesting precise details. Cam just stood there watching, probably annoyed at the inconvenient interruption of a dying man messing up her day. Beckam honestly didn't care what she thought she knew. A real teammate would've been down on her knees alongside him, administering first-aid instead of judging him and this guy.

"Come on, buddy, at least tell me your name," he urged again, his fingers on the guy's neck where a weak pulse still beat. "Shelly who? Is she your wife? Your daughter? A girlfriend? You got her number? Let me call her for you."

He swallowed hard. He was losing this guy and there wasn't a thing he could do to stop it. The words he'd spoken from his past echoed once again: *Please don't die. Not like this. Not here on the street without someone who loves you by your side.*

The dying man closed his eyes and breathed, "Shell."

"Max! Maxwell Bird!" Joslyn screamed from somewhere behind Beckam.

By then, approaching sirens declared the District's finest had arrived. He stood back when the EMTs took over. Joslyn and Georgia stood vigil, watching while MPD Officer Jim

Tuttle, a regular at Union Station and a friend, pulled Beckam aside for the details.

"Someone dumped him out of their car. No vehicle hit him as far as I could tell," he told the officer.

"Maxwell Bird," Joslyn cried from Georgia's arms. "His name is Maxwell Bird and he worked Thirteenth Street."

Which meant Max panhandled outside Metro Center Station where the red, blue, orange, and silver metro lines converged. Also, where crowds of tourists, businessmen, and other busy people might've tossed him a few coins or a sandwich if he were lucky. The White House lay four blocks to the west; Ford's Theater lay a block south. Until today, Max had been lost in a city of pomp, circumstance, and plenty.

"You think he was running from someone? Maybe this is a hit-and-run," MPD Officer Tuttle suggested. Jimmy was a good man and an excellent officer. Trim, tall, and slender, his dark black skin shone in the early morning sun.

"No, sir. Someone dumped him out of their car. I heard tires screeching, then saw him rolling through traffic." Beckam pointed to where he and Cam were standing when it happened. Why was she still back there? "I'm sorry. Me and that lady over there were passing out donuts to the homeless. We'd just left Joslyn and Georgia behind the station, their usual morning spot. I honestly didn't see anything suspicious or out of the ordinary until I heard tires screech. When I turned, Max was already ass-over-boots in traffic. He finally stopped rolling here at the curb."

"Did you get make and model? Maybe the number off a plate?" Tuttle asked as he scribbled in the tiny tablet he'd pulled out of his shirt pocket.

Beckam shook his head. "Too much traffic, sorry. I was more worried about pulling him out of traffic before someone ran over him."

"His head injuries are identical to the other victims," Tuttle murmured extra-quietly as he glanced over Beckam's shoulder. "Tell your boss whoever's doing this is using something like an icepick near as we can figure. Back of the head. One strike. Same MO as everyone else."

"Damn." Killing homeless men and women made no sense. "But now you know whoever's been killing these people has help. And he's got to be male, strong enough to puncture a skull bone. You're not looking for just one lone guy on the street, either. A vehicle is involved. At least two people. One to drive. Another to push Max out of the car. That couldn't have been easy. This smacks of a gang initiation."

Tuttle nodded. "It surely does, and yes. We've got eyes and ears on all local gangbangers. You tell Houston to back down yet? We got this one."

"No, but I will." Beckam tapped his earpiece and sent Mark a quick update that MPD was on the scene. They'd worked closely with The TEAM for years.

"God bless us all," Joslyn murmured wretchedly from where she was leaning into Georgia. "He's… he's gone."

Yes. Max had breathed his last. The EMTs did what they could, which at this point was simply to wrap him up and transfer his body to their gurney, then take him to the county morgue.

Beckam's heart melted. It only took one look at Joslyn, and she barreled into him. He opened his arms and held on tight while she buried her face in his jacket and sobbed. "I just talked with him yesterday. He said Shelly wanted him to go live with her. Finally. He was going to be happy. He was a grandfather."

"Shelly's his wife?"

She shook her head. "No, his wife died two years ago. Shelly's his daughter. He had two kids, but I don't think Jax has spoken to him in years. He never understood why his successful father fell off the grid like he did."

"Excuse me, ma'am," Officer Tuttle said. "I'm sure sorry about this. I know it's hard losing a friend, and I didn't mean to eavesdrop, but do you have his daughter's or son's number and address? I need to notify next of kin."

Joslyn shook her head. "No, but Shelly lives across the river. Her husband's Sal Goldstein of—"

"The law firm? S and G?" Tuttle asked. "You've got to be kidding."

Joslyn nodded. "Max was a lawyer there. One of their best."

Which revealed a little more of her previous life as well. Beckam didn't know her complete backstory, only that something tragic had pushed her, an educated, genteel woman, onto the streets and into the life of a transient. She had too much class to have ever submitted to drugs or booze. She was the epitome of grace and elegance, like a rich aunt to Georgia's cruder, rougher scrubwoman personality. Joslyn was the lady of the two. Georgia was the brawler, the rowdy redneck. But Joslyn had rubbed elbows with the high-powered law firm of Sachs and Goldstein in her former life? *Interesting.*

Poor Georgia still cried openly, big sloppy tears sliding down her wrinkled cheeks. Beckam waved her over, and then he had an armful of two weeping women.

"Listen, Beck. These ladies need you more than I do," Officer Tuttle said. "If you think of anything else, let me know."

"Thanks, Jimmy. I'll do that."

Georgia sobbed, "Max. My Max." Of all the street people, Georgia had taken each of these murders hard. But then, she'd probably known the victims longer and better than most. She had to be ten years older than Joslyn, and Joslyn looked to be in her fifties. Beckam didn't know that for sure. Street people tended to look older than they were.

The ambulance pulled away. Officer Tuttle was still documenting the scene and taking pictures. Another cruiser had arrived by then. The sun shone through the misty fog, and it was just another day in the District.

By the sounds of things, no one but his daughter and these two ragged women would miss Maxwell Bird. Wasn't that sad? To live your whole life, only to end up nothing more than a fatal statistic on a cold, dirty sidewalk, in a town known for its ability to character assassinate the grand as well as step on the lowly.

Beckam murmured another round of 'I'm sorrys' to the women in his arms. It wasn't until they walked away together that he steeled himself to look for Cam again.

Didn't it figure? Miss Know-It-All was gone.

Chapter Seven

She couldn't breathe. Couldn't think! Had to get away before he looked. Before he saw!

As soon as she could, Camilla grabbed her chance to walk. To run! That man—that Max guy was—d-d-dead. There on the street. He'd died right there on the street in front of everyone. God, oh God, oh God! Only nobody cared! It was like he was just a piece of something to drive around and step over.

But she'd seen him die! She'd watched. She hadn't been able to take her eyes off his face. She couldn't make herself look away. She'd just stood there like the world's most awful voyeur and watched how his pallor turned from bright red to gray then to blue. She'd seen how his chest stopped heaving all at once, how it… stopped moving completely. She saw the thin stream of spittle roll out of the corner of his mouth. How it trickled over his gray whiskers. How he just stared and stared...

And then…

But then…

God! She'd felt him die! She did! She didn't know how that worked, but she'd felt it inside her chest. In her heart. A hollow something that felt like a puddle of cold, dark poison. Like her own heart was suddenly linked to his… or something. She couldn't describe it, couldn't even begin to weigh or measure this terrible emptiness in her gut until—

No! Just no! Camilla rushed to the cigarette ashcan standing outside an all-night convenience store and barely made it in time before she threw up. She had no idea where that box of donuts was. Didn't care where she'd dropped it. Couldn't tolerate thinking of gooey pastries as she—

Threw up some more, retching the vile contents of her stomach into that awful, smelly can of other people's cancer sticks. The humiliation! In public! She, Camilla Brinkman, had officially embarrassed herself to death by vomiting on a public street. Ha. Camilla Brinkman, nothing. She wasn't even that anymore.

A big warm hand landed on her shoulder, but—

"Don't touch me," she choked at her nosy Boy Scout mentor while spitting another mouthful of bile into the can, wishing the earth would swallow her, and…

God, he's seen me puke. Kill me now!

Only she didn't believe in God. There was no such thing as a benevolent overlord. Even if there were, a being like that wouldn't deign to help someone like her, even if she believed in Him. Which she never would. God was a concept created by the wealthy to keep the ignorant and repressed in line. The poor, stupid fools of the world were dumb enough to fall for it. She was neither poor nor stupid. Thank God.

Of course, Boy Scout didn't listen, just kept his big, clumsy hand where it landed. But that personal touch of his did help her gut stop churning. She didn't know how he did it, and she didn't care. She was too embarrassed. And vulnerable.

How totally crude was this, her throwing up in public, on a city street? Where anyone and everyone could see? Like a genuine homeless drunk? All those creepy street people were probably standing in the shadows laughing at her. Maybe clapping at the mess she'd made, taking bets on whether she'd gotten any of it on her jacket. Well, she'd show them, too. She'd show everyone! She would. As soon as she could let go of this ashcan.

"It's okay," Boy Scout soothed in that same deep, rumbling tone he'd used on those two old bag ladies. "Tougher guys than you have tossed their cookies after a hard morning."

"Shut. Up," she gasped at the bottom of that can, now gooey and gray with her latest deposit, even as she shrugged his hand away. "I don't need your h-h-help."

Cough. Cough. Spit. Spit. Ewww! The stench! Her poor nose burned from the rapid exit of stomach acid from her body. Her belly hurt. Her ribs. Her head. Everything! And vomiting always made her cry. But Camilla was damned if she'd let Boy Scout see any more weakness.

"Sorry, Cam," he murmured. Still there, damn him. His voice so soft and low. What was he doing being kind? Why was he standing so close? She stunk. Did he need to make sure that she knew he'd witnessed her making a fool of herself. *Moron!*

Cough. Spit. Ewww...

A clean, cloth handkerchief swiped over her mouth, and then... and then... her stupid Agent-in-Charge tipped her shoulder into his side like she needed someone to hold her up. Which she did. Like he didn't care that she'd made a stinking mess of herself. Which she had. Or that her breath smelled atrocious.

"I threw up the first time I saw someone die, too," he said evenly, his voice a gentle rumble beneath her ear. "It's a natural physical reaction to emotional shock. Go ahead. Cry if you need to. That's how we process tragedy."

Like that stupid advice was supposed to help?

"Just go," she growled. At least, she tried to growl, but... but... Big, fat, burning-hot tears spilled out of her traitorous eyes, adding more humiliation to the steaming slime in the bottom of that can, and... and...

Camilla looked up into Boy Scout's face. Damn, he was tall, especially standing as close as he was. She had to crane her neck to see him. Then she had to blink back tears because all she saw was a blur. But he'd seen that man die, too, and he wasn't crying like some pussy. He just looked steadily down at her, like he usually did. Like a big, dumb rock. A six-foot-four rock with the gentlest sparkle in his blue eyes that made her think he cared. Did she dare?

"Max died," she told him as she swiped the back of a hand over her mouth. Like he didn't know? Like he hadn't been there? Yet for some reason, she had to tell Boy Scout. He needed to know that, "I saw him. On the sidewalk. Did you see it when it happened? Did you feel it, too? Did you see him d-d-die?"

Of course, he'd seen Max die, but Cam couldn't get her mouth to stop blabbering. "He... he just laid there, and he... he quit breathing. His eyes, they just... the light in them just went... out."

A sob hiccupped out of her then. More like it erupted out of her chest like a noisy volcano of embarrassed grief and the oddest sensations of loss and confusion. She covered her mouth with the back of her hand and mumbled around it. "One second he, he was there. The next. Pfffft." She waved a double circle in the air. "He was just... gone, only he wasn't, only he... he was, but..."

Boy Scout's fingers squeezed her shoulder, his thumb digging into her collarbone. And that did it.

Camilla crashed into him. Needing something substantial to hold onto that would make the world stop spinning. He would do. She was bawling her eyes out by then and not talking sense, her face pushed into Boy Scout's chest where no one could see her or laugh at her and wonder why she wasn't good enough. She was, damn it. Just not right now.

His arms folded around her and he pulled her into him. Warming her. Blocking the cold and the rest of the world from view while she melted. And cried. God, she cried! What she'd seen and felt back here didn't make sense. It didn't! She hadn't known that dead guy, and she surely wouldn't have publicly admitted it if she had. Yet Cam had felt his spirit—or his soul—or something—lift out his body and leave. She truly had. It was the oddest thing, like leaves blowing away in a gentle fall breeze. Or… or like ash at the end of a cigarette. He'd just—gone.

It actually hurt to feel something she couldn't see and had no way to quantify or weigh or measure. But that was precisely what had happened. She hadn't dreamed or imagined it. But when whatever lifted out of him and blew away, something got sucked out of her, too. An aching hollowness now lay like a stone in the pit of her gut, and how the fuck did that work? Nothingness aching like somethingness? *Does not compute.*

Jesus! She pushed her face deeper into the warmth of Boy Scout's stupid Carhartt jacket, but still couldn't make her eyes stop seeing that guy die. It wasn't just the bright red puddle of blood under Max's head, or the blank look that had crept over his wrinkled, gray-bearded face while he stared at the sky. It wasn't the way the world seemed to stop turning for that split second, like it was holding its breath. Or the way she hadn't been able to feel the cold or the sun or her hands or her feet. It was the way he'd been there one second, but the next… Max was gone. Just. Gone. Not his body. Just—him.

Camilla was even more embarrassed now. She'd lost control and given it over to this… this man. This Agent-in-Charge man who had no business being in charge of her. He wasn't smart enough!

But breathing hurt. Every rise and fall of her clenched-tight chest—hurt as if she'd been stabbed. Hell, even thinking about that dirty old man lying on a cold sidewalk in the middle of winter while he'd died—hurt so hard. She could barely breathe. Camilla needed time to think. She couldn't begin to understand why. She didn't care about Max. He was just some homeless guy. One of many. She hadn't known him long enough to care. Wouldn't ever have given him the time of day, certainly not long enough to have asked his name. So why couldn't she stop thinking about him? Why did Max suddenly matter so damned much? Why the holy fuck now?

Max was a nobody. A bum! He'd contributed nothing to society. If anything, he'd been just another drain on the District's already stretched-thin fiscal resources. Every last one of these degenerate street people were losers. They were the crazies who'd failed in life or who'd resorted to drugs and alcohol when they were stupid and young. They were the lowest of the low, the dirtiest and the dumbest. She was better than all of them put together. Even Boy Scout.

And enough! Camilla stiffened her spine. She'd been in more humiliating situations than this. She would *not* cry one more useless tear for someone she didn't care about. No more. She'd never admit weakness or defeat. She didn't need Boy

Scout's help or his compassion or—or—or anyone. With her belly full of fire again, she jerked out of his arms and away from that hard, comforting chest.

"Hey," he said the second she caught her balance. His hand still circled her wrist and she hadn't pulled out of his grasp— yet. "It's okay. Come here, honey."

And no one had ever called her honey, nor said it so sweetly or so... so...

"Don't. Touch. M-me," she told him with as much icy venom as she could muster.

Boy Scout's blue eyes were so damned soft and warm that she'd stuttered like an idiot. How could one look from him make her think of white, sandy beaches, turquoise waters, and tropical sunsets? Sugary sweet tequila and being safe inside the circle of his arms and... *Gah!*

Camilla swallowed hard. She lifted her chin in defiance at what he'd just witnessed and wiped the back of her hand one last time to remove what was left of her breakfast off her bottom lip. She coughed, the morning air so much colder when sucked into a vomit-ravaged throat. God, she stunk even more disgustingly now that she could breathe her own breath again. That should make her Agent-in-Charge happy. Garner had what he wanted—her abject and very thorough public humiliation.

But he'd let her wrist go, and that was what she wanted. Right? *You bet your ass.*

Camilla Lopez Brinkman had been brought up properly, and she'd remembered every last humiliating lesson the world had ground into her under its high and mighty boot. Papa was right. She didn't need anyone. Never would. Never again. Not hotshot Agent Garner. Not dumbass Alex Stewart. Not asshole

Heath Brinkman, the liar. Not his prissy mother Penn, short for Penelope-the-Pretentious-Bitch, who'd never let a person forget she knew everything and everyone who was anybody. And never his bastard father Spence, short for salacious, grabbing, groping Spencer Brinkman, the asshat who thought marriage into his family made his daughter-in-law communal property. None of them mattered.

You hear me, world? No one matters but me!

Chapter Eight

Beckam stepped back, not because his junior agent was mad, but because for the first time, he'd seen through her rage, an enlightening first. Cam was unexploded ordnance, and eventually, something or someone would be stupid enough to light that fuse. He didn't want it to be him. He'd finally glimpsed the real Camilla, and she was not what she pretended. If anything, she was fragile and close to shattering. She'd had enough.

Since her first day on the job, she'd made it crystal clear that she was better than anyone else on The TEAM. The way she'd walked, talked, and balked at even the simplest common courtesies had created a hazardous hot spot within The TEAM's normally easy-going office dynamics. Camilla Brinkman was a raging inferno that had only grown hotter and meaner since then. And suddenly, Beckam wanted to know why. What made her tick? What made her burn?

She'd been easy to dismiss. Prickly, bitchy women usually were. They seemed intent on making everyone around them miserable, and Cam had succeeded. But rage wasn't all he saw now. Yes, she was mad on an elemental level he'd honestly never witnessed before in all his years. But he got the feeling that anger wasn't directed at just The TEAM. She was pissed at the whole world and everyone in it. Even herself. She just didn't seem to know what to do with her rage or how to let it go.

Her anger was a bottled-up source of radioactive energy that pounded deep inside her veins. He probably could've heard the throbbing beat of war drums if not for the street noise. Tiny veins across her forehead pulsed, and he was pretty sure she'd breathed fire with that last command to not touch. Which naturally, made him want to. This woman needed to be held and reassured, especially now. Who would have ever thought that Camilla needed to be hugged? Maybe even kissed—?

Ah. No. Someone else could do the kissing, someone who didn't mind getting a raft of porcupine quills stuck in his face when she lashed back. Which she would. Beckam wasn't looking for commitment. He was only trying to figure out the puzzle that was Camilla Brinkman. Obviously, she was hurting. Down deep. Where no one could reach because she'd never let anyone get past her formidable wall of nastiness. Yet even that was a puzzle onto itself. Precisely how many years had this woman been working on that wall? My God. What a sad waste of energy and time.

An automatic sigh breathed out of him. That was it. That was Kah-me-ah's secret. She might act all high and mighty, but her anger was just a mask. She was protecting herself, hiding behind that prickly wall of hers, using snobbery to cover her pain and keep everyone away. Although, come to think of it, what could the wife of the privileged son of a well-connected, wealthy District lobbyist possibly know about pain?

Beckam backed off what had felt like an epiphany there for a moment, but yeah. She was probably just pissed because she had to work for a living. That had to be it. Her hubby might be one of those smart guys who expected her to pull her weight in their marriage, as in not just sit around all day and spend his money.

Yet there she stood, her defiance tossed at Beckam like a glove, daring him to pick up that challenge of a duel and fight her to the bitter end. She'd like that. She'd been picking a fight since day one.

"Are you going to be okay?" he had to ask.

She jerked her elbow out of his hand with a nasty, "How many times do I have to tell you to back off? Jesus! Leave me alone!"

If those black eyes sparked any hotter, he would've been scorched on the spot. Hot damn. With her cheeks flushed and her dark, glossy hair pulled back as tight as it was, she cut an impressive profile that screamed, *'Don't mess with me!'*

But once again, he saw through the bluster. He'd had that uncanny gift as a kid, to know when his dad needed more than just a helping hand on the farm. When his mom needed someone to talk with. And now, facing this five-foot-nothing, Amazon warrior who seemed to think she had to fight everyone who crossed her path, Beckam's eyes were opened again.

Fighting was all she'd done since she'd shown up her first day, when FBI Director Tucker Chase, one of Alex's many FBI nemeses, had all but tossed her to the wolves, or in this case, The TEAM. Was fighting all she knew?

She hadn't been happy then, and she wasn't any happier now. First, Alex told her that her position was only temporary. Then, everyone on The TEAM had backed off from befriending her because, well, because you couldn't make friends with a snarling dog that snapped your head off every time you came within striking distance. Even Ember Dennison,

Cam's cubicle partner, who was the friendliest woman on the planet, avoided her. Which was just plain sad now that Beckam had caught an actual glimpse of the hurt little girl hiding beneath the toughest-bitch-on-the-block, the I-could-care-less persona Cam projected. What was that about? What was she hiding?

Beckam was no dummy. His mom always said he'd come to earth with more intuition than any boy had a right to. Well, he was a man now, and she'd been right. That uncanny childish intuition of his had morphed into a reliable sixth sense that had literally saved his life and the lives of the men and women in his Army company over and over again. He could usually read people, and he knew he was right this time, too.

Cam might've built a wickedly thick, high wall complete with razor-sharp concertina wire to keep people out. She might sound nasty as all get out on her best days, and she could surely make grown men turn and run away. When she scowled, she did look meaner than the scariest mask found in any Halloween store in October.

But this morning, he sensed that she also had her back against a very different kind of wall. One she would never talk to him about or let him pass through. She was Mrs. Jones all over again. That secretive neighbor lady back in Horse Hollow, Oklahoma, who'd accused him of fathering her child, when in fact, her bully husband had been beating the crap out of her for who knew how long. All she'd needed was a safe refuge, for just one person to help her. That she'd chosen a dumb high school boy instead of one of her husband's buddies should have been telling. She'd chosen someone she'd thought she could trust. The town that loved to gossip hadn't known that. No one had. Not even Beck. Because victims like Mrs. Jones tended to project what they needed others to see until—they couldn't.

What a sad way to live.

With a grunt, Cam tossed his handkerchief into the ashcan, not that Beckam wanted it back. He didn't. It was just that most people would've asked before they threw something away that didn't belong to them. But then, Camilla Brinkman was not most people.

He took a full step back and out of her air space, seeing her now with different eyes.

"Let me know when you're ready to roll," he told her quietly, his gaze averted in case she needed to swipe that line of snot running under her nose before it reached her quivering upper lip. That might embarrass her, and he already knew she didn't deal well with negative reinforcement, other than to come up swinging. This moment of revelation helped. It explained things without explaining everything. It gave him a tentative way forward. Well, at least, it gave him a better way around her.

Compound this latest insight with the fact that she, the wife of a guy from one of the District's wealthiest families, didn't need to work for a living. Yet, despite being miserable every day on the job, she hadn't quit The TEAM. Despite being the office pariah everyone avoided and talked about behind her back, she still showed up every day. Which meant that Camilla desperately needed the job she was about to lose.

There came that thought again. *Poor kid.*

She was angry and hurting, especially now, but she hadn't ever been in combat. That scene back there on the street had to have been tough on her. Yes, Beckam had felt Max's death, too, but it wasn't his first, and it wouldn't be his last. The business he and she were in ensured that. But he was willing to bet it had been a rude awakening for Cam. That as tough as she thought she was, she'd had no way to prepare herself for the gut-wrenching impact of an up-close-and-personal death. A vicious murder.

This untrained woman didn't need an old-fashioned spanking like Mary Lou had. Uh uh. Cam needed someone in her corner. She needed someone she could trust to have her back. She needed not to fight the world alone. Only he got the sense she didn't just think she was alone. She believed it.

But why? The woman had everything. Her husband, Heath Brinkman, was the well-connected only son of a distinguished DC lobbyist. Spence and Penn Brinkman were known for their lavish, celebrity attended banquets and parties. They knew people. They wined and dined kings and queens, presidents and prime ministers. If anyone was well-connected, surely Cam was. Or was she?

His mom had a saying: *When Mama ain't happy, ain't no one happy.* Which narrowed things down. Cam wasn't happy at work because she wasn't happy at home, which meant…

"What'd your husband say when you told him you'd be working on the street for a while? Bet he's ready for you to quit Alex and stay home with him, where you'll be safe, huh?"

She grunted, but no snarky rebuttal lashed out at him.

Beckam spared her a quick glance. She'd wiped her nose, but sparkling, black misery stared back, lashing him like a tiny cat-o-nine-tails.

Her eyes were so dark brown it was hard to tell the black pupil from the iris. It wasn't a chocolate fudge kind of brown color, but more like the black/brown from the scorched bottom of Mom's saucepan that Mary Lou had burned because she'd been too busy texting to tend to the homemade fudge she'd insisted on making. Cam's eyes were that same color of sad, scorched, soon-to-be-tossed-in-the-trash, fudge. Maybe—

"What?" she snapped, her gaze now flashing daggers, laser beams, maybe rivers of steaming hot lava, too.

"I won't let anything happen to you," Beckam felt compelled to promise. He'd always been a sucker for pretty brunettes. Which Camilla Brinkman could be—if she ever let herself relax enough to smile. "I know what you're feeling right now. Death is never easy to watch. Murder is harder."

Those pointy, perfectly plucked brows slammed into one helluva nasty V, and man, he could almost hear the door to this conversation slam in his face. "Shut the fuck up, *Senior Agent*. I don't need you or anyone else watching over me."

He nodded, just once. She wasn't ready to talk. Okay. Good enough. Message received. It just wasn't the message Cam thought she'd sent.

Chapter Nine

Big fuckin' whoop. The day finally ended. So what? Camilla found herself back where it started, beside the dirty stained sidewalk where those three old guys squatted all night. Over a vent that blew warmer air up from the metro lines below. Guess they weren't as dumb as they looked. But all their crap was gone. Zack took it, the ass. What was she supposed to do now, sleep out in the open? In this town? At night?

She dropped her backpack near the vent, the bag Boy Scout had insisted she carry, then stuffed with more shit than she'd ever need. But all those bottles of water, the OD green woolen blanket, extra socks, and protein bars made sense now. As did the inflatable plastic pillows. The box of hand warmers. That tiny tin can of breath mints.

But fuck, she was sick to death of this stupid, waste-of-time mission, and it was only the first day. He thought it would last two weeks? God, she hoped not. She had half a mind to sneak out after he went to sleep, hunt the murderer down, and end this game once and for all. Wouldn't that surprise Alex?

By now, Dave and Harold were probably tucked in, nice and warm at Raymond's Kids, the shelter Kelsey Stewart operated. Not like Camilla cared what folks like the Stewarts did. Some uneducated people got lucky and made a few bucks during their pathetic lives. Big deal. So Mrs. Stewart dabbled in helping the helpless? Ha. If she really were smart, she wouldn't have to waste her time like that, would she?

Boy Scout had also said that Bruce declined the offer to shelter overnight at Raymond's Kids because too many others went without. He'd said he'd be fine on the streets, that he'd been doing it most his life. That there were homeless families with kids who needed to keep warm more than he did.

Camilla snorted at Bruce's alleged high and mighty sacrifice. Who was he kidding? She knew better. He needed a bottle, and Mrs. Stewart probably had rules about drinking at her place. That was the real reason he hadn't joined his buddies. He was a drunk.

Boy Scout also said Joslyn and Georgia were safe for the night at Lorelei's Kitchen. Camilla didn't ask how he knew. Asking would mean she was interested in the homeless. As if.

"What now? Are we just going to sit on the sidewalk the rest of the night?"

Instead of answering, Boy Scout tossed a small plastic wrapped bag at her. "Here, blow these pillows up." He was busy pulling things out of the much bigger pack he'd carried high on his back. A flocked air mattress. Some kind of gray pad.

She threw the bag back. "Blow it up yourself."

It hit his chest, then fell to the sidewalk. And there went that thing he did with his jaw. Boy Scout was easy to read. He ground his teeth when he didn't know what to say, and he was grinding those back molars plenty. "Guess I won't inflate your half of the mattress then."

Say what? "My half? You only brought one mattress?" Camilla cocked her head in exasperation. "How stupid are you?"

He shrugged, another one of his go-to, good-old-boy personality quirks. "Remind me to recharge this inside the station tomorrow, would you?" he asked as he pulled two more devices out of his bag. Neither of which was another mattress. He plugged one into the other, stuck the hose of the one into the mattress and—

Oh. A portable air pump and a battery pack. Okay then. Yes, it needed to be recharged faithfully over the next few days or weeks or—fuck—however long this distasteful job lasted.

Camilla walked to where Boy Scout now crouched with his pack in the middle of the sidewalk and retrieved the bag she'd thrown. "Fine," she said, going for meek but not really meaning it. "I'll inflate the pillows. You handle the mattress. How big is it?"

A definite smirk shifted over his mouth. "You're in luck. It's a double."

That figured. He'd only really brought one mattress, which he was unfolding into all its five-by-seven foot, too-small-for-two-normal-size-people, dimensions. He'd probably hog the entire thing, and she'd only get one small corner. But it *was* flocked. That might provide a tiny bit more insulation between the frozen concrete and a person's body than plain vinyl. But probably not.

Once he made sure this plastic piece of junk lay flat on the concrete, while the pump did its thing, Boy Scout looked up. "I talked with Alex," he said, crouched there with his wrists on his knees, his pants wrinkled where those manly, thick thighs joined with his hips and...

Crap. She didn't want to notice his pants or the way the lights from the train station made the turquoise in his eyes sparkle. He looked like he enjoyed the thought of sleeping outside in frigid weather. It was as if he enjoyed bugging the hell out of her, too. But then, Boy Scout was male, most likely eager to crawl in this pathetic sack and *'get some'*. Wasn't that what guys like him thought ninety-nine percent of their pathetic, wasted lives? About getting the girl? Sex? *Well, guess again, asshole.*

Camilla settled cross-legged on the other side of the mattress without asking how it was he'd spoken with his boss or what wisdom Alex had imparted. Instead, she focused on blowing up both pillows, so she didn't have to look at her Agent-in-Charge. By the time she finished, the pump was whining its last gasp even though the mattress was only half-inflated. His half. A definite flat strip down the middle separated it into two very distinct sleeping areas. Damn him. He'd never meant to blow up both sides.

She opened her mouth to call him on that dirty trick, but he beat her to it with, "Don't you want to know what Alex had to say?"

Camilla shrugged. He'd tell her if it were important. That was what Agents-in-Charge were supposed to do. Why should she have to ask?

And right on cue, Boy Scout offered up, "Officer Tuttle called him with the ME's findings. The ME confirmed Max Bird's COD. Blunt force trauma. MPD believes the perpetrator's using something blunt like an icepick. Not a blade, and not sharp, but just as deadly."

Which meant MPD had no idea of the exact weapon used in the commission of any of these murders. Great. She was working with idiots.

"Just like the last six deaths," Boy Scout continued grimly, "Max's clothing, fingernails, and bloodwork harbored no forensic evidence. The only thing linking him to the other victims in this crime spree is that he served in Vietnam. He was Army. Decorated."

That caught her attention. Did that mean…? "This guy's only killing veterans?" Why did she not know that?

Boy Scout nodded. "So far, yes."

"Why didn't you tell me that before?"

Both his shoulders lifted. "I didn't think you were interested."

"I'm on this mission too, aren't I? Don't I deserve to know everything you know? Do you think I'm stupid?"

"No, I think you're smarter than most of us, if you want my honest opinion. But you're not a team player."

That was rude and uncalled for. "I am, too."

He dropped his gaze, his head shaking from side to side. "Exactly when and where?" he asked the concrete before he lifted his chin and those damned sparkling eyes speared her. "I mean really? Give me one solid for-instance."

He had his nerve, calling her out like this. What'd he want, dates and times?

Apparently.

Before she could formulate a proper answer, he went on. "You alienate everyone who comes within spitting distance of your desk, which is odd, since it's The TEAM's customer service desk." Boy Scout lifted his hand, ticking off her shortcomings on his fingers. "You don't type, answer office phones, or help anyone with technical support when asked, yet you claim to be the office expert."

Automatically, she scratched a nonexistent itch on her forehead. *That made four. So what?*

But he wasn't finished. "You openly argue with Alex. You've told him 'no' more than anyone I've ever met. You talk down to everyone, including Alex, whom the rest of us respect, by the way. And you're rude to the other agents' wives whenever they come to the office. You treat everyone else like they're stupid. You—"

"They are!" she spat.

Boy Scout canted his head, his expression more sad than hostile. Rude and accusatory she could've dealt with, but the tenderness blinking back at her was something new. Most people would've lashed back at her or walked away. They'd call her names and they'd laugh behind her back. But he kept talking softer and softer. He was making her mad, but he seemed to be growing calmer while he did it.

"They're what, Camilla?" And that was another thing. He kept pronouncing her name right. Every time. Like he knew how much she hated hearing him say it. "Not as rich as you? Not as smart? Is everyone in the world dumber than you? Is that really what you think?"

Well, yeah. She'd known that for years. Only now... She wasn't sure what this lean, mean, gentle Boy Scout could read in her eyes. In her body language. That had to be what he was doing, dissecting her bit by bit. Piece by piece. Studying her cumulative scores. Taking his time. Interpreting everything she did and said, translating what and who she was into terms he could understand. That was different. A man thinking. Speaking deliberately like this guy did. Possibly wanting to know who she really, truly was instead of what everyone thought she was. That'd be the day. *Damn him.*

Camilla jerked her jacket tighter around her and made sure the zipper was up as far as it would go. The sidewalk was c-cold, and she was sick of the conversation. Sick and damned tired.

Reaching inside his jacket, Boy Scout pulled out a small cellophane packet. Ripping it open, he tossed whatever it was across the half-inflated air mattress at her. "Here, Cam. Warm up while I finish."

Oh, good. A handwarmer. She snagged that lifesaving baby out of midair and kickstarted the chemical process that would provide heat by bending it in the middle. The porous bag of salt, water, activated charcoal, and vermiculite quickly released a hearty dose of exothermic energy, and... *ahh.*

The luscious warmth centered in her palms and then spread up her arms, making her shiver as the gentle wave spread through her body. See? There was no need for God. Just the magic of science waiting to be understood by dimwitted mankind. Science she could trust. Who needed anything else?

"Anyway..." Boy Scout settled his butt flat to the sidewalk, his legs out straight in front of him. Lifting the flat half of the mattress to his mouth, his cheeks ballooned as he blew into the valve stem and—

"You're inflating my side of the mattress? Manually?" *That's just plain crazy. It'll hurt your cheeks. You'll get dizzy. How stupid are you?*

He nodded, his lips pursed and the valve stem tight between his teeth, as—*whoosh*—another mighty breath went in through the narrow opening. How and why he managed a smile while doing that, she didn't know. But he did. Puff after puff, he inflated the rest of the mattress by mouth, then sealed the valve like a good boy scout. By then, the inflated mattress extended over his legs, and his extra-large boots lifted the opposite end off the ground.

For once, she didn't want to fight anymore. Boy Scout wasn't fighting back right anyway, not as nice as he'd been while telling her how much everyone in the office hated her. Okay, he hadn't said that in so many words, but she got the drift. People didn't like anyone who graduated high school years earlier than they did, then went on to graduate Harvard before her eighteenth birthday. Same old story. People with superior intelligence were outcasts in any social circle.

"Umm, thank you," she said. "That was nice."

He shrugged. "It's no big deal. That's what buddies do. We take care of each other, right?"

Yeah, whatever. At least he hadn't called her his girlfriend again. "Sure. Right."

She handed over the two very small plastic pillows she'd inflated. Okay. Maybe they were vinyl, but they weren't much to look at alongside the double mattress he'd inflated by himself. While smiling. With that mouth. And those lips...

Camilla's tongue made an errant, automatic lap around her mouth, skating over her teeth and licking her bottom lip. But only because it was dry and chapped, and she hadn't located her single tube of lip balm yet. Certainly not because Boy Scout had intelligent eyes and a nice mouth. His teeth were white and straight. But those lips were Hollywood, super-stud perfect. Not too lush. Not too thin. They were manly and by far one of his best features.

The scar across his right eyebrow spoiled everything, though. Why hadn't he had plastic surgery to fix that ugly thing? It turned him from a guy with passable good looks into a freak. Who wanted to look at that every morning? Not that she cared what he looked like in the morning, but how hard could it be to talk with a competent plastic surgeon? At least get an honest, professional opinion? An estimate?

Suddenly, she felt inadequate. No, that wasn't the right word. More like… possibly… slightly… judgmental. But she was cold and too focused on keeping warm, and on the atrocious fact she'd soon have to sleep on the sidewalk. That had to be why he'd brought up those mean things. He must get grouchy when he was cold.

Okay, maybe not. He had peeled out of his winter jacket as soon as he'd dropped to the sidewalk and started blowing up that mattress. Still, he had to be starving as much as they'd walked today. Down Constitution Avenue. Up Constitution Avenue. Then over to Independence Avenue, crisscrossing every street that ran between the two iconic thoroughfares.

And she hadn't seen him eat even one of those donuts. Probably because he was one of those self-righteous people who never broke any law or did things wrong.

"Want something to eat?" she offered, trying to be more helpful by digging into her pack for two of those nasty MREs he'd also insisted she bring.

"I was thinking more of burgers and fries," he answered, his big chin nodding. "There's plenty of twenty-four-hour fast-food restaurants inside the train station. What say we at least eat one decent meal every day?"

"And leave our stuff?" How stupid was he?

Yet once again, Boy Scout reached into that magic pack of his and produced another bundle, this one long and blue and black and—

A tent! Small, but big enough to fit that mattress and two people. Camilla let out a hearty sigh of relief as he shook that bundle of plastic sheeting and sticks into a magnificent, albeit tiny shelter. The walls of the tent wouldn't offer more than a deluded sense of safety, and she knew it. Thin sheets of vinyl material couldn't keep a murderer out, but it would make the world disappear for the night. She'd take that thin privacy shield over sleeping out in the open anytime.

"Go eat. I'll stay here with our stuff," she told him. No way was she leaving their camp now that she had a tent to hide in. Why, anyone could come along and steal it. Then where would they be? Robbed and left to freeze to death? No. Just no.

Boy Scout cocked his head. "Come with me. Warm food will do us both good."

He had one of those manly smiles that accentuated the angles of his big chin and his high-set cheekbones. Even his forehead, which, now that she noticed, was nicely covered with a sheaf of dishwater blond bangs that made him look— different. He'd lost his cap today. Or maybe he'd stuffed it in one of his many pockets. Or given it away. He seemed prone to do stupid things like that. But that chin of his had a dimple smack in the center of it. Did he have any idea how much he looked like a spoiled little boy when he smiled like he was now?

She shook her head. "Go. Get something to eat. I'll be fine. Two pistols, remember?"

There it was again, instant sunshine breaking over his face like sunrise at dawn over the gray Potomac River. "I won't leave you behind," he replied, not breaking eye contact.

Camilla felt a lump materialize in her throat. He hadn't said *'can't'*, but *'won't'*. As in *'will not'*. As in, *'I choose not to leave you.'* Boy Scout was a good six-foot, four inches tall. Maybe taller. He probably weighed well over two hundred pounds. A guy his size had to be hungry. But he meant to go without food just because she wouldn't eat with him? Which meant he put his comfort second to hers. Which meant something else she couldn't quantify. It meant sacrifice. Him sacrificing his comfort for hers. *What the fuck?*

She licked her bottom lip, then bit it, unsure and in unchartered waters for the first time in her life. He meant to go hungry? A big guy like him, who probably burned well over three thousand calories a day. Maybe more. Just because she refused to go eat with him? Very strange indeed. Heath never needed companionship. Neither had her parents.

"I'll be okay," she told Beckam firmly. "Bring me something back. Something that's not greasy or fattening or sweet." That ought to do it. He'd leave now for sure. Heath would have. Of course, Heath never would've asked if she'd needed anything in the first place.

But Boy Scout shook his head, his focus still on her. "No, Cam. That's not the way it works when we're together. You stay, I stay. If you're sure you're not hungry, then I'll just—"

"We are not together," she snapped, setting him straight. "And stop calling me Cam."

Growl. Grumble. Growl. Her very empty stomach spoke up. Just as clear. Just as loud. *Damn it.*

"We're together until this operation's over," he told her evenly.

There was no way to back out of his invitation. She cringed, glancing over her shoulder at the still busy street. Washington, DC, never slowed down, well, except when it snowed. And it could happen. It was January. But that was the last thing she needed. "Are you sure our stuff will be here when we get back?"

That manly smile morphed into a grin, but those eyes…

Those bottomless, dark blue eyes...

They were looking right through her.

"Of course!" Boy Scout bounced to his feet as if he hadn't seen her when she knew damned well that he had.

Like a man who'd just gotten his way, he stuffed the air mattress into the now-erected tent, which he'd simply shaken to turn it into a small, two-man-sized hideout that would make sleeping tonight—interesting. Picking both his and her packs up from the ground, he gave her his hand, his palm open, his fingers curled, beckoning her up off the ground. "Let's relocate, shall we?"

She blinked. "You mean, we're not going to sleep on the sidewalk?"

His brows furrowed and those stupid laugh lines at the corners of his eyes crinkled, enhancing the mischief in his eyes. "Nah. That'd be too cruel. I wouldn't do that to you, not when I'm just beginning to like you."

You like me? "You don't like me," she snapped. "You're just teasing. Stop it."

He smiled wider as he picked the tent up and beckoned her to follow him. Across Columbus Circle Northeast they went, him carrying the tent like an inflated briefcase, her tagging along like a nobody. Then across Massachusetts Avenue Northeast. He cut the corner at First Street North East, headed to the shadowy cover of trees in the green space directly across from the station, where bushes lined the sidewalks. Only that green space was covered with a crusty two-inch mantle of last month's snow.

"Here," he said as he pitched the rear of the tent against the leafless shrubbery and in the middle of the snow. Okay, so it was barely any cover at all. But there was less snow here, and anywhere else was better than spending the night on the sidewalk where anyone could see them. Or kill them. "See? No one'll bother us here. So, what do you say to dinner now? Aren't you hungry? Just a little?"

She stalled at an invitation that sounded a lot like a date. With him. Just the two of them.

Digging into his pack, Boy Scout pulled out a thin cylindrical tube and—*SNAP*.

A glow stick. He tossed it inside the tent and all at once it looked lived in, like someone was home in this tiny shelter in the dark.

"You'll see, Cam. The tent will be here when we get back, right where we're leaving it." He rubbed his hands together. "I don't know about you, but I'm ready for a double-cheeseburger and a mountain of cheese fries, maybe a chocolate shake on the side."

For the first time in forever, Camilla acquiesced instead of biting this guy's head off. Gingerly, she took hold of his callused masculine hand. He must've lost his gloves, too. Instant warmth engulfed her much smaller fingers. And there they stood. Palm to palm and flesh to flesh. Something hotter than the heat from that silly handwarmer flashed through her veins, burning her from the inside out. Scaring her.

This day had been full of so many awful physical reactions that Camilla couldn't begin to explain or understand this one. It was very peculiar. Very new. Her body seemed out of sync with her very articulate mind. Frightened, she tugged her fingers free of Boy Scout's fiery grip once she got to her feet.

Time ground to a halt as she stood there with her fingers tucked into her armpits, looking up at him. Him looking down at her.

He really wasn't as dumb as she'd thought. Until he winked and said, "Shall we?"

She would have snapped his head off for that formulaic, very dumb-jock gesture. But like a gentleman, he'd stuck out his elbow as if she should grab hold of it—of him. Like she was royalty or something. But that would make him a prince or at least a gentleman and—

That must be his secret. Boy Scout was one of those old-world gentlemen types. Cavalier. Chivalrous. Always polite to women. Even her. He probably treated all women like ladies because that was how he'd been raised. Like a goddamned boy scout.

Well, no. Just no.

Camilla shook her head, grabbed her bag away from him, and left him standing there beside the tent she knew wouldn't be there when they returned. Not unless they ran inside, were lucky enough not to run into a crowd of hungry, just-arrived travelers, placed a rushed takeout order, actually got that order in a timely fashion, and then ran back outside again.

Yeah, no way. This tent would be gone as soon as they turned their backs on it.

Boy Scout was a fool and she wasn't. End of that stupid story.

Chapter Ten

This woman was hungry. Cam had quickly and efficiently polished off two plain *'hold the pickles, ketchup, mustard, mayo, lettuce, onions, and—oh, my hell. No cheese?'*— hamburgers, a salad without dressing, and two glasses of tepid, *'hold the ice'* water. How on earth did anyone live on tasteless food like that?

"You want dessert?" he asked, eyeing the cheesecake counter beyond Cam's left shoulder. *Mmm. An extra-large slice of New York style would sure taste good before bed. Double topping of blueberries. Whipped cream.*

Cam shook her head with a definite, "No, thank you. I don't eat sweets."

Of course, you don't. This woman didn't have a clue how to enjoy herself.

"Hey, come on. My treat," he cajoled, actually enjoying her company for a change. Which was odd. But she hadn't said anything snarky during the entire meal, which for her, was a record. For him, at least, the meal had been damned filling. Three double-cheeseburgers and an extra-large plate of cheesy fries later, he was finally feeling like himself again. A man burned mega calories on cold, long days like this one. Cheesecake was just what he needed. That and a tall Starbucks venti. Strong and black and hot enough to keep the cold at bay for an hour or two.

Cam's index finger came up as she swallowed the last of her tepid water, then looked across the table at him and said, "I don't usually eat red meat, but those burgers…" Her brows lifted as she looked down at her empty Styrofoam container. "… were really quite delicious."

"But you didn't get any of the good stuff," he told her. "No ketchup or mustard? No pickles? Who actually likes plain, bland burgers?" She hadn't even gotten those buns toasted.

"I eat healthy," she replied with something that—almost, nearly—curled the corners of her lips.

"I saw that," he teased. "You're laughing at me. You think I eat like a pig."

"I do not. I never said that. Although…" Stretching across the table, she brushed the pad of her thumb over his chin, then did something totally out of character. Camilla, *aka Kah-me-ah,* the almighty Grouch of The TEAM (who should not be confused with *Oscar the Grouch of Sesame Street)*, stuck that thumb in her mouth and sucked off whatever mustard or ketchup she'd just scrubbed off his chin. Wasn't that the weirdest thing he'd never seen coming?

It flummoxed her just as much as it did him. "I... I…" she stuttered, her big brown eyes wide and astonished as all get out. "I don't know why I did that. I really don't understand what came… over me."

"I do. You're mom material," Beckam said, grinning at his first glimpse of the real Camilla Brinkman. There were so many sharp, pointy layers to this female Rubik's Cube, layers she obviously didn't realize she had.

"No," she said adamantly. "Not a mom. Not me. Not ever."

Beckam leaned across the table, wrinkled his nose and whispered, "Liar. Every woman wants a baby. Admit it. You're no different than any other gal. You might enjoy working outside the home, but you'd love to have a child, too. Maybe a sweet little girl of your own. A son?"

"No," she answered, her voice gone too quiet, the unprecedented gleam in her eyes now flat. "I'm not… I mean, I can't… I mean, no, damn it. No. Just no."

Instant remorse punched him solid in his heart. She couldn't have kids. That explained a lot. *Why didn't I think of that? Why'd I open my big mouth?*

Her chin came up and her *stay-the-fuck-out-of-my-life* wall came up with it. "How could you say something like that? Are all women just sex objects to you? Do we all fit into some stereotypical notion of what women should and shouldn't be? Is that all you think of me? That I belong in bed or on the floor or on the table?"

Danger! Danger! Will Robinson. Danger! If that wasn't a cry for help, nothing was.

Beckam swallowed past that hard lump in his throat. "That's not what I meant."

"It's what you said." She'd opened her eyes so wide, the whites showed around her pretty brown irises.

He shook his head. "No, what I said was you'd make a good mother. And you would. You've got a light touch, Cam, and you do care. As hard as you try to disguise it, as much as you don't want anyone else to know, I've seen it. I've seen you, and you are a compassionate woman. In your way, you care about people."

"I do not." There went that chin again, which Beckam was beginning to recognize as her cue to shut up and back off. Or else.

So, he did. Reaching across the table, he meant simply to take her trash and toss it out with his. But she pulled both hands away from him, clutched them to her chest, and tipped back in her chair. Okay, that was just plain—sad. Was she afraid of him? He hated that he'd frightened her.

"Are you okay?" he had to ask.

"Why the fuck wouldn't I be?"

"Because you curse more when you're angry."

They were back in combat mode again. Her against him. Maybe her against the world.

Beckam let the moment stretch even as her words came back to him. *'In bed'* he could understand. She hadn't been married long and newlyweds were ambitious playmates. Not that he knew from experience, but he'd heard stories about how crazy two people could get in bed. But *'on the floor'* or *'on the table'*? The way she'd said those two scenarios carried a different weight than the simple sexual play between husbands and wives. Something was definitely wrong in the Brinkman marriage.

Beckam diffused the confrontation with, "Guess we should get back."

Her fisted hands shifted under her chin. Her elbows went to the table. She was holding her head to keep it from shaking. "Yes, we should," she agreed, her nose once more in the air as if her time with a lesser lifeform was over.

"Here. Let me," he said as he pushed his chair back, grabbed the trash from the table, and stalked to the nearest garbage can. Coming back to retrieve his pack, he fluttered his fingers for her to join him. "Come on, Cam. Up and at 'em. Let's roll."

She climbed to her feet, but dodged taking his hand. After grabbing her backpack from beneath the table, she shrugged one strap resolutely over her shoulder, then asked the floor, "You're not getting d-dessert? But I thought…"

He stopped to really look at her. For a second there, she sounded like she cared. But Cam wasn't making eye contact. She was as skittish as a colt in a lightning storm. "That's not the way it works. You stay, I stay, remember? I'm not going to eat in front of you."

A breath sighed out of her. She seemed to be having a hard time swallowing now that he'd put his big feet in his mouth. But damn. It was hard for most men to maneuver the current politically correct environment, much less the emotionally charged subjects of gender bias, feminine equality, or any of the social issues facing the country these days. God made everyone special, not just blacks or whites, men or women. At least that was what he'd been taught all his life. Why'd there have to be a law for everything? Why couldn't all God's children just get along?

But that inadvertent insight she'd thrown at him like a hand grenade had hit hard. Cam was a walking timebomb, the pin already pulled and tossed to who knew where.

"I'd, umm, take a thin slice of plain cheesecake," she murmured, her gaze still on the floor. Her neck muscles worked extra hard. "I mean, if you still want one. I'd… I'd get one, too. Only plain. No top—"

"No, thanks," he interrupted. "Honest, Cam. I can live without dessert. We're buddies. It's not that big a deal."

Her head came up. Were those tears shimmering in her eyes? Had to be. Her bottom lip was quivering enough. "But it *is* a big deal for me," she said. "Please. I have money—"

Somehow, she'd turned his refusal to eat *without* her into a rejection *of* her. God, Beckam wanted to grab this woman into his arms and give her something to hold onto, something beside her crumbling composure. "Well—"

"Please? Let me do this for you."

Beckam never could take a woman pleading for anything. Swallowing hard, he turned around and hit the cheesecake counter, ordered two thin slices of plain, ordinary, unadorned cheesecakes-to-go, paid for it with *his* money—*not hers, damn it*—and swiftly returned to Cam's side with the white paper to-go bag in his hand.

She'd just stood there the entire time, but she'd been crying. Or trying not to. But her eyes were red and her nose was puffy. She couldn't hide that.

He pretended he hadn't noticed as they headed for the lower level and the side exit. "Long day, huh?"

She didn't answer. Didn't say a word as they passed rows and rows of shuttered vendor kiosks between the food court and stairs. Not until they reached the last hallway out of the station in the basement did he tell her to, "Stop. Hold up a second. Let's use the restrooms before we hit the sack."

He expected something rude to jump out of her mouth, but all he got was a quiet, "Good idea."

"There's showers in there," he said, in case she didn't know that about the women's restrooms. "You could, you know, rinse off some of the street grime before we go back to camp. Maybe wash your hair if you want. The showers are private little rooms with solid doors that lock, and everything's coin-operated. So are the hair dryers. There should be shampoo, too. I mean. If you wanted to do that."

Her chin came up then, and Cam said words he'd never heard her say before. "Thanks, Beck. That would be nice. I'd like a shower before, umm, bed."

Beck. She'd actually called him by name instead of Boy Scout, which he hated.

"I'll watch your backpack," he offered.

She shook her head. "I might need something in it. I won't be long. Don't wait for me."

This woman just didn't get it. "I'll be here when you're through," he reminded her again. "Where you go, I go. No worries. Take as long as you need."

She never looked back, just shut the door in his face. No matter. She still seemed to think he'd leave her.

Guess again, Camilla. Beckam crouched outside the restroom door until he heard the shower come on. He settled his back to the wall. Willing to wait. Willing to care. For as long as it took.

Chapter Eleven

Life wasn't fair, and Camilla had accepted that hard, cold truth years ago. She'd had no choice. Superior intelligence always set people apart. It made them different, and it created fences and barriers between geniuses and the so-called *normal* people. Only she'd never felt like a genius. Not even once. As she faced the sad-looking woman in the steamy mirror tonight, everything seemed different. Out of sync. Or something. The face was the same she'd looked at this morning. God, that felt like another lifetime ago. But the person behind that proud Puerto Rican stare had changed, and she didn't know how to get back to who she was. To who she used to be.

The restroom had been busy when she'd come in, but after she showered, it was empty. Good thing. No one could mock her when she told that woman in the mirror what she'd told herself since childhood. "You don't need anyone else in this world, Camilla. You might be the ugly duckling in school, but you are better than everyone. You are smarter. You are prettier. You are a winner. Everyone else is a loser. Remember that. You are enough all by yourself. You don't need anyone else."

The mantra began again. Again and again and again. Then one last time, louder than before. Until she'd repeated the words her father had taught her as a little girl more times than she ever had before. Yet for some reason she couldn't fathom, the words that used to comfort her most of her twenty years, didn't sound so right nor so honest in this empty, tiled-cocoon of a train station bathroom. That man standing out there in the hall waiting for her—actually waiting—had messed up everything in her organized life, maybe even the world, with his generous brand of loyalty and honesty. The planet felt as askew on its axis as she felt on her feet. Not dizzy, but— unbalanced. Off. And she didn't know how to fix it.

Her wet hair straggled down the towel she'd draped over her back, water dripping from the ends into the clean, checkered, blue-and-brown flannel shirt she'd changed into. The old Camilla still stared back at her in the mirror. She was different from everyone else, had always been, and she knew it. People truly hated her. They always had. But tonight, when Boy Scout had listed off yet another multitude of her shortcomings, it hurt.

Yes, she'd always fallen short according to the world's standards, but only because those standards were set so low. And… and…

"And God!" The cry burst out of her. "I am so sick of being alone!" she told that fool in the mirror. "Every day. Every night. I can't live like this anymore. I don't want to."

Her words bounced off the white-and-blue tiles, just like they'd bounced off her empty bedroom and her father's all-too-confident, all-too-knowing ears. She'd always believed he knew better, but the cost of being what he'd always wanted her to be was too high. His goal, so out of reach. So fuckin' hard to attain.

'You are a genius, my precious flower. Such a gift. You're too good for this world. Now go. Make me proud.'

But if she was so smart, why the fuck did everything have to hurt so bad? Why'd everything have to be too hard? Why couldn't she have just one friend? Was that asking too much? Just someone to talk with. Someone to confide in. The little girl inside her cried out in misery for just one person to care enough to let her be who she really was. To not expect so goddamned much more of her than she had to offer. To accept her for who she was. Just as she was. Why wasn't she good enough to begin with? Huh? Why'd her father want her to be someone else? Someone she obviously wasn't?

Just let me be…

But now wasn't the time for self-pity. If she didn't get moving, someone would steal their tent for sure. Nearly too tired to care, Camilla swallowed her misery yet again. It took a quarter to start the hair dryer, another to get the job done. She combed her hair as it dried and left it hanging straight, instead of wrapping it into a nice, tidy knot. For once, she wanted to be ordinary. Nothing special. Normal. Not above average. Not smarter. What would it hurt to step out of line? To not have to maintain an aloof demeanor. To not have to be better or prettier. Just once.

Others did it. Look at Joslyn. Camilla had a feeling that woman wasn't like other street people. Despite her shabby get-up, she had a regal air about her. And she wasn't dumb, not if she'd known that Max worked for Sachs and Goldstein. S&G had worked several of the country's highest-profile cases. They worked miracles, oftentimes pro bono. Joslyn and Max must have been lawyers on the same team. Working for celebrities and government officials. Senators. Lord and ladies.

And suddenly, Camilla was jealous of the way Joslyn had chosen to live. She'd seemed happy sitting there with Georgia, something Camilla hadn't been in a long time. So long, she couldn't remember the day or hour. Except for tonight. Sitting across from Boy Scout. That was kind of—nice. Maybe even—peaceful. Until she'd made the mistake of touching him, and he'd translated her wiping his big, dumb chin into her owning some kind of maternal instinct—which she didn't. *The ass.*

Why'd he have to go there? God, just because she touched him did not make her mommy material. She didn't want a baby. Didn't need one to be a complete woman, either. What kind of person even considered bringing a child into this fucked-up world, anyway? Only the stupidest, that was who. People who let their baser instincts run their lives. Religious men and women, still out to propagate the earth because the Bible told them to.

News flash! It's been done already, people. Ever hear of world population explosion? Declining social infrastructure? Global warming? Congested urban sprawl? Air pollution so thick you can't see the mountains five miles beyond your immediate environment?

God, people were dumb.

That did it. Aggravated at all she'd believed for years—but that hadn't worked for shit—Camilla went against her father's childhood decree to always look regal. To never let her guard down. Fluffing her hair one last time, she tossed her head in defiance that actually made her look better. More alive. Why should she have to keep it pulled tight in a knot, anyway? She shouldn't have to, damn it. She wasn't a kid who needed to be told what to do anymore. She was twenty-damned-years-old!

Besides, her scalp hurt from pinning all that hair up every day. It was heavy. At last dry and sleek, it hung free for the first time in months.

And you know what, Papa? It looks like a thick, black, silky cape on my shoulders. It looks good, and I look like a queen. Maybe if you'd let me be me, you would've liked me better.

She turned her head one way, then the other, admiring her reflection. Really seeing herself. "And I like it," she said out loud "I might even like me tonight, too."

The oddest sense of relief shifted up her spine and over those same stress-tightened shoulders. That, most of all, was what she wanted. To be comfortable inside her own skin.

What's more, she could sleep with her hair like this and not worry about catching a cold or pneumonia. It might actually keep her warm. It was thick and long enough. Okay then. Stiffening her spine against her father's incessant demands, Camilla faced the woman in the mirror one last time. "You're stronger than you know," she reminded herself. "But Joslyn looks happier than you. What's she got that you don't?"

The woman in the mirror didn't answer. Didn't smile.

But whatever Joslyn had, Camilla wanted it, too.

Chapter Twelve

He'd heard Cam talking, but Beckam was no fool when it came to handling emotional women, not after some of the stunts his drama-queen sister had pulled back home. He restrained his need to run into the women's restroom to see if Cam needed help. She might not be fully clothed, but she would be embarrassed. And pissed. And, well, he didn't need her to know he was now certain that Mrs. Heath Brinkman was not a happily married woman.

That hadn't kept him from eavesdropping. *Ugly duckling? Better than everyone else? Smarter? Prettier?* Damn. This woman kept repeating one helluva mantra. But she didn't sound like she believed it. By the end of the fourth iteration, she sounded more depressed than she'd been at the start. As far as motivations went, that one sucked boulders.

But that last line, *'You are enough all by yourself,'* hurt Beckam's heart. He'd seen a lot of shit during his military career, but Cam reminded him of another woman from that singularly sad moment back in his senior year. Mrs. Jones, whose first name he now knew was Desiree. *Was* being the key word. He'd learned a hard lesson that day, but now he knew: Always step up when asked. But when begged? Step up faster. Quicker. Even if you don't believe the person begging for help. Even if what she said didn't make sense. Be there. Reach out. Grab hold and never let go. If he'd acted on impulse that morning instead of judging, if he'd understood one-tenth of all Desiree had lived through before her one and only attempt to run away, she could've died happy. Happier.

"I'm done," Cam said as she pulled the restroom door open and came into the hall, her pack slung over one shoulder and her hair…

Her. Hair.

Beckam scrambled to his feet, his hand out to take that heavy pack. But a silly "H-h-hey," huffed out of his mouth like he was back in high school again staring at the head cheerleader who now looked—fantastic. She'd changed her shirt, and damn. That flannel made her breasts fuller and softer and… She wasn't wearing a bra. It was suddenly h-h-hard to swallow with her hair straight and shiny, the ends of it curled and cradling those breasts like his fingers wanted to. Was it hot in here?

"I said I'm done. Your turn," she said, her chin pointing at the door to men's room behind him. "I'll wait. Don't take long, though."

"You look… umm, different with your h-h-h-hair down," he said, stuttering like an idiot, his man card in question, but his idiot card getting punched big time.

"Should I put it back up?" she bit out. "Is there some rule I don't know that—"

"No. Please, no rules. Not like that." His palms came forward to placate the raging side of Cam before she launched into her Jekyll-and-Hyde routine. "You just look, I don't know, softer, I guess." *And a whole lot prettier. Friendlier. Sort of.*

Of course, she took it the wrong way. "So, I looked like a bitch before, but now I'm, what? Acceptable? Less of a troll? Someone you don't mind being seen with?"

Man, she turned every compliment into a war zone. Beckam sucked in a belly full of patience. "I've never called you a troll, and I don't think you've ever looked like one. Not once in your life. You're a beautiful woman, Cam. It's just that now, tonight, you also look like you've had one helluva tough day, and we're both overdue for a good long combat nap. I'll grab my shower in the morning. Come on. Let's hit the road."

She turned to the end of the hall, walking ahead of him. "Do you always talk like that?"

"Like a hick?"

"I didn't say that."

"I didn't call you a bitch, either," he said sincerely.

"I meant…" She huffed. "I meant what the fuck's a combat nap? Can't you just say nap? Why's everything have some stupid military designation?"

Man, oh, man, oh, man… There were never any mixed signals with Cam. She seemed to despise everyone equally, and you always knew where you stood with her. Well, except for that strange moment there at the ashcan when she'd been crying and desperate enough that she'd let him hold her. She'd been a quivering mess then, burrowing her runny nose into him like a scared little kid trying to hide.

Corky'd done the same thing that time Beckam's father's bull broke into the corn silo. Lucky hadn't hurt the little guy. Hadn't even gone near him, but the sight of that massive bad boy on the loose in the yard and snorting his way to his idea of Thanksgiving dinner, had scared the crap out of the tow-headed little boy. He'd all but crawled inside Beckam's skin the second Beckam ran to him and picked him up. Corky'd been crying then, too. He'd been a quivering, snotty mess. Like Cam. Of course, Beckam wouldn't tell her that.

He sucked in a breath, wishing comforting her could be as easy as Corky. "Every military guy or gal, former or active duty, learns how to grab a quick nap between hostile operations. If they're smart, they set their internal clocks and wake themselves up after ten or fifteen minutes. It's a learned skill. Days get long in war zones when there's no way to fall back to FOBs, err, forward operating bases."

Cam acted as if she hadn't heard or cared what he'd said, not that Beckam expected she would. At the end of the hall, they turned right, then made for the train station exit. The real test would be tonight. If she meant to stay with The TEAM, she'd either buck up and find a way to manage the bitter cold, or she'd desert her post as soon as things became uncomfortable. Which they would.

It was funny. This morning, Beckam expected she would've quit by now. He'd planned on it. Yearned for it. Damn near prayed for it. But now?

He wasn't so sure what he wanted from his junior agent. She'd turned out to be an excellent markswoman. Yes, she still pulled the bitch card out of her deck without much provocation, but she cared about people. A little. A heartless woman wouldn't have cried or thrown up after witnessing a stranger die. Yet Cam had. And no person on earth was born mad and nasty. Mother Nature just didn't work that way. Uh uh. Something had happened to Cam in her short twenty-some years. Something seriously wicked was driving her.

Because she always had to be first, Cam hit the station's basement exit door before he did. True to nature, she didn't hold it for him, just shoved it wide open and stalked out into the bitter cold like royalty, as if she had something to prove, and everyone had better get out of her way.

The door slammed shut in his face. Okay then. He palmed it back open before it smacked his nose. The comradery he'd felt during dinner was definitely a thing of the past. Beckam followed Her Highness, matching the length of his stride to her much shorter steps, while she bee-lined for their still standing and faintly green-glowing tent across the street.

"Hold up," he called after she dropped to her knees at the tent flap.

Either she hadn't heard him or she chose not to comply with his request. Inside the tent Cam went, her heart-shaped ass the last thing he saw before the flap dropped behind her.

Crouching, he pushed the flap aside and peered at the cranky woman inside, her snarly face now lit by the pale green of a fading glow stick. "I was going to suggest we sleep feet first, with our heads toward the tent flap, you know, in case anyone bothers us during the night. It's unlikely, but that way, the first thing they'll run into will be two armed undercover agents. What do you think?"

Her eyes lit up. "Good idea," she said as, on her knees now, she crawled to the rear and opposite corner, dragging her backpack behind her.

Beckam couldn't help smiling. She had to hold her hair out of her way when she crawled deeper into, what was essentially, a pup-tent for two. "You'll also need to sleep with your flashlight, your watch, and a bottle of water close by."

"I'm not sleeping with bottled water. Uh uh." She shook her head. "It's cold. I'll freeze, and I'm too tired for that crap."

"It's the only way to keep water warm enough to drink on an op like this. Take two bottles to bed if you think you'll wake up thirsty during the night." Which made him think. "But if you need to pee before morning—"

"I won't," she snapped. "God, how dumb do you think I am? But if I do, I promise I'll wake you before I do anything or go anywhere, *Agent Garner*." There it was, her snotty 'Agent-in-Charge' card again.

"Coming in," he announced as he stuck his boots through the opening and scooted inside on his butt.

Her eyes lit as she vacated the center of the small tent and made room. "Did you bring, umm—?"

For sure she wasn't asking about condoms. "Sleeping bags?"

"I, umm, forgot, but if you didn't bring any either, then we're going to be—"

"What kind of Ranger would I be if I let you freeze on your very first covert op?" he asked as he settled cross-legged inside the tent flap and dug the two rolled-up-tight sleeping bags from his enormous pack. It took up a third of the air space in this tent all by itself. "Lucky for you, I've brought a couple zero-degree bedrolls that'll keep us warm all night long."

She blinked. "Umm, what? You're a—what?" This woman was civilian to her self-righteous, oblivious core. Here she'd worked with former military for months now, but had no idea what or who any of them were. Had never acted interested or asked. Until now.

"I'm a Ranger, ma'am, as in Army Ranger," he explained as he set the carry-out bag with the two cheesecakes in a safe corner near the flap. "You know. We're like Navy SEALs," he said, thinking the current SEAL craze out of Hollywood might've reached into her pretentious, entitled little world. "Haven't you seen *'American Sniper'*? That was about a SEAL."

Again, the blank look. "I wish you guys spoke English. I never know what you're talking about."

Which explained more of the puzzle known was Kah-me-ah. She had no clue what the steady diet of military acronyms or jargon bandied around the office meant.

"You're kidding! You seriously haven't heard of Chris Kyle? How about Adam Brown? Marcus Luttrell? Where on Mars have you been living?" He tossed a sleeping bag at her. "Keep this dry. You get to carry it from now on."

"Not military. Fish and Wildlife, remember?" she bit out, hugging that still-wrapped bag to her chest, unknowingly doing the mothering thing again.

Why he kept seeing her with a baby in her arms, Beckam didn't know. Motherly was the last thing Cam was, unless all mothers ate their young. But there was something sad and longing about her. Not all the time. Mostly, she was as prickly as a porcupine, but sometimes, like now, she looked like a lost little girl who needed a teddy bear—or something—to hold. Which reminded him of Mrs. Jones again. Maybe it was time for a couple stories.

"Kyle, Brown, and Luttrell are American heroes. All Navy SEALs, Kyle and Brown gave their lives serving others." Like any other man on the planet, Beckam untied his boots, pulled his dogs out of those steel-toed monsters, and let them breathe, glad to be able to wiggle his toes despite the cold. But unlike most other men, Beckam stuffed both boots into the giant-sized plastic bag he'd brought along to protect his footwear in case it rained or snowed. Either could happen. Number one rule of every American soldier: *Take care of your feet, and your feet will take care of you.*

Cam snorted as she unwrapped her sleeping bag, then laid it alongside his. But the uptight woman rolled it the wrong way. After a quick, furtive glance at him, she growled and flipped it, putting the opening at the tent flaps like he'd requested.

He could clearly read the flash of, *'Fine. There. Are you happy now?'* in her dark eyes. Just as clear was her embarrassed regret that he'd seen her mistake. Which wasn't really a mistake at all. Which meant her pride—or something—ruled everything she did. *Interesting.*

He might be wrong about story time…

"Not suggesting anything unprofessional here," he said as he coughed to clear his throat, but going to put it out there anyway. "If you want to conserve body heat or if you get too cold during the night, feel free to take your jacket and pants off, and—"

"No," she interrupted, her hand in his face. "Don't even ask. I might have to sleep in close proximity to you, but I'm keeping my clothes on, and I reject your stupid come-on. You stay on your side of the tent, and you can be damned sure, I'll stay on mine." Her head came up, the snark with it. "Any other questions, Boy Scout?"

Man, she was actually quite pretty when she was mad. Those pretty eyes came alive with fire. He was pretty sure he saw sparks. Beckam couldn't help the grin spreading across his face like heat lightning on a hot summer night in Horse Hollow. This woman took everything he said the wrong way. Intentionally. It was another kind of deterrent to keep people from getting too close. A force field.

He cleared his throat again, because, little by little, he was peeling away the eye-watering layers to this feisty onion. "Not suggesting anything improper, ma'am. But the ground gets extra-cold this time of year and—"

"And don't. Just, don't," she snapped, her head turned to the side but her tiny gloveless hand right in his face again. "Don't lie. I know what you want, and you're not getting it from me. Jesus Christ! Back off or I'll scream sexual harassment. Rape!"

Rape? As in me raping you? His big mouth blurted, "In your dreams, junior agent. I'm just Army, remember? And us ignorant, brain-dead grunts did whatever we needed to in order to stay alive in whatever harsh environment we were sent to. Which includes the Arctic and the Antarctic, where it gets a blistering fifty below on a sunny day, and that's if the wind isn't blowing. But it never included rape."

And enough! Beckam was done trying to get along with his tent-mate. "Don't flatter yourself, Brinkman. You're the last woman in the world I'd come on to. You're married, remember? And I'm not that kind of stupid. I'm just a Boy Scout, remember?"

It was plenty warm inside this little tent now.

There went that bristly wall again. Cam turned the rest of her body to him. Still dressed in her boots, jeans, and jacket, she'd be warm enough for a while, but then…?

She'd probably be too proud to snuggle up to another warm body, which he'd done plenty during those desperate Arctic training ops. It was just what guys did when they hunkered down in the worst of times. When they needed some shuteye to survive the night. Ask any grunt what it meant to spoon with another guy while swathed in layers of cold weather gear, maybe a woobie. It meant nothing more than surviving. Okay, maybe it meant something different to the few gay guys Beckam came across, but even then, it registered a big fat zero on the romance Richter scale. Body heat was simply a resource, and guys did what they had to do to get the tough jobs done. So there. End of one lame-assed story that wasn't the one he'd wanted to share anyway.

Guess the cheesecake was a no-go, too. Exhausted from the drama more than all that had happened today, Beckam stuffed his bagged boots into the tent corner, then unzipped his sleeping bag and climbed inside. He kept his holstered weapons in place, just in case. He would've slipped out of his tactical pants to be more comfortable, but opted not to because of her remark. The nerve of this woman.

Snapping a couple foot and hand warmers, he stuffed them into his socks and under his arms. They'd last until he fell asleep. Finally, he grabbed three bottled waters out of his pack and slid them inside his sleeping bag, situating them between Cam and him, mentally noting he'd have to buy more tomorrow. Doffing his jacket, he rolled it into a pillow just as—

"Here." Cam stuffed one pathetic, inflated plastic pillow into his face like a gift.

"No thanks," he replied. "Good night." Weary of the drama, he pulled the top of the sleeping bag up and over his head, prepared for sleep. If she could dish out rejection like a pro, she could take it.

What Cam didn't realize was that, even though she'd put the opening of her bag near the tent door, she'd still positioned it wrong. While the zipper to his bag opened to his left and the outside wall of the tent, her zipper opened at Beckam's back. She'd be facing him if she didn't make that adjustment. And she'd better hurry. The light from that glow stick was fading fast.

Sure enough. Grunting and huffing, she crawled to the back of the tent and flipped her sleeping bag over. Beckam didn't offer to help, just let her work her current problem out by her lonesome. Yeah, story time could wait. It was a dumb idea anyway.

Chapter Thirteen

God, it wasn't even ten o'clock and it was already freezing. Shivering beside the tent, Camilla smoothed the wrinkles out of her sleeping bag, her fingers turning into icicles with every passing second. She'd lost her gloves, probably after dinner, and couldn't yet stuff her hands into her pockets to keep them warm, not until she crawled inside her bag and laid alongside her Agent-in-Charge. Damn him. Boy Scout, his sleeping bag, and gear took up a good two-thirds of the floor space. And there wasn't much.

Her long hair was driving her nuts. A tie or something would surely come in handy, but she'd put her backpack at the foot of her sleeping bag where no one could steal it. She wasn't about to crawl across the tent just for a hair tie. She needed inside this bag. Right now. This stupid tent was fuckin' cold. Talk about idiotic ideas.

At last, Camilla had her sleeping bag repositioned, but shimmying her big ass into it with limited room to move was something else. Then the zipper refused to budge. It wouldn't go down. She'd have to climb in the hard way, with her boots on and still fully clothed. She hadn't brought an extra bag for her boots like Boy Scout had, and it was too damned cold to take them off. Boy Scout didn't know everything. Her boots were staying on, where they'd do the most good. So was her jacket. She'd show him. She'd be warmer than him.

But damn, it was hard shoving booted feet into a flannel-lined sleeping bag. Her jacket rode higher on her back with every inch into the bag she gained. At last, she was fully inside, but by then, most of her jacket was neatly rolled up near her shoulder blades rather than covering her back or her fat ass.

Another struggle commenced. Cam elbowed and hip-checked Boy Scout's back and butt with every turn, twist, and wiggle. But goddamnit, finally, her jacket was down where it belonged—mostly—and she was inside the stupid sleeping bag. Cold but covered. Make that still damned cold. And tired. Frustrated far beyond her boiling point, which was set pretty low these days. Ever since she'd lost her position with Fish and Wildlife Services. Damn FBI Director Tucker Chase for that stab in the back. He'd purposefully set out to destroy her.

But holy shit, getting settled for the night was a lot of hard work for nothing. Peeling her hair out of her mouth, off her face, and away from her eyes, Camilla gathered all those strands into a ponytail and commenced braiding her thick tangles into a tight twist for better control. Why the hell had she left it down? It seemed a good idea at the time, but now…

She'd seen that look in Boy Scout's eyes when she'd come out of the bathroom. What'd he say, that she looked softer with her hair loose on her shoulders? What the fuck did he mean by that? Did he think she was a pushover? Easy?

She growled loud enough to wake him even as she elbowed his back again. She'd show him, the dumbass. News flash! She was no pushover. Never had been. Never would be.

By the time her braid was done, she needed to hit or kick something. Boy Scout would do. Only he was asleep, snoring softly beside her, and he made a wall there in the dark, a great big wall of Beckam.

'I don't need you or Alex Stewart or Tucker Chase,' she mentally told his back. In her mind. Where she could still think anything she wanted, no matter what Stewart said. He didn't own her. No one did, and damn anyone who thought they could!

A gentle wave of warmth wafted off Boy Scout, distracting her vengeful, rambling rant. Damn, he smelled good, but how had he fallen asleep so quickly?

She couldn't get to sleep, not as cold as it was in the middle of fuckin' January. *Jesus Christ, this was a stupid operation, and damn you, Alex Stewart, for bossing me around and doing this to me. Ugh. This is all your fault. I hate you and your perfect TEAM. Every last one of them. But* you *most of all. You pretentious, egotistical selfish man!*

"Do you feel better now?" a tired, deep voice rumbled beside her.

Cam slapped a hand over her mouth. Had she said that last bit out loud? "I'm fine," she snipped, hoping to shut Boy Scout up once and for all. "But Stewart is an ass."

"I thought we'd already established that." The Great Wall of China beside her came down as the man who also answered to Mr. Stewart, flattened to his back, then rolled that big body of his inside his sleeping bag until he faced her. "Here," he said as two bottled waters appeared in front of her face. "Would it help if I snapped another glow stick, so you could see?"

"What do you think I am, a baby?" God, why didn't he just chew her up and spit her out instead of being nice? That she could have handled.

"No, ma'am, but I do think you're a new operator who hasn't adjusted to the demands of her job yet. Tonight you're cold, and I'm pretty sure you forgot what I said about keeping a flashlight, watch, and a couple bottled waters handy. Right?"

"Yes," she answered, trying to sound meek instead of ready to fight as she accepted the bottles he gave her. Both were already lukewarm, not frozen solid like hers were. *How'd he do that?*

"First rule of Arctic training 101," he answered as if he'd read her mind. "Stay hydrated, but don't eat snow. The water content in snow is too low to supply an overworked body with sustainable hydration. Plus, snow is ice, and ice is cold. It depletes a soldier's body temp, the last thing he or she needs on an active op. Keep those bottles under your arms or between your legs, some place where they'll be surrounded by body heat. Might sound dumb, but dying from dehydration is dumber."

Camilla was too cold to argue. She slid the bottles between her left arm and side. Awkward, yes, but Boy Scout seemed to know what he was talking about. This time.

"Another thing," he whispered. "You'll sleep more comfortably, and you'll be warmer, if you lose the winter jacket and boots. Might sound counterintuitive, but body heat is all you need inside that sleeping bag. It's engineered for sub-zero temps. If you're comfortable doing it, slide out of your jeans, too. Relax. Trust yourself, Cam. You've got this."

Oh, that was rich, him telling her to undress again. Was that all he thought about, getting her naked? "Did you take *your* jacket off?" she taunted. "Or is this your idea of foreplay?"

Shaking his head, he blew out a long, disgusted sigh. "Yes, I took my jacket off. It makes a better pillow than plastic balloons."

"Your pants?"

"No. I'm not that stupid. But understand this, Junior Agent. Rape is a vile, vicious act of violence perpetrated by men who despise women and hate themselves. It's ugly and it's nasty, and that comment was uncalled for. If you're too good to work with male agents, go home."

Camilla lay there staring at the dim light from Union Station across the way filtering in through the pointed ceiling of their nylon tent. Thinking. Wondering. Wishing she had better control of her mouth. But not going home. Not now. Not ever. If anyone turned tail, it wouldn't be her. But Beck was the one with the toasty warm bottled waters. Maybe she should've listened to this guy.

"I, umm…" Her throat contracted around her words. "I shouldn't have said that. Rape, I mean. That was uncalled for and…" She swallowed again. "I don't think you're that kind of a man, Agent Garner. At all. I don't. Honest. I'm… I'm sorry."

His voice came to her with a quiet rumble. "I accept your apology, Cam. But that was quite a nasty threat. Too many women think they can trash a man's reputation with that word. It only takes once."

She nodded in the dark, staring at the ceiling with tears welling in the corners of her eyes. "It was, err, is an ugly word, and I was wrong. I won't use it again."

"You know, I've seen a lot in my deployments overseas, and in some third world countries, rape, incest, and pedophilia are as common as online shopping is in America. But I've never seen anyone of my guys abuse a woman or a child, not once. Most Americans aren't made that way. Yes, I know it still happens. Too much. But it's not an accepted way of American life like it is in parts of Indonesia, India, and Afghanistan."

"You're a… a gentleman," she murmured.

"I'd like to think so. Yeah, I'm just some guy from Oklahoma, but mostly, my mom and dad raised me and my sister by the Good Book. We know right from wrong. That's just the way it is."

Instantly contrite, Camilla turned to face him. It'd been a long time since she'd believed anyone enough to trust them not to lie. Boy Scout might be honorable enough. He might be right. Hence his stupid nickname. But did she dare follow his suggestion? That would mean sitting up to unlace her boots. He'd know then that she'd fallen for his line—if it were a line. Yet she couldn't sleep like this, stretched out on her back with her boots bound inside this damned sleeping bag.

Swallowing hard, she pushed forward to untie her laces. Which didn't take long. When she finally had her boots off, she took time straightening her jacket. Might as well be as comfortable as possible. Then she set her boots alongside her sleeping bag, between her and the wall of Boy Scout.

"You hungry for cheesecake yet?" he asked quietly. "I mean, it'll keep until morning in this temperature if you're not, but…" He let his suggestion hang.

She remembered his face back in the station. His eyes had it up like a little boy looking forward to a treat. *Well…* "Okay," she murmured civilly. She could do this. "I'm still awake. Why not?"

"I was hoping you'd say that." In seconds, he'd pushed upward and retrieved the takeout bag. "Here you go, Cam," he said politely as he placed her dessert into her cupped hands.

They made quite a pair sitting there with their little plastic disposable cartons of plain cheesecake and their plastic forks. The light from the station offered just enough ambient light through the trees for her to see what she was doing. Boy Scout was so big his head rubbed against the tent's nylon ceiling. He was at least a foot taller than she was. It was almost comical. Them. In the dark. Like two naughty kids about to break the rules.

But damn… the moment that first forkful of cheesecake decadence melted on her tongue… "Hmmmmm," moaned out of her without a filter. He was right. This stuff was good. And she was hungry. But, damn it. Why hadn't she ever tasted cheesecake before?

Because you're Papa's little girl, and you always do what you're told…

Another bite. Another moan in off-the-charts delight. *My God. Whoever invented cheesecake is a god. How could eating something as delicious as this be wrong? It can't be that bad for me.*

But Papa said so…

"You like it, huh?" Boy Scout asked. Was there a hint of teasing pleasure in his question?

Because… Yes. She liked cheesecake. A lot. Now that she'd tried it. "I've never had anything this delicious before," Camilla admitted, inadvertently smacking her lips.

"Man, I know what you mean." He made a deeply contented sound in the back of his throat. "Next time, we'll try the kind with strawberries. Or chocolate drizzles. You'll like that one even more. The one with macadamia nuts and white chocolate is my favorite."

Boy Scout purred like a big, rumbling tiger, the vibration of that masculine sound reaching across the few inches between them. Warming Camilla without touching her. He was a bigger version of her happy tomcat. It was bizarre how a simple thing like plain cheesecake made him happy while she struggled to find anything to smile about every morning. When she'd wake up alone. Forgotten. Again.

Her mind pinged to the giant slice of nut-encrusted chocolate cake she'd glimpsed behind the glass at that cheesecake kiosk. What would Beckam sound like if he'd eaten that fattening piece of artful cuisine instead of this extremely small slice of plain dessert? Suddenly, she wanted to know what else made Boy Scout happy. If he was this easy to please, he must walk around with a perpetual smile on his face most days.

She would've polished off the rest of her dessert, but it was worth savoring. So savor, she did. Tiny bite by tiny, delicious bite. She tried not to eat too fast, but before she knew it, the cake was gone, and just the taste of heaven lingered on her tongue. Only then did she realize Boy Scout was finished and that he'd laid back down. He was watching her in the dark, his elbow bent, his head in his hand, and his features once more lost in shadow. She could barely make out the glow in his eyes.

"Want me to take that empty container for you?" he asked.

She would have rather licked the plastic throw-away clean to get every last crumb, but he'd think she was a pig then. *Can't have that.*

"Umm, sure. Yeah. Okay." *I guess.* Reluctantly, she locked her fork inside the lid and passed her garbage to him.

Boy Scout was careful not to touch any part of her, not one finger. And that bothered Camilla, though she didn't understand why. She'd never wanted to touch him or any of his friends before. There was no reason to touch him now. And yet...

"So tell me about yourself," he said as he stuffed the takeout bag of garbage behind him. "I know you're smarter than most us guys. So, let's start out easy. What's your favorite color?"

"Green."

"Favorite movie?"

"I don't waste my time on movies, television, or theater."

He paused a scant second. "Favorite song? You've got to have a best song, maybe a playlist you listen to over and over again?"

"Tchaikovsky," she enunciated slowly in case Boy Scout had never heard of the master pianist.

"Ah, one of my favorites. Did you know Disney used his music for the Dance of the Sugarplum Fairy in Fantasia?"

"Everyone knows that."

Camilla sensed amusement in his tone. "Okay, I've got a harder one. Were you always a genius?"

"I'm not, umm… a genius." She cleared her throat, wishing he hadn't asked that particular question. "Why do you ask?"

"No reason. We're just working together, and it's always nice to get better acquainted."

She offered the first thing that came to mind. "I'm from New York. My parents still live there, sometimes anyway. They moved to The Palisades on the Potomac last year, said they wanted to be closer to me." *Wish they hadn't.*

He didn't seem impressed at the mention of one of the District's finer neighborhoods. "As in New York City or state?"

"City," she clarified.

"Oh, yeah? Where exactly?"

As if a man like him would know anything about NYC. "Fifty-Seventh Street, across from Central Park."

"Ah, Billionaire Row," he said as if he'd been there. "That'd put you right near Columbus Circle. What do your parents own, the whole block or just a building?"

"The Morning Glory Estate," she replied, needing him to understand just how much better than him she was. How much wealth and entitlement she came from. Which was just plain weird. She'd never answered personal questions before. Mostly because no one had ever asked. Or cared. Yet even as she stressed her elite status, she needed him to know that, "My Papa's Luis Lopez, the sugar magnate from—"

"From Puerto Rico. Yeah, I know. I was part of the clean-up team that went in after Hurricane Maria back in '17. You're lucky your mom and dad left when they did. You probably already know, but there's nothing left of the Lopez plantation. No trees. No roads, either. The storm stripped everything, even outbuildings, from the land. That part of the island's still mostly barren."

"I wouldn't know," she admitted. "I've never been."

"No? Your parents never took you back home to visit?"

She shook her head. "Born in America, remember? Why should they?"

Boy Scout wasn't able to see her response, but he also couldn't see the question in her eyes. Her parents had rarely talked about the country they came from or life on the plantation. She knew nothing of their previous life, only that her father had invested wisely once he'd become a United States citizen. They'd told her she was American, not Puerto Rican. *Be proud. Stop asking questions.* So, she'd done what she was told. As usual.

"Hmm, that's too bad. Puerto Rico was beautiful before Maria struck."

And there the conversation stalled. He leaned back onto his arms, now folded behind his head. Camilla wiggled deeper into her sleeping bag, her feet toasty warm. Her eyes drowsy.

Until Boy Scout whispered, "Shhhhh. Someone's coming."

Chapter Fourteen

Beckam tensed, his senses pinging a high threat level as two sets of footsteps shuffled across the crusted, frozen grass and nearer the tent.

Closer…

Closer...

He scrambled back into his tactical pants, then tugged on his boots when, unexpectedly, an icy cold hand latched onto his wrist, making him jump. "Damn," he hissed, still focused on whoever was stumbling about outside, some drunk or other wayward soul. But now, just as focused on the icicle fingertips gripping him.

"Shhhhh," Cam whispered. Like he hadn't already told her that? "Who is it?" she asked, a definite tremor overwhelming her usually snarky tone.

He hesitated answering that he wasn't Superman and didn't have x-ray vision any more than she did. But he wasn't that cold-hearted. She was worried. Make that scared. And those delicate fingers were now a death-grip. Taking a chance, he covered those frozen digits with his much larger, warmer palm to calm her nerves.

"Probably just someone looking for shelter," he murmured, cocking his head to better hear where those footsteps were headed. Yup, still coming his way. Might just be Bruce, looking for a place to crash. Might be Zack, checking on him and Cam. But they could also be trouble.

Speaking of Cam… She'd scooted closer, the length of her warm body now pressed into his side. He could feel her pulse pounding in the fingertips clutching his wrist.

"It's okay," he whispered. "I won't let anyone hurt you. Promise. Don't be scared."

"I'm n-n-not s-scared." She wasn't very good at lying, shivering like she was.

He lifted his arm over her head and circled her shoulders, pulling her into his side, needing her to believe that he'd keep her safe. By then, whoever was outside had stopped walking. Beckam couldn't hear snow crunching anymore. Only heavy breathing. Which meant they were standing right outside the tent, listening.

Cam burrowed her face into his jacket under his arm. A frightened little sound eked out of her. "I don't want to die."

Yeah. For sure she was no covert agent, and this mission was way beyond her KSAs. Knowledge, skills, and aptitude. Yet here she was, too stubborn to quit even though she was freezing and out of her element.

"Me neither," he admitted evenly. His hand came up automatically, cupping the back of her head, soothing her like he would a frightened colt in a thunderstorm. The time had come to do something besides lay there and wait. "I'm going out. Is your weapon close?"

She shook her head.

Damn. No operator ever slept without his or her loaded pistols, cocked and ready within reach. "Where are your pistols?"

"In my b-b-bag. By my feet."

Beckam bit his lip at that rookie mistake, then unholstered one of his two Rugers and tucked it inside her palm, making sure she held it correctly before he let the piece go. He preferred the Ruger Security-9, a nine-millimeter handgun. The fifteen round magazine and one always in the chamber gave him sixteen rounds of prevention, otherwise known as self-defense. Both pistols came with a Viridian red dot laser. He'd often relied on that tiny red dot to create a few second thoughts among would-be aggressors, and to solve home invasions, anything that threatened him or his family. Which, now that he'd reconsidered the situation, fit Cam for the next week or so. Something felt right about including her inside his family circle.

Okay, then…

"We're going to talk gun safety when I get back," he told her, keeping his voice low. "But for now, I'm getting to my knees. Watch out, so I don't bump you with my elbow or knees. Sit tight and—"

"D-d-don't go," she whispered, her cold hand suddenly on the back of his neck, holding him in place. "Please, Beck, I… I…"

"It's okay," he said, unzipping the tent as quickly as he could. "Stay here and—"

CRASH! Someone hit him across his shoulder blades. Hard. Damn.

Pissed, Beckam tore the tent flap open and—

THUMP! THUMP! The bastard hit him again! Twice! This time connecting with his right arm and hand which Beckam had wisely raised before said bastard struck his head.

"Stop or I'll shoot," he warned, his hand painful and swelling around his trigger even as the Ruger's red dot danced over the wide body of a man, then another, both standing too close to the tent.

Just two kids. Teenagers. Both dressed in black winter jackets and sloppy jeans. Both with baseball caps over long hair on brainless skulls. The nearest boy, the hefty one, held a tire iron over his shoulder, ready to strike again. A baseball bat shifted against the skinnier one's right shoulder, his boots positioned like a batter on home plate. As if this were some kind of game.

Bleeding now and unsteady on his feet, Beckam wiped his free hand under his nose. His fingers came away wet. Great. They'd drawn first blood. Which ramped this encounter into the danger zone. Blood tended to excite cowards who preyed on the homeless and defenseless. Gave them something to brag about to their equally morally bankrupt posse, which might be hanging back in the shadows, waiting their turn.

"You need to think twice," he told the bastard whose big feet were stepping on the corner of his tent. "This is no toy I'm holding. One more step and I will take you down. Drop your weapons, now. Nice and slow, boys." He'd turned his mic off while he and Cam had gone into the station to eat, but he switched it back on now. Turned the volume up high. Told whoever was on duty back at TEAM HQ, "Nine-one-one. Agent under fire."

"Understood, Beck," Zack's voice came calmly over the wire. "Beau and Renner are closest. They're in transit to your location now. Can you last until then?"

"Copy that," Beckam replied as the first swarm of black, sparkly dots swirled at his peripheral. *Hope so.* Help was on its way, but Beau and Renner had better step on it.

"Or what you gonna do, motherfucker? Make us?" the chicken shit standing behind Tire Iron taunted. He was the nervous one. Too scared to step up and take a swing, but twitchy and unpredictable, like he was dying to use that bat, maybe kill someone. Both were teenage-young and twice as stupid. "You one of them piss-ant do-gooders out to save the fuckin' world?"

Beckam kept his pistol on Tire Iron. "Drop your weapons and sit down, boys. You're in my territory now."

"I ain't gonna sit in no snow, and I ain't no boy," Tire Iron shot back, his weapon lowered, but kicking at the crusted over snow like a petulant child. "I'm better than you, you dumb fuck. You ain't even got a place to live. Why don't you—"

"Git your girlfriend out here," Chicken Shit interrupted with a leer. "We know you got a chick in there. We heard her. Let's see if she's any good in the cold, huh?" The teenage loser grabbed his junk like he and his moronic buddy weren't on the losing end of Beckam's Ruger. Like he would ever get the chance to put Camilla in danger.

There was a saying among Rangers. *You can't fix stupid.* God's honest truth.

But Cam must've heard that last comment. She roared out of that tent on her hands and knees, shrieking as she pushed to her feet, "Sit down! On your asses. I said now!" Her pistol's convincing red dot laser centered on Chicken Shit's forehead. Not like these two were smart enough to take her seriously.

"Hey, bro." Tire Iron chuckled. "You got a little red dot on your face. Looks like measles."

"So do you," Chicken Shit scoffed as he stared Cam down, aiming the end of the bat in his gloved-hand at her. "You. On your knees, bitch. Let's get this party started."

Said every idiot ever.

Beckam didn't want to have to shoot these kids, but now he might. Except Cam had taken position between him and them. He wanted to cuss her for not doing what she'd been told, but hot damn. She'd certainly stepped up. Which was more than he could say for Chicken Shit, thankfully, who must've had second thoughts with her death ray in his eyes. He'd stepped back a couple feet, but that little red dot tracked him like he'd been laser painted.

Interestingly, her red dot wasn't dancing as erratically on Chicken Shit's face as Beckam's was on Tire Iron. His right hand might be broken. Had to be as quickly as it was swelling. His fingers were stiff in his glove, and it was getting harder to grip his pistol properly. Which meant these two jerkoffs could still overpower Cam and kill them both. Him, first. Her, after they raped her.

Beckam switched from right to left hand. Mostly, he didn't want Cam to have to kill anyone. Ever. Yes, she put on a good show, but she was running on red-hot adrenaline now. He was pretty sure she'd never shot a person before, maybe not even a pheasant or rabbit.

But damned if the world didn't decide to tip sideways then. Beck tilted with it. Damn it. Not good. Him going down. Leaving Cam to fend for herself. He turned his chin into his two-way without taking his eyes off the idiots and murmured, "STAT."

"Hang on, buddy," Renner answered this time. "Just two more minutes."

As if she understood how bad things were, Camilla stepped into Beck's hip to steady him, her weapon still on target like the professional target shooter she was. "Drop your weapons or I'll shoot you right goddamned now, boys," she hissed.

Chicken Shit sneered. "I ain't no boy. 'Sides you're just a dumb bitch. Bet you couldn't hit a bus if—"

BLAM!

Dayam… Cam had just put a warning shot between the idiot's black boots, then had that red dot back on his forehead before he screamed, "Don't shoot! Don't shoot!" Probably wet his pants, too.

"Then drop your fuckin' weapons!" she yelled like they weren't standing ten feet away and couldn't hear her.

"Better do it, boys," Beck advised. "She's fast with that pistol and now she's mad."

"I'm not just mad, you assholes. I'm fuckin' mad," she hissed.

Beckam almost shivered at the level of snarky ice in her tone. He'd heard it plenty in the office, but tonight it was different.

Thud. Thud. The tire iron and bat hit the ground, followed swiftly by two sets of teenage knees.

"We didn't mean nothing," Tire Iron sniveled, his hands clasped at the back of his head and his cheeks shining in the ambient light. "We was just funnin'. Honest. Weren't we, Ev?"

To which idiot Ev said, "Yeah, sure. We didn't know anyone was sleepin' inside that tent."

"You lying sacks of shit!" Cam bellowed. Okay. So her delivery needed a little less venom and a lot more professional calm, but her shooting stance was perfect, and that laser dot had never strayed from her kneeling target, which was Tire Iron now. "You hit my partner. I saw it! You knew damned well we were in that tent. You meant to kill us. Now sit your dumb asses in the snow and freeze your balls off!"

"B-b-but it's cold," Tire Iron whined as he settled said balls to the ice.

"Shut. Up!"

Beckam didn't mean to, but he leaned into Cam a little bit more, enough that she shifted her position to keep him upright while her left hand circled his waist. Man, that felt good.

"You okay, partner?" she asked out of the corner of her mouth, her red dot the most obedient little piece of LED magic he'd ever seen. Not only was she steady with a pistol, but Beckam got the feeling she meant what she'd said. She would kill these punks if they didn't shut up.

He didn't dare pass out before Beau and Renner arrived. Couldn't. They might not go easy on Cam. Hell, she might not go easy on them. And heaven help these two teenage bullies. She might kill them if he succumbed to the night creeping in on him.

Tire Iron couldn't keep his mouth shut. "Listen, bitch. Maybe we could work a trade—"

BLAM!

Oh. My. God! She'd fired that round right between Tire Iron's knees. Three inches higher and he'd be singing soprano.

"Ow, ow, ow. You shot me, you cow!"

"It's called shrapnel, pussy boy," she whined right back at him. "I put one round between your legs, not into your tiny little balls. It kicked up ice and dirt that stung your tender, baby-soft, flabby thighs. Shut the fuck up or the next one goes between your eyes. Understood?"

"Y-y-yeah. G-got it," Tire Iron whimpered, rubbing both hands over his wounded manhood. "G-g-got it."

"You?" she snapped at Chicken Shit.

"Whatever," he grumbled.

"Do you understand that I *will* shoot you and your boyfriend here to defend myself and my Agent-in-Charge?" Damn, she was relentless. Beckam had to give it to her. Cam was fierce in battle, and she meant business. When someone pushed, she pushed back—hard. Maybe a little too hard.

Just then a siren howled from Capitol Hill to their south. Metro PD was on their way. Beckam hoped Officer Tuttle was working the late shift. Which was doubtful, but still. A man could hope. Other tires screeched out on Columbus Circle Northeast, followed by the hump-thump-grunt of a heavy-duty vehicle clearing the curb and heading straight for him. Renner and Beau had arrived.

"Renner Graves is on scene," Beckam told Cam before he lost what was left of the shadowy light he was standing in. "That's him behind the spotlight. Beau Villanueva, too. They're here to assist you. Us, I mean. Please, Cam. Be nice to them. Okaaaaaaaaaay…?"

And down he went.

Chapter Fifteen

Camilla didn't want anyone's help. This was her chance to prove she had what it took to be a TEAM player. Only she did need help. And she knew it. Especially since Beckam had just face-planted at her feet. She went down on one knee with him, but wasn't fast enough to keep him from falling, since she had to keep her pistol on these idiot teenagers. The air wheezed out of Beck as he came to rest on his belly, putting them both at risk. And she was mad all over again. These two piece-of-shit bullies hurt him!

"I ought to kill you right here and now," she hissed as someone from The TEAM SUV spotlighted the boys, the tent, Beckam, and her. "Do you hear those sirens? That's the police. You're going to lockup for the rest of the night. Hope you have fun with the big boys downtown. I hear they like fresh meat."

"Shut your pie-hole, bitch," the skinny blond who'd held the bat shot back at her. "You don't know nothin'."

Bitch, the name all degenerates called women who were smarter than them. Which was a really stupid thing to say to a really angry woman with a loaded gun. Agent Villanueva and Agent Graves hadn't climbed out of their vehicle yet. They weren't here yet. They couldn't see what might happen next. Justice could be served before they even made it across the park. Her trigger finger itched for vengeance. She could do it.

She wasn't Camilla the timid anymore. She was Cam the courageous. Only... only…

Beck had asked her to play nice. Playing nice was not her strong suit, but because he was her Agent-in-Charge, and because he'd asked instead of ordering, Camilla paused to rethink her impulse to kill first, ask questions later. She'd just met a guy with rock-solid morals and the spit-and-polish shine of a boy scout. Make that a choir boy. Did she really want to throw that away over two worthless shitheads?

Both Renner and Beau had tumbled out of the SUV by then, Beau with an AR snug under his chin and Renner with his pistol drawn. That was kind of nice, them coming to their rescue as fast as they had. Probably more for Beck than her, but still. Renner and Beau were here, and they weren't pointing their weapons at her.

Cam took a deep breath to steady her thinking and her racing heart. Okay then. She could do this. Instead of exacting vigilante justice for what might simply be Beckam's broken nose and maybe a broken rib, she told her fellow agents, "These two assholes attacked us. That bat and tire iron…" She pointed her chin at the weapons now on the ground. "…are evidence. I've been holding these bastards until you and the police arrived. Bag that shit, but keep your eyes on those two. They're fuckin' murderers."

"Way to go, Cam," Renner replied evenly as he holstered his own pistol and knelt with Beckam. "Not sure why Beck even called us. Looks like you've got everything handled."

"Not really. C-can you help him?" she asked. She'd never forgive herself if Beck died.

"You bet," Renner breathed as he peeled his gloves off and placed one hand at Beckam's throat, feeling for a pulse, his other hand cupping the back of Beck's head.

Meanwhile, Beau walked straight at the boys, the buttstock of his rifle snug in his chest, his body coiled like an angry, black-eyed snake about to strike, and the barrel of his rifle aimed at the sniveling, chubby kid with blue balls. He kicked Bat Boy's boot.

"You're the two creeps who just hit Dupont Circle," he said, not asked. "You left an elderly woman behind. She's bloodied, but guess what, assholes? She's still alive, and she had a lot to say about you. She ID'd your punk asses, right down to your size-ten rubber boots."

Bat Boy stuttered, "N-n-no, sir, we n-n-never b-b-been—"

"I've got witnesses! With cell phones! Who took videos instead of stopping you little maggots!" Beau spat, standing over the two kids now, the business end of his weapon in Bat Boy's skinny face. "They caught you in the act of beating that poor woman damned near to death. The police have everything they need to put you away for attempted murder. You're gonna be a big star. Run, you murdering little asshole. Run!"

Instantly, Bat Boy morphed from mouthy asshole into sniveling, quivering, sphincter-clenching asshole, hugging his knees. "B-b-but you're gonna k-k-kill me if I r-r-run."

"You bet your ass I am," Beau promised, taking a step between Bat Boy's boots, threatening him with every billowing puff of his frosted, wintry breath.

Whoa, this man was magnificent. So fierce. Definitely angrier than Cam at what these kids had done, but damn. Beau cussed almost as good as she did. He looked like a pissed-off dragon who wanted to eat these two jerks for a midnight snack.

Like he *could* breathe fire and brimstone and melt them where they cowered.

She bonded instantly with this dark-haired, dark-eyed, over-the-top intense man with hatred etched on his ruggedly handsome face. How had she not noticed this monster back at TEAM HQ? Why hadn't she known about his total disregard for Mr. Stewart's rules on how to apprehend suspects? Not that she knew what those rules were, but Stewart probably had hundreds of politically correct rules to protect dirtbags like these two. He was one of those detail-oriented bosses who made sure everyone crossed their Ts and dotted their Is. He probably had more rules than MPD, but, yeah. Camilla liked Beau's cook 'em and eat 'em style. A lot.

Go, go, go. Shoot these motherfuckers. End them. I'll help hide the bodies.

"Ah, Beau. Buddy," Renner called out as he log rolled Beckam gingerly onto his back, his hands moving expertly over Beckam's head, then down his neck and over both shoulders. "Not positive, but there's a slim chance MPD wants these jokers alive when they get here. You know, just in case they want to call a lawyer or something. Just my opinion."

MPD being the District's very capable Metro Police Department.

Beau rolled his shoulders as if he didn't care what Alex, Renner, or MPD wanted. Camilla could swear she heard his spine crack all the way from where he stood, hulking over those two blubbering teenagers who were on their way to jail. Maybe prison, if justice were truly served. Both should be arraigned as adults. Not juveniles. She guesstimated they were around seventeen. They were old enough. They needed to pay for what they'd done.

"I couldn't catch him when he fell," she said quietly to Renner, so the mean boys couldn't hear.

"'Course not. Beck's a big guy. Probably twice your weight," Renner agreed easily, still focused on his buddy as he asked, "You okay, Beau?"

Beau had stepped back from those teenagers, but he hadn't yet lowered his rifle. "Yeah. Sure. Course. But I'm not here to do MPD's job. Sure wish these little bitches felt lucky, though." He jumped a half-step at Bat Boy, freaking the kid out. "Then I'd show them what happens to bullies where I came from."

Well, good, Camilla thought. *Scare the hell out of them.*

Renner didn't seem worried that Beau might go rogue and execute these kids like Camilla had considered doing. Whoa. Another epiphany. She and Beau had something in common. Neither of them liked assholes.

But of all the other agents in the office, Camilla had liked Renner Graves from the start, even though he'd mostly avoided her like everyone else. Soft-spoken with sandy brown hair, he didn't often say much to anyone. But when he had, he'd drawn negative attention away from her. Never confrontational or one to argue, he'd made things easier for her at the office. He wasn't passive, just one of those peacekeeper types who interjected himself into her line of fire. Not so much a friend. More like a frenemy. He was a lot like Beckam— everything she wasn't.

Only Renner was shorter than her Agent-in-Charge. Not bulky-big like Beck, either, but wiry and quick on his feet. Quick with a smile, too, but why not? He'd just gotten married, and he seemed truly happy about it. Best yet, he and his new bride Tara had invited Camilla to their New Year's Eve wedding. Not that she'd accepted. She hadn't. Couldn't. Wouldn't have dreamed of it.

But she had been honestly surprised that they'd asked, and that inclusion had felt—nice. It made her, kind of, almost, their friend. Didn't it? But it would've also meant going alone, and if she had, people would've asked questions, and knowing this group, someone would've figured out... *That.*

No. Not going there.

So, she'd RSVP'd her declination as quickly as their invitation hit her office desk. That was her way. Send a quick, strong signal. Leave no doubt, and be done with pretense. Then, because that invitation had touched her in a way she hadn't expected, she'd ordered the most expensive set of crystal wine goblets she could find. *Simone Crestani.* What else? Had them wrapped and delivered express. And with that, her problem was solved. Well, *that* problem was solved. The other problem in her life was another, deeply-tangled mess altogether.

"Stop it," Beckam growled as he came to, blinking and shaking his head as he batted Renner's hands away from his face.

Camilla nearly swallowed her tongue. Was he talking to her? Had she lost her mind and spoken that last thought out loud? Did he know about Heath? Was he telling her to stop and forget about that mess? Stop crying about it? If not... *Jesus Christ, stop what?*

"Stop messing with me, Renner," Beckam said groggily as he twisted his neck and peered at Beau. "Glad you guys made it. I was worried, maybe those two assholes would get the jump on Cam and—"

"You were worried about me?" she bit out, relieved that she hadn't opened her big mouth again. "You were the one who insisted on going outside. If we'd—"

"Damn it, Cam," he muttered, his eyes squeezed tight like his head hurt. Which it no doubt did. He had hit the ground hard and these jerks had hurt him. "Give it a rest. Please."

"Just lie still," Renner ordered, his palm on Beckam's broad shoulder, holding him flat. "You've got quite a knot on your forehead, but the back of your head's bleeding. Concussions are kinda sneaky. Let's not induce a brain bleed, shall we?"

"That's my fault," Camilla explained. "I couldn't catch you when you fell."

Renner placed a first-aid kit on Beckam's chest and was busy wiping the blood off his forehead. "Good thing I restocked my blow-out kit this morning. I'll leave it with you."

"Forget my head," Beckam muttered. "Got anything for my hand?"

"You think it's broke?" Renner asked.

"No," Beckam answered too quickly. "Just mashed a little."

Renner took hold of Beckam's right hand and squeezed.

"Yeah. A little. Ouch! Shit!"

"Just mashed, my ass," Renner deadpanned. "You need x-rays and this needs to be casted."

"Don't hurt him," Cam ordered sternly.

"'S okay, Junior Agent," Beckam told her. "Stand down. D-don't shoot our friends here."

Not like she was going to, but *Junior Agent*? Nobody'd been smart enough to call her that before. She liked it.

"No cast," Beck told Renner. "No ER, either."

Beau was talking into his two-way, still standing over the boys, his rifle still pointed at Bat Boy. "Copy that. Yeah, I see them now. MPD's here. You know it. After we give our statements, we'll go to the ER with Beck and Camilla, make sure they're still good for duty. Okay, will do."

He had to be talking to someone at TEAM HQ. Her ears pricked at her name being pronounced correctly. That was nice. But Beau's dark eyes were on her now, his gaze intense. One side of his upper lip twisted as if he didn't approve of her.

He wasn't so bad. Just intimidating, grouchy, and dark most of the time, at least until one of the other agents chatted him up. Maverick seemed to gravitate toward him, and Beau liked the agent everyone called Cowboy. Not Cam. She tried not to talk to anyone at work. Mostly because she didn't know how.

But Beckam had told her to play nice. Not told, but asked. He'd even said please. Okay then. With her heart climbing up her throat, Cam met Beau's stark and obviously negative appraisal as she told him, "Thanks, Agent Villanueva. I'm glad you and Renner are here and will stay with us until this is over."

He didn't answer, which was embarrassing, just stood there and stared at her like she was a freak or something.

She swallowed her discomfort because she was a freak. Damn. Being nice wasn't easy. Maybe Beckam was wrong, and this wouldn't work. She bit her bottom lip, wondering what else she could say to bridge the ever-widening gap between her and Beau, when—*I'll be damned.*

He nodded. At her. Just once. His head dipped like he actually appreciated her answer. His lips did something, kind of like a reluctant smile, but kind of a grimace, as if he didn't know what to say to her, either.

He's just like me. Cam thought as she nodded back at the hulking agent. Message received. *You're not as bad as I thought you were, either.*

"I don't have a concussion," Beckam fussed, his head and shoulders lifting off the ground again. By then, Renner had wrapped his right hand in a thick casing of gauze and tape. "Those boys aren't big enough to—"

"To what? Nail you with a tire iron?" Cam interrupted. "Bet me. That sneaky rat bastard meant to kill you. He hit you hard. You're bleeding. Lay down and do what you're told."

Renner's brows went up. "Man, she's got your number," he said through a cheesy grin. "And she's right. You won a free ride to the ER tonight, Beck. Might as well take it easy until we get you checked."

"No ambulance," Beckam said. "Not going."

"You sure? Just in case—?"

He shook his head. "I got dizzy. That's all. I've been hurt worse. Honest."

"Which might indicate a previous concussion," Cam pointed out. "Did you think of that? Have you fallen before? Have you taken a hit like that, say, in the last couple of weeks or months? When was your last physical?"

His uninjured hand settled over his face as he squeezed his temples, hiding from her. "Let it go, Cam. Please. I'm fine. Really."

And then she knew. He had a secret too, one she'd just stumbled across. This wasn't the first time he'd passed out, but he was still her Agent-in-Charge. All man. One hundred percent alpha. This discussion needed to take place privately, not in front of those two thugs or his fellow agents.

"Well, I say ambulance," she still told Renner and Beau. They weren't so bad. "His head might be okay, but his hand's injured."

"I second the motion," Renner added, a twinkle glittering in his eye as he lifted to his feet. "What say you?" he asked Beau.

"ER, just to play it safe," Beau called out from over by the two MPD officers who had arrived. He'd stuck his rifle into his back holster by then. "But first, these officers need to talk with you, Cam. Then you, Beckam. You up for that?"

"I said no ambulance," Beckam growled again, his free hand still shielding his face. "Yeah, Beau. I'll talk to anyone. Just not going to any ER."

Cam dropped to his side, worried at the odd pitch in his voice. "Are you sure? Don't you want to make sure that hand and your head are okay?"

His fingers parted enough she could see his eyes. "Don't you get it? These punks aren't the murderers we're after. If we leave, we won't be back. Alex will pull us off this op, and we'll lose any street cred we made today. As a couple, I mean. You really want to give that up? Now? When we finally have a clue who's killing these vets?"

We have a clue?

"Stewart'll send us back out here," she assured him, glancing over her shoulder at the sad little tent behind her. She and Beckam had actually talked together inside that cold, cramped space. Like real people, not like Heath talked to her. At her. Down to her.

Yes, she'd been overly defensive with Beckam at the beginning of this op, and okay, he hadn't held back everyone's opinions about her, either. True, enough. But when these two bullies arrived, she'd been worried. Make that scared enough that she hadn't thought twice about rolling into his side or grabbing his arm. It was a silly reflex thing, something she'd just automatically done. Because she knew he'd take care of her. Despite all her weapons training, she'd never hit anything but paper targets before, and targets didn't bleed or die. Although, when that kid with the tire iron hit Beckam, she'd wanted him to bleed. And die.

And yeah, Beckam might have been shocked when she'd grabbed onto him in the tent like she had, but he hadn't ridiculed her or pushed her away. And she *had* felt something rare and odd when he'd put his arm around her. Not like he was Prince Charming or anything utterly stupid like that, but he had been—kind. And big and strong and—yeah, kind, even though she hadn't been nice to him. Ever. Not like he could've been anywhere else inside a crowded pup tent, but he'd pulled her close, and he'd promised he wouldn't let anyone hurt her, and…

Cam swallowed hard, not understanding why that small act of chivalry affected her like it had. Beckam had no PhD. He was a dumb Army captain, had probably never gone to college a day in his life. Hadn't written one thesis, much less three. Okay, so she hadn't exactly written hers, either, but still. She was smarter than him. Wasn't she?

"No, Cam, he won't. You'll be back at your desk feeling useless before you know it, and I'll be squaring my last after-action report with Mark or Harley for the hundredth time. Damn it." Beckam reached for her then, and it was almost as if he knew what she was thinking. He intertwined his unbandaged fingers with hers like he needed her to believe him. To have—what'd everyone say—his six? "Stay with me,

Cam. We can do this, I know we can. Together. But if I end up at the ER…" He was looking straight at her by then, his other hand off his face, his dark eyes seeing through her. Challenging her. "The murderer will get away. Is that what you want? Because I sure don't. We have to see this through. It's just you and me, kid. Please. I can't go to the ER."

Just you and me, kid? Wow. A silly warm glow climbed her body. No one had ever called her kid before. He'd made it sound like an endearment.

"Okay," she whispered, still tracking Renner and Beau. Both were engaged with the two MPD officers now, the teenage delinquents already seated in the back of two separate patrol cars. "But once we're alone, you have to tell me why no ER, got it? No more secrets, Boy Scout. I want to know everything you know. We're partners from here on out, okay?"

She could have died and gone to heaven when his face blossomed like a warm, inviting sunbeam breaking through this bitter, cold night. The way his lips curled, not with hurtful cruelty, but with honest appreciation. Lips she wanted to taste.

He nodded, squeezing her fingers. "Deal, partner." Only he said 'pardner' with that deep, rich country twang of his. Like that made her a buddy. *His* buddy. Maybe even his friend. "Now help me up, so we can get back to work."

Cam did something she hadn't done since the evening she'd accepted what she thought had been a dream-come-true marriage proposal, but had ended up being just another lie. She smiled, too. Then she took hold of his big, callused hand and said, "Okay, Beck."

Chapter Sixteen

It wouldn't be easy, but Beckam was determined to get back inside the tent before his buddies dragged him off to the nearest ER. That was not happening.

With Cam staunchly at his side, holding him up, he made it slowly to his feet. But instead of letting her keep that feminine arm around his waist, he stiff-armed her once he was upright. Not that her arm around him didn't feel, *well, really good.* But because a man on a mission had to stand on his own two feet without help, and hopefully, without face-planting to maintain credibility. The last thing Beckam needed was for Renner, Beau, or anyone else on The TEAM to know he'd been within shrapnel-hitting distance at that bombing in Pakistan six months ago. If he went to the ER tonight, they'd take more x-rays, then MRIs and CT scans. They'd realize that shockwave had not only blown his eardrums, but that he was pretty sure he'd cracked his skull when it threw him into the wall of that stone mosque. And no. Just no. His headaches were fewer and farther between. He could hear again. Rarely relied on lip-reading. He *was* getting better.

He just didn't need Alex knowing that the bombing he'd survived had also forced him out of the Army. Not that he'd willingly taken the medical discharge without arguing his case. More like he'd been sternly told he wasn't fit for duty and would damned well take that medical discharge or risk court-martial. Which was his politically-minded CO's way of clearing the ranks of guys he didn't work well with. Namely, anyone who didn't bend over and kiss his hairy ass on command. Which Beckam had refused to do, especially when that ass-kissing got people, civilians or soldiers, killed.

As far as court-martial, Major Brad Parker had no evidence to support it. But Beckam had seen the liar do it before. Parker was a modern-day Frank Burns of *"MASH"* sitcom notoriety. A kiss-ass himself, he'd attached himself to more generals' backsides than remoras did to sharks. Which gave him the inside track and political clout Beckam didn't have, as well as a rep Beckam didn't want. Parker had zip to do with leadership or vision, but everything to do with stepping on enlisted men and women on his way to the top. He made Frank Burns look like a hero. But hey. When Beckam agreed to call it quits rather than fight his conniving CO, Parker *was* already on the short list to make colonel. He might just make general, too.

"Hey, hey, hey," Renner guffawed when he caught sight of Beckam up on his feet. "Where do you think you're going?"

Beckam waved Renner's cocky comradery away. "Back on the job. I'm good," said every hard-headed Ranger ever. "Time to give my statement to these officers and get to work."

Beau cocked his big, square head until it was nearly resting on his broad shoulder. That alone said, *'How stupid are you?'* But then he topped it off with, "Like hell, Garner. Sit your ass back down. You're not going any—"

"Knock it off, Agent Villanueva. He's right," Cam spoke up, her snark set on high. "We've got a job to do, and we're going to finish it. Back off."

Oops. Wrong way to handle Beau. The man had a wicked temper, had in fact tested Alex's patience until he'd nearly fired

Beau last year in the middle of hunting the serial killer, Catalina Montego. But in the course of that desperate hunt, Beau had also saved Maverick Carson's life, rescued Doc Fitz from the crazy woman she'd thought, at the time, was her aunt. The woman ended up being one of the many mentally ill sisters of the woman McKenna had also discovered was not her biological mother…

Yes, that was a mess of confusion in the middle of one of the hottest ops The TEAM had ever worked—and bungled. But Beau had been there that day when he, Alex, and Gabe discovered and rescued the twenty-some men whom Montego had tortured and held prisoner in her abandoned warehouse. In fact, Beau was the reason Maverick was still alive today.

Somewhere in the maelstrom of Beau's first few months working with The TEAM, he'd not only transformed the recalcitrant man everyone called Cowboy, into a genuinely happy man, but Beau had also come to a truce and understanding with Alex. They actually liked each other now. But Beau still didn't like Cam. Not one bit.

Beckam headed off the upcoming confrontation between these two mouthy troublemakers with another, "Really. I'm good, Beau. No problem. Just needed to catch my breath. You know how it is when you get sucker-punched. Any questions, officer?"

A hefty billow of frosty breath snorted from Beau's flared nostrils at Beckam's attempt to distract him. Man, he looked like Lucky, Beckam's dad's bull back home. Ready to charge, maybe even scrape a deep furrow into the earth beneath his boot, slam Beckam into the ground and pin him. Beau could do it, too. He was built like that bull, all muscle and brawn. Only he was smart, too, and hands down one of the most stubborn operators Beckam had ever worked with. Could he take him on the mat? Beckam wasn't so sure. But that'd be one helluva wrestling match if push ever came to shove.

Grunting to get Beckam's attention, the sturdy-looking female MPD officer gave him a stern once over, then fired several questions at him. *Where were you when you were first hit? Why aren't you in a designated homeless shelter like you should be? This is a park, not a campsite. Move along or lose your tent, is that understood?* In other words, *I'm the law here, and what I say, goes.*

Yeah, I don't think so…

At which point Renner jumped into the fray with both feet and a polite, "Excuse me, ma'am. Officer. You might want to check with Mayor Tillis before you evict my Agent-in-Charge from this location. These folks are not just more homeless street people. They're with me and we're working at the mayor's request to help stop the murders among the District's homeless population. This tent is only here to attract the same people you're looking for."

"Hmmpf," she huffed, her cynicism evident in the way she stuck her chin at Cam and asked, "I suppose that's why she's here, too? What's she do, type your reports in that POS tent?"

The tiny hairs at the back of Beckam's neck prickled to attention. That glint in this officer's eye was downright predatory. And she was blatantly sexist—against a woman. What was her problem? Had she recognized Cam from somewhere or did she just not like women in general?

"No, ma'am," he answered politely before Cam could claw the officer's eyes out. "Cam's a qualified private investigator, and she's one of Alex Stewart's best. We work together." Okay, that was an outright fib, but name-dropping Alex might win

Beck a few points. Everyone in town knew who Alex was, if not by reputation, then by the frequency with which TEAM successes hit the front page. Some people even liked him.

Beckam squinted, needing to catch this prickly officer's badge number or her name. *Ah, Officer Lark.* "Is there anything else we can do for you, Officer Lark?"

"Keep this area clean," she ordered, her swagger on high and her gloved index finger stabbing at him like a one-tined pitchfork. "No littering. Clear your shit out every morning. You need back-up, you call me first, understood?" *Stab.* "Train station's my beat. My rules." *Stab. Stab. Stab.*

"Yes, ma'am." He nodded, not willing to debate who he'd call first if trouble came knocking again, but fervently wishing Officer Tuttle worked twenty-four-seven. Jimmy understood street people. Lark here seemed to think she owned them.

She grunted, turned her back on him, and walked to her cruiser. Once MPD left, Renner's feet were still firmly planted. Looked like he intended to stand guard for what was left of the night.

That was Renner for you. The whole sadistic torture thing that Catalina Montego had brought to America had also turned him into one badassed protector. He'd already been known to look out for the younger military members and homeless veterans. But now he'd turned into everyone's big brother. Extra protective. Extra fierce. Extra ready to throw down at the slightest provocation.

Beckam knew for a fact that Renner and his new bride Tara had invited all Montego's victims to their New Year's Day wedding. Quite a few, mostly the ones that could walk, had actually shown up. That alone declared their allegiance to this guy. And their love. Renner was in that rare, good place all men strived for. He could easily start his own security business with the number of men who adored him for saving the last of Montego's victims' lives.

Which meant Renner and Beau had to go.

"No need for you guys to stay," Beckam insisted. "We'll be fine."

Two might puffs of frosty 'WTF' billowed from Beau's flared nostrils. He was another one of those prolific cursers. But Beckam was willing to bet Cam could best him.

"You sure about that?" Renner asked, worry clearly etched at the corners of his eyes.

"'Course he's sure," Cam interrupted, her hand possessively on Beck's forearm. "Now beat it, guys. Get back to work. It's too cold to stand around and talk. We can't do our job without sleep, can we?"

Renner grinned. "Copy that, Cam. Stay in touch, Beck."

"*I'll* stay in touch," she snapped. "He needs to rest. I'm on this mission too, in case you didn't know."

There went that cocky smile again. Renner seemed to enjoy sparring with Cam. "Wouldn't have it any other way," he said as he stripped off his gloves and tossed them to her. "Keep those pretty fingers warm. Glad we could help."

She caught the pair, then stuttered, "Th-thanks, umm, Agent Graves, for getting here so fast and f-for the gloves. I, umm, seemed to have lost mine."

He grinned. "Stay frosty, kiddo."

"'Night, guys," Beckam grumbled, needing her to get inside the tent before everyone linked hands and started singing Kumbaya.

"Later," Renner said as he and the strong, silent, grumbling type at his side turned back to their vehicle.

Beckam waited until they left before he dropped to his knees and ordered, "Inside. Step on it."

Of course, she had to argue. "You first."

"Just get inside," he snapped. Then added, "Please."

Lucky for him, Cam did as he very much needed her to do. Finally, thankfully, he climbed in behind her and zipped the flap up tight. While she turned her flashlight on and fussed with her gear bag, he doffed his boots and jacket, took off his pants, and stuffed himself back into his now frigid sleeping bag. Rolling his jacket into a makeshift pillow, Beckam stuffed it beneath his head and finally relaxed. He was damned cold and tired, but their cover was safe.

His head hurt, and Renner had given his hand a shot for pain. That would last a few hours. It'd be morning by the time it faded. Maybe Cam wouldn't mind humping over to the free clinic with him then. That way, they could check in on Bruce and Dave next door at Raymond's Kids. Maybe get that x-ray of his hand and another shot for pain. Kelsey usually served a daily hot breakfast. She might be Alex's wife, but Beck knew she'd keep confidences, too. He'd seen how well she'd worked with Renner during that Montego op. He trusted Kelsey. Everyone did.

"Would you mind if, umm…?" Cam was still on her knees. She'd located her gloves and pistol, both bottled waters, her flashlight, and watch. All were laid out on her sleeping bag, the zipper side still toward him.

"What do you need now?" he asked, as weary as he'd ever been.

"I, umm, think you were right. We should conserve body heat."

Say what? Beckam lifted his weary head off his jacket/pillow. "Okaaaaay…" he said slowly, needing her to spit out precisely what she meant before he jumped to conclusions and got his head bitten off.

"Would you mind, umm, if we zipped our bags together? You know, like you suggested before? Just for tonight, I mean. Not like forever or anything crazy, but…" Her gaze shifted over his bandaged hand and then to his head. "You're hurt. That way I can, umm, monitor you through the night. Make sure you're, umm, breathing okay. Not like you're going to die on me or anything but… Would you mind?"

"You're sure?"

Her head bobbed, jostling all that shiny silk now coming undone and spilling over her shoulders in tangled dribbles of shadowy black. "I'm cold. Aren't you?"

"Well, yeah, but…" What could he say? His body temp had suddenly spiked with a fever. Because she was not just some grunt trying to survive arctic training. If anything, Cam was a splash of burning hot cayenne pepper, strong and powerful enough to water his eyes. *If* he were dumb enough to touch her. Which he'd done, but not like he'd be touching her once those bags were joined. "Yes. Good idea." Then, just to keep any hint of anticipation out of his voice, he added, "If you're sure you want to."

"I'm sure. Just don't know how—"

"Let me," he said, as once again, he peeled out of his sleeping bag. But damn. He was only dressed in his undershirt and boxers, freezing his balls off. As hard as it was working with one hand, Beckam zippered her sleeping bag with his while she slipped out of her jeans and boots. He paused to allow her under the cover first, then carefully maneuvered his much longer legs and larger body inside, making sure to keep to his side of the bag and not bump her. Which didn't last.

Shivering, Cam crowded him, tucked her head under his chin, and snaked her hands around his ribs, which, okay. That hurt. Maybe he'd been wounded more than he'd thought. But when the rest of her delicate and nearly naked self aligned with his belly and legs...

Okay, that wasn't going to work. Shivering now, he stuffed enough of that zero-degree bag between their bodies to hide the erection that had sprung up between them like a steel rod. Damned thing seemed to have a life of its own. And now it ached, too.

"Hmmm," she breathed. "This is better. I can listen to your heartbeat all night now. Just to make sure you're okay."

Well, yeah, she could hear his heartbeat. It was pounding loud enough. Felt like a pair of out of control bongos in his chest. "You're freezing," he told her as he looped his arms outside the joined bags, careful not to make any more physical contact than necessary. This was definitely not his brightest idea, but there he was, almost groping his junior agent inside what had become their all too intimate quarters.

"There's a draft," she complained. "My neck's still cold. Can't you fit your arms inside?"

"Sure, but then..." *Bandage or not, my arms are long enough that I'll be clutching your backside.*

"Oh, come on," she growled, wiggling against him. Teasing him whether she meant to or not. "Loosen up. I'm not going to bite you."

"Cam..." he breathed as he squeezed his eyes tightly shut, concerned that some very significant TEAM protocols were about to be breached. Despite everything he'd told her about how often he'd slept with other grunts, he'd never before put himself into this position with a female soldier. Not once. Yes, there'd been opportunities, but Army captains were held to a higher standard. At least, he'd held himself to a higher standard because of his rank. Leadership meant something. The last person he wanted to emulate was Major Parker.

"So talk," Cam ordered once he'd shifted his arms inside the bag, looped them over her shoulder blades, and covered his bandaged hand with his good hand, keeping them as far away from her butt as he comfortably could.

He hedged. "About…?"

She bumped his chin with the top of her head. "About why you refused to be seen at the emergency room. What happened? Were you shot? Does anyone know? And why not? Don't you Army guys, what'd you call yourself, a Ranger? Don't Rangers need regular physicals, too?"

"It's not that simple."

Dead silence. She cleared her throat. Then, after swallowing so loudly he could hear it, she asked, "Would it help if I told you my secret first?"

He closed his eyes, nearly too tired to care what secrets she harbored. But he said, "Sure. You tell me yours. I'll tell you mine." Maybe he'd fall asleep by then. He hoped.

Her shoulders wiggled against him, which in turn made her breasts mash into his chest, and it was dominoes once again. All the blood in his brain vacated the premises, headed south to man-land. His breath got caught in his throat. Erotic scenarios played out in his all-male head. Scenarios that had her moaning beneath him, her nails scratching his back while he sank into her slick, warm body, and…

Damn. He scrunched more of the sleeping bag between Cam and his very hard equipment. Yeah, she'd hate that. It'd probably set her off on another hateful tangent, and he just wasn't up for the drama.

"Umm…" She stalled.

"Not easy, huh?" he taunted, wishing she'd let it go. "We can always save this conversation for tomorrow."

"No, but… I don't know. You've been nothing but decent to me tonight, and I know I'm not the easiest person to get along with, and… Well, umm…"

Understatement of the year. "Just spit it out, Cam. Who knows? Maybe you'll feel better once you tell someone, even if it's just me."

"That's the thing. I've never told anyone what I've suspected… Err. Umm…"

Beckam didn't think, just pulled her tightly against him. "Scout's honor, Camilla Brinkman. I don't share confidential information. Whatever you need to say, just—"

"That's another thing. I'm, ah…" She blew out a puff of breath. "I'm sorry about calling you Boy Scout instead of using your name. That was rude and uncalled for."

"I've been called worse. Don't worry about it."

"But I am sorry."

"Apology accepted. Now…"

"Okay, so, I, umm, don't think, umm, my degrees are, err, exactly valid." Her shoulders bunched beneath his palms. "I mean, I might've fudged a little on my finals, and well, I had some, umm, help, writing my dissertation and…" She sucked in a deep breath. "…defending it."

"How could you possibly fudge on a final or dissertation? Isn't that some kind of a face-to-face interrogation?" He knew damned well it was. He'd looked into graduate school, but was a long way off from hitting that mark. He'd only recently completed his General Ed requirements, headed for doctorates in both Bioagricultural Sciences and Pest Management Specialization. They'd come in handy when he retired to Oklahoma. Unless he went into Animal Sciences. Cattle breeding, genetics, and livestock behavior piqued his interest, too. He just had to decide.

"Well…" Cam shifted against him, once more lighting his body up in ways she might not have meant to. "I had help. It's not like I cheated, but…"

He kept his mouth shut. In his book, if you had help during a final exam or dissertation, you cheated. No ifs, ands, or buts about it.

With another gulping swallowing, Cam admitted, "Maybe I did. Because I'm pretty sure Papa paid my advisors and my masters' committees to accept my dissertations. I was so sure I'd failed, but then… yeah. I didn't."

Advisors? Committees? She'd cheated more than once? "But surely when you submitted your written dissertation, they approved it and—How many are we talking about?"

"Three, but I never submitted anything, Beck. It all just happened. One morning I'd get called to the dean's office. He'd tell me he'd never seen a woman with my IQ before, that I was at the head of my class, that I was welcome to attend the commencement ceremony if I wanted to. Or something along those lines. They all made it clear I didn't need to do anything more. Honestly, I got the impression none of my deans wanted me there."

Beckam stilled.

"So, yeah," she said quietly. "I never attended any graduation bullshit. It seemed useless. Besides—"

"Besides what?" he asked, fully aware that Cam had just admitted to defrauding her college. Or colleges. As well as every deserving kid who'd actually worked for their education.

"No one cared. It's not like I was popular or anything." She huffed through her nose. "I was always the girl in the wrong place at the wrong time."

He bumped the top of her head with his chin. "Explain."

"All my life, Beck. I've been that too-smart-for-her-own-good kid at school. It started in fifth grade. The principal at my private school said I was advanced, a genius. Which made Papa happy enough to insist the principal let me skip a few grades and go straight to high school. Which sucked. I was a ten-year-old stuck in a class with mean-mouthed fourteen-year-olds. Then I skipped to twelfth. I flew through that, and two years later, boom. Me, a freshman in college. Do you know how many friends an awkward thirteen-year-old makes in college? With eighteen and nineteen-year-old walking bags of testosterone and estrogen who can all drive and drink and... other stuff?"

"Umm, none?" he answered, hoping he was wrong.

"Give the boy scout a prize, err..." Cam had the grace to cough. "Sorry. Didn't mean that the way it sounded, but yeah. I wasn't just a fifth wheel, I was the local walking pariah. Even my advisors avoided me. You'd think I'd had the bubonic plague or an STD or something."

Which made sense. Beckam knew Cam was smart, but she'd never displayed any genius at work. Only at the range. There, she'd excelled. So what was he missing?

"How many PhDs do you have?"

"Three. One in Jurisprudence, one in Geological Science, and the other..." Her head bobbed against his throat. "You'll laugh."

Not with his heart lodged up high in his throat like it was. If what Beckam was hearing was true, someone had defrauded not only the universities Cam had attended, but her as well. She'd be a laughing stock if this ever became public knowledge. She'd be ruined before she got started. "Try me."

"Forestry. Funny, huh? But I actually liked those courses, and I think my professor liked me. But then..." She drew in another big breath. "Same old story. The dean called me to his office. Said I'd aced all my courses, that he's never seen anything like me before. Blah, blah, blah. Here's your diploma. No need to waste time on the commencement ceremony. Goodbye. Good riddance."

"He didn't really say good riddance, did he?"

"Might as well have."

Well, damn. Beckam hated to ask. But he did. "Do you really believe your old man, umm, bribed those deans and counselors? That he had someone else take your tests, and, I don't know, falsify your dissertation?" Was that even possible?

She shook her head against him even as she murmured, "That's exactly what I think. I just don't know what to do about it."

"Damn..." he breathed. "Me neither, but that had to be miserable, you stuck with a bunch of older kids in school, then adults. College kids are the worst party animals, and you were just a kid."

But it also explained a lot about the prickly Rubik's Cube in his arms. No wonder Cam acted as if she were fighting the world. She was.

Chapter Seventeen

She knew the second she'd admitted what she'd suspected her father had done, Beckam would pull away. Maybe shove her out of their joined sleeping bag and tell her to get lost. He'd tell Alex, who would surely make her quit The TEAM. Which, believe it or not, had only just today started feeling like it might be her TEAM, too. Like she belonged. But Beckam wasn't breathing evenly anymore. His arms were both still around her, but his breath came in sharp, hard gulps like he couldn't believe what he'd heard. This was the end. Only this time, she'd be more than just a pariah. She'd be a confessed liar and fraud. Worse, she'd just outed her father. He could go to jail. Alana would hate her for ruining her glamorous, entitled, sequined, make-believe life.

But Cam had carried this awful secret long enough. Beckam was right. Even if he hated her for it, the secret was out. She still couldn't relax enough to draw in a deep breath, but she did feel better.

Yet she truly didn't know who was the worse liar, her father for pushing her too hard, then paving the way and making her believe, for a while there, that she really was smarter than everyone else. Or her, for needing his approval and love so badly that, once she'd suspected the deceit, she hadn't been brave enough to confront him. She'd gone on to her second, then her third PhD. To this day she didn't know if she'd been rebelling even then, pushing him to his limit. Daring him to stop what had turned into an outrageous charade for them both. An outright lie. She'd lived with deceit most of her life. Her father's lies, yes, but somehow, somewhere, she'd bought into those lies and made them hers.

Which led to other questions. How many college administrators had he bribed? And why? What had Luis and Alana Lopez stood to gain by betraying their one and only daughter? By presenting her to the world as a genius, when she was fairly sure she was barely above average? Her future? Was that what this was all about?

'Well, Papa,' she wanted to tell him now, *'That didn't work out very well for you, did it?'*

Unless...

Fuck. It all made sense now. Luis and Alana Lopez were tight with Heath's parents, Spence and Penn Brinkman. Now her archenemies. Her worst nightmares.

Cam could barely draw in enough air to sustain her by then. She was trapped between family and prison. If her father had done this to her, would he also have planned for the day she came to her senses? Had he covered his tracks and made everything look like she'd committed this fraud all by herself?

Beckam must've sensed her pulling away. His arms crossed over her back, his fingers splayed as he held her fast and murmured, "When did you suspect you weren't precisely the genius your father wanted you to believe you were?"

She could've cried at the gentleness in his tone, but bit her bottom lip instead. "I always hated school," she whispered. "Every fuckin' day of it. No matter how hard I tried, I was never smart enough, even in grade school. But he insisted I was excelling, that I didn't see the forest for the trees. That I was better and smarter than everyone else. That he would prove it to me."

Beckam's uninjured hand moved to the back of her head. "Breathe," he murmured, his voice deeper than she'd ever heard.

That broke the dam, and Cam started to cry. Big sloppy tears she couldn't hold back. Not anymore. Years. She'd been masquerading for years, and Beckam sounded like he believed her after just one day together. One day! Who did that?

"You poor thing," he whispered, and—

Her heart broke with a tortured, *Wah. Just wah!* Cam buried her face in his shirt even as his body curled around hers, cupping her like a kitten in a quilt. Enfolding her. Comforting her.

"Leave me alone," she cried even as she clung to him, her fingertips digging into his poor, battered body.

"Shush," he whispered into her hair. "Just shush for a minute, will you?"

She bobbed her head, willing to hear him out. There was nothing he could tell her that would top the sin she'd just confessed. Nothing. Until he said, "So, umm, my secret. You still interested?"

Not really, but okay. She still had no way forward, but this wasn't about solving her problems. This was only about sharing. Wiping her nose with the back of her gloved hand, Cam nodded. "Might as well. Can't be any worse than mine." At least not the secret she'd shared. But that other one…

Had to take a number. She couldn't dare reveal more of her pathetic life. Beckam would know what a fuckin' loser she was then. Because Alex Stewart was right. She wasn't any good at customer service.

Beckam started slowly. He'd been going to tell Cam how he'd hurt his head and why he'd taken a medical. But she seemed to need a story with more heart so he said, "Once upon a time, there was this high school kid who'd wanted to be a Ranger all his life. His dad was Army and this kid loved his dad, like his dad was his first and only hero. Anyway, he took the ASVAB, the Armed Services Vocational Aptitude Battery test, then signed up early with the local Army recruiter. Hey, are you still awake?"

Her head bobbed. "Ah huh, keep going. I'm listening."

"Good. Well, anyway…" He took a deep breath. "This kid had a neighbor lady, and her name—"

"Just to be clear. This kid is you, right?"

"Well, yeah. This is my secret, so of course the kid's me." He drew that out, teasing the unhappy woman snuggled into his side. "Anyway, his neighbor's name was Mrs. Jones, umm, Desiree. One day in May of my senior year, Desiree had an accident with a Holstein heifer in front of my parent's home. She was running away from her husband, and she hit one of the neighbor's cows. She was only going maybe thirty miles an hour, but she broadsided the poor animal, which made an ungodly mess, and well. You don't need to know about all that. But the thing is, yeah, I'm that high school kid, and that was the day I learned something the hard way. Something I've never told anyone. Only you. Now."

Beckam cleared his throat. He knew he was stalling, but the morning Desiree died came back to him in vivid technicolor, complete with aroma vision. "The thing is, she had her twins with her, and when she hit the cow, all the stuff in that poor animal's gut came in through the broken windows and covered Corky and Carrie with, you know, cow shit."

"How awful! Those poor kids."

Beckam nodded. "Yup. Sure was, but Carrie's everyone's sweetheart and Corky's the cutest little guy. They're growing up too fast, but wait until you meet them. You'll fall in love and…" Damn. Why'd the crazy notion of her meeting them tumble out of his big mouth? Like that would ever happen? Like she'd even want to go home with him to Oklahoma? Not likely. She'd been pretty definite about not being mom material. Although now, Beck wondered. If Papa was as sneaky as he'd sounded, what was her mother like?

"Anyway," he continued. "I got the twins out of their booster seats and into our house where my sister cleaned them up and quieted them down. Then Dad and I were able to get Mrs. Jones out of her car and away from the car without hurting her too much. By then the sheriff had arrived. EMTs too."

"You're her hero," Cam whispered. "You saved her life."

"Umm, no. I'm not and I didn't. Wish I had, though." He shook his head, never more certain he was anything but Desiree's hero. "You see, the minute I set her down, she grabbed my arm and said, 'I told him it was you'."

"What was you?"

Beckam gulped as the biggest failure of his life rolled back over him. "She'd told her husband, Brent Jones, who everyone thought was a real nice guy, that the baby she was carrying wasn't his. That it was mine."

"Shit. You knocked up a married woman? You were screwing around with… Umm, wait. That doesn't sound like you, Beck."

He sighed in relief. Cam was finally using that big brain of hers. Didn't hurt that she'd called him Beck, either. "It wasn't me. I didn't do that. Only ever talked with the lady once after one of my high school wrestling matches. Only once. But you've got to understand, that day of the wreck, she was desperate. She'd hit that cow hard, and she was bleeding internally. She was in a lot of pain, and she was miscarrying, Cam. There was blood everywhere. All over her, on my hands and arms, my shirt and pants." He paused to catch his breath, his words tumbling out too fast and furious. Truth was he'd been covered in Desiree's blood and too inexperienced to feel more than frightened that he'd killed her by trying to help her.

Inhale. Exhale. Start again.

"The sad thing is no one believed her. Right then and there, I flat out denied her accusation to her face. My dad backed me up. In the end, no one believed her. No one was on her side. I wasn't wrong, but that didn't make what I did to her right."

"What are you saying?"

Beckam ran his bandaged hand over his face, needing something to sop up the extra moisture leaking out of his tired eyes. "I'm saying that after that crazy lie, while she was lying there dying on our porch, she also said her husband was going to kill her unborn child. A little girl, Cam. Desiree knew she was having a baby girl. But it seemed so far-fetched. So unreal. I mean, Brent was a good guy. Sure, he worked hard, and he probably didn't have two extra nickels to rub together, but that day, I chose to believe him over her. I'd heard all the town gossip. Brent was one of the good old boys, but she was from the city. She was the sinner, the cheating wife, not the other way around. Certainly wasn't her faithful, hard-working husband, the guy everyone loved and believed they knew. And there she was, pregnant with some other guy's kid to boot. I honestly thought I knew everything I needed to know to judge her. But God…"

And there he stopped, reliving the anguish in Desiree's teary eyes all over again. Standing over her like an executioner while she gave up her last hope—him.

"And then…" Cam hinted gently, her fingertips tapping his collarbone.

"Desiree died on the way to Saint Joe's. They saved her baby, but yeah. She died. Brent was there. They told him the good news, that he was a father again. That his little girl was premature, but she was going to make it. That he could see her as soon as they cleaned her up and ran a bunch of tests. Only the first chance he got, Brent strangled that tiny baby with his bare hands. Broke her neck. Couldn't have been hard. She was so small. Never said a word, just killed the baby Desiree asked me to save."

The baby I should've, could've, God in heaven, wish I'd saved…

"Oh, Jesus," Cam breathed. Her arms tightened around Beckam, her sweet breasts warm and full and somehow, the comfort he needed in the middle of this gruesome story. "What…? How…? Who's the real father?"

Swallowing hard, he told her what he'd forever wish he'd known then. "In the legal nightmare afterward, Brent ended up at Big Mac, the state prison in McAlester, Oklahoma. But the court awarded custody of Corky and Carrie to Brent's parents, who were so much worse than him. I was already at Fort Sill when I heard the news, and I came unglued. I mean, how could they turn two innocent kids over to the parents of the man who'd killed their little sister? Who'd scared their mother so bad that she'd run away from him? So, yeah…"

He blew out a long breath, wondering why he'd ever wanted Cam needed to hear this. "So, I called my parents. Figured I'd catch the next bus home. Told them I meant to adopt Corky and Carrie, that those little kids were more important than anything I could do for Uncle Sam. I owed Desiree that much. Didn't matter. There was no way I was going to turn my back on them like I did their mom. I couldn't let them grow up in the same kind of hell that made Brent."

"But why? That baby wasn't yours. Neither were Desiree's other kids. Terrible things happen, Beckam. Doesn't make you responsible for other people's stupid decisions."

Man, he loved the sound of his name on her lips. But she was wrong about Mrs. Jones.

"Yeah, but Mrs. Jones wasn't stupid. She was just scared to death for her baby, and that baby *was* mine, Cam. Don't you know? Maybe not literally or biologically, but think about what you're saying. We *are* all brothers and sisters in the Lord's eyes. You might not believe the same as I do, but we *are* our brothers' and sisters' keepers. Every day. And I owed Mrs. Jones that much, especially after I'd all but called her a liar in her time of need. She'd reached out for me to save her, Cam. *Me. Just me.* But I let her down when she needed me most. I didn't save her, and because I was more worried what the sheriff and his deputy were thinking, I didn't save her baby, either."

"There was no way you could've known that. And even if you had, Brent was legally that baby's father. The hospital would never have let you see her, certainly not instead of him."

"I know all that, but…" Beckam closed his eyes, still trying to un-see the desperation in Desiree's sad eyes when she'd told that terrible untruth. When she'd besmirched his pristine, but totally worthless, teenaged reputation and threatened what he'd thought then were the dreams of a lifetime. Truth was, the thrill of being a Ranger had never compared to the thrill of looking into Carrie's and Corky's pretty blue eyes every time he went home. Eyes that would forever remind him of Desiree's last desperate wish and his worst failure.

"But that's what I should've done, Cam. I should've claimed that unborn baby girl right then and there, and told the world, loud and clear, that yes, by God. She was mine. I should've realized then that no woman in her right mind would've made such an outrageous claim unless she was desperate. Desiree would've at least died happy, err, happier. And what would it have hurt, huh? Yeah, people would've gossiped behind my back, but they did that anyway. And who cares what small-minded gossips think? I mean, whether she'd planned it or not, Desiree turned me into a father that morning. That little girl could've been mine. She should've been. I owed that mother and baby then. I still do."

Which was not a great leap for Beckam. He'd always wanted to be just like his dad.

"But you were just a kid. How could you have known what to do? Oh, my God, you're kidding me? You did it, didn't you? You adopted them."

He shook his head. "Not me, but Mom and Dad did. They hadn't told me then, but yeah. Right after I went to Fort Sill, they petitioned the court to reconsider their decision to place those kids with Brent's parents. It only took a few seconds for my parents, Carolyn and Ross Garner, to step up to the plate and do what was right. In the end, Brent's parents relinquished custody of those two little angels sight unseen. That's right. They'd never even met their only grandkids. Turns out, they didn't want the burden of raising one-year-old twins."

But Beckam did. Every chance he could. Corky and Carrie might live with his parents, but in his mind, he was as much their father as his dad. A good portion of every check he earned went to their care and keeping. Of course, his mom and dad were the very best parents for those two little orphans. Because of their generosity, Corky and Carrie were growing up strong and happy back in Horse Hollow, on a ranch where they could run and laugh and dance to their hearts' content.

They might not wear the latest fad or have their own Echo Dots, but the last time Beckam saw them—and that was just Christmas—they'd been full of spunk. Laughing. Dancing around the Christmas tree in the pajamas he'd brought them. Just kids doing what they did best—growing up too fast and being kids. Being the best medicine for this tired, old world.

"Damn." The only swear word he allowed breached his lips. "Not sure why I told you all that."

Yet he did know. Camilla Brinkman was a lot like Desiree Jones. All she let anyone see of her was the tip of an iceberg. But what lay beneath that snarky surface was a boatload of heartache and despair. But really, what did anyone know about Cam? She'd thrown up so many nasty defenses since she'd come to work with The TEAM that no one was close to her.

So, he explained, "The good folks in Horse Hollow, you know, the ones who go to church every Sunday but who still gossip behind everyone else's backs? Well, none of them ever knew that Brent slapped Desiree around at home. Not that an abused woman would share that kind of misery with just anyone. Not that she had friends in Horse Hollow. Which makes her death even sadder. It took Brent killing that motherless baby to wake everyone up. The sheriff called the medical examiner from Tulsa. He did an autopsy. Found previously broken bones in Desiree's arms, fingers, and her leg. Her skull. Which meant living with Brent had been Hell."

"Yes, it was," Cam said quietly. Her voice had grown softer. Sadder. As if she knew precisely what Desiree had suffered.

Which Beckam suspected she did. He finished the sad tale. "But Gus Butler, the rich kid in town, knew all along that little girl was his. He explained it in his suicide note, the one old man Butler found after his one and only child hanged himself from the rafters in his garage. Right next to his fancy car. Gus wrote how much he loved Desiree. He knew she was pregnant. They'd made plans to run off to his dad's vacation home up north in Canada. Gus thought she could apply for immunity there, that he could raise those three kids like they were his own. The only reason she implicated me was because she didn't want to get Gus into trouble. You see, everybody in Horse Hollow loves the Garner family, but not the Butlers. Guess because the Butlers are rich, and we're more like everyone else. She fingered me because she thought her baby'd be safer if we had her. Ended up, she was right. Corky and Carrie are safe and sound. Just wish I'd been man enough to be who she needed that day. That unborn baby might still be safe, too."

Beckam stilled then. Because Cam was crying.

Chapter Eighteen

The more he rocked and held her, the more Cam's heart broke until… "Fuck," she cried. "Fuck. Fuck. Fuck!"

"I'm sorry. I didn't mean—"

"Shut up. Just. Shut. Up!" she begged, the rest of her lies ready to spill over the dam she'd built and rebuilt, strengthened and disguised for too many years. That story he'd told could've been her life. Except for the broken bones. She couldn't remember when she'd built that dam to keep people out. Only knew the less people knew, the easier it'd been to lie to herself and the world. Not like anyone ever cared enough about her to dig deeper, to look for the real Camilla. Not like she would've let them if they'd tried.

Her chest hurt deep inside, like she'd been stabbed through and through. Make that gutted. Speaking her smaller sins out loud of defrauding those universities, had done her in. Hearing the words, giving voice to all her awful suspicions about her parents, made her suspicions real and true. She *wasn't* better than everyone else. She wasn't smarter or prettier or, or… God, she wasn't better at anything!

Only once she'd actually said it out loud and heard it, once she'd shared it with the man she'd wanted so much to hate when this mission started—she knew in her heart it was true.

God! Her inner diva recoiled at the salty, sweaty smell of Beckam even as her nostrils flared to draw more of that masculine scent into her soul. She didn't want to need anyone. Ever!

But that poor Desiree Jones... She'd needed someone just as desperately that day as Camilla did now. Her poor, poor baby girl. God, why were people so mean? So cruel? So gawddamned vicious and deceitful and... and...

Desiree had reached for Beckam because deep inside her mother's heart, instinctively, she'd known back then the same thing Cam knew now. That in every way that mattered, Beck was too fuckin' good to be true. Honorable. Patient as fuck. He would've loved that poor baby girl, not broken her neck like she was nothing. Cam knew it in the darkest, deepest, hidden depths of her battered soul. He would've loved her baby, too. He would've nurtured and protected it, and... and he wouldn't have let anyone take it away from her. Not even Alana.

Oh, God, oh, God, oh, God!

Cam could barely see him in the dark, yet Beckam was still there, his heavy breathing a comfort despite the tragedy he'd shared. She could barely stand the tenderness in his touch, but he continued holding her gently and carefully, his poor, hurt arm around her as if she might break if he let her go. Like she was valuable, important to him—of all people.

Not Heath. Certainly not Luis nor Alana Lopez. Never her in-laws, Penn and Spence Brinkman. God, how she hated them. Cam wasn't who she'd been made to believe she was, not even as a child. She wasn't special. Despite everything Papa had drilled into her foolish, little girl head, despite all the brainwashing, feel-good mantras, and bullshit he'd insisted she learn and repeat and repeat and repeat... It wasn't true. None of it. She'd never been more than a pawn in his devious chess game of mind over matter. Of money over morals. Of pride over family. Over… *me.*

Her eyes squeezed tight against the hot tears spilling down her face. She didn't want to break down in front of the same guy she'd once believed she'd needed to best. That was just this morning, back when he was nothing more than her Agent-in-Charge. When she'd thought she'd hated him.

Because she didn't hate him. Couldn't. Not Beckam Garner. Didn't know how. Not anymore. Not after that stupid story about that dumb woman who… who's… *Who's just like me. Was, damn it.* The woman he'd felt responsible for then, even as a kid, enough that he'd fought for her twins. Who does that?

"Are you going to be okay?" he asked, a full note of reticence in his voice.

She got that a lot. It was all she deserved. People tended to pull back and protect themselves when she was around. All she had to do was open her mouth and be as mean as the rest of the fuckin' world, and everyone shied away from her. *Hear that, World? Fuck you!*

Only now...

Cam drew in a quivering breath, and along with it came the musky, heady, male scent she was beginning to crave. "I didn't want to do it," she whispered to her only friend. Swallowed hard. Wiped the back of her hand under her runny nose. Beck didn't need any more snot in his shirt.

"I'm sorry," he murmured. "Never should've shared that stupid secret, huh?"

"It wasn't stupid. At all. Actually…" God, this was hard, but she trusted Beckam now, and that was a fuckin' first in her life. "Actually…" she repeated, needing someone to know the real Camilla Lopez Brinkman. That the two names attached to her were both cruel and unusual punishment. Like Desiree's tiny dead baby, her hardest secret begged for one short breath of life. Just one.

But instead of giving it the light of day, she buried it like she'd done for years. She locked it away and simply told Beckam, "I'm glad you told me about Desiree Jones. I wish I'd known her." *You know, because two birds of a feather and all.* "I, umm, think I understand why she chose you."

"She picked me because she was drowning, Cam, and she needed someone, anyone, to believe her. I was just her last straw. That's all."

Cam shook her head against his broad chest. "No, I think she chose you because you really are a Boy scout. And I don't mean that to be mean, but you've got, I don't know, this incredible sense of honesty and honor inside you. It's like the sun shining through a stained-glass window. It comes through all the colors that you already are and lights you up, makes you gold."

He purred like a cat. "You're saying I'm a rainbow?"

She could tell he was smiling, the brat. Smiling in the face of her despair. And that was okay. Because he really was golden. "Yes. You're a rainbow, and I'm a fuckin' unicorn."

The second her retort slipped out of her mouth, she felt him cringe, and wasn't that telling? Cam lifted her chin, trying to read his eyes when, right on cue, her own personal Boy Scout said, "I sure wish you wouldn't cuss, Cam. Especially not that word. You're such an elegant woman, and you dress like a million bucks. People look up to you, but when you say things like that—"

"People don't look up to me. Get real. You just want me to change who I am," she breathed, wishing he would. Daring him to challenge her simply by asking. By saying the right thing, like 'please'. Not telling. Certainly not by lying.

His head bobbed. "Yes. I guess, in a way, I do. It's just that, I don't know, you project so much anger into that ugly word. Maybe I'm old-fashioned, but when two people who love each other hook up, it's called making love. That other word is what animals do in the barnyard and the mud. It's crass and it's vulgar, but cursing isn't the real you. It's just a shield you use to make everyone back off. And they do, but is that all you really want?"

"No," she replied breathily, swallowing past the hard knot climbing up her throat. So close to Beckam's face that she could smell his breath. So near, she could almost taste his lips… his mouth. Still. Needing him to say the word…

His shoulders scrunched. "I know the rules on free speech, Cam. You're entitled to say whatever you want. I get that, I do. But while we're working together, would you mind curbing your inner unicorn, say, just until we catch the guy who's murdering our veterans? Then, if you still want to, you can go off on him like a sailor on shore leave. No holds barred. Deal?"

God, she wanted to kiss this man. He made everything sound easy. Well, easier. As if she really could restrain the mean little girl inside, who'd believed her father loved her when he'd just been using her. Like Heath had. God, like everyone in her life had.

"Yeah, okay. We've got a deal," she finally answered through her tears. "I promise I'll refrain from swearing like a sailor around you, but, umm—"

"Oh, oh," Beckam muttered. His muscles bunched under her fingers. Was he holding his breath? "Here it comes. Let it go, Cam. Let me have it."

That made her smile enough to tell him, "You need to know, umm…" *Big breath. Be brave. Just let it go…* "I'm, umm, not married anymore, Beck. I divorced Heath almost a year ago. Hated to do it…" *Not really.* "…but I couldn't live with a man who can't keep his pants zipped." Or who won't, as Cam had discovered when she'd caught Heath rutting like a pig with his latest flavor of the month in her bed. On her pillow! *Damn him.*

"That explains a lot," Beckam said. "I'm sorry. Did you love him?"

"I thought I did," she answered, still wiping her emotions off her face. "At first. But I was so young, and he's a player, and besides…"

Beckam stilled. Waited. She could almost see him rolling his eyes as she debated telling him the rest of this part of her sordid little life. So she did. "I'm pretty sure Papa made a deal with Heath and his parents, you know, like a dowry or something. Heath got rewarded for taking me; Papa got inside Brinkman's inner circle. My marriage was a farce from the start."

Beckam breathed a growly, "You're kidding me? What exactly is your dad into that he treated you so badly?"

She shrugged. "I always thought it was sugar, but now…"

Beckam's arms closed around her.

"…I'm not sure."

"You said something before. Maybe it's nothing, but…" His chest expanded with a big breath. "Did Heath ever hit you?"

She shook her head. "No, why?"

"Because you said *'Yes, it was,'* after I told you how Desiree's life with Brent had to have been Hell. Which, now that I know what your ex was like, made me think that maybe living with him was Hell, too. You sounded sad, almost pensive. Am I right?"

Fuck, err, umm, damn. Jesus, cursing was going to be a hard habit to break. Beck was extraordinarily observant if he'd caught that tiny slip. But, yes. As he'd shared Desiree's story, Cam had felt as if she and Beckam's neighbor were sisters who'd both lived lives they'd never wanted. Like Beckam felt connected to that murdered baby girl, Cam felt a connection with Desiree.

Only her baby had been sucked out of her body while it was still so tiny that she'd never known its gender. Never got to feel it bumping around inside her tummy, or watched in wonder as its tiny knee or head travelled under her skin. Talk about Hell on earth.

She'd made her share of mistakes, but loving her shy neighbor boy, Hector Solomon Rojas, Junior, hadn't been one of them. Only sixteen-year-olds when Baby Rojas happened, they'd been foolishly in love and adventurous enough to think they could face their brave new world together. That they could stand against their mothers' wrath after Camilla hadn't had a period for three months. That their secret rendezvous when their parents weren't home, had gone unnoticed.

They were wrong. Once Alana got together with Martina Rojas, Hector's fiery-tempered mother, the decision was made for them. Martina sent Hector back to Mexico, never to be heard from again. Alana had marched Cam to her overly solicitous family doctor, who'd smiled while she'd attached the

IV to the back of Cam's left hand. Who'd told her everything would be okay when she knew it would not. That Cam had nothing to worry about.

All lies. When she came to, her legs were still spread wide in cold, metal stirrups, and there was no more Baby Rojas. Only bleeding that wouldn't stop, and a broken heart that was still raw and wondering to this day. Did Hector ever think of her? Had he ever really cared about his baby or her? He'd never called or written, not even once. Worse, how could Alana have done something so wickedly cruel to what would have been her first grandchild? Just have him or her sucked out of that warm little nest inside Cam's body and flushed away?

After the frantic doctor had finally stopped the hemorrhaging, Cam went home, changed in ways she'd never imagined. Ways she hadn't believed possible. The naïve, trusting, little girl shed once been was gone, replaced by a bitter, betrayed, and utterly useless young woman who could no longer bear children. Alana's doctor said it was the only way to stop the bleeding. Alana said it was best that her ovaries were gone. That children were nothing but trouble and heartache. But Cam had stopped living that day. Not like anyone noticed...

"Much of my life hasn't been…" *What? Not like everyone else's? Not filled with family that loved me?* "I guess I've just always wanted what other girls had, you know? Father/daughter dances. Romance. A husband who couldn't wait to come home to me. Just to me. Unrealized expectations. That's all." And a shitload of regret for ever having been born.

Beckam shifted, tucking his bandaged hand protectively against his chest as he settled. His big body filled their scrap of a tent. His other hand brushed over her face, bumping her nose and making her smile, then settled around her head, cupping her jaw. Better yet, he drew his face closer to hers, his breath warm and his lips so close she could've licked them.

"You know what you need?"

God, yes. She knew what she needed, and it was him. Every minute. Every breath. Every inch. He was the first person to care in a very long time, and she was starved for his brand of attention. But like an addled girl with a teenage crush, she asked, "W-what?"

"This." He pressed a chaste kiss in the center of her forehead. Just like a damned Boy Scout.

Relieved he hadn't taken their tenuous friendship to the next level, yet hurt that he hadn't, Cam closed her eyes, her fingers hooked around his wrist and her heart pounding. Wanting more than she could ever deserve, but thankful for this tender interlude, one of so few in her life.

But how she wished he'd never pull back, that he'd get carried away with her. Now. Here. Maybe lose the scrubbed, polished gleam behind his ruggedly handsome looks.

Alana's prophetic, ugly words still rang true: *'What goes around, comes around, Chica. You cheated behind my back with that Rojas boy, now you got what you deserve. That's why you lost his baby. Liars and cheaters don't get to keep the babies they make. Don't blame me for your mortal sins.'*

What despicable words for the innocent act of two teenagers getting carried away and creating a baby. *Mortal. Sins.*

Cam let Beckam's wrist go, convinced Alana was right. Because once she told him this most terrible secret, he'd never kiss her again.

Chapter Nineteen

Beckam knew there was more to Cam's story, but until he could ask Mark or Beau to run in-depth background checks on Heath Brinkman and Luis Lopez, maybe Spencer Brinkman, there was nothing more to be done. Even if there were, Brinkman and Lopez were not his nor Cam's immediate mission. Neither were the young men he'd tangled with earlier. The TEAM still had a murderer to catch, and Beckam meant to do that after he rested. He'd gone a good twenty-four hours without sleep. While that happened frequently on active duty, he'd gotten used to the nine-to-five routine of The TEAM and the eight hours of shuteye that went with it. But mostly because he didn't want to tell Cam about his concussion. She looked up to him. He liked that.

Easing off his sore shoulder and flat onto his back, he told Cam, "We'd better stop sharing stories and go to sleep."

"Yes," she breathed, her tone husky and…

Was she as turned on as he was? That kiss was not the smartest thing he'd done, but it had felt right and proper and…

Damn. What he was thinking of doing to Cam had nothing to do with being proper. At least the sleeping bag they shared was thick enough to conceal the happy boy in his boxers. Morning would come soon enough. He planned to hit the men's restroom before she opened her pretty eyes. No sense in her seeing his morning wood right off the bat. And wasn't that an interesting double entendre? He certainly felt like he could knock one out of the park right now.

"I mean, unless you have more unicorn and rainbow stories to tell. I might fall asleep, but I could listen for a while."

"Tomorrow," she mumbled. "You still haven't told me all you know about these murders, or why you won't go to the ER, or…" She yawned. "…everything else I need to know to be a real junior agent."

She wanted to be a real junior agent? Best thing she could've said.

"Until tomorrow then," he promised. "Night, Cam."

"Night, Beck."

With that, she pressed herself into his arm, her body warmer now. Softer. Infinitely more tender. And there they lay, spooned like lovers, but just enough to keep each other company in the middle of a bitter, cold night. Yeah, right. Beckam kept his bandaged hand high between her shoulder blades. While his mind raced away with feverish images of him and this fiery woman locked together, their legs tangled together in silken sheets, and the rest of their bodies doing plenty more than spooning.

This was not one of his brighter ideas. But when she rubbed her nose into his shirt...

When her belly expanded into his ribs with a deep breath…

When she let loose a breathy, feminine moan that sounded like contentment…

Lord, help me, Jesus. It was all he could do to not tip her chin up and kiss her mouth. But he didn't. He couldn't. Not and respect himself in the morning.

Somehow, Beckam nodded off once or twice that night. When he woke, it was early morning, and he was feeling fairly content himself. Cam had actually talked to him like a human being last night. Better yet, she'd confided in him. She'd told him things she'd never told anyone, and she'd actively listened, then asked questions when he'd talked. They'd finally conversed, and wasn't that a shock?

Okay, so she'd also argued, but now he knew that was her go-to-hell way of making everyone back off. Only she would've used a different word, but still. Last night her arguments weren't nasty, but said more to convince him that he'd done nothing wrong the day Desiree died. Which, yeah, he got that—intellectually. He was not the reason Mrs. Jones ran into that cow, and there was no way he would've ever killed her baby. But in his heart? He knew he could've done more to help her before she'd died. He just couldn't imagine what that something more was.

The sun wouldn't be up for another hour or so. That would give him enough time to dash across Columbus Circle for the train station restroom, maybe grab a quick shower before Cam woke. Quietly, Beckam unzipped the tent flap and then eased his wide body out from beneath his sleeping companion. Silly woman moaned, then snuggled into his side of the sleeping bag, which hit his heart. Damn. He hated leaving her, but Mother Nature said go. So he climbed to his knees and tugged his shaving kit out of his bag. After he wriggled into his pants, he lifted to his feet, sealed the tent, and, despite aching like a son-of-a-gun, he jogged over to Union Station.

Early morning came in the guise of more hectic, loud traffic on Massachusetts Avenue NE and Columbus Circle NE, both designated one-way streets to accommodate the heavy flow of the thoroughfare. He'd always pictured Columbus Circle like an octopus with its back plastered against the front wall of Union Station. The high-traffic arteries that fed the Circle were its grasping tentacles, radiating outward, then drawing the hectic, pulsing vehicles into its cavernous beak, to be devoured or spat back, depending on their destinations. In truth, the roundabout only facilitated the heavy traffic into and away from the station.

Even now. While a couple POVs, as in personally owned vehicles, honked at foolhardy pedestrians who'd dashed illegally across the streets, like Beckam, an army of buses screeched to a squawking halt in the designated loading zone nearest the station's entry. Looked like more heavy equipment had moved onto the street during the night. Wouldn't that put the cherry on this hot fudge mess of traffic?

Once inside, Beckam set a quick clip downstairs. On the way, he contacted TEAM HQ to update Alex on what went down last night, but he got Mark Houston instead.

"You should've gone to the ER. Better to be safe than end up sorry."

Which told Beckam that Mark hadn't yet dug deeper into his DD214, his discharge paperwork from the U.S. Army and discovered the underlying reason for him not wanting to visit the ER. Probably because Mark was busy investigating Cam, and Beck hadn't given him a reason to look deeper. He cringed at his deceit. It might be time to come clean—after this mission. Instead he told his senior agent, "I'm good. But I do need a favor. Is Ember back from leave yet?"

"She came in late yesterday, why?"

"I need her to look into Luis and Alana Lopez, Spence and Penn Brinkman, Heath Brinkman, too. Not sure what they're involved in, but I've got a bad feeling."

"Why? What's going on?"

Beck hesitated, not willing to betray Cam's confidence, even with Mark. "That's not my story to tell. But there is more to Camilla Brinkman than meets the eye."

"Finally," Mark breathed. "She's opening up, isn't she? Is that what you're trying not to tell me?"

"Err…" Beck stalled at that unusual question. *Maybe.* "Yesterday was tough." *On her and me both.*

"Sorry about Max Bird. Officer Tuttle sent over a copy of the police report. But Renner said Cam acted differently last night. Said she handled her weapon like a pro. Sounded like she handled Beau like a pro, too."

That made Beck smile. Beau was another tough nut to crack, yet Cam had handled him quite well, hadn't she? "She's proficient with a long rifle, pistols, too. That woman can shoot. Surprised the hell out of me."

"Sure wish she hadn't padded her resume." Mark sounded pensive. "Still looking into her academic records. Something isn't adding up. Alex already has me looking into her parents. I'll add the three Brinkmans to the list. Need anything else? Pain pills? X-rays?"

That was a hint if Beck had ever heard one. "No, really. I'm better this morning. Renner gave me something last night for the pain. Swelling's almost gone."

"Would that be the swelling in your hand or your head?"

Beck chuckled. "Both, *Mom,*" he teased. "I'm not worried. As long as I can shoot, you shouldn't be either." Which was not entirely a fib. He could shoot—left-handed. "Hey, one more thing. You ever dealt with MPD Officer Lark before?"

"Renner said she answered the call last night. Why do you ask?"

"She tried to roust us out of her area, and talk about rude. And sexist, not against me, but Cam. What's her problem?"

"Cam, huh?"

That made Beck smile. "Yes, she's Cam. I'm Beck. We got past the whole call-me-Kah-me-ah-or-die routine early yesterday."

"Good. That's why Alex wanted you on this op. You've got a light touch. But to answer your question, I have no idea what's going on with Lark. You do seem to have a knack with difficult women, though. Maybe you should team up with MPD next."

Beck about swallowed his tongue. "Yeah, no. Counseling women's not my MOS. So, why's Alex late?"

"He's already been and gone. Had an early meeting with Mayor Tillis. Should be back before noon. You need to talk with him?"

"Nah, just surprised when you answered his line. Everything quiet last night?"

"Yes, Max was the last. You read the file. There's a pattern here. All victims were Vietnam vets. All homeless."

"Which means our killer's got access to DoD records, and he's tracking them down."

"Or he knows them. Might be homeless himself."

"Not if he's driving." Beckam pursed his lips. "Pretty sure there's more than one person behind these murders. Max was definitely rolled from a moving vehicle. Although, now that I think about it, Cam and I were walking west. The vehicle was behind us, headed toward us."

"Which puts the passenger side toward the curb—"

"Which makes it entirely possible that the driver shoved an already dying man out of the vehicle."

"Yes, it does. Beau spent all day yesterday checking traffic cams near the station. He narrowed it down to a gray Honda Pilot. Couldn't see through the tinted windshield or get a clear read on the plate, though. Traffic was too congested."

"It's worse today. Road construction. Listen, I've got to go. Call if you need anything."

"Same with you, Beck. Tell Cam we're proud of her." Leave it to Mark to know what to say.

"Copy that."

By then, the smells of breakfast wafting through the station were overwhelming. That fueled Beckam's need to rush through his shower and get back to the tent before Cam stirred, hopefully with breakfast biscuits, fries, and coffee in hand. Wouldn't she be surprised?

But Karma was not on his side this morning. The shower stalls were already full when he arrived at the men's room. A dozen or so men waited in line in the hallway. Decision made. He'd shower later.

Beckam hurried through an abbreviated early morning ritual, washed at the sink, brushed his teeth, and combed his hair. Shaving would wait. Finally done and his time running out, he collected his shaving kit and hit the hallway to level one. Taking the stairs two at a time, he scanned over the heads of the noisy but orderly morning crowd, searching for the source of that tantalizing aroma. Mmm, coffee and bacon, his two favorites. Once again, his gaze fell on the kiosk where a young woman in a pink shirt, black pants, and a frilly white apron restocked shelves with cheesecakes, donuts, croissants, and—

Man, he was hungry. But choosing breakfast for Cam was not going to happen. He had no idea what to buy that she'd eat.

Damn it. But okay. New plan. Get back to the tent, grab that sleepy woman, and get her back here in short order. He chuckled to himself at that unintended pun. Short order, ha.

Back outside, he actually felt halfway decent, despite the increased throbbing in his injured hand as he maneuvered across the crowded way. He'd been careful to keep the bandage dry, but his hand throbbed enough that he kept it raised and against his chest. Overall, it didn't hurt as bad as it had last night. His shoulder was tight, though. He'd intended to work that muscle under a hot shower, but he'd manage.

He'd been shot once while deployed. Fortunately, it'd only been a crease, but yeah. That bullet had nicked his hard head enough that it left a nice little divot over and through his left eyebrow. Which resulted in a concussion that earned Beckam a couple days downtime. At first. It hadn't really been a serious injury. Yes, he'd been evac'd out of the valley in the Philippines where he'd been sent to end a known Al-Qaeda affiliated terrorist. But the PJ traveling with Beck's USMC squad at the time patched him up, gave him a shot of antibiotics and a plastic vial of pain pills, told him to take two and call if he ever blacked out or got dizzy.

PJs were Air Force Pararescue Jumpers, the real heroes, the guys who delivered battlefield care and rescue, and who were as crazy a bunch of special operators Beckam had ever known.

That should've been the end of it, but then Parker decided to end Beckam's career. Damned nosey politician. To make matters worse, Beck had struggled with headaches and dizziness, just like that PJ had said he might. But admitting it made no sense. Beckam could overcome just about anything, even his own hard head.

Shoving those memories away, Beckam ran the distance from the street to the tent, his heart singing for a new day that promised more revelations from the former Mrs. Brinkman.

Until he peeled back the flap and Cam was gone.

Chapter Twenty

Where could he be? Cam dodged another crowd of blank-faced men and women on her way to the food court where she was sure Beckam had gone. But shit, she couldn't see over or around the rushing crowd. Even when she lifted up on her toes. Being short sucked. But then—

Oh wait. "Joslyn!" she called to the women walking up ahead of her. "Wait up!"

Joslyn turned and blinked. Her head cocked. Was she lost, too?

Cam waved, then squeezed between the man and woman in her way. *Jesus Christ, just shut the f----. Umm. Just shut up and get out of my way. Please. With sugar on it.*

Joslyn saw her then. She waved, and… *whew!* Cam wanted to pat herself on the back for remembering she'd promised Beckam no more swearing. *Wonder if that meant no shits or Jesuses or hells or damns, too?*

"What are you doing out so early?" Joslyn asked, her gray eyes wide. "Have you seen Georgia?"

Oh, great, Georgia, the smelly part of this twosome, was missing, too. "No, have you seen Beck?"

"Yesterday. With you. Is he on duty again today?" Interestingly, Joslyn was wearing the same corduroy pants and turtleneck sweater as yesterday. Her gray hair had been combed and she still looked semi-clean. But Camilla looked closer. Was that dried soup dribbled on her chin?

Anxious now, she scanned over Joslyn's shoulder, hoping to catch sight of her Agent-in-Charge before he spotted her. She'd woken up alone and cold in that tent. Which she'd assumed meant he'd simply dashed over here to take a shower like he said he would last night. Only he hadn't been downstairs, and none of the guys in the long line outside the men's room had seen him. She'd asked. The man who had checked inside for her had insisted no one fitting Beck's description was there. Not that she'd believed everything everyone said. Beck could've still been inside one of the shower stalls. Naked and wet. All lathered up and…

F-f-f… Damn! That mental image was not helping. Cam shook it off. Besides, if the men's restroom was like the women's, there were only five shower stalls. What were the chances he'd have gotten that lucky, that'd he'd been inside scrubbing those manly muscles and biceps? Those thick, wide shoulders? She could almost picture him standing under the spray with his bandaged hand held high and protected from getting wet, his rugged face tipped upward, water sluicing down his back and over his ass and… Cam growled at the way her wayward mind wandered over Beckam's body every chance it could. Not good! Determined to get back on track, she'd hurried back upstairs, thinking for sure he'd be stuffing his face with cheesecake by then, or something equally decadent and filling.

"Oh. Oh. I don't know what happened. She was just here," Joslyn said, her fingers knotted together, twisting each other like worried vines. "Where could she have gone?"

"I'm sure she's here somewhere," Cam answered, more worried about Beckam than Joslyn's ornery friend. *Wait.* Could it be possible? "Is she a veteran?"

Joslyn's head twitched up and down, more like nervous tremors than a definite affirmative. "Years and years ago. Max was a veteran, too. He served in Vietnam. Oh. Oh. You don't think her going missing has anything to do with his m-murder, d-do you?"

Cam froze. Georgia's vanishing act couldn't be connected with Max's death, could it? No way. "I don't know. How old is she?"

"She turned seventy-one a couple months ago."

The math was right. Georgia might be as old as Max. She certainly looked older than dirt. But that didn't mean anything. "Did she serve in Vietnam, too?" Were women even allowed to serve in combat back in the sixties and seventies?

By then, Cam had tugged Joslyn out of the crush of the morning crowd. They'd taken refuge near a busy magazine kiosk where harried businessmen and women jostled briefcases and large covered paper cups of coffee while perusing the latest daily press offerings. None of which Cam ascribed to. There was no sense in it. Why read corporate propaganda?

"Yes," Joslyn replied. "She was in for quite a while."

The first quiver of anxiety blossomed in Cam's stomach. Georgia and Max. Both veterans. Both the same age. Both homeless. "Did she work with Max?"

Joslyn shook her head. "No, she never mentions anything about her service. Neither did Max. That was a long time ago."

But Georgia was a veteran, and she was missing, like Max had been before—you know. Cam forced the still too-vivid memory of her one and only meeting with Maxwell Bird out of her head. Where the hell was Beckam? They needed to talk. She was sick of being the outsider on this fuckin' team. She wanted to know everything about this mission, and she wanted to know it yesterday!

"Oh, oh," Joslyn said yet again, to herself. "She can't have gone very far, could she?"

Not unless someone grabbed her and means to kill her, Cam thought. But she said, "Not if she was just here a couple minutes ago. Was she?"

"Yes. We'd walked from Lorelei's Kitchen." That nervous nod again. The cords in Joslyn's neck turned into taut wires beneath her crepey skin. Her knuckles whitened beneath the clenching assault of her fingers. "P-please, Cam," she murmured, the whites of her eyes showing. "She means well, but she'll never make it on her own. She needs me."

That frightened stare spurred Cam to do something she'd never done before. Closing those few steps between them, she put an arm around Joslyn's shoulders. "There, there. She probably just zigged when you zagged. Does she like cheesecake? Or chocolate? I know Beckam does. Maybe she's over there pigging out with him. Let's go see. Then we'll check the other vendors. Maybe someone'll remember seeing her." And maybe Beckam will have shown up by then, too.

"Oh," Joslyn whimpered, her elegant fingertips to her mouth. "Oh. Oh."

That little word was quickly grating on Cam's nerves. It seemed like Joslyn's automatic response to everything.

"Come with me," Cam ordered before Joslyn could utter those two letters again. "She can't have gone far."

"But what about Beckam? Shouldn't he be with you?"

Well, yeah, but… "Don't worry about him. He's a big boy. He'll catch up while we search for Georgia."

"You'd do that?"

The disbelief in Joslyn's tone irked Cam. "Sure. Why wouldn't I?" she said, biting her tongue at all the reasons Joslyn might throw at her even as she pulled Joslyn back into the morning crush.

"Be-because you're busy. You're important."

"I'm never too busy for you," Cam said what she imagined Beckam would've said if he'd been there. "You keep an eye on the left; I'll watch the right. Move it."

Okay, that came out a little harsher than she'd intended, which was an odd thing to think. She'd never cared if she'd been harsh before or what anyone thought. Only now that she'd gotten to know Beckam a little better, Cam realized she meant what she'd told him last night. She didn't want to be bitchy anymore. Instead, she wanted him to tell her she was pretty and elegant. She wanted that man's mouth on her lips, not her forehead. She wanted him to get his ass in gear and show up, damn it.

Searching for Georgia helped Cam focus on the task at hand. Yet her mind strayed to worst-case scenarios. What if Max's murderer kidnapped Georgia? What if Georgia and Max were part of a diabolical scheme to destroy America? What if Joslyn was next? Oh, indeed.

On and on she and Joslyn went along the busy, crowded kiosks edging the food court. Between the pizza kiosk, past the pastries, then onto the table and chairs where she and Beckam had eaten just last night. Another couple sat there now, twin dark-haired girls tucked between them, both in matching pink snowsuits with fuzzy bunny booties and…

Cam stepped back in time, staring at those pretty little faces that could've been hers. So pink. So pure. Okay, so they were too young to have been hers, and there was zero chance an aborted fetus could've, would've ever been seen again. Yet she couldn't make her heart stop wishing for what would never be. What would her baby look like today if she or he had been allowed to live? For certain, that child would've had dark hair and olive skin. But would she have had Hector's bushy eyebrows? His quick wit? Or would she have been dainty and short like her mother? Would she have wanted to be an astronaut like his dad once said he'd wanted to be? Or a ballerina? A forest ranger? A mom?

Cam's free hand went automatically to her tummy, rubbing the empty place where another life had once blossomed like a tiny, unseen flower… Another life with Hector. A different version of Camilla Lopez. She'd never have become a Brinkman then. She'd have been Mrs. Hector Rojas. A handsome boy's sweetheart. Somebody's mommy.

Oh, for fuck's sake! Who am I kidding?! Cam wasn't anyone's mom. Never would be. She wasn't nice and… What was she doing holding hands with some old bag lady who'd lost her stinky friend and probably her mind? Huh? *Answer me that, World! Just get the fuckin'….!*

"Camilla!" a strong male voice bellowed from somewhere up ahead. "Cam! I'm here. I see you. Look at me!"

Beckam! She saw him then. His poor bandaged hand lifted high over his head, waving. His eyes were extra-bright and black, his brows knitted. The crowd parted as he shouldered his way toward her, then he started to run. To her. To—*me. He's actually running to me.*

For several heartbeats, something sizzled between them, something warm and erotic. It hung like the shimmer of a fleeting miracle. A mirage. She could feel it, taste it. Smell it. It all came back to Beckam. The turquoise sparkle in his eyes. The salty smell of his skin and the minty scent of his breath. The big heart beneath all that rugged physical male beauty. She wanted him any way she could have him. On his back. On her back. Or her belly. Just…

Now. She wanted him right damned now.

Cam dropped Joslyn's hand. She wasn't sure what she was doing, but she sure as hell wasn't going to think twice for once in her overly-organized, controlled, mess of a life. Her leg muscles bunched automatically. Her eager heart whispered, 'Go to him! Hurry!'

She sprang off the balls of her feet, needing more than just hope and wishes to live on. "Beck!" she cried out. "Damn you! Where have you—?"

Cam never got to finish cussing him before he lifted her off her feet. Bracing his wounded arm around her shoulder, he swung her in a circle, and then…

Oh, God. His mouth crashed into hers, and his tongue speared her, filling her with something no TEAM Agent-in-Charge should have done in public, but… *Jesus Christ.* She'd wanted this forbidden taste since the first second she'd laid eyes on him. She wanted it now more than ever.

Because *dayum.* Boy Scout could kiss. Not only were her feet off the ground, but he was very thoroughly palming her backside with his good hand, pressing her into his hips and his cock while his tongue tangled with hers. Holy fuck! Every last feminine muscle in her body responded with heat and longing so sharp, tears sprang to her eyes. Beckam was dominating her.

In public. Filling her mouth. Clutching her ass. Growling and—

She should've been scared. It hadn't been long since Heath had slapped her around. But were those tears dripping into her face? She tipped back in Beckam's arms, needing to see him as well as taste him. Sure enough. Tiny crystal droplets glistened on his velvety thick eyelashes even as he gave her a lopsided, embarrassed smile and whispered, "Sorry about this, but, Cam. Cam. My God, I… I thought…" He choked. Shook his head like a little boy who couldn't believe what he'd done.

Neither could she. He'd actually said *God.*

Breathing hard, he finally set her down, his uninjured hand hot and sweaty but still circling her wrists. "I, I…" He scrubbed his free hand over his head. He could barely speak.

She'd never noticed before, but the ends of his dark hair were golden. Sunburned. Bleached.

"When I got back to our tent, you were gone, and I thought… Damn, I thought you might've been hurt or taken or… something. Here." He dug a small black wire out of his jacket pocket, opened her hand, and handed her a—

Oh. An earpiece. Cam looked down at what was obviously a peace offering, then peered up into his handsome face. "You weren't there when I woke up," she explained, keeping her voice as low as his. "I thought you came over here for a shower and food, but then I ran into Joslyn, and she needed help finding Georgia and—"

His head bobbed at every excuse she gave him, then, curiously, he circled the back of her neck and pulled her into him, her forehead to his forehead. Beck was shaking. Trembling. Panting in her face. That *was* sweat beaded along his hairline. Why? Had she scared him by not being where he'd left her? Was this just panic? Or was it—more?

Or didn't he trust her? Was that what this emotional display was really about? Didn't he think she was capable? *The ass.* She'd show him. She wasn't just some dimwit on patrol. She'd remembered her gear bag and her pistol this time. She still had possession of the handgun he'd loaned her last night, too.

"You're mad at me? Is that what this is all about? That stupid kiss? You're pissed because I—"

She didn't see it coming. But... *Ah. Yeah.* He came in fast and sweet again, caught her by surprise. Covered her opened mouth and swallowed every last bit of her snark, absorbing her futile attempt to resist with a mouthful of sweet surrender. He nipped her bottom lip, then licked his way into her mouth, and Cam melted into him, boneless and utterly incapable of logic or why she'd been upset.

Jesus, this man could kiss. He tipped her backward into his wounded arm, his other hand still firmly cupping the back of her head, holding her. Kissing the life out of her as if they were the only two people in the station. As if Joslyn wasn't there. Making her forget to remember—something about Agents-in-Charge and breaking TEAM rules and...

Whatever.

God, he smelled so good, of coffee and toothpaste, deodorant and soap. Of clean male sweat, which meant he still hadn't gotten the shower he'd passed up last night out of deference to her.

She understood then. Beckam Garner wasn't mad at her, and this wasn't him being distrustful. Not at all. This was him caring and being scared that she might've been hurt or lost. That was what this meeting of mouths and lips and tongues was about. He honestly cared. About her. Wasn't that a kick in the head?

Chapter Twenty-One

This crazy, sweet woman thought he was angry? Okay. Yeah. Maybe he was, a little. At himself. At first. But more than anything, Beckam was relieved, and yes, embarrassed that he couldn't seem to stop kissing Cam. Her mouth was so warm and sweet, and she tasted like the honey he used to suck from the wild clover that grew along the creek banks back home. But most of all, he was just so damned thankful she was safe and happy to see him. He'd never seen a glow as hot as the one in her bright, brown eyes when she'd first spotted him. She'd lit up. But he should've known. Cam was a tempestuous firecracker with a short fuse.

He'd run all the way back from their tent, and hell, yes. He *was* breathing hard. His face was probably bright red, and he knew he was covered in sweat. He could taste it. His lungs were on fire, and he also tasted copper, the bloody by-product of that last burst of panicked speed. But she was here and safe—thank God—and that was what counted most.

Taking a long, ragged breath that didn't come close to slowing his heart rate, he set Cam on her feet again, holding her steady with one hand, because, man. She was shaking, too.

"You okay?" he asked, still craving the silky slip of her hair through his fingertips. His nose flared wider, searching after every last molecule of her uniquely feminine and very lovely scent. The spicy taste of her mouth lingered on his tongue. He couldn't stop licking his lips. What she must think of him, smelling like a pig and mauling her like one, too.

Might have been the adrenaline coursing like a wildfire through his system. Or the panic attack that hammered his heart at the mere thought of anyone kidnapping her. Whatever. He'd never had this strong of a physical reaction to a woman before. Ever. He also had one heck of a hard-on, so yeah. Could just be the adrenaline. Or it could be her.

"You're giving me an earpiece?" Cam asked breathily, her lips still wet and shining from his kiss. "Me?"

He hadn't let go of her yet, not completely. "You earned it," he murmured huskily, lifting his good hand to her cheek, running the pad of his thumb over that juicy bottom lip. His fingers still trembled. Damn, his entire body was shaking with voracious need. But the last thing he wanted was for anyone from The TEAM to catch him being an idiot. Yet here he was, his heart stuck up high in his throat and him breaking every last one of Alex's rules on fraternization.

"You're not… mad at me?" Why did her eyes glimmer with disbelief? Or was that fear?

Beckam shook his head. "Just worried. Didn't think I was going to be gone that long. Fully expected you'd still be asleep when I got back. Almost bought breakfast for you, but I wasn't sure what you'd eat and—"

"Breakfast?" she asked, her snark gone and something else glowing in those pretty brown eyes. "You were actually going to bring me breakfast? Like… breakfast in bed?"

"Sure, why not?" He shrugged. He'd been known to do that for his mom and dad on their special days or when one of them was sick. Why not Cam? "But you're a picky eater. How could I?"

"I'm not picky," Cam snapped, but just as quickly as her snark roared to the surface, it evaporated into a shy, genuine smile. Her lips pinched like she wished she could unsay that last remark. And wasn't that a sight worth waking up to? The Cam from the office was an entirely different person. The perky woman staring up at him now seemed gentler. The blush on her cheeks glowed. There was a definite spark in her eyes, and for once, it wasn't disdain. She looked—alive.

"Umm, okay. You're right," she offered softly. "I do, umm, tend to get bent out of shape easily. Sometimes. But what would you have brought me? I mean, for breakfast, if I wasn't particular about what I put into my body?"

'Me,' sprang to his mind, but Joslyn interrupted with a relieved, "Oh, there she is!"

Cam blinked, and the moment to tell her about his ideal breakfast in bed was gone. Beckam licked his lips, never more aware of a missed opportunity than right there and then. He shouldn't have kissed another agent. Shouldn't have let those erotic images of her moaning beneath him, her mouth on his body, or his hands in all that hair...

Sheesh. Beck raked a hand over his head, very aware of Cam's feminine side. Damn, she was just plain lovely this morning. Totally, delectably, delicious.

But Joslyn had stopped whatever had almost happened between him and Cam. Felt like trust, or something just as powerful. Also felt like Heath Brinkman was an ass for never spoiling his wife by giving her something as simple and easy as breakfast in bed.

With a small whimper, Cam eased out of his arms and turned to face Georgia, who'd walked up behind them as if nothing were wrong. "Where have you been?" Cam asked as patiently as Beck had never heard her. She almost sounded sincere. "We've been looking for you."

"I don't answer to you," Georgia grumbled, her face wrinkled with scorn. "You ain't my friend, and you sure ain't my keeper. Buzz off."

"But we were worried," Cam said without a titch of snark in her tone. If she kept this up, Beck might have to sit down before he fell down. "Ask Joslyn if you don't believe me."

"We have been looking for you," Joslyn confirmed, hugging herself with her hands tucked in her armpits, her eyes glistening. "I thought something happened to you. One minute we were walking and talking, the next you'd disappeared. Where… Gosh, George, where on earth have you been?"

Georgia tugged a crumpled bill out of the pocket of her grimy jacket and waved it under her friend's nose. "Couldn't let this get away, could I?"

"Well, err, no, but… You stopped to pick up a buck?" Joslyn asked.

"No, I stopped to pick up ten bucks," Georgia corrected. "See? It's a ten, not a one. You'd've done the same. What the fuck is your problem?"

"Nothing," Joslyn said sadly. "It's just that, with Max dying like he did, I thought… I mean, I was afraid…" The tears brimming in her eyes changed their color from gray to silver. "Oh, honey. Never mind. Just please, if you can't resist stopping, at least let me know why you stopped or where you're going. Tell me to 'hold up' or 'slow down' or something. Anything. This town isn't safe, and I—"

"It's safe enough for me. You's the one what's got the problems."

And there it was. Georgia believed Joslyn needed her more than the other way around.

"Hey, ladies," Beckam said as he pulled Cam into his side, his heart hammering. He couldn't get over how much better he felt with her safe and accounted for.

Joslyn steamrolled over him with, "You're right, Georgia. I am the one with the problem. I know that. L-let's just try to be kinder to each other as long as we're together, okay?"

"Yeah. Okay. I guess. But I ain't letting any loose change get away from me. I find it, it's mine. I ain't stupid."

Georgia was definitely the tougher of the two, but Beckam suspected her indifference to Joslyn's gentler feelings was a smokescreen. In some ways, Georgia was like Cam.

He tried again. "Anyone hungry? I'm buying breakfast for us four." He made a circle with his index finger to indicate the foursome he meant. "Take it or leave it. Breakfast burritos or corned beef hash. The *Greasy Pig*'s on me."

Joslyn's mouth dropped. "Beckam, you're hurt. What happened?"

"Nah, I'm good—"

"No, he's not. We were attacked last night," Cam replied. "Two brain dead teenage boys hit him with a tire iron. They were out to roust whichever homeless people they could find. Beck got the worst of it."

Damn. Not what he wanted to talk about. "Cam's right. But it's no big deal. I'm good."

Joslyn reached for his injured hand. "Oh, Beck. What'd you do?"

"Called for back-up," he admitted. Then chuckled. "Had to. Cam was going to hang those two idiots from the first tree she could find. You should've seen her."

She nodded vigorously. "You bet. I was mad. They deserved to get shot for what they did to him."

Joslyn still held Beck's hand. "I'm surprised anyone got the jump on you, son. Are you okay?"

"'Course," he replied. "Just took too long getting out of the tent. No worries."

"Damn Sweetie Pie," Georgia chortled. "You were in a tent together? Sounds like you and Chica got something going on. She always that frisky in the middle of the night?"

Beckam looked down at the woman still standing close to him. Cam seemed to be waiting for his answer. Georgia might be right. He and Cam did have something going on. He'd thought he could fool her, covering up by being open about it. But there was a soft light in Cam's eyes this morning. A glow that, for once, had no venom in it.

"Hope so," he said honestly, clearing his throat when his reply came out ragged and rough. "Partners always got their buddy's six. Right Cam?"

She blushed, then turned to her favorite bag lady and stammered, "It's… it's just our cover, Georgia. Trust me. We need to look like a real couple to catch whoever murdered Max." She turned back to Joslyn. "Come on. Let's go find the Greasy Pig. Sounds, umm… interesting."

She laughed. Cam actually laughed. Beckam cocked his head, wishing she'd do it again, even as his crazy heart whispered, *My girl.*

Wouldn't everyone back in the office come unglued talking about this? Him and her? That kiss? But yes. *My girl.*

"It's over there," Joslyn pointed into the crowd. "See the neon-pink, flashing pig? Right next to *Brats and Beer*? Come on, kids. Cam and me'll save a couple chairs for you slowpokes."

Beckam cocked an elbow for the grumpy lady still in his midst. "Shall we?"

"You betcha," Georgia replied, hooking her arm through his, even as she stuck her chin at the two women ahead of them. "Better watch your step with that one, sonny. I don't trust her. She's not right in the head. She's odd, know what I mean?"

"Who? Camilla?"

"Well, duh. I ain't talking 'bout Joslyn."

Beckam could've laughed, but that would've been impolite, and Georgia was just playing Mother Teresa. "Trust me. I keep a close eye on all my junior agents."

Georgia harrumphed like she knew better.

Beckam let her think she was right even as he smiled over the top of her red ballcap to the two women walking ahead of him, their arms intertwined like two old friends.

Cam might not have been right in the head—yesterday. But everything seemed to have changed since then. Maybe it was because she'd been there when Max died. Maybe it was just time for her to face reality. Her taking Beck into her confidence had to have been extraordinarily difficult. He got the impression she'd been closed off for a long, long time. Maybe most of her childhood. Yet he couldn't help thinking she'd also been prepared to finally let someone in. He was just glad it was him.

Until last night, she'd wielded her anger like a club, aiming it at anyone who came too close. But Cam wasn't the real problem. If what she'd said was true, her folks and Heath Brinkman were behind her evil princess routine. She'd just learned to hit first and strike back before anyone could hurt her again. When a child grew up being manipulated, compromised, or abused, fighting back was instinctual. Cam's snark was her first line of defense.

But the more she'd revealed about her life last night, the more she'd relaxed. And the more she made Beck think of the monarch butterflies he'd seen at Joint Base Pearl Harbor-Hickam, Hawaii. He'd been temporarily assigned to Naval Special Warfare Group 3, SEAL Delivery Vehicle Team 2, for a joint Army/Navy training exercise. During that long, hard week, he and rowdy SEAL Team 2 hiked the rugged, four-mile Crouching Tiger Trail on Oahu's east shore.

The hike was beyond amazing, but of all the rigorous climb's steep drop-offs, fantastic views of the turquoise-blue Pacific, and the thick, lush rainforest wrapped around them like a living, verdant blanket, Beck remembered the monarch butterflies best. He hadn't expected to see so many of them that far from the mainland. Yet there they were, clinging to the undersides of a stand of leafy ferns beside the waterfall where Team 2 had decided to cool off. All those butterflies had fluttered their wings like living jewels of amber and gold and black, just like stained glass windows.

Cam was the same as those butterflies, still trying her fragile wings in a strange new world of kindness and restraint, instead of the bullying and betrayal she'd lived with. Yeah. He'd keep an eye on her, all right. A very up-close and personal eye. Because now, her heart might finally be in the right place.

Chapter Twenty-Two

Breakfast was nice. Georgia ate like a pig. But instead of telling her to shut her mouth when she chewed so people didn't have to look at the gooey mess in her mouth, Cam ignored the old woman and chose to do something that would put that sappy smile back on Beckam's face again. Anything. She just wanted him to be happy with her. When he smiled, she felt like there was a piece of sunshine stuck in her chest. The sensation hadn't gone away yet. She couldn't help wishing it wouldn't. It'd be nice to feel this good all day, every day.

So she'd dashed back to the kiosk for more coffee when cups ran low. She also brought back more napkins and extra salsa for that ginormous egg and bacon burrito Georgia was stuffing into her face.

Mostly, Cam tried not to stare at Beckam. But he'd sat next to her, and there wasn't much room on this octopus-like contraption, not with four plastic seats attached to the metal arms radiating from under the table. Every sideways glance at him tightened the knot in her belly. Every time he brushed his arm against hers, or bumped his knee into her thigh, her entire body thrummed with the oddest sensations. Felt like hope. Lust. Both mixed with anxious wonder that he'd kissed her like he had. Thinking about his mouth on hers made swallowing her vegetarian egg-white omelet difficult. Made breathing tough, too.

After the meal was over—which didn't take long for four hungry people—she cleared the table of trash. Beckam said their goodbyes. Joslyn and Georgia went one way while Cam and Beckam picked up their bags and exited through the station's basement. The lines at both restrooms were gone.

Clearing her throat, Cam asked, "Aren't you going to take a shower?"

She earned a grin for that. "Why? Do I stink?" he teased.

"Oh, no, I just..." *Just what? Want to join him? Well, yeah.* That idea had crossed her mind. "You were kind enough to let me take mine last night. I know you want to be fresh for the day. You go ahead. I'll wait for you."

He cocked his head, his blue eyes extra blue under the fluorescent lighting. "I hate leaving you out here alone."

Aww... As nice as that sounded, it was still ludicrous. She'd been left alone more times in her life than he'd ever know. "Trust me, I'm used to it. Go. Take your time. I'll be right here when you finish."

"Promise?" he asked, a sweet, sexy sparkle in his deep blue eyes. God, a girl could get lost in there.

"Yes," she told Beckam as she dropped her bag to the floor and settled to her haunches beside it. "I promise."

He held up his bandaged fingers. "Five minutes, Cam. That's all it'll take. Be thinking of the questions you wanted to ask last night. I'll fill you in on everything I know once we're back on the street." And he was gone.

Cam drew in a sigh. She almost believed him.

It didn't take Beckam long to run under the shower head, towel dry, and dress in the same clothes he'd worn yesterday. Clean, dry socks were the only change he made. In less than the promised five minutes, he and Cam were back on the street, both carrying backpacks, both headed to their tent before Officer Lark did something foolish to their camp.

After they loaded the tent and sleeping bags into their gear bags, but before they hit the street, Beck asked Cam, "Where's your earpiece?"

She made the cutest frowny face, her smile all but turned upside down, the tiny crow's feet at the corners of her eyes stretched wide. "Forgot. Oops. Sorry. I'm not used to wearing one. How's it work?" she asked as she tugged the device out of her pocket.

That brought their show-on-the-road to a full stop. While still semi-hidden by the wintry bare shrubs and trees, Beck took just enough time to get her wired up. After they were walking again, he explained how she needed to keep her cell charged for the earpiece to work. He showed her how to turn it off and how to interpret clicks if they had to go silent. One click meant 'no', two clicks meant 'yes'.

"What about three clicks?"

"Good question. Three's an SOS. It means all-out war in progress or agent down, come quick, do not pass go. Try not to use it, Cam. Ember Dennison's already tracking our whereabouts through the GPS in our phones. If you send an SOS, the entire team will converge on our location."

"But tracking us is against privacy laws," Cam breathed. Which was different. The way she'd said that. Quietly. Not argumentatively.

"No, it's not. It's SOP for any TEAM agents in the field, that's standard operating—"

"I know what SOP means." She chuckled, another reaction Beck hadn't seen coming.

"I'm just explaining things instead of burying you with military jargon."

"That's nice. Thank you. So, you're telling me Ember's tracking us now, but only while we're on the job, right?"

"Yes, which will be twenty-four-seven until this op's over. But she can also track missing agents, their wives or children, anyone using our cells. Like Tara Graves last month, when her ex kidnapped her and—"

"Tara was kidnapped?"

Beck looked closer. "Well, yeah. Where've you been? On Mars?"

Her lips pursed as she frowned. "At work. Like everyone else."

"No one told you?" He couldn't believe Cam didn't know about Renner and Tara's very near disaster. She worked closely with Ember, didn't she? Why hadn't Ember told her?

Cam's head shook in short, hard bursts that resembled shivers more than denial. "No one tells me anything."

Well, damn. Now Beck was embarrassed. He'd walked by The TEAM's customer service counter several times a day once he'd returned from Oklahoma. He could've told her, but he'd assumed she'd been kept up to speed like everyone else. Guess not. Alex had granted generous leave over the holiday. Most people took off for vacation with their families.

"You didn't work over Christmas, did you?" *Please don't say yes.*

She sniffed. "No. Mr. Stewart told me not to come back until he called. I thought he was going to fire me, so I stayed home waiting for the phone to ring."

"All Christmas?"

Her head bobbed. "Where else was I going to go?"

Damn. She'd spent Christmas alone. But worse, she made it sound like it was no big deal.

Beck wanted to hit his own hard head with a tire iron at that news. Of course no one told Cam about Tara. Until yesterday, she hadn't cared about anyone but herself. No one told her anything. He changed the subject. "You know what? None of that matters because from now on, Junior Agent Brinkman, you're—"

"Lopez," she corrected him. "I'm changing my name. Call me Junior Agent Cam Lopez from now on."

He wanted to ask, 'Not Kah-me-ah?' but he settled for, "Good plan, Lopez. Start fresh. Man up and take your life back. You get to brief Alex."

"Damned straight," she replied with confidence that sounded genuine. "Speaking of which, you were going to tell me why no ER."

Aw, that again. He put his index finger in his ear, motioning her to turn her earpiece off.

Once she did, Cam whispered, "Are you afraid what they'll find?"

Beckam rolled his tender shoulder. "No, I know what they'll find. Pretty sure I banged my head back in—"

His cell phone vibrated to life in his inner jacket pocket. Palming the phone with his other hand, he caught the caller ID. Damn. It was Alex. Man, that guy had ESP or something.

"Yes, Boss," he answered, scanning the heavy Department of Transportation equipment and orange cones blocking the confluence of Columbus Circle Northeast and Monument Drive. Traffic had narrowed down from three lanes to one this morning, creating a giant parking lot as all those northwest flowing vehicles came to full stops. A flagman stood along the line of flashing barricades, motioning drivers to keep moving. What a mess.

"Camilla's father was shot this morning in front of his home. He's at Sibley Memorial. Not expected to live. Mark's on his way to pick you and Camilla up now."

Beckam's gaze fixed on his junior agent. "I had no idea they lived near here. Where?"

"Ward three, The Palisades."

Oh, yeah. He remembered now. Cam had said that her parents moved to be closer to her. "We know who did it? Why?"

"His wife. One to the heart. No motive yet, but she missed. He's still alive, but barely." Alex paused, then said, "Turns out they aren't from Puerto Rico after all, Beck. Everything we thought we knew about them is a lie. They ran with Torino's daughter back in the nineties, were nearly caught in the military coup d'état that ended President Estevez' rule in Honduras. No one knew for certain what happened to them, but after one of their daughters' body washed ashore, everyone assumed they'd died at sea. Daughter was an infant. Sealed in a plastic bag. Off Belize, near Punta Gorda. Someone tied Alana's wedding ring to her wrist."

Trina Torino, a known drug runner who'd also dabbled in counterfeit USA currency. Rumor had it that Torino funded the army general behind the coup. Punta Gorda was a small seaport on the Caribbean Coast of southern Belize, located across the Gulf of Honduras from the northernmost part of Honduras. Not Puerto Rico.

Cam stood there on the sidewalk, tapping her toes like she was impatient to get on with being a junior agent. Like she still had the life she thought she had.

Beckam swallowed hard at what he'd soon have to tell her. "Another daughter? How did Mark not find this intel during initial discovery?" Discovery—the in-depth research into every TEAM member's background.

"Yes, they had two daughters, but Mark missed it because he kept hitting dead ends when he searched on their aliases, Luis and Alana Lopez, which was all we had to go on. But since you mentioned them along with Penn and Spence Brinkman again this morning, he figured it was urgent and tagged Ember as soon as she came in. She found out, don't ask me how, that Lopez isn't their real last name. It's Escobar."

That name carried a wealth of notoriety and condemnation with it. "As in Pablo?"

"No, as in Molina. Not related to the Colombian drug lord, but just as bad. Molina Escobar, aka Luis Lopez and Trina Torino were cousins on their mothers' side of the cartel. Both families were heavily involved in drug and gun-running, as well as counterfeiting. That's where Luis made his fortune, but get this. Alana's worked her own little sex trade on the side. She's been running high-end prostitutes out of their home on—"

"Damn. Billionaire Row, New York City."

That got Cam's attention.

"You got it. Fifty-Seventh Street, right in the middle of Manhattan."

Beckam, swallowed hard. "Right across from Central Park. But Boss, I was in Puerto Rico after Hurricane Maria. I saw the devastation to the Lopez plantation."

"Yeah, well, do you know what a pied-à-terre is?"

Beck shook his head, knowing full well Alex couldn't see him, but afraid to say anything more with Cam standing so close and listening.

As if he'd read his mind, Alex explained, "Plain and simple, it's a tax shelter for the obscenely rich. It used to mean a small, secondary residence, but the tycoons in the world today turned it into a financial device to shelter their mansions and their billions from localities where it might be more easily seized. Like China, Russia, the Middle East, and South America. That's what most of those properties on Billionaire Row are. A pied-à-terre is simply a tool for tax avoidance, also money laundering. In short, Escobar used that acreage in Puerto Rico, not to enrich the local community by providing jobs for people who needed them, but as an investment to disguise the fact that he actually lived in Honduras, also to establish a second, cleaner identity in the States. Claiming Puerto Rican citizenship, albeit illegally, gave Escobar the ability to enter the United States at will and without applying for citizenship. All he and Alana had to do was switch their documentation from Escobar to Lopez. Which, by the way, means your junior agent is now an illegal immigrant since her parents never naturalized."

"A shell company," Beckam breathed. "The sugar plantation was just another lie."

Cam cocked her head, studying him now.

"Everything we thought we knew about that bastard Luis Lopez is a lie. The only thing Camilla's got going for her is that

Ember can't find anything anywhere that proves Camilla knew what her parents were into or that she committed crimes for them. She stands to lose her reputation, Beck, if not her mind when this hits the fan. But she is not a criminal, and I have all the proof I need to defend her. I'm damned glad she's working for me. Listen, I'll let you break the bad news to her when and however you choose to handle it. I trust you. In the meantime, Flanagan's on his way with Mark to relieve her. She's not agent material anyway."

And just like that, the world shifted under Beckam's feet. The stars realigned. His spine stiffened. "Yes, she is," he told his boss with certainty, his back erect and his spine stiff. "Don't do that to her. Not yet. Let me talk to her first. Call you back in five."

He did the unthinkable. Beckam hung up on Alex.

"What's going on?" she asked quietly. "You were talking about me, right?"

Pocketing his cell and fully expecting it to buzz in his jeans pocket again, Beck reached out, took hold of Cam's shoulder, looked her in the eye, and gave it to her straight "I'm sorry to tell you, but your father was shot this morning. He's at Sibley Memorial. Mark's on his way here to take you to see him in the hospital."

"Just me?" she asked, her voice suddenly small and very un-Camilla-like.

The bleak shadow in her eyes stabbed Beck's big heart. He couldn't bring himself to tell her everything. She hadn't even asked, 'How's my dad?' Not 'Is he still alive?' either. Nor had she cried out, 'Oh, my God, I need to get to him right now.' Just... *Just me?* Beck knew what he'd be doing if he'd gotten a call that his father was dying. Certainly wouldn't be standing around thinking about it.

"I'll go with you if you want," he offered.

"No, I… Alex wants me to go, doesn't he? He doesn't want me on this job. He hates me."

Beckam shook his head as he watched The TEAM SUV approach the gridlock that was Columbus Circle. Had to be Mark behind that wheel. "Alex doesn't hate you. None of us do. In fact, he just told me he's glad you work for him. He just expected you'd want to be with your dad at a time like this. He's sending Agent Flanagan—"

"To replace me. I get it, b-b-but…" Cam paused. She'd also spotted Mark. "What if I don't want to see my father? He's dying, isn't he? He might already be dead. It might be too late."

"Possibly."

She inhaled a deep but shaky breath. "What difference will it make if I go? Alana will be there."

"No, Cam…" There was no way to hide the truth. She needed to know. "Your mother's the one who shot him. She's probably in county lockup. Trust me, she won't be at the hospital."

"But I'd rather stay with you, I mean, here, at work. Please don't make me go." She was blinking big, brown eyes, not brimming with tears, but filled with something else Beckam couldn't quite read. Not guilt. Fear maybe? Did she already know who her parents were? Was she part of their web of lies? Or was she frightened of her mother? That actually felt more right.

"I'll fight to keep you on this mission," Beckam told her what he'd tell any other agent. "You've proven yourself. But think twice, Cam. Luis is your father, and this might be the last chance to see him. Whatever happened between you and him, it's in the past. At least spend time with him before he passes. Forgive him. Be there. That way you'll have no regrets."

"He lied to me," she whimpered. "Beck. All those years, he lied. I'm not sure I even know who he is."

"But he's still your dad. He probably just wanted the best for you," Beckam told her, hoping he was at least a little right. "Trust me, Cam. I'm okay with whichever decision you make, but if you decide to go, do it for yourself, not him."

Mark was at the curb by then, waiting, flashing his headlights.

Cam blew out a frosty puff. "I didn't make you go to the ER."

And there it was, his line in the sand. Either he trusted her or he didn't.

Beckam's world shifted yet again. Luis Lopez, aka Molina Escobar, had definitely betrayed his daughter many times over. There were no two ways about it. He might've had good reasons behind his twisted idea of parenting. He might've truly wanted the best for her, so much that he'd bought the appearance of a prestigious, higher education to help her get ahead. But Beck doubted it. Drug runners and cartel bigshots focused more on the high risk of social networking with other criminals instead of spending quiet evenings at home with their families. Big deals made big money. Little girls did not. Escobar's lies had simply caught up with him. Cam's refusal to be there for him in death proved that. The man didn't deserve her then. He deserved her less now.

Beck's hand still rested on her shoulder. He could feel the tremors rattling over her through his fingertips. So he gave Camilla Lopez the one thing he suspected she'd needed since the day she was born. "Like I said, I'm okay with whatever you decide. I've got your six. You go, I go. You stay, I'll stay. What'll it be?"

"*We* stay," she breathed on a sigh, her dark eyes still troubled, still not believing.

Beckam made it a done deal. "Good enough. We're staying. Let's go tell Mark."

"But he'll make me go."

Beck knew better. "Not Mark. He thinks you walk on water."

"Oh, he does not."

"He does. Talked with him earlier when I called in my sitrep. Said to tell you he's proud of you."

"You liar," she muttered. "He's not proud of me. No one's ever been—"

"Scout's honor," Beck said as he raised his right hand, bandage and all, to the square.

But damn. Things were unraveling fast for Cam. Her life was about to be upended, not only her fraudulent PhDs, but now her family. Her heritage, for Pete's sake. Not only was she not Puerto Rican, she wasn't even Camilla Lopez. Worse, her parents were involved with a wicked Honduran cartel that specialized in gun running, drugs, counterfeiting, and prostitution. Could things get any worse?

Chapter Twenty-Three

Agent Flanagan winked at her through the SUV window, but Cam ignored the tall, slim redheaded junior agent riding shotgun with Mark Houston. She had to bite her tongue, and she clenched her fingers to keep from swearing or flipping him off. She was a TEAM junior agent now, and Mark even smiled like he was proud of her. It was funny knowing she'd made two friends in the office. That seemed to tip the scales a little in her favor. She almost wished she had a TEAM badge. Beck had one. He wasn't wearing it now, but she'd seen it on his belt. It made him someone. She wanted to be someone, too.

Just as Mark Houston cranked the wheel away from the curb, he leaned past Flanagan and called out, "Good job, Cam. Keep it up."

She stood there dumbfounded. He'd actually complimented her out loud. In front of Beck and Flanagan, whose first name she couldn't remember, because, well, he was new, and she hadn't cared who came and went at TEAM HQ. Until now.

Beck hip-checked her, nearly knocking her into the curb as the SUV roared away. "Told you he likes you."

She wanted to respond with something snarky like, *'Well, of course. I always do good work,'* but that cat was out of the bag. Beck knew better. Still... Cam swallowed the strange, pleasant feeling swelling in her chest and simply replied, "Let's get back to work."

To which Beckam asked, "Why would your mother shoot your dad?"

Oh, that. Cam's cheeks ballooned as she blew out a big breath. "Because Alan always hated him. They never got along. I'm just surprised she used a gun. Thought she would've used a knife and cut him into little pieces like she always said she would."

Beck seemed to take that in stride. "Why'd she hate him?"

"Money. He never gave her enough, least that's what she said. You have to understand, Alana has expensive tastes. Only the best, she always used to say. Why settle for less, another one of her rules."

"You need to know Alex is on your side," he said quietly.

She turned and looked at him then. "No, he isn't. The only reason he gave me this job is because of that FBI creep, Director Chase. He pawned me off on Stewart to get back at me. That much I know for sure."

"I can't speak to what Tucker Chase hates or not, but Cam. Stop." Beck raised his palm as he came to a halt. "Alex might be fed up with the way you treat everyone in the office, but you've earned that bad rep, and it's up to you to change it. Trust me when I tell you that he's not going to fire you. I've seen him in action. Alex is the best guy in the world to have on your side."

She caught the earnestness in Beck's tone. "Why? What's going on? Why do I need him on my side?"

The penetrating look in his eyes turned her blood to ice.

"He found out about my PhDs, didn't he? That I'm a fraud? He knows I'm not married anymore, doesn't he? God—"

"Cam, there's more."

"More?" Oh, God, Alex knew about the abortion. He'd told Beck. And now...

"I was sixteen," she ground out as that awful day came back and slapped her down all over again. Once more, she heard the deathly quiet, seemingly benign background music in the waiting room. She smelled the sting of the antiseptically sterile exam room. She heard the conniving lies that Alana whispered. Emptiness settled into the hollow hole inside Cam's barely developed teenage chest where a tiny heart had grown. Where it had been ripped out and flushed away with her baby. "I was just sixteen," she told him again, shame raining down her cheeks, dripping from her nose, and off her chin. God! "It wasn't my fault! Alana said it was a normal, prenatal exam. I didn't know they were going to kill it!"

"Stop," Beck ordered as he mashed Cam into his chest and under his chin. "God, just take a breath, will you? I don't know what you're talking about. Slow down. Breathe. Just breathe, honey."

Yet Alana had done to Cam's unborn baby precisely what she'd always said she do to Cam's father. She'd had that unborn baby sliced into tiny, convenient pieces.

Cam sank into Beckam's hard contours, ashamed and embarrassed and so fuckin' tired of carrying the weight of the world with all its lies. Was there no relief? Shit!

"I never knew she'd do that to me. You have to believe me! You know what? Never mind. Jesus Christ, I quit!" she yelled, the shit finally kicked out of her, and too weak to fight back anymore. What difference did it make? The damage was done. Her heart would never heal. "Let me go. Just let me go. Damn you, I tried, but I can't do this anymore!"

She meant every vicious word, but instead of releasing her, Beckam wrapped those big, strong arms around her and held on tight. "No, stay with me, Cam. Trust me on this, you're going to be okay," he soothed, his breath warm on her cheek, his uninjured fingers in her hair, gentling her all over again. Making her believe that somehow, she deserved better when she knew damned well she didn't deserve anything good. Nothing! Not now! Not ever!

"No, I'm not," she cried, her palms flat to his chest, pushing him away. Needing to run. To hide. She'd just outed herself in the most despicable way, of the worst crime imaginable. She'd had an abortion. She'd killed her baby, and now he'd leave, and she couldn't blame him. She'd been stupid and so fuckin' needy back then. She'd actually believed Alana was helping her with that prenatal check-up. That finally, Alana loved her. At least, that she'd loved her grandchild. But no. Alana had only ever loved herself.

"Don't fight me," Beckam growled softly, still holding her against him. Refusing her impulse to run away. "What's done is done, Cam. Stick with me. We'll figure out whatever this is. Trust me. I'm here for you."

That's what you say now…

She gave in to her despair then, ducked her forehead to that honorable chest and closed her eyes against the hopelessness sweeping through her like a wrecking ball. Destroying the little bit of self-esteem Mark Houston had just blessed her with. Taking out everything in its path, then swinging back around to make certain there was nothing left. Not like Cam had much faith in herself to begin with. She'd never been confident, not as hard as school or making friends had been. But in the darkest night, she'd actually found two lights, Beckam and Mark. Only now…

God! She'd opened her fuckin' mouth and doused those bright lights for good. They'd never look her in the face again. Goddamnit, she didn't want to face herself, either. "Let me go!"

"Shhhhh, Cam, just shush," Beck soothed, still as gentle as ever. Still so damned kind. God, he had to be the dumbest fuck in the world, holding onto a degenerate woman like her. Acting like he cared.

"I quit," she whined again. "I'm leaving The TEAM. You guys don't need me. I'm not good. Let me go."

For the first time in her life, suicide seemed like a viable answer. Not that killing herself made sense, but it seemed a good enough way out. The perfect solution to all her problems. Why not? It'd put an end to the unending misery that was her entire fucked-up life. There seemed to be no other way out of the train wreck headed her way. No one could hate her if she wasn't here, right? It made sense in a desperate sort of way. It felt right. She'd be out of everyone's way once she was dead. They'd be free of her, and she'd be free of them. Best solution all around.

Cam swallowed the despair choking her. She'd give Beck the key to her apartment before she did it, though. He wouldn't mind taking care of Hector, would he? "I have a cat," she told him as if that explained her way forward. "His food's on my kitchen counter. Don't scare him when you go over there. He's a stray, but he's a good boy."

"Shut up and sit down," Beck ordered, still gripping her shoulders like she might bolt.

But the time for running had passed. All she needed now was for Beckam to keep being the noble man he was. He'd find this murderer, and when he did, she'd slip away while he was distracted, and she'd never be seen again.

"Knock it off," he told her brusquely as if he'd heard her ugly plan. God, she had a lot of secrets, but yeah. Suicide actually looked bright when all hope was lost.

Angrily, yet tenderly, Beck tugged her off the sidewalk and forced her to sit alongside him on the frozen grass, across from the train station. They hadn't done anything mission-related today. Breakfast didn't count. Maybe Alex would fire both of them. No, on second thought, he'd never fire Beckam. Beck was over six feet of pure, solid goodness. An archangel, just like the stone statues Cam remembered from some New York cathedral she'd visited as a little girl. That time she ran away from home. She was the sinner. Alex would surely fire her, unless she killed herself first. Yeah. That'd work.

Cam sat still as stone, afraid to breathe. There was no rescue in sight this time. Mother Nature's cold was nothing compared to the rock called her heart.

"I know what you're thinking," Beck told her.

No, I don't think you do, she thought wearily. *Not this time.*

He pulled her into his side then, forcing her butt to slide the distance between them until they bumped hips. "Kiss me," he ordered, his uninjured hand curled around the back of her neck.

"No," she whispered, leaning out of his reach. His kisses were poison. They'd make her believe, and then she'd tell him this secret, and his kisses would turn to hate, and no. Just no. She couldn't bear that.

"Damn it, then talk to me," he muttered as he tugged her head back toward his mouth and kissed her cheek.

Ah, he was breaking her heart just by being him. Just Beck. His lips were soft and his breath warm, almost like a breath of life. Almost. But not quite. Nothing could save her now, not even Boy Scout.

"Please. Tell me what happened when you were sixteen," he breathed against her skin. "Please. I want to know. Who hurt you? Tell me, and I'll hunt them down and hurt them back."

You have no idea...

"Rangers never give up, Junior Agent Cam Lopez. Did you know that? That's what you told me to call you, remember? Well, maybe it's time Junior Agent Cam Lopez started acting like a Ranger. Fight back against the hateful people who hurt you for a change. Fight your parents for what they both did to you. Prove they were wrong. Stop letting them ruin your life. Tell them to go to Hell. You ever think of that?"

Yeah, well... Fighting Alana hadn't worked the last twenty years. Oddly, Cam felt better now that she'd made her decision. Hector would be fine when she was gone. He was an alley cat when she'd found him. He could be an alley cat again. Even if Beckam didn't want him, he'd still be okay. He was tough. Alley cats knew how to take care of themselves, and maybe, someday he'd find a family with little kids who'd love him and snuggle him and—

A sob squeaked out of her at the thought of Hector finding an actual loving home. If anyone deserved one, he did.

Cam turned her head away from Beckam, so he wouldn't see her fall apart. Kids. The worst hurt in her heart had come to her because of a kid. A child. An innocent baby with no gender and no name. A baby to this day she still called… Hector. She couldn't breathe.

"Camilla," Beck said, speaking her name with two Ls. Teasing her. Thinking he could get her to answer by making her mad. But it didn't matter what anyone called her now. *Slut. Murderer. Baby killer…*

"Please, honey, believe that I'm here for you," he whispered earnestly, his good arm around her shoulder, her body pressed tight into his side while they sat together like a couple idiots on the cold DC sidewalk and watched DeWitt Construction equipment do whatever they were doing across the way. January seemed an odd month for road repairs. Must be an emergency.

And what the fuck? Who cared what DeWitt Construction was doing? Cam didn't. It was time. Past time! *Just say it and get it over with. Go home. Feed Hector. Listen to him purr. Snuggle him and tell him you love him. Then leave him in the kitchen and go hang yourself in your closet where he can't get to you.*

Cam lifted her hand and scratched her forehead, glad for the way her fingernails dug into her skin and made her feel. Pain. That was what life was all about. Layers and layers of pain. Shittin', fuckin' pain… But she had to make Beck leave first. It'd be better for him if he did, so she sucked in a gut full of air and blurted her last ugly secret.

"I had an abortion, okay? When I was sixteen, I had an abortion. I was naïve and stupid enough to believe that Alana loved me, but yes. She wanted me to get an abortion so I had one, Agent Beckam Garner. And when I woke up, my baby was gone, but Alana was happy again. Well, as happy as she could be. So there. Now you know everything. I'm a cheat and a liar and a baby killer. Hate me all you want because, trust me. I hate me, too." She didn't mean for those last words to sound so pitiful.

Beck's breathing hitched like someone had just punched him in the chest. But instead of pushing her out of reach and running away, he curled her inside his strong arms and whispered, "Oh, my God. You poor, poor thing."

Yup. There he was, saying God like he had a right to. Like he actually ever talked with Deity. Like there really was such a thing as a benevolent Being in the universe who watched over idiots like her. But what would it be to be loved unconditionally like that? Despite her sins? Despite herself? What a fuckin' lie!

"No! I'm not a poor thing," she growled, pushing back. Needing him to listen instead of feeling sorry for her. Wanting him gone from her life, so she could throw it away once and for all, and, Jesus! Just be done with it! What the fuck did it matter if she lived or died? No one would miss her. No one ever had! "Didn't you hear me, you ass? I killed a baby. My helpless, perfect, little…" A damned hiccup jerked out of her. "…b-b-baby."

Beckam's chest heaved like a blacksmith's bellows, but still he pulled her into that damned Carhartt jacket and smothered her face into his chest.

She melted. "I killed my baby," she cried into that cheap, shapeless jacket, as payment for the crime she'd held onto for so long came due. With interest. "I didn't want to, Beckam. Honest, I didn't understand what Alana was doing until it was too late, b-but—"

"Then *she* killed your baby, not you, Camilla." That time he said her name right. "This one's on your goddamned mother. You poor little thing. How old are you anyway?"

He cursed. Beckam actually cursed.

"T-twenty," she stuttered. "Almost twenty-one."

"Damn, you're not even old enough to drink. That's just four years ago. How old were you when you married?"

She hated to admit how young and dumb she'd been. How gullible. "Eighteen and a h-half."

"I'm so sorry," he whispered, his lips in her hair, kissing her temple like it could somehow make her perfect again. Fat chance of that. The world was too fucked up for her to ever be good again, much less perfect.

"You were only a baby, a little girl," he told her softly. "Hell, you're still just a kid, and you should've been able to trust your mom. Of all people. How could you ever have known she'd do something so evil? To you?"

Because Alana had never been anything but cold and hard, and evil was the best word for her. Cam's tears were impossible to hold back now. He sounded amazed that a mother could be as cruel as Alana Lopez. If he only knew. "I never understood why she hated me, but she did. She used to curse me and scream that she'd gotten stuck with the ugly, stupid one."

"What's that supposed to mean?"

"I don't know," Cam whined, her heart breaking all over again for the love-starved little girl she'd been all her life. She sniffed hard. "And I don't care. That's why I didn't want to go to the hospital. In case sh-she's there."

"Who was the father?"

"H-H-Hector Rojas," she admitted. "My neighbor's son. We were both sixteen, and I was lonely. So was he. I thought I loved him, and I know he loved me, and—"

"Where is Hector now?"

"His mother packed him off to Mexico the same day Alana took me to her lady doctor friend." Cam ran a finger under her nose. This damned operation had turned into one hell of a crying jag.

"So he doesn't know his baby's dead?"

His baby, not *it* and not just *the baby*. Damn Beckam for being thoughtful every damned time. Cam loved that Beckam didn't use politically correct words like 'the pregnancy was terminated' or 'the fetus' or ridiculous lying half-truths that only whitewashed the pain she'd lived with since that day. Dead. Her baby was dead. The baby she and Hector had made and wanted with all their foolish teenage hearts was dead. Murdered! And Alana had done it.

"I never heard from him after again," she explained quietly.

Until now, she hadn't wondered whether Hector knew his baby was dead or not. She did now. Did Hector ever care, or had he assumed she'd decided to raise their baby by herself? Did he think she didn't want him? Her head hurt with all the twists and turns in the insane hairpin road that was her life. How had everything gotten so fucked up?

But like the kind, honorable man that he was, once again Beckam tucked his arm around her waist and hauled her onto his lap. Once he settled her head under his chin, he hugged her and just rocked. Back and forth they went. Not talking. Just sitting together.

Cam pressed her ear to the solid wall of his chest, listening to a good man's heart. He'd make such a good father some day and… *Jesus Christ. Where'd that stupid thought come from?* She shoved it out of her head, her future already written in stone. Headstones...

After a couple minutes, Beckam said, "I talked with Mark and Alex earlier today. There's a lot you don't know about your parents. Do you remember the day you arrived in New York?"

Stupid question. She shook her head, bumping his chin. "No, because I was born there."

He drew in a deep breath. "Actually, no. You were born in Honduras, not New York City. Your parents fled Honduras when you were a little girl. Which explains why they never went home to visit. Puerto Rico wasn't home to them any more than Honduras was home to you."

Unbelievable. But with parents like Luis and Alana Lopez, it sounded likely. "What else?" she asked, hating the pitiful bleat that came out of her mouth in the guise of a question.

"Your father's name isn't Luis Lopez, either. It's Molina Escobar. And I know what your mother was trying to tell you. You had a baby sister, Cam. Alana and Luis never told you, but it's true. She must've died the night your parents fled Honduras, because her body washed ashore in Belize the day after."

"I—what? A sister? That's what Alana meant? I'm the ugly, stupid one?" Oh, God, yes. That had to be right. Alana ad wanted her sister. Never Cam. Which was probably why her father had favored her, only he hadn't. Not really.

"Who knows what your mother thought. All Alex knows is that the authorities found a drowned infant in a sealed plastic bag with your mother's wedding ring tied to her wrist the day after Escobar fled the country. At any rate, because of that dead baby, Molina Escobar and his entire family were presumed dead."

"What was her name?" Cam knew it was a stupid question the moment it spilled out of her mouth.

He shook his head. "Only your mother can answer that, honey. Sometime later, your parents made it to New York City where they already owned property on Fifty-Seventh Street. By then, they'd changed their names. Then Hurricane Maria came along and wiped out the sugar plantation in Puerto Rico. That only strengthened their position. I'm not sure what their losses were, but bottom line, if Molina still owns that chunk of property in Puerto Rico, when he dies, it'll go to you."

"Morning Glory Estates," she murmured.

"No, I'm talking about the sugar plantation. But yes, I imagine the New York estate would go to you, as well as any property Molina and Alana still own in Honduras. It might've been nationalized. Unstable governments tend to do that. I'll ask Mark and Ember to check into the legal issues now that your mom's in jail and your dad's been shot. I'm sure Alex will help, too."

"I don't want anything of theirs."

He kept rocking.

"What's that guy over there doing?" Cam asked, wiping her nose with one hand while pointing at a construction worker standing across the street. "Is he taking pictures of us with his phone."

Sure looked like he was. Beckam waved at the man. "Hey, you in the orange vest. Can I help you?" he called out over the traffic, his voice strong and pumped full of in-your-face authority.

The nosey, short guy stared at Beck a second longer, then stuffed his phone in his pocket and turned his back on Beckam. He looked both ways, crossed Columbus Circle Northeast, and disappeared into the chaos of the construction zone.

"That was odd," Beckam said before he changed the subject. "You named your cat Hector? You still love him, don't you?"

Cam nodded. "Yes, I love my cat, not sure about Hector Rojas, though. We were so young. He probably doesn't even remember me."

"Mind if I ask Ember to track him down, see what he's been up to? Who knows? He might be holding a torch for you."

"Why are you doing this? Why would she ever help me?"

"Because you need closure, Cam. Trust me. Ember's a good person. She'll be thrilled to help you find your old boyfriend. It'd be good for you and it's important he understands what happened to his baby. You're a fighter. Just having a bad day, is all. Trust me, you've got more people in your corner than you know. I'm not the only one."

She couldn't help it. Cam pressed her face into Beckam's shirt and wept all over him, never more sure than now how little she deserved all this man was doing for her. But finally willing to believe him. Maybe even willing to believe in herself for a change. She'd been foolish to have considered suicide. Beckam was right. She hadn't killed her baby. Alana had out of the bitterness of her cold, dead heart. Throughout Cam's entire life, Alana had destroyed everything precious. Even that other baby girl, Cam's sister. How sad.

"Umm, Beck?"

"Yes?"

"You're right. I should go see Papa. If he's still alive, he might be able to answer some questions. If not..." Her shoulders lifted. "I won't be any worse off than I am now."

Beckam nodded and away they went.

Chapter Twenty-Four

"You can turn your earpiece on again," Beckam told Cam.

After her last meltdown, they'd gone back to Union Station to use the restrooms. She'd freshened her face, but still looked unhappy. Now, they were walking the National Mall where they'd meet up with Renner and Beau. Mark was on his way to rendezvous with them, then he'd transport Cam and Beckam to Sibley Memorial.

Cam nodded that she'd heard. Taking off one glove, she fingered the earpiece and turned it on. She wasn't making eye-contact yet, but she'd agreed to visit her father. Beck doubted she'd get the answers she needed from him. A man who'd lied to his only child all her life was a bastard. He didn't deserve one last visit from the child he should've loved and protected.

Another wintery storm had rolled in, dropping the temperature ten more degrees and turning the day gloomy. Tiny soggy slush pellets blasted their backpacks as they speed-walked. Beck had slowed his gait so Cam could keep up. She'd taken the upsetting news about her family better than he'd expected, possibly because knowing the truth somehow confirmed what she might have suspected all along. But he had a sneaky feeling a bigger storm than the one Mother Nature had unleashed was coming.

He could feel it in the air around them. Smell it. Taste it. Like ozone after a lightning strike, it had a presence most people shrugged off as nothing worth worrying about. Not Beckam. This was a precursor. A premonition. Something wicked was still headed his way.

At first, he'd assumed the niggling sensation climbing up the back of his neck was because he'd dropped too much crap on Cam's slender shoulders. He'd suspected she'd survived some kind of physical abuse from her parents all along. But having an abortion forced on her at sixteen? Inconceivable. His fingers curled into hard fists at the pain she'd endured during and after that ugly procedure. How could anyone do that to a teenage girl? To their daughter? Their little girl? To that unborn baby?

The whole thing made him sick. He'd been brought up in the heartland of America by hard-working parents who'd loved him and his sister. The Garner family went to church together every Sunday, and Beck honestly believed in and tried his best to live the Ten Commandments. The Golden Rule was a hard, fast rule in his parent's home. It was the common thread in every lesson the preacher taught from his pulpit, dumbed down from God's level to the working man's level. That was what his dad and mom did. They lived and breathed the Golden Rule. Look how happy they were. So, yeah. He'd never understand folks like Molina and Alana Escobar. But then, he didn't understand terrorists or the need to blow oneself up just to prove a point, either.

But damn. As sophisticated and confident as Cam was, she was awfully young. At thirty, but feeling like eighty on a bad day, Beck was an old man trying to keep up with a kid instead of the other way around. He glanced sideways at her, looking long enough, just not long enough to get caught. But remembering the heat and taste of her sweet mouth when they'd connected at the station. The way she'd wrapped her long legs around his waist and clung to him when he'd lost his mind and scooped her into his arms as if he'd had a right to. He hadn't expected to also feel the heat of her core against his belly, but he'd been running and had unzipped his jacket. And yeah. He'd felt enough of her delicious body to know she'd wanted him. And he wanted her. Still did.

Earlier this morning, he'd been scared out of his freakin' mind that he'd lost her. But when she ran at him like that, what else could he have done? So, yeah. Big time Agent-in-Charge blunder, check one. And that was just hours ago. Beck knew it to his soul. He was in big trouble.

She was a scared and overwhelmed kid. She'd been lied to all her life by the very adults she should've been able to depend on. Instead, her parents had both used her. Abused her. He couldn't do that to her, too. Wouldn't. So even as they walked westward together, he made up his mind to end this thing between them before it went any further. She needed the experience of working an active operation, but he was not the Agent-in-Charge she needed. Maybe Mark. Maybe Zack. They were both older married guys with children. Even Harley would be a better fit.

As if she'd sensed him mentally distancing himself, Cam grabbed hold of his hand. "Talk to me," she said. "Am I going to jail for what my parents did?"

He shook his head, returning the handhold. "Not in this country. You never defrauded the schools you went to, never bribed or paid off someone to let you graduate with honors. Unless you ran drugs or guns—"

"God, is that what they did?"

"That's what we know that your parents were into so far, but this is a new investigation, so we don't know everything. Not sure if the State Department or Homeland Security will task Alex to handle this mess, but I suspect by the end of it, we'll find out that your parents were into more illicit crap than just those."

"I should get a lawyer."

"Well, about that…" Beck pursed his lips, wondering what Alex meant when he'd said he was glad Cam worked for him. "Let's talk with Alex first, see what he thinks."

For once she didn't grunt or come back with a snippy comment about her boss. "I should hold a press conference, though. Be upfront about everything. Tell the world what I know about my parents, and when I knew it. That's what they'll want, right?"

"Cam, no. Forget that. The press these days is not about reporting the news. You'll never make the media happy. Every last one of them will smear you and your family's name from Hell to breakfast and then back again. Sure, they'll couch it as 'investigative reporting', but not a one of them is after the truth, not unless it's sensational, matches their propaganda machine, and makes a profit. They're muckrakers, pure and simple. All of them. Their lies are something you're going to have to endure, so get ready for the gossip stalkers. Paparazzi, too. It'll be a circus for a while, but in the end, someone else will stumble, and the press will jump on them like a pack of jackals and hyenas. They'll forget you ever existed. I swear, they're worse bullies than your parents were."

She sniffed at that, and Beck turned his head to take a good look at her. Damn. She was crying. He regretted his words.

"Come here," he muttered as he stopped walking and tugged her under his arm. "I need to learn when to shut up."

"No," she murmured, "It's okay, I just… I mean... I have no place to go. My mortgage is overdue. I can't pay my bills and..." She broke down. Again.

Beck dropped his nose to the top of her head and breathed. This poor kid was tearing his heart apart. "Where do you live now?"

"The Palisades. That's why my parents bought a home there. Not to be closer to me, but to be near Spence and Penn Brinkman. Their mansion is a half-mile up the river. You know. Thick as thieves?" The river being the lazy Potomac that wound its way south of Washington, DC.

"How long's What's-His-Face been gone? A year?"

She nodded, sniffing. "Yes, and I, umm…"

Beck dug a tissue out of his inner pocket and handed it over.

"I'm not making enough to live there anymore and…" She took the tissue and wiped her poor, red nose. Took a deep shuddering breath. "I need a new home and… and a new life."

"The real estate market's hot right now. Should be a good time to sell." Why was she telling him this?

"Yeah, well…" She dabbed at her nose again. "I don't know why I've hung onto that place this long. It's too big, and it's not full of good memories. Only…"

Here it comes.

"I can't find an apartment that'll let me keep Hector."

And there it was. She needed a home for the cat she'd named after her teenage lover. Somehow, the fact that she'd fallen in love at least once in her life and had gotten pregnant from that juvenile encounter, added another decade of gloom to Beck's day. He sucked in a gut full of cold air to clear his head. He was not one to mope or digress into an emotional ball of pity, but damn. She *was* young and he *was* old.

"You need someone to take your cat while you move, is that it?" That shouldn't be too hard. He lived alone. Cats were quiet, self-sufficient creatures. Might even be fun.

"You're such a sucker," she said shyly. Wasn't that the truth? "I didn't mean you. He's an alley cat. I'm sure he'll be fine if I just open the door and let him go."

"Uh uh, no way. I'll take Hector for as long as you need me to. Look. There's Mark." He pointed at The TEAM SUV parked at the corner of Fourteenth Street SW and Jefferson Drive SW, between the Washington Monument and Smithsonian Castle. Both side doors were open, both Renner and Beau half-in, half-out, their long legs in view, not much else.

"Wonder what's up," Cam said as they closed in on the rear gate and—

Someone else's feet were visible. Shabby, worn out mismatched boots. The seats inside were folded down. Mark was on his knees applying first-aid to an unconscious— Georgia?

"Damn. What happened? Where's Joslyn?" Beck asked the second he'd shouldered his way inside the trauma team. Georgia lay deathly still in the back of the SUV. Her skin was gray, her head bloodied, and her quilted jacket sleeve was torn. Mark had applied several butterfly bandages to her forehead while Renner squirted an antiseptic wash into a two-inch laceration on top of her scalp. Other than that, she looked no worse for wear. Her breathing was steady and nothing looked broken.

"Found her in the middle of the street, screaming but not making sense," Beau answered. "Joslyn wasn't with her. By the time Renner and I got to her, she'd fainted."

"They left the station together," Cam informed him with a titch of attitude in her tone. "Right after breakfast. We ate with them. That was about two hours ago."

Beck didn't blame Cam for reverting to her usual snark. It had been one helluva day.

Beau cocked an attitude right back at her. "Where have you been since then?" he asked pointedly.

"Cam got some bad news, that's where we've been," Beckam interrupted before she could fire back more hostility. "Her dad's been shot. We were meeting Mark here for a ride over to Sibley Memorial when we saw you guys."

Beau grunted in that accusatory way he had, but Renner piped up, always playing peacemaker. "Hey, guys. Whoever hit Georgia is not our killer. This isn't his MO."

"How do you know?" Mark asked as he applied one last butterfly.

"Because our killer doesn't rob his vics. I checked Georgia over right after she fell. Her stash of challenge coins is gone and her pockets are empty. Might be a simple mugging."

"She did find a ten-dollar bill back at the station," Beck said. "Someone could've seen her waving it under Joslyn's nose and heard her bragging. You guys know how she is."

"Then where's Joslyn?" Cam voiced what everyone was thinking. "My God, if she's—"

"Shut it," Beau hissed. "Joslyn's smart. She isn't—that."

"How do you know?" she challenged him sharply.

Beckam stared over Cam's head at Beau, uncertain for the first time if anyone was smart enough to elude this killer. "Max and Joslyn both worked at Sachs and Goldstein. Is it possible our victims crossed paths somewhere in their previous lives? At S and G maybe? Could our murderer have worked there, too?"

Mark smoothed an antiseptic wipe over the last trace of blood on Georgia's forehead. "I'll have Ember check. She's already running possible links between our victims. The only thing she's uncovered so far that the murdered men have in common is they all served under the same CO in Vietnam. Captain Seymore Gharst from Missouri, US Army Fifth Division, between 1969 and 1970. And before you ask, no, he isn't a suspect because he's in Arlington. He died from Agent Orange related cancer a little over three years ago."

"Joslyn never served a day in her life," Georgia murmured groggily as she came to and tried to push up onto her elbows.

Renner wasn't having any of that. "Just rest another minute while I finish stitching your scalp," he soothed as he pressed both palms to her shoulders to make her lie flat. "You'll do that for me, won't you, sweetheart?"

Her eyes rolled back in her head as she tried to see who was behind her. "Oh, hi Wren. For you, sugar dumpling, I'll do cartwheels in my birthday suit."

He winked at her, the dog.

"Where is she then?" Cam pressed. "She left with you."

"Pshaw," Georgia grumbled. "It's not like we're joined at the hip, you know. Cripes sake, she ain't my sister. Joss wanted to go pray at Saint Pat's, but I had better things to do. Told her I'd meet her at Lorelei's for lunch. Crap. I'm late. What time is it?"

"Just after noon," Renner said. "Do you remember what happened? Who hit you?"

She growled. "He didn't hit me. Little punk ran me down with his bike. Grabbed my coat sleeve when he flew by and swung me 'round like a ragdoll. That's when I slipped and hit my head. Then he jumped off his bike grabbed one sleeve, damn near pulled me out of it. Crap." She palmed her chest, then her pockets. "That little asshole stole my stuff! Get off me, guys. I need to—"

"No, ma'am." Renner told her patiently, still holding her down. "You're going with Mark to the hospital to get your head checked. Right now. Whatever that thief stole, he's long gone."

"We'll give you a ride," Mark assured her.

"But my money," she argued, blinking back tears. "He's got my dollar and my… my money."

"How many challenge coins did you have?" Beckam asked gently. She'd shown her *money* to him often enough that he knew she wasn't talking about actual currency. Only her treasure.

Her lower lip quivered, the thin line of whiskers beneath it, too. "It ain't the coins, Beck. For God's sake, it's them guys what gave 'em to me."

"You served?" he asked, not sure why he didn't know that.

"Yeah. Back in seventy-two, right before we deserted our friends and let Saigon fall." Hurt echoed in her tone. "They were my friends, too, but we… we just left 'em all behind."

"Army Nurse Corps?" he asked.

Her head bobbed. "Until 1973, when they made the last of us nurses leave. Biggest mistake we ever made, going. Should've stayed. Those people needed us, and everyone knew it."

"And those coins…?"

"They give 'em to me when I visit 'em, Beck. I don't steal 'em, if that's what you're asking. But them guys stuck in the VA hospital are lonely. They got no one else, and neither do I, and we talk about back then, you know? We sit, and we remember, and we cry, and..." Her shoulders quaked with the shudders she was trying to hold back. "It helps sometimes, you know, just being with people who were there at the same time as you."

Beck's eyes filled. Yeah. He knew how absolute those friendships forged in fire were to his peace of mind. Which was precisely why he worked for Alex. The TEAM was his band of brothers and sisters, his sounding board and his comfort. "It does, Georgia. You visit the veterans' home in the District, don't you? That's how you collected your coins."

She nodded. "Only now, I got nothin'."

Unexpectedly, Beau chimed in with a growly, "But a ton of good memories, ma'am. And good friends wherever you go."

"Yeah, but them coins was all I had to hold onto. Kinda helped me make it through the night." Georgia was outright bawling by then. "Helped me remember the guys I lost and the guys I saved."

Beau wasn't known for being affectionate, but he reached past Beckam for her hand and squeezed it. "You got us, sweetheart," he murmured sincerely. "I promise you, Georgia, you'll always have us."

A sob wrenched out of her. "Yeah. You're right. I still got you. I got all my boys, don't I?" She arched to see Renner again.

"Sure do, sweetheart," he told her with a wink.

"And we'll help replace those coins. Least I will," Beau said solemnly.

"We all will," Mark said as he tipped back onto his haunches. "Now let's see if that head of yours is as hard as you think it is, Georgia. You guys coming?" he asked Renner and Beau.

"No," Beau growled. "We've still got work to do here. Might swing by Lorelei's to make sure Joslyn's okay, though."

"Right. We've got a full schedule," Renner agreed.

"Tell her to stay put, if you see her. I'll be there as soon as I git done with the hospital," Georgia said.

"Or we'll bring her to visit you," Beau said as he and Renner climbed out of the SUV. Mark and Beck got Georgia up and steady onto her feet, then converted the SUV back into a passenger vehicle while Cam watched over Georgia. Cam had grown quiet again, and that was okay. She still had to face her father.

Beck ushered Georgia up front with Mark and made sure she was belted in before he climbed in beside Cam in the backseat. Renner and Beau were on foot, already walking away.

Cold rain splattered against the windshield, and Beck was thankful to be inside where it was warm. But he couldn't help watching out the side window, knowing he was safe while so many others weren't. That same sneaking feeling slithered up his neck. A storm was coming...

Chapter Twenty-Five

Cam didn't know how much she could take. This TEAM operation had turned into a fuckin' marathon heartache. But there she was, putting on her brave face as she prepared to meet her dying father for, what she hoped, was the last time. She had no idea how to feel anymore. Angry or sad, relieved or anxious. There'd been a day not too long ago she would've run to Luis and climbed onto his lap at the end of an exhausting day of trying to be his perfect daughter. She would've snuggled into his arms and smelled the rich aroma of the finest Cuban cigars he smoked. He would have asked her how her day went, and, like a good girl, she would've lied and told him, "Perfect, Papa."

Because that was what he'd wanted to hear. No excuses. No whining or rationalization. Just his perfect daughter, reaffirming her perfect place in his idea of a perfect world. Back then, she would've believed everything he'd told her. Not anymore.

Not now that she knew he was really Molina Escobar, a liar and a deceiver. A man who dealt in blood and murder. He was no better than the killer murdering the homeless veterans. But God, what he'd done to her. It hadn't taken Cam long to realize she could never belong to The TEAM now, because, guess what? She was officially an illegal immigrant. Not only that, but wouldn't the federal government seize her parents' holdings once they declared Alana and Luis to be criminals? Wasn't that how the system worked?

In the end, she'd be not only as dumb as everyone else, but as broke. As worthless. As ugly. She'd be a bag lady, too. Yes, she had her own bank accounts, just more outlays than income at the moment. She might have to stop shopping in high-end stores. Maybe visit Target or Wal-Mart or—shit. The second-hand clothing store she'd thought Joslyn and Georgia would do well to shop at. A full-on body shiver wriggled up Cam's spine at what lay ahead.

"Hey," Beck murmured as he reached a hand to her shoulder. "You ready?"

She hadn't realized Mark had already come to a stop in Sibley's underground parking, that he was also watching her in the rearview mirror. Cam swallowed hard and nodded. "Yeah. Sure." How hard could being treated like crap by her father again be?

"Why don't you leave your gear with me? Call when you're finished," Mark told Beckam. "I'll run you back to the station."

"Good idea. Let us know how things go for Georgia. Joslyn too," Beck told him as he offloaded everything but his holstered pistols. "See you later."

"Copy that," Mark replied.

Georgia snorted, but eyed Cam as she stashed her gear bag, eased out of the SUV, and dropped off the running board to her feet. "You remember what I told you, Beck. Watch your backside."

Whatever that meant. Cam could care less what Georgia thought of her. She was on a different mission, aiming for the parking garage elevators by then.

"Hey, wait up," Beckam called out as he ran to catch up.

So she did. The kindly woman at Information told her Luis Lopez was in Room 131, ICU. "Don't be surprised when you see him. He underwent emergency surgery only this morning. He may still be too doped up for visitors."

"Will he live?" Cam asked bluntly.

"I'm sorry. You'll have to ask his surgeon," the woman said gently.

"And that would be…?"

She checked her computer. "Dr. Money. Chisolm Money. He's one of the best."

"Of course, he is." Papa never settled for anything but the best. "Thank you."

Finally outside her father's room, Cam stalled as her bravado fled. She didn't want to know what Luis or Molina or whatever name her father went by today, knew. She didn't want to face him. Didn't know if she could.

How did one approach the man who'd deceived her for twenty years? *Oh, hey Papa, how's it going? You'll never guess what I found out today. Jesus Christ, I'm one lucky daughter, huh? Broke as fuck. Don't know fuck. Might as well be named fuck since you've only ever fucked me over. Oh, what? Alana shot you!? You don't say. Why would anyone want to kill a man as wonderful as you? You fucker!*

Beck's big warm hand landed on her shoulder, squeezing her but not pushing. Just being there like Georgia did for those veteran friends of hers. Which was kind of him. Cam had never felt more worthless than she did then. Everything in her already messed up life had changed. Every. Goddamned. Thing.

"Remind me why I'm doing this," she said as she faced the closed door between her and the man she'd lovingly called Papa while he'd lied to her face.

"Because you want to know your sister's name. Maybe ask why only her body washed ashore. Find out how she died. Who put her in that plastic bag? Who tied your mother's ring around her wrist? How did anyone even know that ring belonged to Alana? Was it engraved or registered? Insured?"

Oh, yeah. Her baby sister's death. All *those* lies. Different lies, yet still the same lie she'd been living. Why hadn't her father ever told her she'd had a baby sister? What would that have hurt? For that matter, why commit fraud just to give his only living daughter the appearance of an elite education? Why not just pay for one good and solid education? At a trade school? Or a community college? There were enough of them in this country. Why cheat and lie, goddamnit? So many questions.

Drawing in a long, deep breath, Cam put a sweaty hand to the door, turned the knob, and entered the private room. There were no blinds on the tinted windows, only glaring lights overhead. Humming equipment. Wires and cords and tubes that snaked out from under his blankets to various machines and places unseen. Her father, silent and still, lay on his back with an oxygen cannula taped to his face and IV lines running into his arms. Drawn and more helpless looking than she'd ever seen, he seemed smaller against the stark white sheets. Older. Grayer.

Gone was his deep, dark tan. His dark mustache was missing, too. Pasty. He looked pasty white like a cadaver. If his monitor hadn't been lit up with various stats, she would've known she'd come too late. But the screen still beeped for each beat of his heart, and his life line undulated like a wave on a peaceful ocean.

Damn it. Luis/Molina Lopez/Escobar wasn't dying anytime soon.

Still standing at the open door, she asked, "Papa?"

Beckam eased around her and walked straight to the quietly beeping monitor. "His stats are bad, Cam," he said as he read the display. "O_2 saturation is less than fifty percent. I doubt he can hear you. Come on in. Pull up a chair. This might take a while."

Heart pounding, she obeyed. But as she placed her hands on the armrest and her backside into that molded plastic, all she could think to say was, "I'm glad it's not you in that bed, Beck."

"Hey, me, too," he said softly while he pulled up a chair and sat alongside her. "Quite a shock, seeing someone you love right after surgery, isn't it?"

"I don't love him."

"Sure you do, honey. He's your dad. He might not have known how to show it, but fathers love their children, and kids can't help but love their dads."

Cam doubted that. Tucking her hands into her armpits, she nodded. It was either hold onto herself or grab Beck like the hysterical woman she felt herself slipping into. Maybe sit on his lap like before. Of course, she'd just learned how little her parents had ever thought of her then. She'd been nothing, just another pawn to sacrifice in their back and forth power plays. Just someone else to manipulate and use.

Beck had been the only one in a lifetime of bullies who'd actually reached for her—not past her—just for the sake of pulling her onto his thighs and into safety. For a moment back there, beside that frozen sidewalk, she'd felt safe, even as her world fell apart. With Beck's arms around her, she'd thought she could endure whatever life threw at her. Now, about to face her father, Cam wasn't so sure.

"I shouldn't have come," she whispered, glancing at the still open door.

"It was always a longshot," Beck reminded her. "But at least now you'll know you've done all you could. Ball's in his court. Either he'll wake up and tell you what you need to know, or not. It's that simple."

Small consolation. "Guess you're right."

"Listen. You stay here in case he opens his eyes. I'll go grab us a couple coffees. If nothing happens while I'm gone, we'll talk. You can tell me about your cat. We've got time. Okay?"

"But we should both be working." The last day had been a blessing of sorts, working with Beck. Walking. Having a real job. "Hurry back."

He'd no more than left the room when a nurse peeked in. "Mrs. Brinkman, you have company. Do you want to talk to her in one of our family conference rooms?"

"Her?"

"Yes, me, Camilla," Alana Lopez/Escobar snapped as she pushed the nurse aside and stalked into her husband's room. "My, my, look what the cat dragged in. Our precious little princess. What'd you do, lose another job?"

Cam jumped to her feet. "Alana. No, I…"

"Ladies, please…" the nurse interrupted.

"It's time you knew the family business, you little rag," Alana hissed as she stalked Cam. "Time you gave something back instead of always taking. Time you—"

"Ladies. Please!"

"Like what? My baby sister?" Cam shot back even as she tipped over the chair she'd been seated in. "Is that what I took from you? The little girl you never had the decency to tell me about? You stuffed her into that plastic bag, didn't you? Of course you did. It was your ring tied to her wrist. Who else would've done something so cruel and cold-blooded?" The rage Cam had held back for years spilled out of her mouth. "What'd she do, Alana? Cry too loud? Breathe too much? Interrupt your shitty life like my baby would have if you hadn't killed it first?!"

By then the nurse had left, probably to call security. But she was too late. Alana lunged and, in a split second, had her long fingers around Cam's neck. Her nails dug into Cam's throat, her thumbnails stabbed up under Cam's chin, and red-hot hatred blazing in her eyes. "It should've been you who drowned that day!" she growled down as she shook the life out of her daughter. "Not Acindina. It was all your fault!"

Shake, shake, shake. "I loved her. But you. You!"

More shaking. More choking. More spitting. "You weren't even his! It should've been you! Molina's brat! Not his!"

Cam clutched her mother's wrists, digging her own nails in, trying to undo the damage Alana was doing. Trying desperately to breathe. But Alana was older and meaner. She knew precisely what she was doing. Darkness hovered all around. Cam's knees turned to jelly. "Alana, stop. You're… you're killing me."

"You're already dead. Trust me! If there's one thing I know how to do, it's kill!"

It had been a long time since Cam had seen her mother this close. Longer since she'd realized how much the poison spewing from Alana's lips sounded exactly like what had recently come out of Cam's mouth.

Alana had never changed. Neither had one strand of her expertly coiffed black hair, her stiletto thin, perfectly plucked brows, or the icy-cold stare in her flat-black eyes. How interesting. Her eyes were rimmed with kohl—also Cam's favorite color. Only she saw it differently now. Kohl was the color of Death. It helped make Alana who she was today. She made that witch in the movie about skinning Dalmatian puppies look sweet and kind and good.

But Cam had changed. With her last breath, she rejected her only role model, and, without ever having believed in God, she asked Him to, "Please, save me."

A feeble voice called from the bed, "S-s-stop, Alana. Please. Stop. Let Camilla go."

Papa was still alive. Not that he could help, but maybe…

"C-C-Carlos was here," her father sputtered. "For you. He came for you."

Who the hell is Carlos?

Alana looked over her shoulder. "Liar. You'll do anything to save your precious brat."

Only then did her grip loosen. Just a little. Just enough. Cam slid her fingers between her neck and Alana's vicious grip, so she could breathe. Pursing her lips, she sucked in a breath. Then another. Air. She needed air.

"It's true," poor Luis murmured. He sounded so weak.

"Prove it," Alana snapped. "If Carlos really came to visit you—"

"Not me. You. Stupid man thought you'd be here with me." Luis lifted a trembling hand and pointed to the tiny closet across the room. "He left something… for you. Look. See."

"If this is just another one of your lies…" Alana growled even as she loosened her fingers, then shoved Cam away. "I'll kill you, Molina. Dead this time."

Cam fell to her knees, gripping the back of the nearest chair barely in time to keep from kissing the floor.

Swiftly, Alana stalked to the standalone closet and jerked the door open. "Oh," she murmured softly as she pulled a rose-colored leather album from an inner shelf. "He left this for me?" God, she could switch from evil to sounding innocent and sincere so fast.

Another hissed, "Yes…." wheezed from Luis. "But I have something for you, too, my love."

"Your love, my ass," Alana scoffed as she backed against the wall opposite Luis and opened the album. "I was never your love."

"Yes-s-s-s. You. It was only ever you."

"Ahh, he remembered," Alana whispered like a love-struck little girl. Another page turned. Another dramatic sigh followed.

Cam climbed onto the chair and sat, holding her poor aching throat and wishing Beck or that nurse would hurry back.

Lovingly, Alana turned another page, then another, caressing them as if they contained treasures. But whatever was in that album, Cam was sure it had nothing to do with her. While she watched the mechanics of her parents' toxic relationship, she wondered why they'd stayed together this long, and what they'd seen in each other in the first place. Had to be the money or the evidence each one had on the other. Couldn't be their children. Certainly wasn't love.

"He still loves me," Alana said huskily. "After all these years, Carlos still—"

"But I loved you first," poor dying Luis rasped.

Cam watched Alana's upper lip twitch. Then her nose. And sure enough, the softer side of Alana morphed back into the vicious troll she'd been just moments ago.

"Come to me," Luis whispered, his voice so frail and weak. "Be my love again. One last time, Alana. Please?"

Her head tossed as she snapped the album shut. "I was never your love, old man," she snarled, taking took long, deliberate steps to his bedside. Looking down at him with the album clutched over her heart, she told him, "You'll never live through this, so why don't you—?"

His lips moved, but Cam couldn't hear what he said.

Neither could Alana. "Speak up you stupid, old baboon. Be a man for once in your life. What'd you say?"

His index finger twitched for her to come closer.

Alana leaned in, her nose out of joint and her mouth twisted with malice as—

Chapter Twenty-Six

Beckam paused at the Intensive Care Unit's nurses' station and set the two paper cups of hot-damned coffee on the counter. Note to self: use those funny little cardboard sleeves next time. But right then, he needed to call Alex with a sitrep and beg forgiveness. The entire mission had gone sideways, and he was ready to admit he needed a quick assist from a skilled agent. He and his much younger companion agent were more involved in her personal life than getting the assigned job done. Things needed to change. As much as Beckam wanted to help Cam, he needed to get back to work. It might be time to revisit the idea to swap her out with Agent Flanagan.

Beck called TEAM HQ, hoping Zack would answer like he had last time, but no such luck.

"Stewart." The tone in that voice in itself was troublesome. Alex was at the customer service desk answering Cam's phone. Was everyone else out of the office?

"Hey, Boss. Thought I'd call in for a vector check. Sorry, but Cam and I are still at Sibley Memorial. Nothing to report on our murderer."

"Copy that. Last night was quiet on all fronts. Except for the skirmish between you and those teenagers. How's the hand?"

"I'm good," Beck answered, swiftly deflecting any concern. "Mobility's fine. Reconsidering your suggestion on Flanagan, though. Might be—"

"No," Alex said flatly. "Mark reported you're making progress with Camilla. Keep it up."

"Yes, but Boss—"

"But nothing. You're right where I need you to be."

"No, I'm not. I'm at Sibley Memorial hospital, miles away from my post at Union Station. Not watching over any homeless people, not even within shouting distance of where I should be. How's that doing my job?"

"What exactly do you think your job is?"

Was Alex serious? "To catch the guy killing Vietnam vets. Remember? Instead I'm babysitting a woman who may need serious counseling once this mess with her parents comes out in the press. She's got serious issues to deal with. In short, I need someone who can keep up."

"Are you saying Camilla is slowing you down?"

Duh. "I'm not where I should be, am I?"

"As I said, you're right where you need to be."

"But Boss—"

"But Beckam…" Alex's lack of charm radiated across the miles. Damn, he could put more venom into two words than a snake could inject into its prey. "Your service record is why you're there. You're a born leader and an honest man. Only you can reach Camilla, and you've already proven that. She's actually talking with you, not at you, and for once, she's not spitting in your face, either."

"But Boss—" *You have no idea what we're really going through.*

Damned if Alex didn't laugh in Beck's ear. "You should hear yourself. It's not like you to make excuses. What's really going on?"

The question of the day. Beckam shut his big mouth, not willing to admit how important Camilla Brinkman had become to him. Not yet. He was old enough to know better, and common sense told him to walk away from her. Now. Fast.

Not only was she a mess, but ten years! She'd been a ten-year-old child when he was fighting in Iraq on his first deployment. He couldn't fall for a kid, and Cam was simply that. She couldn't even legally go into a bar and order a mixed drink or a beer. This was him trying to do what was right and walk away without hurting anyone, especially her, any more than he already had. But could he dare tell Alex? *Uh uh.*

"You got time for a story?" Another odd thing for Alex to ask. What the heck was up with him today? The man was a hundred eighty degrees different since the bungled operation with Catalina Montego ended last month.

"Sure," Beckam answered easily. Why not? Anything was better than confessing he'd already stepped on those pesky office rules about kissing another agent. Which he'd done, and which he thought about doing again. Cam certainly hadn't kissed like a child, not with those long legs of hers opened wide and wrapped around him like she'd wanted to eat him up. Not the way she'd opened her mouth and all but licked his tonsils. Man, he'd love for her to do that again.

"There was a time I was as pissed at the world as Camilla is now," Alex admitted quietly. "That's who I see every time she lashes out. I see me, Beck. Me, right after Sara and Abby died. I see all that pain and self-hatred again. I can almost taste it. I can smell it. I thought I'd lost everything then. You never get over losing your wife and daughter; you just learn how to carry yourself, so no one knows you're dying inside. So the hole in your heart doesn't bleed quite so much. It's son of a bitchin' hard, but when I look at Camilla, I also see a woman worth saving. She needs us, Beck. She needs The TEAM, and she needs you. Especially now that she's finally cracked open the stone façade she's been hiding behind. You're the first one in this office she's confided in, and that says a lot about you. I'm willing to bet she can count her friends on one hand and have fingers left over."

"She's only mellowed because she was there when Max died."

"Maybe. Just know that you're doing precisely what I need you to do while we're catching this latest killer. It's just a matter of time. The entire team's actively searching. Hell, I've got more men and women on this case than the police force has. But I've only got one agent mentoring Camilla, and that's you."

Beck grunted at that unexpected compliment. "Mentoring, huh?" *Does that include mouth-to-mouth resuscitation? Fondling? Wanting to back her into a wall and make her really, really happy?*

"Yes, mentoring. Do what you do best. Teach, and she'll learn. Lead, and she'll follow."

Oh, if you only knew. "That's what I'm afraid of. She's divorced, Boss. I'm working with a single woman with a shitload of trouble headed her way, and she's looking for someone to have her back." *And oh yeah, we're sleeping in pretty close quarters now, too. Not sleeping together as in sleeping together. Barely sleeping at all, come to think of it. But yeah. That.*

"She's divorced? Since when?"

"Since a year ago. Plus, she's losing her home, her credentials are fraudulent, and her parents are scum."

"Son of a bitch. I didn't know she was divorced." Alex went silent for a heartbeat. "What's the deal with her credentials?"

"Mark will find out soon enough, but she's pretty sure her father bribed every school she ever graduated from, probably as early as grade school, to make her appear smarter than she is."

"Hmm. Maybe I should swap you out with Izza."

"Wait, what? Swap *me* out?" *And keep Cam on the op?* "No way."

"Then you'll deal with this *babysitting* job?"

Damn it. Alex played dirty, throwing Beck's words back at him. "I didn't mean babysitting per se. Just wanted you to know I wasn't accomplishing anything operational-wise."

"Yes, you are. You're growing my team, Beck. You're saving a life worth saving. This is no different than what you'd do in the middle of combat. You'd run into hell for one of your soldiers, wouldn't you?" Alex made it sound simple.

"Well, yeah, but—"

"But Camilla needs saving, too."

Beckam wanted to curse like a sailor instead of like his dad, who'd almost never used bad language. *Damn. Damn. Damn.*

Alex kept going. "Mark saw how you dealt with Montego's victims the night she died. You impressed him. Keep it up, and you might impress me."

Beck bowed his head into his good hand, covering his eyes to keep anyone from seeing the turmoil hidden there. All his life he'd lived to serve. His mom and his dad. His country. Every last one of the soldiers who'd fought with him. Now Alex Stewart and his TEAM of damned good former snipers. He honestly didn't know how to do anything else. But this time Alex was asking a lot.

"Is there anything you need to tell me? Anything going on that we haven't covered?"

Beckam knew what Alex was really asking. "No, Boss. I'm good. Even if there were anything going on, trust me. I'm too old for Cam, and she's too broken for me."

"Cam, huh? I thought that about a lady one time…" Alex paused. Took a breath. Then said, "Good job, Beck. Keep me informed."

"Copy that, and thanks, Boss," Beck said tiredly. He pocketed his cell, picked up the coffee cups and—

BOOM! Gunshot!

He ran to Luis' room.

Chapter Twenty-Seven

Cam shoved her chair backward so fast it hit the wall behind her. Luis had just shot her mother! He'd shot Alana! The tiny handgun was still in his shaking hands. He'd shot Alana! Right through her photo album.

The next few seconds rolled by with unreal slowness. The astonished look of awareness in Alana's bright black eyes. The way her red-painted lips opened and closed like a fish's mouth. The way she gasped for air. The way her knees buckled before her long, skinny fingers clawed at the blankets as she slid to the floor. The bright red, bubbling blossom spreading over her blouse behind the album, spreading downward over her belly and skirt, her legs and—

"Mother!" bleated out of Cam's mouth as she ran to catch her mother in her arms as Alana folded limply to the floor. Then the word she'd rarely ever used, "Mama!"

The door burst open. Finally, Beckam was there. Two men in matching gray uniforms and pistols shoved him aside. "Put your hands up!" the one bellowed at Cam.

"Not her. He did it," Beckam declared as he swiftly disarmed Luis and handed the tiny snub-nosed weapon to one of the officers.

But it was too late.

"Mama," Cam cried again, clutching her mother to her chest, wishing she hadn't witnessed her father's most evil crime. Loving the woman who'd only ever hated her.

"Never... never you... you worthless piece of trash," Alana gasped, her bright eyes gone flat now, the color bleak, her light fading. "Acindinaaaa... was Carlos' baby. She was everything... But you..." She arched her back, writhed, and groaned. "You only ever belonged to—"

"Me," Luis murmured hoarsely from where he lay dying in his bed.

A dozen or so people scrambled into the tiny room then, filling it with crash carts and the urgent noise of first responders. Lifting the now lifeless Alana out of Cam's arms. More police. More nurses and doctors. Cam found herself pulled off the floor and locked inside Beckam's arms, standing over her father, Luis/Molina Lopez/Escobar. The man she never really knew.

"Papa, why?" eked out of her.

His chest expanded. He wheezed. At last he hissed, "Because she would've killed you, my little princess. Alana..." Deep, rasping breath. "Alana loved an American journalist. Carlos Salas..." Another gasping breath. "A reporter. He came to Honduras for a story, but instead, he stole my wife's heart. They fell in love. They made a baby. Acindina. A beautiful little girl, like you. She thought she could trick me. She lied and said the baby was mine, but I knew better. Look at me, my precious princess. Don't cry. Please. I did this for you. But do I have blue eyes?"

Cam cried anyway. "No, Papa. Yours are brown. Like mine."

"Si," he whispered sadly, his voice fading. "You are mine. Acindina was not. She had her father's pale blue eyes. The moment she was born, I knew. But I loved you both."

"Did you kill her?" Cam had to know.

"No, baby. I have done many wicked things in my lifetime, but I would never hurt another man's child. Him, I would kill, and Alana deserved to die. But a child? An infant? What harm could an innocent do to incur such evil retribution? No. It wasn't me. In the chaos of our escape from Honduras and the political purge that followed, your little sister slipped out of Alana's arms and fell overboard. That is how she drowned. But it was not your fault or mine. It was simply a tragic accident. Only Alana never forgave herself. She chose to blame me, and because she hated me, she blamed you, too."

The nurse intervened. "Please. You need to leave so I can help this man."

"No, you go. It's eternally too late to save me." Waving her away dismissively, Luis sucked in a quivering breath and continued. "Stay with me, my perfect princess. Please stay. You must believe me, Camilla. I tried to save Acindina that night. I was the only man there who jumped into the water to save my baby, and I did it the second she rolled over the edge. I dived until I thought my lungs would burst. But she was so tiny, and..." He choked. Coughed. Tears drenched the wrinkles in his face. "Poor little thing probably died the second she hit that filthy water. It was dark and cold. We were trying to get away undetected. In the end, the price we paid was dearer than we'd thought possible."

Cam took hold of her father's icy, wrinkled hand. "I believe you."

"The water was terribly polluted near all the docks, full of flotsam and diesel. A much larger boat sped by too quickly, and we rocked hard in its wake." He drew in another strained gasp, clinging to Cam's fingers. "It's yours, Chica. All of it is yours now. Everything I did, I did for you."

She nodded that she understood, though she knew she never would. "I love you, Papa," the lost little girl inside of her whispered.

"Ah, my princess," he wheezed as he closed his eyes. "Words I thought I'd never hear again. You have given me all I ever wanted, my littlest love. My heart. Ahh… Ahh…" His fingers tightened for a strong second, then relaxed. Then went limp. His chest stopped moving. A hundred alarms screamed and beeped, and an intense team of nurses and doctors squeezed Cam out of their way and took over.

But they were too late. Luis Lopez was gone.

Chapter Twenty-Eight

Beckam tugged Cam away from her father's bed. In doing so, she stumbled over her dead mother's foot and started to sob and—enough. He dipped down and lifted her into his arms and strode quickly out the door to get her away from the crime scene. Once in the hall, he called out, "I need a nurse!"

Cam whimpered like a child under his chin, her nose pressed into the hollow of his neck, her breath wet and warm and…

"Nurse! I need a nurse! Damnit!"

Who he got was Mark Houston, coming toward him in the hall at a dead run. The big guy skidded to a full stop. "Alex said to get to you fast. I was still in the ER. What's going on?"

"Luis Lopez just shot his wife," Beck said, nodding backward at the mayhem behind him. "We need a quiet room before the police show up. Please. Cam's had enough. She needs help."

"Was she shot? Is she hurt? Physically?"

Beckam shook his head, "I don't think so, but I'm not sure of anything right now."

Wasn't that the truth? The tiny woman in his arms clung to him like a child, but damn, did he know better. She was no little girl, but thank God, she was warm and alive, and every fiber in his being wanted to keep her that way. Damn Luis and Alana to hell. They deserved each other.

"Right this way," a stern, prim woman in a black business suit said as she gestured across the hall. "FBI Special Agent Holloway at your service, gentleman. Come with me. You can stay in this conference room as long as you need. I've been using it for my office while I investigated Mr. Escobar. Please. I'll track down a nurse for you."

"She killed him," Cam sobbed hoarsely, her chest heaving wretchedly as the FBI agent left. "Only she didn't and now he's killed her. I don't understand, Beckam. All my life is—fuck! It's all been one lie after another!"

"Shush," Beck whispered into her hair. He took over the first chair he came to, still pressing Cam into his body as he sat down and settled her on his lap. Still reassuring her in every way he could. "I'm here. You got me. We'll get through this. You just hold on as tight as you need to, honey, and let me take care of you. You're safe, Cam. I've got you."

"She killed my baby!" Cam cried as she collapsed into him. "Because her baby died, she killed mine! That's why she hated me. Just because I lived. I don't even remember that night. I was her baby, too!"

"Yes, you were. I know, I know." Beckam didn't understand such awful hate, either, but Cam needed comfort, and she was going to get it. She'd thumped her forehead into his chest, her hands full of his shirt like she needed to shake something—or rip him apart. And that was okay, too. He was a big guy; he could take it. He was there for her, ready to jump at her command, ready to die for her, too.

Meanwhile, Mark still stood in the hall, looking into the room, staring at Beck and Cam like a deer stared into the headlights of the MAC truck about to roll over it. Damn. Mark was smart, and right then, he was taking the scene in, dissecting and analyzing. Seeing the way Beck had taken over Cam. The way she'd melted into him. The fact that both his hands were on her, that he clearly had no intention of letting her go.

But instead of judging them like most people would, Mark's eyes were also warm and tender. Understanding. Palming his cell to his ear, he simply said, "I'm calling Doc Fitz. She'll know what to do."

Doc Fitz was Beau Villanueva's wife and Alex Stewart's physician on staff. If she wasn't at TEAM HQ handling agent physicals or routine exams, she'd be at her pediatric office treating infants and teaching new mothers.

Cam had curled into Beckam by then, her arms around his neck, her face pressed into his shirt. Breathing hard. Trying not to cry but failing. "I don't understand. All my life..." She sucked in a painful hiccup. "She's hated me all my life." Big wretched sob. "I was a baby. Only a year old. A baby!"

"I don't understand, either," he crooned as he tipped forward and leaned backward, needing to calm her however he could, but not knowing what that magical something was. His one resource, Mark Houston, both a husband and father of daughters, had just stepped into the hall and left him high and dry. But Beck would've settled for Alex right then. He'd know what to do, what to say. So Beckam told Cam what he knew. "I've seen you in action. You are not your father or your mother. You're so much better. So much smarter and kinder." *Unless you want to be like them. In that case, I'll shut up and start over.*

"I had a baby sister," she sobbed. "And my own baby. Now I have nothing."

"You have me," he murmured honestly, his bandaged hand at the back of her head to hold her steady while she cried. "I know I'm not much, just a bossy Agent-in-Charge. Just a Boy Scout, but—" *God, I think I'm falling for you.* Words he could not, should not, say. He swallowed hard to soften what he'd already told her. "Everyone on The TEAM is on your side, Cam. Every last one of us." There. That ought to do it. Bring the entire team into it, not make this just about him.

It almost worked—until she said in a very quiet, frightened voice, "I love you, too, Beck. You're my only friend."

Aw, damn… He couldn't say it, and he wasn't ready to admit the feeling rolling around inside his heart. Yet neither could he deny it. She needed something to believe in, so he simply kept silent and let her believe in him.

Mark pushed the door open then and strode briskly to where they were still sitting. "McKenna's on her way. We're lucky, guys. She was over at Medstar Georgetown." *Nice touch, calling Beckam and Cam guys.* "Now let me look at your throat, Camilla. You're bruised and it's hard to talk, isn't it?"

"Yes," she rasped, straightening to allow Mark's much bigger hands around her throat. "She… she strangled me."

Beckam growled, "Why didn't you tell me?"

Which was the wrong thing to say. Cam was already in tears. She didn't need more confrontation. "I… I…"

"Never mind, sweetheart. Forget it. I tend to ask stupid questions when I'm scared," he murmured, nuzzling the side of her head. "I was just worried for you. My bad."

She sagged back against him while Mark finished his cursory exam. "Can you breathe easily?" he asked. "Can you feel your trachea? Any sharp pains? Here…?" He pressed his fingers gently on her Adam's apple, then put the pads of his thumbs up under her chin. "Or here?"

"No. It's just really sore," Cam whispered. "Is anything broken?"

He shook his head. "I don't think so. Your trachea is made of cartilage, but let's let McKenna decide for sure."

"Okay," she murmured so softly Beckam had to strain to hear her. Which made him feel like an ass all over again.

"I'm so sorry," he told her sincerely.

"It's okay, Beck. I get scared, too."

"Why was McKenna at Medstar?" Beckam asked Mark. "Anyone we know over there?"

"Yes, Bruce. Kelsey convinced him to get help for his pneumonia. Last I heard, Dave and Harold are still at Raymond's Kids getting healthy."

"How about Joslyn? We find her yet?"

"Renner and Beau rounded her up, and she's downstairs with Georgia now." Mark grunted as he lifted to his feet. "Those two fuss at each other like a couple crabby old ladies."

"I like them," Cam whispered. "They're just like me."

Mark took a knee alongside Beckam again and gently tapped her forearm to get her attention. "How do you figure, Camilla? You're still young. You have your whole life ahead of you."

"Because no one wants them, either."

"Aww, damn, that's not true," Beckam said as he tightened his hold. "Not true at all."

"Don't lie. Just don't. Stop it." She pushed away from him, her voice growing squeakier with every word. "I don't need anyone. I never did, and now I know why."

"Too son of a bitchin' bad, *junior agent*!" Alex boomed from the doorway. "We're here and we're not leaving."

He stood there like a massive brick shithouse blocking the door. Alex had never looked so fierce nor so certain, dressed for war in his tactical vest and sidearms, scanning his agents with a dark once over, then a darker twice-over. And oh, damn. He'd seen everything.

But Beck didn't care. Not this time. He'd betrayed one desperate woman in his life, and once was one too many. That long-ago lesson with Mrs. Jones had stuck to him like white on rice. Let the world look all they wanted. Let the world know. Beckam protected the weak and the frightened, the abused and the lost. Didn't matter whose wife they were or what enemy he had to kill to keep them safe.

As if he'd caught Beckam's mental declaration, Alex changed back into a human being. Or maybe he changed because he'd just ushered Kelsey into the room alongside him. Either way, Beckam didn't care. He was here for Cam. Nobody else. Not even for his boss.

But talk about change in that cantankerous boss. Alex looked down at his pretty brunette wife as if she'd just descended straight from heaven. Beck knew it then. That was the kind of connection he wanted with Camilla. That devotion. That utterly sappy transition from badass to lover.

Kelsey waved across the room, her smile as kind and tender as Alex's face was grim. "Hey, you two. I've been so worried. Anything I can do?"

Beckam nodded at her, but said, "No, ma'am," with conviction. "Not for me." *But Cam could sure use a girlfriend.*

As if she'd read his mind, Kelsey stepped around her husband and came straightaway to where Beck and Cam were sitting. "Aw, sweetheart," she said as she dropped to her knees and reached for Cam. "I'm so sorry."

Cam did the unexpected again. Still wiping her face, she simply collapsed into Kelsey's arms. Then Beckam was holding two women while they cried together. Damn. This intervention was killing him.

By then, McKenna was there, too. Mark talked with her briefly before she knelt with Cam. Kelsey stepped back to Alex's side while McKenna checked Cam's throat, listened to her heart, and wiped the tears off her cheek. "You're going to be fine, Camilla," McKenna told her in no uncertain terms. "Your throat will be sore for a couple days. Warm drinks will help, but take a couple Tylenol if it gets too bad. Mark, could you please get Cam a glass of tepid water? I have some Tylenol with me. The sooner she takes them, the better she'll feel."

"You bet." Mark was back with that water within minutes.

The look on Cam's face was priceless. It was enough to tear a guy's heart out. She seemed so much like a lost little girl with those tears in her big, brown eyes and her lips pinched into a pout. She'd probably never had so many people fussing over her at the same time. Probably didn't know there were good people in the world who actually took care of each other. Even Mark was acting like a mother hen.

And damn, the entire TEAM was showing up, all of them squeezing into the room around Alex like they'd come for staff meeting. Big, bad Zack Lennox. Goofy Harley Mortimer, with a magnificent silver Malinois puppy straining against its sturdy leash. The Mahers, Connor and Izza. Rory Dennison. Which meant Ember was most likely on call at TEAM HQ. But Taylor Armstrong, Gabe Cartwright, and Maverick Carson, too?

Beckam couldn't believe this show of support. By heck, Adam Torrey was there, too. He stood out in the hall talking with Hunter Christian, while Lee Hart ducked inside with Eric Reynolds on his six. Talk about old home week.

Jake Weylin gave Cam a shy, "Hey there," while cocky Ky Winchester strode straight across the room, reached out and bumped knuckles with Beck. "How you doin', man?" he asked as he nodded to Cam.

"Doing good," Beck answered, very aware that Cam might have pushed out of his arms but she was still sitting on his lap. Old home week indeed.

Seth McCray bellowed a cheery, "Hoo-rah!" when he entered, just before Renner and Beau showed. Last but not least, Mark's blonde and beautiful wife, Dr. Libby Houston, walked briskly into the room like she owned the place, her long white lab coat swishing at her knees and a stethoscope hanging around her neck. "Hey, gang," she said cheerfully. "It's been a while since I've seen you. How was everyone's Christmas?"

While several TEAM agents filled her in on their time off, Alex asked Mark, "Where's everyone else?"

"They're on their way. Mei stopped for bagels, and Devereaux McCray's downstairs loading up at Starbucks' kiosk."

"Breakfast?" Cam murmured out of the corner of her mouth. She leaned back into Beck again. "Everyone's coming here for breakfast? W-why?"

"No big deal," Beck told her. "Standard TEAM protocol when an agent's down. We show up, that's all."

"But... but..."

"But nothing. The call went out that you were in trouble, so here they are. Look at these guys and gals, Cam. You're surrounded by some of the toughest USMC snipers, Navy SEALs, soldiers, sailors, and hardcore patriots in the world. In a few minutes, the wives will be here, and they're bringing food. You might not know these men and women, but not a one of them knows how to quit—on you or anyone."

"Which means you now have more firepower at your back than the president of the United States," Alex declared with authority. "You got a problem with that?" Badassed to the core, he seemed to understand exactly how to reach Cam. Head on. In her face. Daring her to fight back.

"No, I... I just..." She bowed her head onto Kelsey's shoulder.

That earned him a warning look from his wife. Damned if Alex didn't back right down. "Good job, Cam," he said. "You and Beck make a good team. I'm proud of you."

That made her cry harder. Which must've tugged Harley's heartstrings, too.

"Hey, there," he said softly as he took a knee beside Kelsey. "I, umm, brought you something, Camilla." He took extra care pronouncing her name correctly, while holding out the leash to his handsome, bouncing puppy. "Brought a little buddy of mine to meet you. This here's Sonic. She's a female Malinois. Thought you might need a furry friend because, you know. Dogs might not be diamonds, but I know they are women's best friends."

"A dog?" she asked, her back stiff and her body rigid. "How's a dog going to fit in our tent?"

When Kelsey lifted to her feet and stepped back, a warm glow scorched Beck's cheeks. That *our tent* comment was revealing and embarrassing, but it also felt right. Made him feel like he'd finally found where he belonged in the world.

"Oh, no. Sonic's not a working dog, not yet anyway. This here rascal flunked K9 training. She's just not mean enough.

So I thought maybe… I mean, I was hoping…" Harley rolled one shoulder and cleared his throat. "Sonic needs a good home. A special home. You see, she's also deaf in one ear, and I was hoping you might, umm, adopt her?" He made that a question. "You know, to protect your family, umm, if you got one. I'm sure she'll do that, but if you'd rather not…"

Beck was embarrassed for Harley. He was trying so hard to make friends with Cam. Contrite and humble, he always gave back more than most folks coming back from war ever did, or ever would. From his steady volunteer work on the streets with the homeless, to his regular visits to the local veterans' homes and hospitals, to the top-notch German Shepherds and Malinois he trained for the local police, Harley's life was all about service. Even now, he was reaching out to the woman who'd disparaged and humiliated him daily in the office. Yet here he was, leading with his chin again. Still trying to make friends, and offering up one of his pedigreed pups to do it.

"A puppy? For m-m-me?" Cam stuttered. "You're giving me one of your dogs. Just for me?"

Beckam wanted to cry at the ragged disbelief in her voice. Hadn't anyone ever given this woman a gift without expecting something in return?

"Well, shucks, yes, darlin', err, I mean, ma'am, err, Camilla." He carefully enunciated that name again. "Sonic's yours if you promise to love her and take good care of her." His head bobbed, his unruly hair bouncing into his warm hazel eyes. He offered the leash again. "If you want her. Every dog needs someone to love. That's how God made 'em. They never give up on us."

"God? Well, err…" Tentatively, Cam took hold of the looped end of the leather leash. "But I have a cat."

"Good. Sonic likes cats. We got tons of them in our barn. She likes little kids, too, but mostly she likes—"

The crazy puppy jumped up onto Cam's lap, and who could resist? Not even Cam. Beck leaned back to make more room for the pup.

"I don't know what to say, but… th-thank you, Agent Mortimer," she said, snuggling the fur baby in her arms. "Umm, thank you very much."

Harley's grin could've split his face. "'S okay, darlin'," he said earnestly this time, the bright light in his hazel eyes enough to make a grown man bawl. "I was gonna say Sonic likes hugs, but looks like you figured that out. She flunked aggression, but she's a natural comfort dog. And you're holding her just right. Heck, if I'd known you just needed someone to love, I'd a brought this baby into the office a whole lot sooner."

If Harley only knew what he'd done by filling Cam's arms. Tears sprang to Beck's eyes for the infant she'd lost. Which explained why he'd sensed that she'd make a good mom. Because she already was. Any woman who missed her unborn child as deeply as Cam did, was made for motherhood. Even if she didn't know it.

"You can change her name if you want," Harley said, still so damned humble it hurt to look at him. "Later, when you're home, and if you don't mind, I'll bring her AKC paperwork by. I'll show you how to register her, and you can change her name then. I'll bring her food and toys, too. Her crate. Course you're gonna need a bigger crate real soon. Her mama's Kingston's Gold, one of the country's best police K9s. We call her Goldie, but she's a big female. You, umm, are always welcome to come see her. I mean, if you want to."

"I love Sonic already," Cam said quietly. "A lot. Thanks, Harley. Yes, I'd love to meet her mama, only…" She cleared her throat. "I don't why you're all here." Her voice turned squeakier and squeakier. "I mean, I've been kind of, umm, harsh, and—"

"Kind of?" Zack, God bless him, choked. Loudly. Mocking her like only a burly big brother would. Teasing her before she dissolved into tears.

Everyone else held their breaths. But then Camilla admitted, "Okay, yes, Agent Lennox, I deserved that, but… Please." Her voice cracked. "Just… please…"

"Be nice," Zack finished for her. "The rest of you guys be nice. Isn't that what you're trying to say, Junior Agent?"

All she could do was nod.

Chapter Twenty-Nine

The impromptu TEAM meeting astounded Cam. Everyone was so kind, and she didn't understand why. She'd treated most of these people badly. Even Alex and his wife. Yet no one here seemed worried or mad about that, not even Kelsey. Or Zack, who suddenly wasn't cold to her anymore. No one seemed to hold a grudge, either. That alone was interesting. When the rest of the wives showed up, they'd brought not only large bags of bagels and a dozen thermoses of coffee, but enough breakfast sandwiches and burritos to feed a small third world country. The men all dug in, and damn, they could eat. The food went as quickly as the coffee.

All the while, friendly conversation flowed. Husbands gravitated toward their wives. Wives to their husbands, either sitting at the conference table or taking up the chairs circling the room. FBI Agent Holloway had returned long enough to gather her briefcase, then politely left. Harley had taken Sonic back to his house.

By then, Cam had distanced herself from Beckam. Not that he'd asked her to, but because she didn't want to make things any uglier for him once they were back in the office. She knew how people talked, and everyone had seen.

He and Agent Flanagan were the only two bachelors in the room, but her sitting on Beck's lap when most of the agents arrived, made it look like they'd hooked up during their one-night operation. Which they hadn't. To make things crystal clear, she took a chair at the opposite end of the long conference room table, far away from Beck. If only her eyes would stop searching for him.

He'd taken up post alongside Alex, Mark, Renner, and Beau, all standing at the door, discussing what had happened the night before. Man, it seemed like a week ago instead of just last night that those teenagers had ambushed Beck. Yet he stood there like nothing happened. Like he didn't have major bruises on certain parts of his body. His very muscular, sturdy, handsome body.

She sipped her coffee, imagining things she had no right to think about. How his mouth tasted when he'd kissed her this morning in the station. It had felt so right, like two lovers crashing together after a miserably long absence. Beckam's large, capable hands had all but covered her ass when he'd manhandled her like he had. She liked the firestorm he'd ignited in her body. Butterflies still fluttered down low in her stomach just thinking how his one-day growth had scraped and tantalized the sensitive skin on her chin and mouth. Her lips. Beck was no little boy. He'd known precisely how to hold her. She wanted more of the smell of him, of wind and soap and worry and...

"May I sit here?" Doctor Fitz asked even as she dropped into the chair beside Cam.

Ordinarily rude on first contact, Cam bit the sarcasm ready to drip off her tongue. "Sure. Help yourself."

Doc Fitz was one of those intuitive women who read people's minds like most people read books. Not only was she smart, she was also married to someone Cam actually liked. Beau Villanueva. His attack-first, apologize-later work ethic matched hers to a T. If that wasn't enough, there was something vaguely familiar about the gruff, grumbly man, in a déjà vu sort of way that Cam couldn't put her finger on. It was as if he'd walked the same hard road she had once upon a time. Which just wasn't possible. No one could've had a harder childhood than hers.

"It must be difficult, sitting across the hall from where your parents just passed away," McKenna said kindly.

Well, yeah. Cam swallowed hard. Only they hadn't *just* passed away. Like two wolverines locked in a death match, they'd killed each other. This whole day had been one fuckin' hard day, err, damn hard day. Was damn a curse word? Probably not. Beck used it.

Her lying eyes automatically scanned the room for him, as if he would've caught that mental slip of her tongue. She'd promised him that she'd stop cursing, only she hadn't, had she? When life fell apart, she fell with it, sinking back into her mean, old self. Only now, things were different. She didn't want to be like her parents or Heath or his parents, either. For the first time in her life, Cam wanted a fresh start. She wanted to be like Beck or maybe Beau. Maybe even like sweet, gentle Kelsey or even McKenna.

Beck thought Cam wasn't anything like her parents. He thought she was better, smarter and kinder. She desperately wanted to believe him. He'd been right about everything else on this stupid, waste-of-time operation. He had to be right about that too, didn't he?

Oh, God, yes. Only, there was the irony. Cam didn't believe in God, yet she'd always cussed His name as if He were real. She didn't need an almighty Anyone watching over her, but she knew Beck believed. Jesus, was he right about that, too? Christ, she couldn't seem to curse without bringing God into it. Shit!

Dropping her gaze to the paper cup in her hand, the one her fingers were squeezing to death, she whispered, "It is hard. Only…" She drew in a deep breath, needing someone besides Beck to know just how miserable her life had been. Might as well be McKenna. Everyone seemed to trust her. "I never really knew them. My parents, I mean. Not sure I want to now."

McKenna nodded like she understood. But she couldn't, and this was the stupidest conversation Cam had ever had. Confiding in a stranger like they were BFFs. Really? Talk about dumb. She drained that coffee cup and—

"A few of us come from messed-up families," McKenna said before Cam could push away from the table and run. "Take my handsome husband for instance."

Say what? Cam's gaze scrolled back to the huddled mass of Chippendale-worthy men still in conference with Alex on the other side of the room. Alex himself was buff in a tall, trim, take charge kind of way. With his number one alpha personality, he totally dominated any room he entered like no one Cam had ever met before.

On the other side of all that outrageous testosterone, Renner stood at Alex's right, quietly nodding in agreement. Wiry and hard muscled, Renner was the kind of guy who always led with a smile, as if he enjoyed life in general. But Cam had learned early not to mistake that congeniality for weakness. It was Renner who'd ended the notorious serial killer from Cuba, that psycho, Catalina Montego. In the process, he'd rescued not only his sweet wife, Tara, from Montego's clutches, but a handful of the young military men Montego had tortured. Renner might look sweet and cuddly from a distance, but up close, he was every bit as lethal as any one of these guys.

Beau and Beckam were built much the same as each other. Broad shouldered. Tall. Ruggedly masculine. Thick-chested and thick-necked. Well-muscled with deeply veined arms and hands. Like they'd lifted weights all their lives. But while Beau carried himself like he had a chip on his shoulder and wanted to knock someone down and out just because they were breathing, Beck stood relaxed and casual. He'd leaned his butt to the edge of the table, had one ankle cocked, and his arms were loose at his sides as if everything in life came easy to him. As if he knew, deep inside, he could handle anything the world threw at him. Even her.

"You like Beckam," McKenna breathed, her head down but smiling as if they were two girlfriends telling secrets. "Am I reading you right?" She crooked her index finger from Beckam back to Cam. "You and Beck…"

Cam dropped her head, embarrassed she'd been caught eying Beau, as well as Beckam. "He's…" She swallowed hard. "Beck, I mean. He's been nice, umm, easy to work with."

"Nice, huh?" McKenna bumped shoulders into Cam. "I see how he keeps glancing over here at you. I think he's a lot more than nice. I think he's interested."

"No, he's not. He's just my Agent-in-Charge, and, you know. He had to tell me this morning that my mother tried to kill my father." *A bunch of other ugly stuff.*

McKenna persisted. "Hey, girlfriend. You can trust me. I know how to keep a secret. And you're right. Beck is nice, but so are the rest of these guys and gals. If you ever need to talk, feel free to reach out to me. I know what it's like to have a crazy mother, and Beau…" She pointed her chin at her husband's muscled back. "That man had the childhood from hell, but look how good he turned out."

"Excuse me, he what?" *Hell, err, heck.* Cam didn't know that story, mostly because she didn't know any of her fellow agents' stories, except a smidgen of Beck's. And that made her precisely like her parents: thoughtless, unfeeling, uncaring, and just plain mean. "Why do you say that?"

"Because…" McKenna drew in a deep breath and whispered. "Poor kid was abducted as a baby. His family was traveling through Nevada on their way to Washington state to pick apples when they pulled into a rest stop. Beau was asleep. One of his brothers was left behind to watch him. That was when a drug dealer reached in through the open window and stole Beau to make his crazy, heroin-addicted wife happy. Guess they wanted a cute little Hispanic baby to slap around. His brother ended up traumatized, but poor Beau…" McKenna lowered her voice even more. "He went from being the happy, adored baby boy of two loving parents to the punching bag of a drunken bastard. Honest, Camilla. Beau came from one of the most abusive situations I've ever seen. And I'm a pediatrician. I've seen enough."

"He did?" Cam couldn't believe her ears. Beau seemed so solid and sure of himself. So manly. Okay, so he also could be one mean son of a b-b-b—gun. He'd certainly scared those two teenaged thugs last night. But kidnapped as a baby? How awful.

"Yes. Poor kid grew up feeling like he didn't belong to that messed-up Jennings family. Problem was he had no idea where he did belong. He lost his little sister, too. Just like you. Not like they were biologically-related. They weren't, but he didn't know that then. He was a little boy and he loved AJ just the same." McKenna hmphed. "Almond Joy. Those two lowlifes named her after a candy bar. Is that messed up or what? But he called her AJ, and he loved her like any good, big brother would."

Cam hated to ask. "What... what happened to her?"

McKenna's lips pinched into at a hard, thin line, her pretty blonde hair shielding her face from most everyone else in the room. "Poor little tyke died. Not sure precisely what happened, but somehow, someone mixed heroin in her formula. Killed her, then blamed it on Beau. He's still got scars from what Jennings did to him that night. You know, I used to be quite the pacifist. I never believed in violence, but if I could, I'd kill that rat bastard Bass Jennings with my bare hands for what he did to that sweet little boy over there. I would. I swear to God I would."

That sweet little boy must've sensed his wife's passionate love for him. Beau scanned over one hard, muscled shoulder for her. Frowned. *And look out trouble.* Beau turned his back on his boss right then and there and marched toward Cam like a pissed off, heat-seeking missile.

"What'd you say to my wife?" he asked her, his brows arrowed at the ceiling and his brown eyes gone black as sin.

"Me?" Cam asked. "Nothing. I—"

"She didn't do anything, honey. I can take care of myself, remember? Be nice," McKenna replied sweetly, tossing her head while she wiped a tear off her cheek. "I was just telling Camilla she and you have a lot in common. That's all."

"We do not," he bit out, casting another evil if-looks-could-kill glare at Cam.

Which she deserved. She blinked and looked down, not ready to admit that he might have her beat in the abused child department. At least she'd had the comfort of believing that her father had once loved her, but she wasn't ready to admit it. Not today. Not to a wife and husband who obviously adored each other and had each other's back.

Hell—um, heck. All these men and women had someone to go home to.

"Yes, you do, honey," McKenna insisted. "Come sit with us awhile."

Beau swung a chair around and straddled it, hugging the chair back. "Like what?"

"What do you think?" McKenna asked softly. "If anyone has a right to be angry—"

Oh, great. Just what Cam didn't need, personal time with Beau and his loving wife. McKenna might mean well, but Cam couldn't take anymore. Okay, so Beau's little sister died. That did not make him her friend. He'd made it clear that he had no use for her. Anyone could see that.

"I have to go." She jumped to her feet, instantly dizzy that she'd stood up too fast.

She would've run for the door, but Beckam was all of a sudden beside her. "Got a minute?" he asked while his fingers shackled her wrist and held her steady.

"Yes," she all but shrieked at him. Anything to get away from more sharing. The mess called her life would be all over the news by this evening. Beau could wait and hear about it then, like everyone else.

A shadow shifted through Beckam's dark blues. "Are you okay?"

Her heart ached to tell him how miserable she felt, but she bit out, "Why wouldn't I be?"

He nodded like he understood what she really meant, but how could he? Had his parents killed each other? Hell, no. God, she needed out of this chummy, stupid group called The TEAM.

"There's someone here to see you."

"Jesus Christ, what now?" she muttered, sick to death of her life.

"Not sure, but this guy says he knows you."

Cam let Beckam usher her across the room to the huddle near the door. Alex, Mark, and Renner looked up at her, all of them serious as the tall, dark stranger talking with them came into view. Expensive business suit. Perfectly combed, shiny black hair. Seriously handsome. The world seemed to tip on its axis. It couldn't be.

"Hector?" She would've collapsed from the shock of seeing him again, but Hector pushed Renner aside in his haste to get to her. And suddenly, she was in her childhood boyfriend's arms and sobbing like a baby. Not because she'd missed him after all these years or that she still loved him, but because this day had been too fuckin' much! Too weird! Every last one of her sins had come back on her all at one goddamned time. And here stood the father of the baby she'd killed. How much more could she stand?

"What are you… doing here?" she asked between sobs.

He seemed earnestly worried, stroking her head as he held her cheek tight against his chest. "Your mother told me you might be here."

"But Alana's dead," she explained as she dragged his fingers out of her hair. God, that was annoying, being petted like a dog. And he was smothering her. Fuck. He needed to back off. "When did you talk to her?" *How could you? Why didn't you call me?*

"The nurse in the hall told me what happened to your mom and dad. I'm so sorry. I know you were close to them."

Mom and Dad? Close to them? Me? What the hell was he thinking? Needing to see Hector better, she pushed out of his arms. He was still as handsome as ever. Only taller. Older. Suave instead of bumbling. More mature—or something. Yet he made Alana and Luis sound like loving parents, when he knew damned well they'd been anything but.

Hector kept explaining. "Alana called me earlier today. I was just going out the door to my meetings, but she wanted me to know you'd finally divorced your husband. That he'd been a pig to you."

"Just to be clear, I divorced Heath Brinkman a year ago, Hector. But Alana just called you with that news now? Today?" *Un-fuckin'-believable.*

His head bobbed. "Yes. It's true. She thought you'd also come to the hospital to visit your father one last time. That this might be my only chance to see you. That I needed to hurry before it was too late."

"Well, of course she'd think that. She's the witch who shot him!" Cam filled in the little detail Alana had obviously left out.

"Yes, yes, I know." Hector's head of tight shiny locks bobbed. "She'd just been released on bail. She said she needed to make amends. With you."

"I doubt that. But, but how?" Cam asked, the world still reeling, and her once dull, boring life now as unstable as a shifting ice floe in an arctic storm. "How did you get here so quickly?" Simple. He couldn't have. Not all the way from

Mexico. "You were already here, weren't you? You were in DC?" *Since when? How long have you been here?*

Hector nodded, his dark eyes soft and warm. He looked so much like the boy she remembered, and yet—he didn't. Guarded reservation glimmered in those beguiling eyes. "Yes, I'm only here two more days on business, but I can stay. I *will stay* for as long as you need me. Please. Let me take you home. There is so much we need to talk about."

What he meant was 'Where's my child?' Her heart sank like a rock in concrete, stuck forever for all to see. She'd have to tell him the truth, but she meant to do it privately. Away from all these kind, prying faces. It was time to leave. No one here needed to hear her final horrid secret.

"Yes, home," Cam said quietly. "Take me home, Hector. We'll talk there. Mr. Stewart? This is my, umm, friend, Hector Rojas. Hector, my boss, Alex Stewart."

Of course her boss and the rest of the guys had overheard every word, even poor Beckam. Cam couldn't bear to look at him.

Alex crossed his arms over his chest and nodded solemnly, his icy blue eyes extra-tender today. "Understood. Take the rest of the week, Camilla. Rest. Get your head back in the game. Stay in touch."

"I will," she promised. And for once, Cam meant it.

Chapter Thirty

Well, damn. All Beckam could do was watch Cam walk out of his life holding hands with her teenage lover, Hector Rojas. The jerk who hadn't cared enough the past four years to contact the young woman he'd gotten pregnant. The toad who'd let his mother run his life and whisk him off to Mexico instead of manning up and handling his parental responsibilities. The tall, dark jerk who was also James Bond handsome with the same debonair, *je ne sais quoi* of an over-confident, wealthy, entitled male. Man, he was good. But Beck had been around enough to see through that handsome, devil-may-care disguise. Rojas was also a player. Not just any player. A professional, hired-gun type of player.

He'd just palmed the conference room door opened like a polite gentleman. Cam and he were on their way out as a couple, and Beck had to admit, they looked good together. Both olive-skinned with big, dark eyes and gorgeous. They were a matched set, him with his slender but well-toned build; her with all that shiny, dark hair tumbling down her back. Like matching bookends, they looked like they belonged with each other. They certainly had a history together. He might have been wrong about Rojas.

Only Cam wasn't smiling. She'd said all the right things when he'd first grabbed hold of her. Heck, she'd even asked

Alex for permission to leave, a definite first. But something wasn't right, and Beckam wanted to know what.

But by then, Hector had a firm hand under her hair, his fingers flexed and wrapped around the back of her neck as if he was afraid she might get away. Beckam recognized that for what it was, an openly possessive alpha male signal for other males to back off. That Hector considered Cam his. Which made sense in an immature, juvenile way. They had been intimate once upon a time. Despite the years between then and now, this could be a happy reunion in the making if Cam worked it right. Their reconnecting might be precisely what she needed to salvage what was left of her life.

It certainly cleared the way for Beckam to get back to work and hunt down the latest DC killer. But why were the tiny hairs on the back of his neck standing on end? And his gut hadn't stopped screaming that something was off about Hector's timing. Why, out of the blue, had this audacious male suddenly strutted in to claim the woman he'd deserted years ago? Why today? Why not years ago when she'd needed him most? And why was she going with him like a lamb to the slaughter?

"Cam," Beckam called out at the last possible second.

She looked over her shoulder, her sad eyes glimmering and her long hair loose on her shoulders. "Yes, Agent Garner?"

Agent Garner. Not Beck. Damn. Things were worse than he thought. Compound that official greeting with her not introducing him to Rojas in the first place, and Beck's heart sank. His sense of loss made no sense since he knew damned well she was too young for him. If anyone, Rojas had more right to her. They were the same age.

"Did you need anything?" she asked, timid and so un-Camilla-like that it hurt Beck's heart.

Was there hope in her tone? There certainly wasn't any snark. Not after the godawful comeuppance this day had dealt her. Anyone who'd disliked Camilla Brinkman enough to wish harm upon her, had certainly had their wish granted today. She'd not only been thoroughly cowed and publicly humiliated, but outright destroyed. Damn, Karma was a bitch.

Beck crossed the distance between them, remembering how small Cam had felt in his arms just this morning. How delicate. How precious and warm and—hungry for affection. Make that starved. She'd been so happy at the train station that she'd run into his arms and kissed the hell out of him. She'd been so much like a little girl, all trusting and loving and ready to give herself away.

Why was there no enthusiasm for this meeting with Rojas? Why no tender, I'm-so-glad-to-see-you-again kiss? Not even a hug? *Because she still has to tell him about the abortion...* Again, that made sense, but Beckam couldn't help himself. He reached for Cam's hand, needing her to give him some sign that she knew what she was doing.

"Give us a minute?" he asked Hector.

"I don't think so." Rojas shook his head and pulled her out of Beck's reach. The guy had his nerve. "You've done enough. Look at her. She's sick with grief. I'm taking her home."

"Then why didn't you ever call her if you were so worried?" Beck asked.

A sad, half smile curled Cam's pretty mouth. "It's okay," she murmured. "I'll be okay. Just... go find that murderer before he hurts someone else we love."

Beckam nodded, his heart in his throat. Nothing about this goodbye felt real or good. "Are you sure?"

She nodded. "I have to go. Talk to you later."

Somehow, he doubted that. But what could he do? Call Rojas a liar when Cam seemed willing and ready to leave with him. Demand that Cam stay just because his gut wouldn't shut up? "Yeah, later," Beck mumbled, his gut working at that ulcer. "Let me know if you need anything."

There went her sad smile again and she was gone. It was Kelsey standing at his elbow when he finally tore his eyes off the closed door. "She's in trouble. You feel it too, don't you?"

Beckam didn't know how he felt. But something was definitely wrong with Rojas's unexpected showing. Only with Cam's array of masks, it was hard to distinguish dismay from relief. Or how to save her from herself. "It's been a tough day," he admitted, then coughed to clear his overly dry throat. "But I've got work to do. It'd be good if we could catch this killer before she gets back."

"She likes you," Kelsey murmured. "I can't believe she left like that."

Neither can I. "She's a fighter," Beckam said a little louder than he meant to. "She'll be okay."

"She's probably kicking that kid's ass right now," Izza Maher declared just as loudly.

"Or telling him to F-off," Zack replied, though even he sounded as unsure as Beckam.

"Son of a bitch," Alex spat, his index finger at his earpiece. "Mayor's office is on the line. We've got another dead transient."

"Where?" several agents asked at once.

Steely blue eyes zeroed in on Beckam. "Union Station. Get back to work. Let's find this bastard. Today, damn it."

"Copy that," came from the entire room.

Beckam needed to know. "Who is it?"

Alex stared him down. "Your buddy, Dave."

A collective sigh lifted from the agents. Everyone knew Dave. Kind-hearted to a fault. Boisterous. Down on his luck. Damn. Poor Dave.

"Shit," Zack growled. "Thought he was staying with Harold at Raymond's Kids?"

"He was there when I left," Kelsey replied, her voice breaking.

"Well, he's on his way to the city morgue now," Alex said gently. "I'm sorry, sweetheart, but we need to go. Gear up, TEAM. We're Oscar Mike until this bastard's dead or behind bars."

"Copy that," Beckam promised. Oscar Mike, grunt speak for 'we're on the move', which fit Beckam's plan perfectly. With Cam, hopefully on her way to happily-ever-after, he needed the twenty-four-seven diversion of hunting this murderer down and ending his killing spree.

He bee-lined for Mark. "Where'd you park? I need my gear."

Mark nodded toward the door. "Right this way."

Chapter Thirty-One

Cam sat silent while Hector adeptly maneuvered his Lincoln Town car through the busy District lunchtime traffic. For a man supposedly from Mexico, he certainly drove an expensive vehicle. Gunmetal gray and polished as if it had just been washed and waxed, this car boasted a heads-up display, and the same blind-spot detection and cross-traffic alert system Heath's pricey ride had.

Just like Heath, Hector knew his way around the District, not like he had far to go to get from Sibley to her house. As if he'd driven it before, Hector turned south on MacArthur Boulevard NW and then drove straight to Malcomb Street NW. Then right onto Malcomb toward Potomac Avenue NW, all without following a GPS or asking directions. Wasn't that interesting?

Cam starred off to her right where Canal Road ran parallel to Potomac Avenue NW. That road, and the green space between it and the Potomac River, offered a calming interlude that kept boaters from annoying the elite well-to-doers sequestered in their high and lofty mansions where people like Alana lived. She'd never liked living so close to the nation's capital. She'd always whined to return to New York City. Said life here was too centered around politics and drama. Like NYC wasn't?

Yet here in the land of Alphabet Soup, Cam had finally found herself, first working with FWS, doing a job she'd truly loved. Then during that two-hour stint with the FBI. True, Director Tucker Chase had only lured her into DC's pretentious FBI Headquarters to fire her before he'd hired her. But even that was directly because of her failing. Just hers.

She'd pissed him off, and she'd known it while she was doing it. But, by hell, it was her mistake. No one else's. She owned it, and while it was nothing to be proud of, in a way, Cam was. For once, she'd accepted responsibility for her actions. In a harsh way, she'd learned a useful lesson from that fatal mistake. *Don't bite the hand that feeds you.*

That's what Chase had been trying to tell her the day he'd thrown her at Alex Stewart. Working with Beckam Garner had further emphasized Chase's crude attempt at coaching. What had Beck said? *'You don't get to verbally abuse me just because you can't restrain yourself. Your rights end where mine begin, and I have the right not to be badgered or bullied by another person, including you. Understand that and we'll get along fine.'*

How right he'd been. At the end of her first horrendous day working an active operation, she'd finally been traumatized enough to listen. And seeing Max die like he did changed Cam in ways she couldn't explain. The battle between right and wrong was real. There were no special cases, no spoiled brats at the end of the day. Life was hard, and if you thought yourself above the law, it was harder. You truly did reap what you sowed. And possibly... maybe... there really was a God. That's the only thing that explained those internal feelings of loss at Max's death. Besides, Beckam believed in God. He'd been right about everything so far. What would it hurt to explore the possibility?

Down in her heart, Cam had always known there was something intrinsically wrong with her family. No house should hold as much venom as did the empty house of Molina and Alana. Could it be that all who'd lived there were morally bankrupt, godless liars?

Yes.

Thoughtfully, Cam cast a sideways glance out the driver side window past Hector, to the stone façade of a home of the family who'd never loved her. That was the lesson today. They'd never had any real love for her, only the need to use her. As sad as that was, knowing she was not like them was also a solid point in her favor. A relief. They'd made their mistakes. Now, she would make hers. In the end, she would also learn something. With every mistake made from now on, she'd grow as a person, and maybe someday, good people like Beck could forgive her.

Hector gripped the steering wheel with long slender fingers, turning his car as he coasted into her driveway. Everything about him seemed too good to be true. His trimmed hair, still lush. Dark, and long enough she wanted to run her fingers through it. His elegant, expensive looking business suit. Beautifully polished leather shoes. Crisp white dress shirt. Even the scent of bergamot wafting off him. There was no doubt about it, he was polished this time around, no longer a fumbling teenage boy with acne. No longer shy, either. That was what had attracted her to him in the beginning, his quiet, timid way of pleasing her. Of showing up at the gate of Morning Glory Estate and asking the guard if he could please see Cam.

But that was a long, sad time ago.

Wasn't it ironic? She finally made her own money, and despite her propensity to sabotage herself, she had owned her own home for over nine months now. Nine months. The same number of months it took to have a baby. But Cam? She'd soon have an eviction notice for her effort. Might have to join up with Joslyn and Georgia on the streets of DC.

Hmmm. I wonder if my cat would mind living out of a bag? That might work…

Turning his broad shoulders to Cam, Hector killed the ignition and said, "We're home."

"I'm home, you mean," she corrected him, cocking her neck, somehow irritated with his false assumption that this was his home, too.

Something like a smirk quirked his mouth. "Whatever. Let's get you inside."

"Let's," she muttered, trying to keep her sarcasm at bay. But really. Who did he think he was with that cozy 'let's' comment? Her keeper?

Cam opened her door and had both feet on the ground before he made it around the car. Without waiting, she headed for her house and pressed her thumb to the biometric keypad to open the front door. Silence greeted her instead of her cat, but he might be sleeping, the lazy boy.

"Hector," she called out. "I'm home."

The other Hector now in her life closed the door behind him. "No need to yell. I'm right behind you."

"Not you. I'm talking to my cat. His name's Hector, and he's the only one who lives here with me. You're just visiting." Might as well get that straight from the start. Hector the cat lived here. Other Hector did not and never would. There was something different about him. He needed to leave.

He made a funny sound deep in his throat. "You named your cat after me?"

"I did," she replied as she breezed into her kitchen, glanced at the still filled cat food and water dishes, then continued through her dining room into the lavish family room where she spent most of her alone time with her cat. There he was! Her good boy had curled up in the corner of their often-shared sofa. His big gold eyes were instantly wary as he arched his back and stretched out a rumbling, "Meow."

"There's my baby," she crooned as she folded herself around him, lifting him into her arms and onto her lap.

Other Hector took the leather chair opposite the sofa. Heath's chair. The one Cam never sat in and intended to dispose of as soon as possible. He sat looking at her with his elbows on his knees, and his stern dark eyes taking everything in. Trim and lean, he looked like the perfect businessman. Not ruffled at all. More calculating. Sizing her up.

"Why are you here?" she asked.

He turned away from her, looking down the short hallway to her office and bedroom. "Alana said you had something for me. Where's your computer. You do have one, don't you?"

Not what Cam expected. "Alana was wrong. I have nothing to my name except for what you see, and I don't own a home computer. You'll have to be more specific. Precisely what did Alana say I was supposed to give you?" *And why didn't you ask about our baby?* Not that Cam intended to bring up the child she'd lost. He'd have to prove he cared about that baby before she would discuss a hurt so deep. He'd have to explain why he'd left her without a word and why he'd suddenly returned.

His brows narrowed. "Interesting. Maybe Alana didn't have time to tell you."

"What? Before she shot my father?" Oh, that was rich. Alana stopping by to chat. Fat chance. "She lived three doors down, but we never talked. Now what do you want, Hector? This house? Something in it? You can have it. All of it. Take it. I'm about to lose it anyway."

He shook his head, still not making eye contact. Still parsing her home as if looking for something. "Do you mind?" he asked, unfolding those long legs. Other Hector lifted to his feet and walked toward her. "I'm afraid I'm allergic," he said softly as he lifted Hector out of her hands.

"What do you think you're doing?" she protested, jumping to her feet. "If you're so allergic, why are you holding him? Give him back."

Other Hector blessed her with the same patient smile he'd used on her in the hospital, as if he were dealing with a child. Damn him. He headed for the front door with her poor cat swinging like a ragdoll in his hand, and he—tossed her cat outside.

"No!" she yelled. "He'll run away! You shouldn't have done that. He's mine!"

Hector whirled around, his soft eyes gone hard as flint, his jaw set in concrete. "No more games, Camilla. Tell me where your goddamned computer is!"

Chapter Thirty-Two

Mark let Beckam out of his SUV at Union Station. At the end of the block, construction workers were busy jackhammering the concrete street, kicking up a fine dust in the chilly evening air. Blocking traffic. Making too damned much noise. It'd been a hard day, and just like yesterday morning when Max was killed, rush hour traffic clogged the thoroughfare. Impatient drivers laid on their horns as if making more noise in any way helped the situation. The eerie similarity of yesterday morning with this evening's circumstances disquieted every last one of Beckam's ragged nerves. Cam's absence didn't help. She should be here, finishing what they'd started together. Doing her job. But she wasn't, and Beck couldn't get past the premonition creeping in his bones. Something was very wrong with the way this day was ending.

Instead of jogging over to the station for a late-night meal like he should have, Beck opted for circling the area to clear his head. Eating alone was a downer, especially after breakfast this morning with his three favorite ladies. But mostly, he missed Cam. She'd been a surprise. Without her, the day was just another day. Dinner could wait.

He crossed Columbus Circle, dodging traffic, not like that was hard to do in what had become a veritable parking lot. Rounding the station, he left the noise behind and focused on his job. First Max. Now Dave. Two deaths and both in the same area. Both on Beckam's beat. Both on his time. The odd coincidence clawed at him.

With the added drama of Cam's personal problems today, all TEAM agents had been pulled off task. Ember still hadn't had time to draw any conclusions or investigate what any of these victims had in common, other than their service time under Captain Seymore Gharst from Missouri. Which gave Beck an idea.

Palming his cell, he rang TEAM HQ instead of using his earpiece, hoping for Ember, but willing to talk with whomever answered.

"You've reached TEAM Headquarters in Alexandria, Virginia. How may I direct your call?"

Thank goodness. Ember! "Hey, it's me, Beck. Got a question. Did Gharst have any family? Any sons?" It'd take a strong man to kill these victims the way they'd been murdered. If Gharst left a son, could that younger man be carrying a vendetta against the men who served with his father?

"No, Beckam, I already checked Gharst. He has one daughter living in Hawaii with her husband and Gharst's six granddaughters. Sorry, no sons or grandsons. Anything else?"

He shook his head, sick at what this day had done to Cam. "No, just can't get my brain to stop working this puzzle."

"Mark already has me researching links between the victims. If I find anything new, I'll let you know."

He liked working with Ember. "Thanks. Have you found anything yet between Spence Brinkman and Molina Escobar?" The rats.

Ember all but purred over the connection. "Only that the FBI has an open case against Spencer Brinkman and his son. Both Spence and Heath are being investigated for money laundering, gun running, and a little thing called distributing cocaine. Don't ask me how I know, just be glad I do."

"Good." Beck would have crowed at that news if not for the premonition about Camilla lurking over him like a Halloween ghoul. The lingering tension he'd felt all day would not let go. "Where's everyone tonight?"

"Zack and Jake are over at Judiciary Square handing out gloves, hats, and blankets. Mark's making his usual rounds, reaching out to any homeless who are sick or who've had too much to drink. At the moment, Alex and Adam are with MPD in the middle of a hostage/robbery situation in Chinatown, but according to reports over the squawk box, it's a done deal now. MPD has the alleged bad boy in custody. Last I knew, Renner and Beau were still at Sibley Memorial, making sure Georgia and Joslyn stayed there tonight. Guess Joslyn was suffering from an infected toe. Somewhere along the line she got a staph infection. They're keeping her overnight for observation. Everyone else is mobile, reporting in as usual."

"A toe? I wish she would've told me. I would've helped."

Ember chuckled. "You know how it is when you get older. It's hard to admit you need help."

And there it was again, his age. "I'm not that old."

Teasing laughter rang in his ear. "Aren't we touchy?"

"Did all the wives make it safely home?" He had no idea why he'd asked, just wanted to be sure none of the ladies were on the streets tonight.

"You bet. Harley and Judy took Kelsey home instead of letting her go back to Raymond's Kids. She's upset about Dave's murder, but Lexie needed her mom."

"That wasn't Kelsey's fault," Beckam insisted. "We can't make these guys do something they don't want to."

"I know that, but survivor's guilt…" Ember cleared her throat. Coughed. Then said, "Survivor's guilt's a killer. We all carry it for things we had no control over. You can't just snap your fingers and wish it gone. You know that, too."

He nodded, remembering Mrs. Jones and the lie she'd told about him to save her unborn baby girl. And suddenly, he was telling Ember about that long-ago tragedy, how her husband had eventually murdered her baby, and how he, Beck, had suffered for those two deaths more than any he'd witnessed during combat. He'd seen good men and women die. Good soldiers. But that single tragedy still haunted him, just like the ghoul haunting him tonight. Which made him wonder if these ghosts were related. If he wasn't sensing two ghouls—as in the spirits of two infant girls—come back from the dead to wreak revenge on those responsible for their deaths. It felt like something Karma would do. But it also felt like something out of a Freddy Krueger movie.

Yeah, no. He shrugged off the icy cold fingers tapping up the back of his neck. Crazy things like that just did not happen.

"Wow. A baby girl…" Ember murmured. "That had to be so hard on you."

You have no idea. He cleared his throat, wondering what the hell he was doing and why he'd told Ember. Why couldn't he shake his sense of impending doom? "Cam's in trouble, Ember. I can't prove it, but I know it just the same."

"Yeah, well about that…" Ember lowered her voice. "I've been looking into this Hector Rojas dude like you asked, and nothing he told Alex or Camilla is true. He's not here on business. He lives in Crystal City, Beck, and he works for Penn and Spencer Brinkman. He's their financial counselor, and he runs his own business. Only it's called Brinkman Securities, not Rojas Securities, which is odd, don't you think?"

"Want to bet he's knee-deep in their crimes, too? Damn it, I knew that son of a bitch was lying… Err, sorry. Didn't mean to—"

Ember snorted in his ear. "Knock it off. I've heard worse and I've said worse, too."

He knew that, but she'd never heard worse from him. "I'm still sorry. Won't do it again. What's Cam's home address?"

Ember gave him the street number on Potomac Avenue. "Be careful," she murmured. "You do understand I have to tell Alex where you're going."

"Tell him," Beckam replied. "It's no secret how I feel about Cam. I love her. You weren't there today, but you might as well know."

"Aww, I'm so glad. I had a feeling this operation would be good for her. Trust me. I'm going to make friends with that woman if it's the last thing I do. Honest."

He didn't doubt Ember at all. "Listen. I've got to go."

"Hold on a sec…" Ember answered another line, then came back on quickly. "Sit tight. Renner and Beau are on their way to you. They've got a lead."

"Are they driving? Better be, because I'm not waiting."

"Running, Beck. They are both running to you. Should be at your location in…"

"Beck!" A loud baritone bellowed over the noise of road construction. "Wait the fuck up!"

Had to be Beau. "They're here," Beck told Ember. "Talk to you later."

"Copy that," she murmured. "I'll tell Alex what I found on Rojas. Stay in touch."

Beckam hung up as Renner and Beau all but ran over him.

"He's gotta work for DeWitt," Renner wheezed through the great gusts of frozen breath billowing out of him. "Our killer. All these deaths…" Big breath. More frozen vapor. "Every last one… has something more in common."

Another blast of frozen vapor and Beau took over. "They all happened in the vicinity of DeWitt Construction road projects. All of them. Even Dave's murder today."

Beck glared over his back at the steady din of repair work taking place on Columbus Circle, looking for that short guy who'd taken pictures earlier. "You got a name? A mugshot to go by?"

Still breathing hard, Renner dropped his hands to his knees and shook his head. "No, man, but Ember should have something real soon," he said to the sidewalk. "Alex is contacting her to cooperate with DeWitt now. Urban DeWitt's cooperating with MPD. They'll pass all DeWitt employee records to her as soon as they get them. Alex wants us to keep close tabs on these workers while she works over DeWitt's employment roster."

"I might know who we're looking for. One DeWitt worker took pictures of Cam and me this morning. Right here from this site. Across the road." Why did that realization send shivers up Beckam's back?

Renner looked up at that, his brows knitted with worry. "You recall what he looked like?"

"Bald. Squat. Glasses. Danny DeVito kind of short."

"He took pics of you two? Why?" Beau asked.

"Not a clue. Cam noticed him. At first, I thought maybe he was scoping out the area for whatever roadwork DeWitt is doing, but now—"

"Can't be our killer." Straightening, Renner shook his head. "Doesn't fit the profile. You might be a vet, but you're from the wrong war, and you're way too young. So far, all vics have been Vietnam-era, in their late sixties, early seventies. Same CO. Same Army division. You're OFS. He couldn't have been after you."

OFS, as in Operation Freedom's Sentinel, the current mission in the United States' Global War on Terrorism.

Another icy finger skated over Beckam's shoulders and slithered up his neck. "But what if our killer's escalating, and he's at the point where killing anyone will do? Maybe that's why he's here, to clean up the streets of all homeless people."

"Or maybe he's planning to kill a couple kids to throw MPD off his trail," Beau offered darkly, glancing over his shoulder. "Asshole's probably watching us right now."

"Asshole's also got a car." Beckam pointed his chin at the blinking red taillights from all that stalled traffic. "That much I'm sure of, and he may not be acting alone. Take your pick, guys. We might know this guy's motive, but we've still got nothing solid to go on until Ember does her thing and—"

BRINGGGGGGG! Beck's phone vibrated in his hand. He hit SPEAKER and answered, "Ember?"

"Beck. Hi. Listen. I'm working a hot project for Alex. DeWitt has one employee who might be our guy. Jaden Williamson. Moved from South Carolina to Washington, DC, two months ago. Hasn't checked in with his new probation officer yet, but get this. He's Bruce Williamson's kid."

"Bruce? Our Bruce has a son?" Beckam asked.

"Yes, our Bruce, and yes, he has two sons, Jaden and Wilson, both in their mid-forties, but Jaden's the felon. Wilson works for, crap… Oops, sorry." Ember blew a soft whistle over the connection. "Guys. You're not going to believe this. He works for Sachs and Goldstein."

Beau growled. "That ain't no coincidence."

"Maybe not. Find out if they're working together on these murders, Ember," Renner ordered. "I know you can do it. Anyone with wheels close to our location in case we need to run?"

"Copy that, I'll check," she replied easily, the sound of her fingertips tapping her keyboard audible.

"Felony what?" Beckam asked.

Ember came back quickly with, "Date rape. His rap sheet includes a dozen or so bar brawls, assaults, threatening to kill his live-in girlfriend, beating the shit out of her, stuff like that. All with his bare hands. This guy's mad at the world. In one instance, he nearly choked a guy to death in a bar fight. And get this, that victim was another Vietnam veteran."

Incredible. And this guy was still not in prison? "Same CO?" Beckam asked.

"Hold on. I'm checking now… Yes, Beck. Wow. Same everything. Jaden started fighting as a teenager. Don't ask me how I know." Which meant she had light fingers and a way into sealed juvenile records. "Listen, guys. It seems to me Jaden's after everyone who knew his old man. Bruce, Dave, and Harold were all in Fifth Division's Alpha Company, mortar platoon, during their tour. So were the other vics. All drafted."

"And all crapped on when they came home," Beck added. *But no enlisted officers were victims, hmmm. That was interesting.*

One ugly way the Vietnam Conflict, its official designation, stood out from other wars was the internal war its drafted ranks waged against brain dead officers who showed up with nothing but rank, book learning, and big ideas that often got those grunts killed. Green college graduates with no combat experience tended to order troops into harm's way just to look good. Many inexperienced officers were only after their next POS promotion. Vietnam was a power trip for officers who stayed safe in the rear echelon, or who had no concept of how to lead men. Many never saw combat because some grunt they'd nearly gotten killed fragged them back in camp or shot them in their tents. In some cases, it really was the law of the jungle out there.

"Which means Harold might be next. Look into Dave's, Harold's, and Bruce's time in service, Ember," Beckam requested. "Find out where they were stationed. What'd the Fourth Platoon do while they were in country, and who'd they do it to? Who'd they kill? Who'd they piss off? You're sharp. See if anything odd stands out in their records. Did they R&R together? Were they in trouble at the same time? Anything."

"Jesus Christ, where's Jaden Williamson now?" Beau wanted to know.

"Sheesh, Beau, I'm not clairvoyant," Ember grumbled, "but I did notice he and a couple guys from DeWitt all have the same address behind a rundown strip mall off Whitehurst freeway exit. Sending coordinates to you and Alex now. Maybe you'll get lucky and he'll be there."

"That exit's close to Rock Creek Parkway," Renner added. "A lot of homeless people congregate there every night. Ember, alert Alex that those good folks may need TEAM coverage tonight."

"But if Jaden's using DeWitt Construction as a cover-up—" Ember started to say.

"He might also be using a DeWitt vehicle to move throughout the city without being noticed," Beckam finished.

"Wanna bet we'll find blood evidence, maybe the murder weapon, in one, maybe two cars in DeWitt's fleet?" Renner added. "You did report that Max was rolled out of a moving car, right, Beck?"

"Right," Ember chimed in. "Traffic cams in and around Union Station showed no trucks, only cars and SUVs in yesterday's morning traffic. Hold on, I'm searching DMV records… Looking for all DeWitt vehicles… Okay, here we go. DeWitt's fleet includes an even dozen company automobiles, one stretch limo, eight trucks, all this year's model Fords. Wow. Looks like he swaps out his fleet every December. Even the limo's brand new."

Which meant any blood evidence from crimes committed earlier than December was now lost. Beck ran a quick hand over his head. Damn. This simple operation had morphed into a typical day in combat. Chaos. Everything happening at the same time, all of it squeezed into a thirty-six, going on forty-eight-hour day of one surprise after another.

"Do you want a list of DeWitt's heavy equipment, too?" Ember asked. "I can do—"

"Not tonight," Renner chimed in. "Trucks and cars blend into normal traffic better than bulldozers. This'll give us enough to start with."

Ember came back with DeWitt's corporate address off Indian Head Highway in Maryland, but Beck cut her off. "No, we need DeWitt's construction yard. That's where most company vehicles will be parked." Most but not all. Work crew supervisors might take a company vehicle home with them.

"Darn," she growled. "I know that, just got carried away, and… here. Go to this address. Wow. It's not that far from where you are now." She provided a number east of National Harbor. Just a hop, skip, and a jump on I-695 over the Anacostia River and past Joint Base Anacostia-Bolling. Hell, the freeway made both those locations a thirty-minute drive from Union Station.

"Hold on, guys," Ember murmured. "I've got another call."

"Let's roll," Renner ordered. "I'd like to sleep in my own bed tonight. If we can find that evidence at DeWitt's, then we'll contact MPD and go after Williamson at his place."

"Yeah, but…" And there Beckam stalled with his cell in his hand. DeWitt's yard lay to the south, but Camilla's home was due west along the Potomac. He swallowed hard, not as anxious to end this murderer as he was to get back to her side, to make sure she was safe.

Those same icy fingers tapped at the base of his skull, reminding him that something wicked was afoot in the District tonight.

It seemed a simple request, him leaving Renner and Beau to go check on Cam, but his guys needed him now. Not an hour later. One shooter in the right position could mean the difference between success and failure in any op. And this was war. If Jaden Williamson was their man, he needed to go down tonight, and finding that blood evidence could put him behind bars.

Besides, Cam had made it clear that she trusted Rojas, and that should've been good enough for Beck. He didn't really know Cam well enough to second guess her. Two days. They'd worked together just for just two long, heartrending days. That was all.

Yet that same heart told him to run to her. To rescue her. To at least stand for her the way he should've stood for Desiree Jones years ago. Maybe she wouldn't be haunting him now if he had.

"Hey, Beck." Renner snapped his fingers in Beck's face. "Where'd you go, man? We've got to get moving."

"Now," Beau growled. "Strike while the fire's hot. Get that bastard before he knows he's been made. Move your ass, Army."

Beckam stared at Beau, looking through him. Seeing Cam in every shadow. "Did you ever have a feeling that where you should go, wasn't where you needed to be? That someone's life might be irrevocably changed because you deliberately chose wrong?"

Beau ceased growling. "Fuck, yeah. The night my little sister died. I should've been there for AJ. She needed me. Then again, the night McKenna damned nearly died. I almost got to her too late. But yeah, I had a creepy feeling both times. Who the fuck are we talking about this time?"

"Camilla," Renner breathed, ever on target. Ever as insightful as a well-tuned radio antenna. The man was damned intuitive for a guy. "She means something to you," he stated, not asked. "You think she's in trouble."

"I don't think it; I know it. Rojas works for the Brinkmans and they're crooked, plus he's lived in DC instead of Mexico, like Cam thought. He's not here on business like he said." Beckam nodded, then made it perfectly clear in case there was any doubt. "I know what you're thinking. Camilla's the office pariah, a spoiled brat and an entitled rich kid who thinks everyone should kiss her ass. But she's not, not really, and she means something to me. Sorry, but I can't go with—"

"Then where are we going, bro?" Beau declared as if Alex wouldn't mind if his three closest-to-the-scene operatives didn't run with this latest intel to end the murder spree.

"Now wait a minute, guys," Renner interceded in his best levelheaded, I'm-in-charge way. "We've got a job to do, and if we do it right, if Ember's correct, we could end this murder spree tonight. At least we might have solid evidence within the hour if we're lucky. Think about it. Jaden might be driving out of DeWitt's parking lot right now. We could apprehend him before he kills again."

Beckam took a deep breath. Renner was right. The job came first. He knew that, only…

Renner slapped a palm to Beckam's shoulder. "Come on, Beck. Let's end this son of a bitch once and for all. Then we'll go with you to check on Cam. But first things first, okay?"

It sounded like the only answer. The best answer. Renner *was* right. DeWitt's construction yard wasn't far away. The winter storm hadn't dumped its forecasted snow yet. Roads were still clear. If things went well...

But therein lay the rub. The chaos that erupted during combat wasn't called fog of war for nothing. Even the most articulate, best-laid plans and carefully detailed intentions never survived first contact with the enemy. It was Murphy's law at its worst. But the truth was that every strategy was only theory and wishful thinking until it became real. Every soldier knew that when lead started flying, and you went up against a bloodthirsty army intent on martyrdom, chaos reigned supreme. Friendly fire was a real thing in the midst of Armageddon. Anything could happen.

Renner looked to the south. "I'm not in charge, and I'm not telling you guys what to do," he said quietly, "but I'm going after Jaden Williamson. If you guys can't go with me—"

"Guys! Guys! Listen up. I'm still here! You'll never guess who just called me. Direct." Oh, yeah. Ember was still on speaker.

Beck had totally forgotten her. He lifted the cell to his ear. "Who?"

"Urban DeWitt! He owns DeWitt Construction, remember? And he's former Army like you. He's a Ranger! He wanted us to know that he installed GPS locators in every fleet vehicle after a couple guys borrowed his cars and he never got them back. He gave me all I needed to triangulate the location of all DeWitt vehicles. And one of the cars I told you about is parked off Whitehurst freeway exit at that rundown strip mall right now. Want to guess who signed out for it?"

"Jaden?" Beau growled.

"Yes! Alex is on his way to you. Stay put. ETA in—"

"There he is," Renner called out, pointing toward the half-filled parking lot nearest their location where two TEAM SUVs had just jumped the curb, both headed his way with engines roaring and headlights flashing.

That settled it. Cam had better be right about Rojas, because she was on her own.

"Damn it, let's do this," Beckam ordered.

Chapter Thirty-Three

"And I'm telling you I don't have a computer!" Cam screamed at Other Hector for the hundredth time. By then he'd not only slapped and punched her to make her confess, he'd also dragged her by her hair into the bathroom where he'd filled her tub with cold water. She cowered on the floor near the toilet. Seeing double. Scared for her life. But mad as hell.

The only thing he had on her was his size, strength, and weight. He might think that was enough, but she'd been in this exact position before. Because Heath liked to play twisted, mean games too, Cam had equipped every room in her home with enough hidden knives that no predator could stay safe for long. It was just a matter of time before this liar grabbed her again. When he did, he'd be sorry. One of the tiny Swiss Army knives she'd taped to the floor under every counter edge and beneath every wrap-around toilet rug in this house—her house!—was now in her trembling fingers. She would not die today. But this jackass would.

Cranking the faucet off, he turned and looked down at her with his hands on his hips as if he was her lord and master.

Get ready, she told herself, wishing she'd attended those self-defense lessons like Alex Stewart had asked her to since the day he'd hired her. Zack Lennox taught them. How hard could it have been being man-handled by the big, teddy bear who'd had the nerve to tease her today?

"Alana said you were a stinking liar. You gonna tell me where your laptop is or are you gonna make me do this?" Rojas gestured at the half-filled tub as if it were a table laden with desserts.

Get set.

"You're the liar," she declared. "You've never once asked about our baby."

He shook his head in that patronizing way arrogant men had. "See? Another lie. Tsk, tsk. Alana said you'd say something like that, you couldn't be trusted. Look around. I see no evidence of any baby in this lousy place. Come on. It's time." He fluttered his fingers at her as if this weren't going to hurt. "I'm done asking. Get up, so I don't have to make you."

Go. "Make me," she growled, her knife handle hidden but in position, the blade pointed down for swift, hard strokes that would disable him. She needed to get past him to get the door. This had to work.

His jaw hardened. He sneered. With one long step, he was on her, and Cam did it! She stuck that blade in his neck, then… *Bam! Bam! Bam!* Three more times in his chest, shoulder, anything she could hit! Running on fear and pure adrenaline, she pushed him into the tub with that last stab. Blood drenched his white shirt. He bellowed like the stuck pig that he was. Over he went, hitting his head on the opposite tiled wall, but damn it to hell!

He grabbed her forearms at the last second, and down she went with him. Into the water. Under him. One hand circled her neck while he slapped the knife from her fingers and disarmed her. Kicking and thrashing subsided when he straddled her, his knees at her hips, his weight holding her under, his hands around her neck.

Cam swallowed a mouthful of ice-cold water, then inhaled, struggling for her life. To breathe. Her lungs filled. They burned with the reflexive panic that would now kill her. Restrained and drowning, all she could think of was Beckam. Her one true light. Twenty years of living was not enough! She wanted more. She wanted him.

Suddenly, she remembered. She did have a computer. At work. And like every trusted TEAM member, Alex had given her a key to his building. God, she owed him so, so much for trusting her.

Lifting her clasped hands out of the water, Cam begged for her life.

Rojas jerked her head high enough she could see.

Sputtering, she wheezed, "At, at w-work."

"At work what?" he hissed into her face.

She blinked to see him better. Oh damn, she'd cut him good. Not deep enough to kill him. But enough that he was bleeding and mad as hell.

"I have a com-computer… at work…" Spit. Sputter. Breathe, breathe, breathe.

Sliding off her hips to her thighs, Rojas squeegeed one big, rough hand over her face and ordered, "This better be good, or I'll kill you. I swear I will. Only I'll strip you naked and then drown you in the fuckin' toilet!"

"W-w-work," she stuttered again, so cold and frightened she could barely get the word out. "I… I have a w-work computer. Honest. At my office. Let me up. I'll… I'll take you there."

Grimacing in pain that she'd caused, he cocked his head as if he didn't believe her. She could barely see him through the wet, tangled hair in her face. His lips thinned into a mean hard line of determination even as one hand tightened on her shoulder like he meant to shove her back under.

Cam sucked in one quick bellyful of air.

But he asked, "Where's work?"

"Al… Alexandria. T-TEAM Headquarters. I have a… a k-k-key. I can get us both in. No one else will be there," she lied, knowing full well that someone smarter than her had been on-site handling trouble calls and coordinating TEAM resources since this operation with MPD began. Maybe Zack. Maybe even Alex. God, please, let it be Alex.

And there she was, relying on a Being she didn't want to believe in. Yet she did. Because Beckam did.

Again with the dirty look. "You'd better not be lying, bitch," Rojas spat, rubbing his punctured neck and shoulder, his shirt stained pink with diluted blood.

She held her breath, afraid he'd need to make her bleed, too.

Reluctantly, he lifted to his feet then dragged her to her knees while he climbed out of the tub. Still in the water and shaking, she waited for what would happen next. But instead of a punch, he knotted one fist in her hair, then wrapped his other around her neck and lifted her to her feet. He was strangling her while he helped her. But not choking her hard enough she couldn't breathe, only hard enough to prove what he could and would do if or when he wanted. That he was in charge, and he meant what he said.

Out of sheer panic, Cam latched onto his wrists for support. She knew it then. Once he had whatever Alana had promised him, he would kill her. She'd stabbed him. Such insolence would not go unpunished.

Hector grunted as he lifted her over the edge of the tub and set her on her feet. He tipped his face into the side of her head and whispered, "You've got ten minutes to change into something dry. But understand this. I will kill you next time, and it will hurt worse than these little pin pricks you gave me. Trust me. I know how to keep you alive long enough you'll scream to die."

But until then, she thought bravely. *I'm still alive, and Beckam will come. Somehow. He knows I need him. And then, you'll be sorry.*

Chapter Thirty-Four

Two SUVs full of pissed off former military should've been enough to take down one, maybe two, felons. But when Alex didn't turn right off M Street Northwest when Adam, Renner, and Beau did in the other TEAM SUV, Beckam's heart started pounding again. He could breathe. He didn't have to ask to know that his boss was just as hellbent on getting to Cam as he was.

"Hurry," Beckam murmured past the lump in his throat. "She's in trouble. I can feel it."

"Then why the fuck were you still on task?" Alex yelled, his heated breath fogging the windshield. "Every last one of my agents is right this son of a bitchin' second zeroing down on Jaden Williamson. Several are on their way to DeWitt's yard for the evidence we're sure is there. Others have already converged on his address and are waiting for MPD's signal to take him out. MPD's engaged to the hilt. So's my TEAM. The moment we've got hard evidence, we're going in. They didn't need you."

"But I don't bail on my guys. Ever. I had a job to finish," Beckam explained. "We had to end this killer."

"And we will!" Alex drew in a terse, short breath. "Damn it, Beck, you're not in the Army anymore, and you're not the only man on my TEAM. From now on, family comes first, you understand? I don't care if the President of the United States is under fire. You ever choose duty over family again, and I'll kick your ass."

Beckam nodded, so damned grateful for Alex's brand of butt chewing. Tears sprang to his eyes at the harsh understanding his boss just dished out, but he hurried to swipe them away.

Too late.

Alex shot him a quick glance and caught Beck sucking his worry in, the back of his hand still on his face.

"Don't worry," Alex said just as gruffly. "We'll get there in time. I had Ember run a quick background check on Rojas the minute he left with Cam. Son of a bitch is from New York City. Lived in the same wealthy neighborhood Cam did, just stayed out of sight. Bastard never went to Mexico. That was all a cover-up. Camilla's mother was one shit piece of work. She set him up, an eighteen-year-old adult male, with her sixteen-year-old daughter. Jesus Christ!" Alex roared, his knuckles white on the wheel. "That bitch paid him to get Cam pregnant. That's why the son of a bitchin' liar romanced her and made her believe he was her age. Don't worry. I've got the name of the physician who did the abortion. I know everything."

Beckam was not so far gone that he failed to notice that Alex called Camilla, Cam now. She was officially part of The TEAM.

"I'll kill him," Beck promised, his soul set on saving her from yet one more disaster. Alana was dead and in the past. Soon Rojas would be, too. Whatever challenges the future held depended on these next few minutes, on whether he and Alex could get to Cam in time. On her being strong enough to survive whatever Rojas was doing to her now.

As if he read Beck's mind, Alex floored the accelerator, sending the SUV roaring through Georgetown, past GW University on Beck's right and onto Canal Road Northwest. The Potomac lay cold and dark on Alex's left, but headlights and taillights were all Beck could see ahead. His better judgment was now on hold. Only instinct and the inherent sixth sense of a stone-cold sniper ruled him now. The hunter within was alive and on duty, his eyes sharp as he alertly quartered each intersection, searching for Cam's pretty face behind the windshield of each vehicle flying past.

"Rojas is driving a gray Lincoln Town car. This year's model."

"Copy that," Beck replied, his mouth dry when a dark-colored sedan came into view. Brown, not gray. Tinted windows too dark to see beyond. Not Rojas.

His eyes instantly jumped to the next vehicle, then the next until Alex veered right onto Arizona Avenue NW to Potomac Avenue NW. By then the lush green space that separated the District of Columbia from Northern Virginia isolated the residential road, darkening the intervals between fewer and fewer passing vehicles.

Damn, but she lived in a nice part of town. Concrete and stone walls lined the sidewalk at Beck's right, the lavish stately homes beyond more mansion-like than laid back places to raise a kid. This was a subdivision of the rich and famous. Packed onto crowded lots, each home boasted unique architecture, some colonial, some ultra-modern, but all too damned big and pompous for Beckam's tastes. He'd never been a fan of landscaped yards and prissy, trimmed hedges. Or curb appeal. These weren't homes. They were monuments to fame and fortune. No kid belonged here. Certainly not Cam.

Beck needed to do something. Anything. To run. To fight! To end Hector Rojas and whatever devious plan Alana had left behind to hurt her daughter. Beck had never known such maniacal hatred until he'd served in far-off Afghanistan and Syria, where radicalized mothers raised their littlest children to become suicide bombers. And were proud of it. Alana was not so different.

Faster.

At last! Luis and Alana's palatial home came into view, then three doors west, what had once been Cam and Heath Brinkman's place. Not as large as her parents' estate, more like a mausoleum than friendly. Certainly not warm and cozy. Which was precisely how Cam had been until yesterday morning.

As Alex pulled to the curb, Beck stuck his fingers into his nitrile work gloves. "Boss? You ever change your mind about something you thought was an absolute truth, only it wasn't?"

Alex cast a knowing look over one shoulder as he shifted the SUV into neutral. "I'll tell you what I do know. Life can change on a dime. Don't waste it. If you care about someone, show up and be there when they need you. Not when it's convenient or when it makes sense. Follow your goddamned gut, Beck. Every son of a bitchin' time. That's why God gave it to you. You ready?"

Beck answered by opening his door and dropping both boots to the ground. "Yes, sir. Let's do this."

He took a deep breath of January's frigid air. Fresh off the river behind him, it invigorated him down to his warrior's soul. With Alex on his left, they approached the elegant home built of sharp, concrete lines and less of invitation. No wonder Cam had been cold and hard. This place looked like a museum. Or a morgue.

The instant that thought registered, Beckam regretted it. Offering one quick prayer to the wise, all-knowing Man Upstairs, he prayed for forgiveness for his ego and the blessing of the swiftest reflexes to keep Cam from ending up in a morgue. He prayed for spot-on targeting and the ability to know one shadow from the next. He'd never killed an innocent. He didn't intend to now. But Rojas, the pig would die if he'd hurt Cam. And he'd die hard.

"Meowwww," someone's cat yowled from the scrawny shrub just outside Cam's front door. It might look better come spring. Beck surely hoped so, but what was a cat doing in that stack of broken twigs and stubby branches? It couldn't be.

"Hector? Come here, kitty kitty. Is that you? You okay?"

Damned if the cat didn't start purring and rubbing against Beck's ankle. Bending over, he snagged the furry feline under its belly and hauled Hector—damn, he hated that name—up against his chest. "What are you doing outside, buddy?" Now that was a good solid name for a tomcat. Buddy. That Beck could get used to. "Where's Cam? You didn't make her mad and she threw you out, did you? Is she okay?"

Like that silly cat would answer.

Alex's cell vibrated. "Son of a bitch. What now?" he asked as he lifted the lighted screen to his face and growled, "Back off. She's not here. She's at headquarters with that asshat Rojas."

Beck's gut fell. "How do you know?" *And why don't I know that?*

"I know because my security system just pinged an alert," Alex explained as he headed back to the vehicle and handed his cell to Beck. "Ember's there. She'll send the video feed next."

Sure as hell, the live feed on Alex's cell showed an up-close view of Cam's frightened face while she keyed in her passcode to the TEAM lobby elevator. Hector Rojas stood at her side, his hand around her neck again. She looked bad. Dark circles shadowed her eyes. Her hair hung loose and tangled. She couldn't seem to make her fingers hit the correct buttons. Something was very wrong. What the hell?

Beckam jerked Alex's cell closer to his nose while Cam's cat snuggled under his chin. "Is her hair wet? Is that what I'm seeing? God, what's he done to her? Look at her. Cam's lips are swollen. Look at her chin and cheek. She's covered in bruises. He beat her. I'll kill him! I'll kill the son of a bitch! Hector Rojas is mine, Boss. He's all mine!"

Alex never argued. Never said a word. They had no more than climbed back inside the SUV with the cat and strapped in when his phone beeped a different alarm, and an automated voice clearly declared, "Shots fired."

"That's coming from Williamson's location," Alex said just as calmly. "Our guys and MPD are now engaged with the suspect or suspects."

"Shit!" Beckam hissed, frustrated he couldn't be in two places at once, yet knowing without a doubt, that he and Alex would now respond to The TEAM's call for back-up. Cam would have to wait. *Please God, make her strong enough!*

Alex hit the gas, pulled a squealing K-turn, then headed back the way they'd come.

Shit! Shit! Shit! Beck had now lost control of his impeccable restraint. He sounded just like Alex. Even Cam's cat had climbed out of his hands and into the rear seat, hissing.

Yet once again, Alex passed the turnoff for Rock Creek Parkway. Sailed right by it.

Beck pointed to their left as the street they should've been on went by. "The guys are that way. They... they need us." *Don't they?* Man, it was hard letting go of years' worth of military thinking.

"Goddamnit, Beckam Garner," Alex growled. "What'd I just tell you about family coming first? I didn't train my team all these years to fail me now. This is what they do best. Let them take Williamson down. That's what I pay them for. Right now, Cam needs us more than Mark, Zack and the rest of my TEAM."

"Then hurry," Beckam cried. "Goddamn it, Boss, hurry!"

Chapter Thirty-Five

Cam fumbled keying in the code to The TEAM elevator in the lobby again, her fingers numb from the cold, her whole body trembling even as Rojas pushed closer into her side and threatened, "If this is another one of your lies—"

"N-no. Honest. I do have a computer here," she answered, praying to the God she didn't believe in, and that Zack would somehow know she was down here. That he, *oh, please, oh, please, God,* was on duty tonight and would come prepared to save her. Surely no one could get by Zack Lennox. He was so much bigger than Hector.

"Then make it quick," Rojas hissed as he collared her neck yet again and shook her like the rag doll she was turning into.

She'd never been more scared that she'd end up dead.

Suddenly, the monitor over the keypad lit with Ember Dennison's bright, smiling face. "Hey, Camilla," she said cheerily, even pronouncing the name correctly which, oddly, Camilla could have cared less about. "What's up, honey?"

Cam's eyes teared up at that tender endearment coming from a woman she had yet to be kind to. "N-nothing much," she answered as evenly as she could. "Umm, is Zack up there?"

"No, he went to the hospital, remember? To see you. Whatcha need, honey?"

Why was she being so nice?

"Oh, yeah, umm, darn. I saw him there, I just forgot." Cam stalled. "It's just that I left something at my desk, and, darn, I was hoping he could run it down to me. My fingers are too cold to key in the right numbers. C-can you let me up? P-please, Ember?" *God, I'm so sorry I ever treated you like a skank.*

"Hey, girlfriend. You and I both know that whatever Zack can do, us girls can do better, right?" Ember cocked her head and asked. "My, oh my. Who's that handsome stud with you?"

"Just a guy come to comfort his long-lost girlfriend," Rojas supplied smoothly, easing Cam to the side, so Ember could get a better look at his lying face. "Hey, listen. Ember, is it? Well, I'm Hector Rojas. You're a very beautiful woman, and I'm genuinely sorry Camilla forgot to introduce us. But it's very cold down here, and as you know, this lobby of yours isn't heated. Can you let us up or not?"

Ember's face split with a smile. "Sure! It's been a slow day, well except for you, huh, Camilla? You okay?"

Cam nodded like a dolt. Ember really was a gorgeous woman with all that blond hair and her Marilyn Monroe full-figure. Yet she never seemed to notice the way men's heads turned when she walked by them in the office. The way her hips swayed no matter what she was doing. Ember could've been a wealthy star, she was that kind of sexy. Only she was too kind and too nice for Hollywood. They didn't deserve her any more than Cam did.

Cam tried to smile back at her, but surely Ember had noticed the swelling and bruises her poor face sported by then. Or the desperate look she was trying to send The TEAM's genius techie through ESP. Or the fear and outright terror that had to be obvious in Cam's teary, black eyes. The lighting in the lobby wasn't that bad.

Yet Cam nodded bravely and replied, "Yes, Ember. N-now that Hector's here, I'm f-f-fine." *Just fuckin' fine.* "But first..." She stalled, not wanting to put Ember in the same danger. "Umm, maybe you could just give me the code and—"

Hector shoved the barrel of his gun under Cam's chin and put a quick stop to that plan. "I said step on it, or this one dies."

The live feed showing Ember's pretty face went blank and the elevator doors slid open.

"Now move," Hector ordered, shoving Cam into the elevator. "Do something stupid like that again, and I'll cut her to ribbons and make you watch."

Oh, God. Oh, God. Oh, God.

At last! Alex stomped on the brakes and the SUV shifted into a slide that put them alongside the stairs leading from The TEAM's underground parking lot up into TEAM HQ. The vehicle had no more than settled on all four tires when Beckam was out of the door, his boots on the ground. After he made certain Cam's cat was shut safely in the rear of the SUV, he ran for the stairwell with Alex on his six. They already knew Hector Rojas was inside with Cam. Ember had activated Delta Protocol, which had not only fed the live feed of her conversation with Cam from inside the lobby, but had also alerted all TEAM members, as well as Alexandria's police force, of a burglary/home invasion in progress. Not that Beckam needed or wanted APD on-site when he killed Hector Rojas.

For now, two APD patrol cars waited on standby one block north of TEAM HQ, which also put them near the King Street metro station. Thankfully, January's cold temps discouraged tourism, and at this time of the evening, streets were, for the most part, empty of pedestrians. The full brunt of the latest forecasted storm still lingered off the East Coast. It was a damned good night for Rojas to die.

Beck slowed his steps at the second level landing where TEAM offices were, breathing hard but ready to engage. The bright LED lights overhead went out, but just as quickly as darkness consumed all sight, emergency generators kicked on and emergency lighting with it. Wherever Ember was, she was safe and manipulating TEAM resources to Beck's and Alex's advantage.

Carefully, he palmed the fire door's sturdy knob, testing to make sure it was unlocked as it should've been. Kicking it in would've made for a damned loud entry. Which he wouldn't have minded, if Rojas had broken into TEAM HQ alone. But Cam was in there with Rojas, and Beck wasn't going to frighten her any more than she already was.

The round knob rotated in his gloved hand without a sound. God bless Alex for every last one of his OCD ways. Nothing dared squeak in his kingdom.

"She's upstairs in the vault," Alex whispered, tapping his earpiece. "Ember. Let's get this done before Rojas knows we're inside."

Stealthily, Beck opened the fire door and proceeded forward to the work bay. Alex closed it silently behind them, then both men hunched low to keep Rojas from catching sight of them over the customer counter.

Back when Alex had first organized his office and this work bay, he'd designed it on a wagon wheel concept, the customer service desk in the center with work stations radiating out from there like spokes. Alex's office, as well as his senior agents' offices, lined the farthest hall. Restrooms and supply rooms were located in the corridor that stretched behind the fire door. The elevator and entry were straight ahead. One level up, a secure vault kept track of all makes and models of firearms and ammo. As far as covert surveillance companies went, TEAM HQ put Alexandria on the map.

"So, where's that blonde bitch you were just talking to, huh?" Rojas asked a frazzled Cam, one palm flat on her desk, his long fingers tapping impatiently even as he glanced over his shoulder and stared into the dark. "Where the fuck did she go?"

That's right, Beckam thought. *Keep looking at that nice, bright monitor. You'll never see me until it's too late.*

"I'm not sure she was even here. Ember's smart. She could be working from home for all I know." Cam ducked, her poor bruised face backlit by the screen, her nervous fingers tapping beneath a monitor filled with garbled pictures and lines instead of documents. "I… I can't make this keyboard work. Look. My computer's on, but all the regular apps are turned off. Maybe it's battery powered and I—"

He leaned in closer, his fingers snarled in her hair. "You'd better figure it out goddamned quick, or I'll hunt your girlfriend down and kill her. Don't think I won't."

"Owww," she cried. "You're hurting me, but I promise. She's… she's not my girlfriend."

Rojas scoffed. "Course not. You never had friends, did you? You were always too good for the rest of us. Doesn't matter. I'll strangle that bitch with her own intestines. You can watch."

But Beckam knew differently. Everything in Cam's life had changed, and Ember *was* her friend. The entire TEAM was now on her side. She just didn't believe it yet.

The old, spit-in-your-eye prima donna was gone. She bowed her face and closed her eyes, humbled to her soul. "O-okay. Maybe Ember is my girlfriend. You could be right. I'll try to get her to answer. She'll know what's wrong with my stuff. E-Ember. Are you still here? Can you hear me?" she called out plaintively. "P-please. I know you're smarter than me, but I need to get something that's on my computer. It has to be here. Please. Help me get into my email, and then we'll leave. We'll just go. P-please."

Beckam shrugged at the distress knotted in his neck. Poor damned kid had no idea that Ember, like him, would never let Rojas walk out of here without fighting to the death for Cam.

"Copy that," Alex whispered into his mic. "Going silent. Good girl." Which meant he'd just communicated with Ember, and from now, they'd signal each other by finger taps and code. "She's coming down and she's armed. Be ready."

Alex didn't have to say more. Beckam knew damned well what to do. Like two well-oiled pieces of military machinery that knew each other's game plans, he and Alex closed in on the customer service counter. Beckam stood at Rojas's left just behind him, close enough to touch the bastard. Alex stood between Rojas and Cam, again behind them but close enough to protect Cam.

The lights flickered on, stark and bright for a split second before they flashed off again. This time, no yellow emergency lights flickered to guide Rojas out of TEAM HQ. He was caught.

"Freeze!" Ember ordered from the hall near the elevator.

Rojas whipped out that pistol and fired six times.

Stupid man. She was smarter than that. Like a fool, he'd only reacted to her voice, not her. And he'd used all his ammo. She was still upstairs. But before the last report echoed through the work bay, Alex had Cam up from her chair and out of range, while Beckam strong-armed Rojas's throat, pressed the business end of his pistol flat against Hector's temple.

"You hurt my woman," he hissed. "You bastard! What'd you do, waterboard her? I'll kill you!"

"I… I… No, I just—"

"He tried to d-d-drown me," Cam declared from behind Alex. "In my bathtub. In my own home!"

The lights flashed on and—*Ping*. Ember was back, God bless her.

Out of his peripheral, Beckam could see she'd come decked in riot gear with two pistols in her hands, a knife sheath at her thigh, and a rifle slung over her back. Like a heat-seeking missile, she ran straight at Rojas. "You hurt my friend!" she screamed both pistols flashing laser dots over his sweaty face. Tossing one pistol to Cam, she told Rojas again, "You hurt my girlfriend, you dickwad!"

He stuttered like the sick bully he was.

By then, Cam had stepped out from behind Alex. Damn, she looked good standing tall with her shoulders back and the loaded handgun in her hand aimed at Rojas.

"You do know Camilla won the coveted President's Rifle trophy in long rifle competition a couple years back, don't you?" Beck asked as he eased the pistol out of Rojas's sweaty fingers. "She can hit the inside of an empty tin can a mile away, and she can do it with one hand tied behind her back. You knew that, didn't you, *Hec-Tor*?"

Rojas's stiff lip curled. "She's your bitch?"

Beckam didn't think. Didn't even know how strongly he'd reacted until—*BLAM!* Rojas was down on his hands and knees, spitting blood and cursing, "Fuck you!" over and over, like an adolescent punk.

"Yeah, well, fuck you first," Ember declared with venom. "You hit any TEAM member, that's what you get. Be glad it's Beckam and not me. I'd kick your sorry ass for even touching my girlfriend."

By then, she stood shoulder to shoulder with said girlfriend. But poor Camilla was crying, either because of Ember's staunch show of loyalty or because she'd been beaten. Tears tumbled down her cheeks and dripped off her nose, yet there she stood for everyone to see. Even the creep who'd used and abused her.

"You knew I was pregnant," she told Rojas softly. "You knew. We talked about how much we wanted to be parents. How much we couldn't wait to see *our* baby. You used to sing lullabies to my tummy. I remember everything."

He sneered. The ass on his hands and knees had the temerity to sneer up at the intelligent woman with the handgun pointing at him. How interesting that Ember had given her a Ruger Security-9 nine-millimeter—just like Beckam's.

"Yeah, well, Alana paid good. What was I supposed to do, pass up easy money? Hell, I was just a broke kid back then—"

"You were eighteen," Alex corrected. "An adult. And you were anything but broke. You lied because Alana paid you thousands to seduce her daughter and to make sure you got her pregnant. You've been on Alana and Penn Brinkman's payroll for years. You're part of their prostitution ring. You're a goddamned pimp."

Rojas shrugged like it was no big deal, but Cam cried at that fresh betrayal. "You got me pregnant? On purpose? But you knew what Alana was like. You knew all she put me through. You knew she was heartless. Why? How could you do that to me? To anyone!"

Interestingly, she'd stopped trembling. Once again, the laser dot from her scope didn't twitch or jump like it would if someone else had been holding the weapon. Uh uh. This was where Cam excelled. Target practice. Hitting bulls-eyes… or assholes.

But Beckam's heart tripped up his throat when she took another step forward, her jaw clenched tight and her eyes gone dark.

"No," he told the woman he loved. "You don't want to kill him. He's not worth it, Camilla." *And I don't want you to end him. Not like this. Let me. It'll be easier for you that way.*

Ember made it worse when she took a step back and said, "Let her, Beck. He tried to kill her, and he took a shot at what he thought was me. He needs to die. Besides, he's the reason she lost her baby."

For once, Alex stayed silent.

"But he's unarmed," Beck explained patiently. He'd never thought he'd be defending a creep like Hector Rojas. Yet there he was. Still too damned stupid to be anything less than honorable. To not do the right thing. Bottom line, he didn't want Cam to carry the burdens he carried after he'd killed men in combat. Hector wasn't worth sacrificing her soul.

The firearm in her steady hand never wavered, but her eyes went mean and scary.

"Please, sweetheart. You are not your mother. You're so much more."

She took another step into Rojas's comfort zone, leaned over and pressed that pistol to his forehead.

"Let me," Beckam begged. "Please, Cam—"

"This is for my baby!" she yelled into Rojas's cowering face. "Mine! Not yours! Never yours, you goddamned coward!"

And—*CLICK*.

Jesus Christ, she'd shot him. Or had she?

Beckam swallowed hard. Thank God. That noise was just her magazine rejecting from her pistol. She hadn't pressed the trigger. Just scared the shit out of the bastard who'd intended to kill her. The man who'd fathered her baby, then lied like the piece of shit he was. Who'd deserted her and probably laughed with Alana behind poor Cam's back after that awful abortion.

Cam lifted her head high, turned and handed her weapon handle first to Alex. "Thank you for being here, Boss. I've learned a lot working for you. I'll never forget you."

Boss. The word Beck never expected he'd hear from Cam. His heart swelled with love for this diminutive warrior. He'd never felt prouder or more humble.

"But I quit." Swallowing hard, she faced him then. With tears gleaming in her soft, pretty eyes, she whispered, "Goodbye, Agent Garner. It's been the greatest pleasure of my life working with you, but I can't do this."

For some reason only women understood, Ember wrapped an arm around Cam's shoulder, and together they stepped into the elevator, and she walked out of his life. Again.

Damn. This was not the storm Beckam had expected. Weather. For once, couldn't it just have been weather?

Chapter Thirty-Six

Beckam had left another voicemail reminding Cam that he still had her cat if she wanted it back. That maybe she'd forgotten that he and Alex had found Hector outside in the cold, the night they'd come looking for her. That she could have Hector back any time that was convenient for her. Just call. He'd swing by after work, and he'd only stay as long as it took to hand over the cat, its perch, food, bed, litter, litter box, and all its stuff. That he wouldn't stay. Wouldn't ask questions. Or would she prefer if Harley delivered Hector instead? Would that work better for her? Would it be easier? *Just say the word.*

Boy Scout would never change. He made everything easy for everyone else, even her, bending over backward, forever accommodating, humble, and still too darned nice. That call made four in the past month. But in each one-sided message, he'd never pushed too hard or nagged. He'd just gently reminded her that her cat missed her. Beckam made it sound simple, but he was wrong.

Nothing was easy these days. Not selling real estate, buying a new home, moving, nor all the legal and financial ramifications that went along with those complicated decisions. The last month had been a jam-packed learning experience for Cam. But Beau and McKenna Villanueva had given her the name of a good real estate agent, and after the sale of her multi-million-dollar home in The Palisades, Cam had more equity than she'd expected. Buying this cute little rambler had been simple after that. At least, simpler. She still had a mountain of unpacking to do. Clothes to wash for work tomorrow. A few dishes to put in the dishwasher.

"Beck again?" Ember asked from the kitchen table, where she sat sipping a glass of white wine, her legs crossed and looking every bit like the fifties sex symbol she resembled.

"Yeah. Beck. Who would've thought a guy could have that much staying power, huh?" Cam forced a note of levity into her voice, as if hearing Beck's strong, masculine rumble in her ear hadn't brought another annoying glimmer to her eyes. She did that a lot these days. One thought, one flashback, just someone mentioning cheesecake, and it all came back to her.

But it was an untrue note, judging by the way Ember's brows clashed when she set her glass down and caught Cam dashing her tears away. "You do know you'll have to see him someday, especially if you want your cat back. You do still want Hector, don't you?"

Cam nodded, that old hurt caught up high in her throat again. It might be easier if Harley brought her cat with him when he came over with Sonic. The old adage, killing two birds with one stone made sense. Harley was safe. Married. Beckam was an out-of-control fire in her gut, and she just didn't need a man like him in her life. Only her cat.

Ember let her off the hook. "Are you keeping that awful name?"

"What, Hector? Heck, no. I've already changed his name to Lucky, because, well. He's been lucky for a stray." And because she'd once overheard Beckam tell a story in the office about his parents' bull named Lucky, and, well... she didn't want to hear that other name ever again and Lucky just felt right. Never mind that the name reminded her of Beck. At least, it would once she had Lucky back and Beck was out of her life for good. Then she could think over their time together and laugh until she cried. Cam swiped the corner of her traitorous eye. Darn things kept watering. She must be allergic to something. Maybe her heart?

Ember had turned out to be a good and sincere friend. Her Hollywood handsome husband, Rory, and their son, Tyler, had helped Cam move out of her home in The Palisades and into affordable housing near them in Silver Spring. They were almost neighbors, only a block and one street away from each other. If Cam looked south from her front doorstep, and through her neighbor's yard across the street, she could see straight into Ember's backdoor and the Dennison kitchen. They could wave to each other if they wanted. If she wanted.

But Cam had yet to do anything so—chummy. *Girlfriend.* There was a word Cam had never expected in her daily vocabulary. Ember was the best, and so were Kelsey Stewart, Libby Houston, McKenna Villanueva, even Izza Maher. Adam's wife Devereaux, too. Harley's wife Judy. Actually, everyone connected to The TEAM had become Cam's proxy family this past month and a half. All the women had gone through some shit in their lives. So had their husbands, and they'd made Cam a part of their unique band of brothers and sisters. She felt normal most days, like she belonged.

But night times were different. She wasn't sleeping. She'd gone through too much, in too short a time. It was hard to decompress after seeing her parents kill each other. She'd actually gone back to that cathedral in NYC one weekend. Even went inside. Looking for something, she hadn't known what. Too bad miracles didn't exist anymore. She'd surely needed one. Just hadn't found one there.

He'd waited long enough. It'd been weeks since Jaden Williamson's reign of terror ended. Tonight he was taking Cam's cat back.

"Sure quiet in the office these days," Renner murmured like he was talking to himself. Only he wasn't. "…now that Montego's in the ground and Williamson's kid is on his way to prison."

"Yeah. Quiet." Beckam gave him that much.

Renner'd said he'd come over to Beck's bachelor pad *just because*, but Beck knew Renner was worried about him. Heck, everyone in the office acted like they were worried he might fall off the deep end, or do something crazy just because Cam quit. Even Alex stopped by his desk one too many times a day to check on him. Unnecessarily so.

Beckam had never been surer of himself. He'd purposefully kept himself plenty busy since she'd walked out of his life. She'd moved on. Well, so had he. That was what soldiers did. The night at TEAM HQ, when he and Alex interrupted Hector's plans, had also ended any stray feelings Beck might have had for Camilla It was that simple. Intense, violent, life-and-death operations and the adrenaline rush that came with them, caused emotional, unrealistic reactions. The lines between right and wrong, especially between men and women, tended to blur during extreme stress. Men got horny.

Women did, too. He'd been there before; he'd be there again. No reason to worry.

It was simply the end of another successful chapter in his life as far as Beck was concerned, and he was glad it was over. Finished. Cam had lived to talk about her near-death adventure. Mrs. Jones hadn't. At the end of the day, that was all that mattered. Cam was alive and doing well. Ember said she'd already moved into a smaller, more affordable home. She'd gone back to church, and, by God, that was good enough for Beck. Damned straight.

"So…" Renner drew that word out. "You're going to have kittens."

Beck shook his head. "Not me. The cat goes home today."

Of all things he hadn't seen coming, Hector wasn't a tomcat. Instead, he'd been a barely pregnant feline when Beck had first found him, err, her. But now, Hector the cat was a rotund ball of orange tiger fur and ready to deliver. Any day now. Harley'd dropped the good news when he'd visited the evening of a particularly dark, much-to-do-about-nothing, Valentine's Day. The stupid day everyone else at the office sent flowers or jewelry to their beloveds. The day losers like Beckam went home alone.

Harley'd given Hector a clean bill of health all right, but then he'd guesstimated—with a straight face—maybe five or six kittens were inside that contented mama's belly.

"Say what?" Beck had asked in outright shock over the top of his bottle of root beer—Harley's choice.

Harley'd laughed. "You didn't know?"

"Never looked. Cam said she had a tomcat. I just figured…" Beck had shrugged because he should've known she wouldn't know which end was up when it came to feline gender. "Damn. That mama's got to go. Now."

Yes, the cat had gotten chubby, but he'd figured that was what lazy felines did when the weather turned frigid. He'd honestly never upended, never even thought about checking Hector the cat's boy-parts. Which Hector didn't have because he was a she, not a neutered male, which made Beckam grin at the joke that the real Hector Rojas was. The man who'd knowingly mislead a sixteen-year-old girl, enough that he'd gotten her pregnant, deserved all he got in prison. He just might end up the prettiest boy on the cell block. Now *that* would be Karma.

But the cat once known as Hector, had to go home where she and her offspring belonged. Now, as in right damned now. Beck knew from the stray cats that moused in his father's barns, feline gestation wasn't much more than sixty days, even if a person knew when those mama cats got pregnant. It was still hard to tell precisely when they'd drop those adorable, fluffy kittens. Which meant time was short. Hence Miss Kitty was packed and ready to go.

"You need a hand?" Renner offered lackadaisically.

"Nope. Truck's already loaded. Just need the cat," Beckam replied as he scooped Miss Kitty up and out of the corner of his couch where she usually—nested. Damn, that was exactly what she'd been doing. Nesting. He stuffed Miss Kitty into her cat carrier. He had to hurry.

"Want company?"

Beck cocked his head at the guy who was probably his closest friend on the entire East Coast. "You offering to ride shotgun and hold the cat for me, or are you just coming along for the ride?"

"Just thought you'd like company," Renner replied. "It's been a tough year."

That it had, but no. "This won't take long. Pop another root beer and hang around if you want. There's plenty left. God knows I don't drink 'em unless Harley's here."

Renner's face cracked into a grin. "Thought you'd never ask. I'll turn on the game. Call if you need anything."

He'd become a different guy since he'd gotten married and joined Alcoholics Anonymous. Not like he kept the anonymous part of that program quiet. But he was prone to crack jokes more often now, and Renner was genuinely happy. He and Tara were good for each other. Damned good.

Beckam put a quick stop to that trip down memory lane. Just because Renner ended up with the woman of his dreams did not mean he would. Life didn't work like that. Not for Beck. He just needed this thing between him and Cam done. Once and for all. Tonight. End of story.

"Probably not," he shot over his shoulder as he and Miss Kitty headed out his door. "I'll be right back."

Chapter Thirty-Seven

"I need to get going," Ember said as she lifted to her feet and set her empty glass in the sink. "Rory's probably wondering where I am, and Tyler will be home from school soon. Did I tell you he's in math lab, and he loves it? He's doing so much better now that he understands what the teacher's talking about."

Tyler was Rory's biological son from his first marriage, and Ember's adopted son. Coincidentally, she'd miscarried twice since she and Rory had married, so she completely understood the anguish Cam still harbored over the loss of her baby. It might never go away, but having someone who could relate to that dark time in her life, was truly comforting.

In the end, Georgia had been right when she'd told Renner, Mark, and Beck that just being with people who knew what she'd been through during the Vietnam War helped. The hollow spot in Cam's heart where her baby had once lived still hurt. But knowing she wasn't the only woman who'd suffered the loss of a child, and that kind-hearted Ember knew what she was talking about, softened Cam's grief. Sometimes…

But then Beck would call and leave another voicemail, and she'd wonder if she'd made a mistake crawling back to Tucker Chase on her hands and knees, begging him for her old job back. Oddly, he'd put one of his big, thick, muscly arms around her that day, and he'd hugged the stuffing out of her, almost as if he actually liked her again. Word must've gotten back to him. Alex must've talked, because Tucker put her back on his payroll pronto. No questions asked. And that was okay. Alex and Tucker weren't so bad. They were safe. Married. Not interested.

But Cam wasn't cut out for a job with former snipers. She'd seen the killer in Beckam's eyes the day he'd apprehended Hector. He'd meant to save her and end Hector if he had to, and he had saved her. But that fierce look of a killer was the same look she'd seen in Hector's black, soulless eyes, the same lightless stare of a man intent on ending another's life.

It scared her. She'd had enough of murder. Hell, in her short life, her unborn baby had been cold-heartedly murdered, then her parents, too. Of course, they deserved each other, so them murdering each other probably didn't count. Unless you witnessed it. Then it mattered. To Cam.

Then there was Max and poor, sad Dave. Once he'd been apprehended, Jaden Williamson had confessed to killing his father's friends. It seemed Bruce's Army group, Alpha Company's mortar platoon, had inadvertently strayed into enemy territory one day, up north past something called the Rock Pile. They'd come across a band of South Vietnamese traitors smuggling chests of stolen treasure out of South Vietnam and into Laos. Rubies from the Mogok Valley in Upper Myanmar, Burma. Gold from the Yunnan province in China and the mines in Tibet. Precious Vietnamese artifacts. Gems. Pearls. Wagons full of guns, cannons, and ammunition.

Surprised, the enemy combatants engaged in a three-day battle. It was a hard-fought tussle, but U.S. forces won in the end. Only Jaden had never believed his father's version of the story. He'd nurtured the few facts he'd been told into a crazy, twisted legend of lost treasures and the US Army soldiers who'd stolen it. Which explained why he'd kidnapped his father's buddies, then killed them when they hadn't a clue what he was talking about. Fiction was stranger than truth.

At the opposite end of the spectrum, Wilson Williamson turned out to be the good son. Until Jaden's capture, he'd haunted his father from one end of the District to the next, trying to take care of Bruce as best he could. When news of Jaden's capture and confession surfaced, Bruce finally gave in and went to live with Wilson and his family. He had two grandchildren who adored him. Or so Tucker had said.

But there were still days Cam's sanity hung by a thread. Living alone was hard, but she no longer contemplated suicide. Never even entertained it like she had back when everything in her messed-up life had fallen apart. Because Beckam was right, too. She wasn't anything like her parents, and she strived to prove it to Tucker Chase and the others in his strange, but friendly office, every single day. Cam now had friends in the FBI, as well as on Alex Stewart's TEAM. She was stronger. More confident. She ate better, and she'd signed up for a yoga class with Ember. She didn't need a man in her life, but her cat…?

Cam ran a hand over the tightly wound bun gathered at the back of her head. She'd have to deal with Beckam soon. The man wasn't the type to give up, and she wanted Lucky back.

"I can tell you're not in the mood to chat," Ember declared as she emptied her glass. "I'm out of here. Call me later?"

Cam waved at the stacks of, as yet, unpacked moving boxes. Only a couple dozen to go. "Might be a lot later. I need to put some of this stuff away. Thought I'd get as much done as possible before morning."

"I'd stay if I could, but I like to be home when Tyler gets there," Ember replied breezily. "Call whenever you can, even if it's late. I'm a night owl, you know that."

"Will do," Cam said as her voluptuous friend wrapped her in her arms and kissed her cheek.

"Night, chatterbox."

Ember had a way of spreading cheer with everything she did and said. To be called something as simple as *chatterbox,* after living a life devoid of teasing niceties, tugged a smile to Cam's lips. "Night," she told her BFF. "Don't forget to tell Rory thanks again for installing my security system. I'll sleep better tonight."

"You haven't been sleeping? What's keeping you awake?" Ember cocked her head nearly to her shoulder. "Do you have a prowler? I can stay if you need company, just have to let Rory know."

Cam shook her head. "No, but that guy at Union Station, the creep who was taking pictures of us that day. He's still out there. How do I know he's not involved with some scam Alana set in motion before she died? It'd be just like her."

Ember's lush, ruby red lips twisted into a sideways pucker that was adorable on her. "But you already know what Rojas was after. He only wanted the Swiss bank account numbers your father emailed you the day before your mother shot him. That's why Alana wanted Luis dead. He had to die if she stood a chance of getting her hands on every last cent he had. But oops! Turned out he'd already given everything to you, and he'd made it legal. The plantation in Puerto Rico. That monstrosity of a museum you called home in New York City.

Everything. If you'd been at work that day instead of out in the field with Beckam, you could've hidden the email where no one would've found it. Lucky for you, I intercepted it before Rojas showed up. I deciphered it, then hid everything for you. Think about it. If you'd been able to get into your computer, Rojas would've made you transfer it to his account, then killed you on the spot and run with your fortune."

Cam inhaled a deep breath, then released it with a sigh. "It's blood money. Alex knows a good lawyer. I might actually be wealthy once the dust settles, but I'm giving it all away. I never want to see Morning Glory Estates again."

Ember grinned. "I know! Isn't he the best boss ever?"

Well, yeah. Maybe. But Cam wasn't ready to admit that. The second she did, Ember might tease her into returning to The TEAM, and no. Just no. Beckam was there.

"When's Harley bringing Sonic by?"

Safe topic! "Tomorrow. I told him I needed to get a room ready and—"

"You're giving your dog her own room?" Ember squealed. "Wow! My little cocker spaniel sleeps with me and Rory on the foot of our bed. At least let Sonic sleep in the same room with you. Else what's the use in owning a big, scary German Shepherd?"

"She's a Malinois, and she's not scary."

Ember giggled. "Trust me, that sweet little puppy can be just as scary as any GSD if some idiot tries to break in."

If, not when. Which made Cam thankful all over again for the alarm system Rory had installed, tested, and then re-tested all day. "Maybe I will," she conceded. "It'd be nice to have something to snuggle with. Now off with you. I've got work to do, then a hot shower and maybe another glass of wine before bed."

"Later, little girl," Ember blew an air kiss from the now opened front door. "Oh, hi there," she said slyly to someone on the porch just out of Cam's view. "Umm… Cam? You've got a visitor." Her green eyes danced with excitement. "Good to see you, too, big guy. Buh-bye!"

And off she went. *The brat.* Because it wasn't Harley and Sonic on her porch. It was Beckam standing there with his big arms crossed over his equally impressive chest. Her lazy, tiger-striped tomcat lay draped around his neck like a fluffy winter scarf that purred. Lucky had yet to make a move. Silly boy acted like he'd found a new best friend.

"Hey," Beck said, his voice hoarse and ragged. He coughed, then lifted a hand to his mouth and cleared his throat. Either he was coming down with a cold or this unexpected get together was just as awkward for him as it was for her.

Why his callused fingers scraping over his whiskers sent a tingle straight to Cam's core, she didn't know. Except for the operation they'd started but hadn't finished, he'd always been cleanshaven in the office. There'd only been a full day of scruff at the end of their time together. Yet this afternoon, Beckam looked as if he'd just come in from a week of living on the streets. With his ball cap perched backward on his head, the rim behind him, his face sunburned, and his hair a little long, he was a sight for her sore eyes. His were wary, though.

Cam wasn't prepared to see him tonight. She thought she'd have more time to disguise her heart. But she couldn't help how her nostrils flared to breathe in those heavenly masculine smells of wind, soap, and coffee in the air between them. All American, manly scents. The spicy musk of men's deodorant.

The menthol sting of aftershave. Or men's cologne. The five o'clock shadow gracing his angular chin and cheeks, and the whiskers prickling over the skin above those luscious lips, declared Beck hadn't shaved today. Why not? Was he already on another mission? Had it been easy for him to trade partners? Did he ever think about the night she'd burrowed under his chin and nearly inside his Carhartt jacket because she'd needed to feel safe more than because she'd been cold?

Her stomach dropped at the memory of their one kiss in Union Station. She'd felt closer to him during that volcanic embrace than she'd ever felt with her ex. In one extraordinarily hard but enlightening day, she'd fallen in love with Beckam Garner, and she knew it. She'd even told him. Yet he hadn't returned the sentiment, and there she'd stalled. Not waiting, just mournfully sad she'd been wrong again. That she'd fallen for a man who hadn't fallen for her.

Cam refused to play the fool this time around. She could get along fine without men in her personal life. They made good mechanics, coworkers, and street sweepers. Garbage men. Soldiers. Friends. Just not soulmates. But she did want Lucky.

"Come in," she told him as curtly as she could manage without squeaking. Her silly heart still pounding too high up in her throat, making it difficult to speak at all. "You're letting all the warm air out." Which he wasn't. She could've stood there all night admiring him and drooling. But because he wasn't there to reciprocate her feelings for him, she needed to move this meeting along. Life was short. She needed this chapter over and done with.

"Yes, ma'am," Beckam said as he angled his wide shoulders through the doorway.

"Me-rowwww," purred *lucky* Lucky, the twice-rescued, thoroughly spoiled little boy who obviously adored Beckam. Didn't everybody?

"Yes, you can come inside, too, you lazy cat," Cam told him pointedly.

Beck doffed his hat while she closed the door and reset the alarm to her security system. Motion within triggered the interior cameras while any tampering with the windows or doors triggered a silent alarm that notified local police. Rory had tested it before he'd gone home, had even called the police so they didn't come running at the false alarm.

"I see Rory's been here," Beck said as his sharp blue eyes quartered what he could see of her tiny home, scanning the blinking cameras posted down the hall and in corners overhead.

"Yes. Right after he and Tyler helped move me in, he installed the best security system on the market. I feel quite safe now."

Beckam tipped his head to her like old-fashioned men did in deference to ladies, way back when. "Good. Better safe than sorry," he said as he unwound the feline from his neck and handed him over, one hand under Lucky's plump butt, the other cupping his big belly.

"My goodness, what have you been feeding him? He's as big as a sumo wrestler." He weighed as much, too. Cam no more than had Lucky on his back in her arm, when she realized she'd need both hands to hold this fat cat.

"Yeah, umm, about that…" Beck scrubbed a hand over his face. His lips pursed a heartbeat before he blurted, "Hector's pregnant."

"He's… He's what?"

"Yes, ma'am. Hector's a female, not a dude, and she's due any day, maybe even tonight. You'll want to keep her indoors from now on. Keep a close eye on her. Call Harley if you—"

"How can you be sure?"

That earned her the lopsided grin she loved. On a good day, Beck could make the sun come out. "I should've checked, but, well," he admitted, that hand now combing through chunks of his lush, dishwater blond hair. "You'd said Hector was a tomcat, and I guess that was good enough for me. After I found him running loose that night, I asked Harley to come check him. Just wanted to make sure he hadn't gotten into any antifreeze or something that would kill him. But then Harley tells me Hector's going to give birth to five, maybe six kittens and—"

"Oh, my, no!" That couldn't be right. Just. Could. Not. What would Cam do with a house full of cats? "Five or six? Right here? In my new house? But it's so small. Should we take him…? I mean her, I mean should I…? Won't she need a d-d-doc… a vet?"

The more rattled Cam grew, the more Beckam's face blossomed into a smile. "If you want to, sure. You could take her to a vet, but most mamas know what they're doing when it comes time to have a baby. Or six."

"Oh, that's real funny. But really. Will she be okay? That's a lot of babies all at one time. What if she can't feed them? What if they won't latch on and nurse?" Did kittens just know how to do that the second they opened their eyes? For that matter, weren't kittens born blind and hairless and… *Oh, darn. What have I gotten myself into?*

"It's okay, Cam. Cats have been doing this longer than mankind's existed on the planet. If Hector, I mean Miss Kitty, has a lick of trouble giving birth, call Harley. I'll leave his emergency number. He'll know what to do. Just keep her warm. She'll be okay. You'll see."

"B-b-but… My house. All those cats…" Panic set in. How could she control a herd of kittens while she was at work? Was that what you called more than one kitten, a herd? Or were they a flock? Whatever. They'd be underfoot all the time and into everything. They'd destroy her home just when she finally had her life back. This was not what she needed.

"Guess you could call a vet," Beckam said quietly. "Have the pregnancy terminated or make arrangements to give the kittens away as soon as they're born. Some people would."

"I am not some people!" Cam spat at him, her Spanish up. *How dare he?!* "I was just… just surprised is all. I would never…" *Never. Never. Never!* Cam couldn't speak, not with her heart in her throat for a different reason than lusting after Beck. Hefting Lucky over her shoulder, she faced her cat away from the evil thing that had just come out of Beck's mouth. Hot tears blurred her vision as she clung to the only creature that had ever loved her unconditionally.

"Damn you, Beckam Garner," she murmured, her soul ravaged all over again for the child she'd lost. "You're an ass! I don't kill b-b-babies. How could you say that to me? Me!" And now her voice had gone tight, and she was squeaking like a mouse. Which Cam was not.

"I never said you did," he replied evenly, his voice a velvet purr that gentled her aching heart.

The need to reach out and touch him welled up into a profound physical pain she couldn't ignore. Maybe it was just post-traumatic stress like her counselor said. Or her bottled up suppression from years' worth of betrayal and abuse. Heath *had* assaulted her. She did suffer from spousal abuse and a lifetime of betrayal.

But Beckam had never hurt her. Not even the teeniest littlest bit. He'd always been a rock. Her rock. His size, strength, and dominant masculinity had shaped her into the woman she was today. He was everything she'd wanted through all those empty, heartless years. And more.

Cam couldn't hold back. She was on fire. Within the space of one poignantly quick heartbeat, she was inside his arms, her and Lucky and… God! She'd needed this man for so, so long. A sob choked out of her in one big hiccup when Beck's big body encompassed hers in warmth and strength, all the things she'd tried to live without.

"I'd never hurt a baby," she choked, holding onto her cat as if she could save Lucky from the cruelty of the world. "I am not my mother."

It seemed as if his whole body breathed a sigh. "I know, Cam. Sweetheart, I know. But you asked. I just answered the question."

She buried her face in Lucky's thick fur, ashamed she'd ever placed things above the love of this sweet feline and the tiny, helpless kittens in her belly. Things had never loved her back. Not Alana's exotic jewelry or one dollar of her father's money. Not even her parents. Only this stray little girl who'd needed a safe home for her babies. Five or six of them. Suddenly, Cam couldn't wait to see those furry little faces. She needed to read up on kittens. But first…

She melted into the heat of her one safe haven, painfully aware that Beck hadn't ever said *we*. Only *you*. "You're not s-s-staying with me?"

He coughed instead of answering.

She burrowed into that jacket, clutching it and Lucky like two lifelines. "Beck, I'm sorry I got mad. I'm sorry—"

"Stop," he ground out. "Just stop, all right, Cam? I didn't come here to stay. I just came to bring Hector back—"

"Lucky. I changed his, I mean her, name to Lucky."

"Good. I always hated calling him, umm, her, that. But good. Okay then." Beckam coughed again. "It's just that…"

Cam would've smiled, but she couldn't. Not yet. Beck was having trouble saying what he needed to say, which was probably goodbye. Like a wooden post with no heart or soul, she stiffened in his arms. Her foolish hopes fled. She, of all people, could handle rejection. Okay, then. She pulled away. *Might as well get it over with.* "Why did you really come here?"

His nostrils flared with a manly puff. "To bring Lucky and all the stuff I've bought for her, back."

"Is that all, Agent-in-Charge?" she asked coyly.

"Yes, ma'am," he answered quickly. Forever the Boy Scout. Forever too damned polite and honorable.

But he was lying. Cam could tell. Returning Lucky might've been Beck's intention when he'd started out for her place tonight. But there was something else in his eyes now. A shadow of heat. A trill of desire. A question he didn't seem to know how to answer—or how to ask. *Hmm.* This man didn't really want to leave. He just didn't know how to stay.

She could've slapped her forehead for not seeing though him sooner. Of course! Beckam didn't know the first thing about come-ons and one-liners.

Okay then. Game on.

Instead of confronting him or calling his bluff, instead of fighting or calling names like she used to, Cam nodded as if she understood perfectly, and as if she totally agreed with that lame explanation he'd offered.

To bring Lucky and all her stuff, my ass. Beckam could've had Harley drop Lucky off. Or Rory. Even Ember would've done that for him. But Beck hadn't asked them, had he? No, because honorable men saw even the hardest jobs through.

"Wait up, Beck," she told him sweetly, "while I shut Lucky in my bedroom and grab a coat. Many hands make work light, isn't that how it goes?"

"Okay. Yeah, right." His eyes actually lit up at that adage. "But there's not much. Why don't you just hold the front door while I carry everything inside? Don't want to let all the heat out."

There was that. A genuine smile blossomed over Cam's cheeks at his polite reminder. She loosened her hair tie and let her tangled masses tumble over her shoulders. "I'll still need a jacket or something," she said without a single hint of tease in her voice. "Be right back."

Beckam's gaze scrolled over those heavy ebony tresses. His chest heaved; he even licked his bottom lip. That was when Cam knew she had him. This man loved her long hair and her full breasts. Well, good. Those she knew how to use.

Chapter Thirty-Eight

Why was he really here? *Good question.*

Beck scrubbed a quick hand over his head, not sure of anything at the moment. He couldn't breathe, not after she'd let that shimmering cascade of ebony curls hang down her back and off her shoulders. Obviously, she hadn't been expecting company, not wearing that lighter than air, simple, pink cotton dress and those strappy, summer sandal things, umm, espadrilles? Wasn't that what Mary Lou called them? The combination of that summery get-up mingled with all that shiny, black, tangled hair, and those long, long legs… Damned if they didn't make Cam look more feminine. Softer and prettier. Definitely better than what she'd looked like in the old lady dresses and pantsuits she'd usually worn in the office. Certainly better than who she'd been in those smelly, cast-off clothes he'd purposefully scrounged out of the garbage for her.

That simple little dress of hers emphasized every inch of the well-endowed and unencumbered rack beneath it. He was a man. Couldn't help that his eyes went straight to the embossed imprint of the hardened tips of her nipples. No dress could conceal the way they'd stood up when she'd set eyes on him. She wasn't wearing a bra, which only made his reaction at seeing her again worse. Or better. He might've even licked his lips at the errant electric volt that nailed his cock, zapping it to life like the randy Frankenstein monster it could be.

Damned thing had a mind of its own lately, and tonight, it seemed to want inside Cam in a bad way. In a good way, too. But officers… Damn it! Officers were gentlemen or they were nothing at all! He had to be strong. For her.

Edgy for wanting a woman he had no right to want, Beck scrubbed a firm hand over his zipper to readjust the brain-dead bad boy in his pants before she noticed. Just what he didn't need this afternoon. Blue balls.

But worse… all the lovely attributes he'd not noticed when Cam had been Attila the Hun at TEAM HQ, made her look younger tonight. Damn it, forbidden fruit might be the sweetest, but ten years was a lifetime. She probably didn't even like hard rock, not that different likes and dislikes were deal-breakers, but… Ten. Years?

Until now, he'd never been particularly drawn to any woman. It wasn't too long ago he could've had his share of wannabe Army wives, but none of them had been as strong, nor as sweet and resilient, as Cam. She'd never looked so, so beautiful. That was the only word for her. She'd all but stopped his heart when she'd dared him to enter her home with that "you're letting all the warm air out" crack. God, he'd missed the lovely disdain she wielded like a monarch's scepter over worthless commoners like him. She really was a queen, and he was nothing but a peasant, ready and willing to grovel at her feet.

Cam's eyes were clear for the first time since he'd known her. She looked genuinely happy, as if she'd conquered her rage against the world. At her parents. As if she were finally content with who she was inside herself. He could still smell the sweet, flowery scent she'd left behind in her wake. Like an aphrodisiac he shouldn't let himself wallow in, it was nonetheless on his hands and fingers. On his clothes. Smelled like heaven, whatever it was. Flowers and hope and, yeah. Heaven.

This house couldn't hold a candle to that mansion in The Palisades in snob appeal, yet everything about it spoke of Cam. She'd decorated her living room in soft earth-tones mixed with ruby red accents. Christmas was long gone, but the woven planter overflowing with live poinsettias, sitting on the hearth of her slate-gray fireplace, made her front room cozy, inviting, and warm. Instead of the ever-popular Venetian blinds most people used, her windows boasted light and airy cream-colored panels beneath heavier, tan curtains, again striped with reds, crimsons, and darker browns. Nice effect.

While the house looked to be only one thousand, maybe fifteen-hundred square feet of livable space, she'd made it a home. And she'd just barely moved in. Once Harley brought Sonic over, Cam would have everything she needed, and wasn't that just perfect? She'd have a houseful of life, while Beckam crawled back to his fortress of solitude to wait for his next mission.

His fingertips set to tapping his thigh at the obvious dichotomy between his life and hers. Between his choices and hers. There was a time not long ago he'd wanted to be the cocky guy selected for every TEAM classified op. He'd pressed hard to be one of Alex Stewart's top men. His small circle of go-to-guys. He'd worked one-on-one with Alex to take down Hector Rojas. Alex was proud of him. Beck could tell, because he was leadership material, damn it.

All his life Beck had strived to be, if nothing else, reliable. Dependable. The chief everyone else relied on and turned to. He'd been an Army captain and a Ranger. In all things, he'd held himself to a higher standard. He'd excelled every damned time. He'd only ever and always been above reproach; a model warrior sworn to uphold the constitution and adhere to all ROEs, rules of engagement. No matter what lies Major Brad Parker spread, Beckam was born to be a hero. He was the living version of Marvel's Captain America, damn it. Only now…

Beckam wanted something else. He looked down the hall and cocked his head, drawn to the music in Cam's sweet voice as she cooed at her cat. Silly woman was probably tucking Lucky into her bed, maybe even under the covers like she'd do with a little kid. Her own baby if she had one…

Hmmm. Maybe it was time to get a cat or a dog. Yeah, no. Stupid idea. Beckam didn't want a pet. He wanted Cam.

After making Lucky comfortable at the foot of her bed, Cam grabbed a hoody out of her hall closet and shrugged it over her shoulders. "Wait right here," she told her fat cat. Not like that mama cat was going anywhere anytime soon. She had a double chin!

Beck stood waiting and stalwart at her front door. "Ready?" he asked, that same puzzled look shadowing his eyes.

"Sure. Let's do this," she answered, fluffing her hair over the shoulders of her hoody and excited to be working with her Agent-in-Charge again.

He nodded once and opened the door. "Wait here. Be right back."

"You bet," she said as she leaned out her glassed-in screen door to track Beckam while he hustled back to his—wow. She didn't know he drove the big red truck always parked in TEAM underground parking. She'd never buy anything that sat so high off the ground. She'd worry it would scrape the low ceilings in parking garages and then she'd be stuck and—

Dayam... it was good to see him. Only she saw him through better eyes now. He really was a Boy Scout, the proverbial straight arrow. He didn't know how to play games, and he didn't deviate from being the gentleman his parents had taught him to be. If anything, he was a mythical unicorn, a legendary miracle that proved good men did exist. Which made her wonder if he was a virgin. That seemed out of character for a man who'd been in the Army, yet for Beckam, it felt right. Nothing he'd ever done hinted at him being a player. Besides, weren't all Boy Scouts unsullied and pure?

Big, big breath. *Dayam... He looks so good.* She licked her bottom lip when he jerked the tailgate on that monstrous truck open, put one hand to the side, and then jumped into the truck bed without effort, flexing that tempting backside. Stretching his jean pockets until she nearly choked. Handsome man. Taut backside. Not an inch of sloppy fat anywhere on that bod.

She was panting. Maybe drooling. She'd forgotten how muscular he was. How tall and athletic. How lithe and wide and—nice. He was her kryptonite.

Carefully, he lowered a ginormous bag of cat food over the side, then a bag of litter, a rust-colored carpet-covered thing that looked like a ten-foot-tall tree, then a rust-colored, carpet-covered box. Lucky's bed maybe? My heck, how much had Beckam bought her lazy cat? He'd only had her a little over a month. But the simple black t-shirt beneath his signature

Carhartt jacket emphasized every last detail, right down to the rigid valley between his pectorals. And those shoulders...

She remembered snuggling into that body one cold, wintery might.

Beckam finally jumped down to the ground with another bag slung over his shoulder. What on earth could that be? Then, methodically, he marched back to where she held the door for him and stacked everything inside her entryway.

"Where would you like this?" he asked, holding the cat tree in one hand.

Cam pointed down the hall. It was a good thing she'd planned on giving Sonic her own room. Looked like she was going to share. "First bedroom on your left, the open one opposite mine."

Something snapped between them at that revelation. Those words. Bedroom. Mine.

Her tongue made a quick lap over her suddenly parched lips. This was crazy, overreacting to every little nuance between them. But, yeah. Now he knew precisely which bedroom was hers, and, oh yes. There was a very nice bed in it.

"Yes, ma'am," Beckam replied smoothly as he tipped the bulky thing on its side and maneuvered it with all its branches into the hall, unintentionally putting on one heck of another show. Whatever aftershave or cologne he'd splashed on set her pulse to racing. Damn, damn, damn, he smelled delicious. Did that even make sense? She didn't care.

"Umm, want me to take your jacket while you're inside?" she offered.

"Nope. This won't take long," he replied, already on task.

Hurriedly, she reset her security system and returned to where Beckam struggled with that three-branched cat tree. The thing was too big. Too bulky. Those padded branches were too long to make the turn into her spare bedroom. After trying a few different angles and grunting to keep from marring her walls, Beck backed out of the hall with it, turned the tree so the longest branch pointed up instead of sideways and started over. But once more, he could not get it to turn corners without scratching the walls.

He backed it out of the hall once again and set it in her front room, dragging his fingers over his head and ruffling all that gorgeous, dark blond hair. "Damn," he huffed. "I made it too big. It won't fit."

"You made it? For me, umm, I mean, for Lucky?"

Beckam frowned. "Well, yeah. Figured he needed exercise. Didn't know he was a mama."

Which made Cam want to laugh. Beckam prided himself on being a farm boy. How could he have missed deciphering her cat's gender? But then, she'd missed it, too.

Man, she could not tear her hungry eyes off his handsome, grumpy face. All hard angles and determination, Beckam looked unhappy. If he frowned any wider, she'd faint, just fall down on her knees and beg him to forgive her for having been so distant and cold.

"Here. Let me help. Maybe two are better than one," she said, squeezing those words out of her desert-dry throat. Trying extra-hard not to moan when her nostrils flared wide at his close proximity, or when her belly expanded, breathing his scent back into her heart. Into her life.

He'd worked up a sweat in that sturdy jacket, the rugged, masculine drift of him inciting her hormones like a red flag to a charging bull. Which was not a good simile at all. She was no bull. But she did want to charge right over Beck, knock that manly ass to the floor, lick that frown off his mouth and wherever else that all-male body might be frowning.

Oh, God. What am I thinking! Just that priceless, illicit picture of having her way with him in the middle of her living room knocked the starch out of her knees.

"Thanks," he answered, jockeying the cat tree back into her narrow hall.

But she lied. Beckam's piece of art woodwork just plain was not going into her spare room. The workmanship was like nothing she'd ever seen, but he'd made it too long and the branches too wide to navigate the hall. It had to have been a tree not long ago, but carved stars and moons adorned every bare length and branch now. He'd tucked the carpet edges between lengths of what looked like polished oak, then attached rubber bumpers to the base to protect her floors. There wasn't a stray cat hair in sight. Not one. Either Beck had just finished this work of art, or he'd kept it covered so Lucky couldn't shed all over it. But he'd made it for her and Cam knew it. To use Ember's favorite word, *wow. Just wow.*

"Let's just put it in the corner by the couch," Cam offered. "I'll move the end table. Lucky won't mind."

"You named her after my dad's bull," Beckam said, not looking at her while he maneuvered the tree for what Cam hoped was the last time.

"I had to. He, err, she… umm, Lucky deserved an honest name. A better name, and well, it reminds me of you."

Something hot like a solar flare flashed between them.

Beckam cleared his throat. "You get the end table. I'll get this monstrosity."

"It's not a monstrosity," Cam corrected as she pulled the end table out of the corner and set it against the half-wall between her kitchen door and the hall. Where it seemed to fit perfectly. She stood back admiring the placement. "I like this better here. What do you think?"

She could've slapped herself. What did he care where her table ended up? He wasn't staying.

To prove it, he barely glanced at the table, but like every other guy in the world, he said, "Ah huh. Looks great." By then, he'd situated the tree in the corner, its branches safely extended along both walls instead of outward where people could run into them. "How's this? Need me to move it? Might as well let me do the heavy lifting while I'm still here."

Cam looked sideways, but—what cat tree? Her mouth went dry at the sight of her very own Agent-in-Charge, standing in her house, scratching the back of his head. He filled the room. Certainly dwarfed the antique sofa and wingback chair she'd rescued from the thrift store. My goodness, what a long way they'd come.

"Looks perfect," she managed to whisper.

And it was the perfect picture because the honest man standing there was all she could see. Her. House. Not Heath Brinkman's. Not Luis nor Alana Lopez/Escobar's. Just hers. And the handsome man who'd only ever mentored and protected her, who'd been there for her when she'd needed him most, and who'd held her so tenderly when life ran her down, was now standing in the very heart of all she held dear.

He looked awkwardly uncomfortable, though, as if he were ready to bolt now that he'd done what he'd come here for. Which he would. Beck was a taskmaster, and when he was done with a job, he moved onto another. Then another. Yet she knew he cared for her as more than just a junior agent. It was there in the true-blue heat of his eyes, which had grown sadder tonight. Not a hint of turquoise sparked. Because he was always and first an officer. *The idiot.*

"Wine," she blurted, then added, "I've, umm, got a bottle of white wine or… or…" *Or something…* Her tongue had suddenly turned to wood.

He shook the invitation off. "No, thanks." *Oh, darn.* "Beer'd be better if you've got it. I'm not much of a wine guy." *Yes!*

"I have beer." She couldn't help the smile blossoming over her face at that little capitulation. How long would it take him to drain one can of beer? Five minutes if he was really thirsty? Ten, if he sat down and shucked out of that jacket while he drank? But what if…?

"Dinner. Umm, have you eaten today? I mean, dinner?" Man, it was difficult speaking with this man around. She tried again. *I can do this.* "Have you had dinner, Beck? Ember brought over takeout earlier. Teriyaki chicken and sticky rice. There's plenty left over, and I was wondering…" And there she stalled like an airplane flaming out of the wild blue yonder, ready to crash and burn.

Beck jerked his head back like guys do when they want you to come to them. His gaze kept darting to her mouth, then away. There was a funny shimmer clouding the blue in his eyes.

"You," he murmured huskily. "I'd really rather have you, Cam."

That was all she needed to hear. In two steps, Cam was in his arms, her mouth opened, and tears trickling hot and heavy down her cheeks while she kissed him. But these were happy tears. So happy. Man, she wanted to eat him alive. Every last inch. Every piece of him.

"Beckam," she breathed between nibbling his lips, loving the scrape of that five o'clock shadow on her chin.

He took her eager mouth by storm, his tongue tangling with hers, dancing! His breath warm and sweet in her nose. Beck might be a Boy Scout, but he kissed like a sinner. Yet there was something pure in the touch of his lips to hers. Something sacred. Every lick and nibble was more reverent than voracious. More coaxing than hurried, as if he needed to gentle her, to reassure her. As if he wanted to take his time tasting her.

For the first time in her life, Camilla felt loved. That was what Beckam was doing. He was loving her first instead of himself. Treasuring her. The care with which he kissed made her want to give him something back in return. Her hands skated over his massive shoulders, needing a better hold while he cupped her jaw.

Still so gentle, his long fingers delved into her hair, while his callused thumbs scraped over the tears on her damp cheeks.

She canted her head to give him better access. To give herself better access to that wonderfully, carefully demanding mouth of his. Coffee. He tasted like coffee and melted caramel.

A whimper escaped at the tempting scent drifting off him. The same aftershave he'd worn on their once-in-a-lifetime operation, only mingled with fresh air and the smell of manly sweat. The erotic perfume of an aroused male filled her senses as he gentled his mouth even more, then fit himself to her. This guy didn't know how to be rough. He held her so carefully. So different than those other guys in her life. Those liars and cheats and—

All at once, what Heath and Hector had done to her rushed over her again.

"I can't do this!" she nearly screamed, frantic to be free. To run!

The pain was still too raw. Too fresh. This was why she'd gone back to the FBI. There was no danger there, because there was nothing and no one like Beck. Yes, they were all honest, hard-working people, but none of Director Chase's people could measure up to the danger Beckam posed. This simple, honorable man from Oklahoma, an unimportant state in the middle of nowhere-America, populated by ordinary people who went to church every Sunday and who believed in God, could hurt her worse than anyone ever had. Because she loved him but he could leave. Would leave. They all did.

Lifting the back of a shaky hand to her mouth, she wiped his kiss off her wet lips. No longer making heartbreaking eye contact. No longer sure of anything. "Please. J-just go."

Beckam backed away. "You said beer."

Well, yeah, but that was then and this is now. She used to rely on ugly words, but her heart wasn't in them like it used to be. She didn't want to hurt this guy. He hadn't done anything wrong. It was just her misplaced anger. Misdirected fear. Cam knew that now. She hadn't missed a one of her counseling appointments. Wouldn't dream of it. She now knew she'd been programmed by unloving parents and their choice of a husband. No more. She'd cried more these last few weeks than she had in her entire wasted life. She was stronger than this. It had to stop.

She just needed a minute to breathe and remember where she was and who she was with. That men were a mistake she couldn't afford to make again. Not even Beck.

Still afraid to look at his handsome face for fear she'd see sadness in his beautiful eyes, she told the floor, "You're right. I do owe you something for bringing Lucky b-back." And now she was stuttering like an imbecile teenage girl on her first date. Which this was not. He'd only come over to—

"You don't owe me anything," he said, interrupting her panic attack. "Honest. Not even a beer. It's okay. I'll leave, but if you ever need help or…"

She glanced up in time to watch his hand make a fast pass over his head.

"…anything. Please Cam. Just call. If you don't want me, I'll send someone from The TEAM. They'll help you. You'll see."

Not want you? The notion stabbed at her heart. Cam lifted her chin and looked him in the eye. He might as well know. "But… but I don't want them, Beck. I want you, too. Only—"

"But all I've ever done was try to get close to you," he said in a whisper. "I've never hurt you. Wouldn't dream of it. What are you so scared of? Me? Do I scare you, Camilla?"

Her head bobbed. "Yes. But only because I'm afraid you'll leave me. I know you will. Someday. Somehow. If we were to get serious, I'd do something you won't like. I'll wake up, and you'll be gone and—"

And she was back in his arms again, his big palm cupping the back of her head as he pressed her protectively under his chin. "No," he choked, his heart pounding in her ear. "Never. I've fought too hard to get here. Every time I called, all I got was your voicemail. But never you. I know you're scared. I'm scared too, Cam, but…" She listened to his throat working through a hard swallow. "Please. I don't have a clue what I'm saying right now, only that I need you to give us a chance. I know I'm too old for you, but—"

"You're too what? Too old?" she asked, drawing just far enough out of his arms to look up and see into his eyes. It was odd how being this close to him instantly quieted her fears. When she'd been with Heath or Hector, she'd wanted nothing to do with them when they came this close. But they didn't stand a chance with Beckam filling her line of sight. The key was keeping her eyes open.

"How... how old are you? Like eighty? Ninety?" she teased, more relaxed now. Steadier. Able to breathe. Because this was Beckam Garner. Her friend.

The thickest lashes fringed his beautiful, sad, blue eyes. Brown eyelashes with the tiniest hints of gold. Gorgeous, like soft sandy beaches accentuating a troubled, turquoise-blue ocean. Were those teardrops glistening on his lashes?

Beckam leaned his forehead to hers. "I've lived ten hard years more than you," he whispered hoarsely. "I'm an old soldier. You'll be wasting your time on me. You're so young and vibrant, but Cam... I've tried to stay away, but I can't. I want you."

The last of her anxiety vanished. "But I'm older than you in other ways," she told him sincerely, threading her fingertips up into his hair, loving the silky feel of every short golden lock. "Maybe even wiser in some respects. You've seen combat, but I've lived it. Every day since I was a child. In my father's house. In Heath's house. At every school I transferred to. In every job I've ever held. Okay, so that's only been three jobs, well, four if you count the FBI twice. But I'm not scared of loving you, Beckam. Only of losing you. Because you're a guy, and one day you'll wake up, and I won't be good enough or skinny enough or—"

"No, no, no." A strangled cough choked out of him. Beck was blinking hard and fast. "I think it's the other way around," he whispered, licking his lips. "You've got your whole life ahead of you. Why on earth would you want someone like me?"

She couldn't help but take that manly jaw into her palms. If ever there was a man who needed a comforting hand, it was Boy Scout. "Are you going into assisted living tomorrow and you didn't tell me? You would do that without me?"

At last, the sunshine in his soul came back out. "Would you go with me if I were?"

And there it was, finally. The starlight in an honest man's heart shining out of his glistening eyes, even while he tried to sniff it away. Ah, men. They hid so much of themselves trying to look and act tough. Didn't he get it? Tenderness was all Cam had ever needed in her life, and Beckam had that in spades. With him, she could breathe. Maybe fly.

"Yes," she told him carefully, her heart pounding at this tremendous step into unchartered territory. "I will go anywhere with you, Beckam Garner. But you need to know I'm not much fun. I'm always scared now, I can't sleep most nights, and I don't trust anyone. Not yet. Sometimes it's all I can do to go out my front door to work in the morning. But I'm seeing a good counselor, and my boss, Tucker Chase, understands what I'm going through. He's been really good to me since I went back to work for him, and I'm trying. Every day's hard, but I'm finally getting things straight in my head. Alex lined me up with a good lawyer, and…" She licked her lips, needing Beckam to understand that age was not the handicap here. The spousal abuse she'd lived through was. The constant betrayals. The ugly things she'd grown up with and had once thought were normal. But he was smart. He'd figure it out if he hadn't already.

"For the first time in my life, I have real friends who don't judge what or who I used to be." Cam almost snorted at that understatement. She had been a bit of a beast. "But you're my best friend. I want you to stay, Beckam. Tonight. With me. Will you?"

Chapter Thirty-Nine

Yes! Yes, a thousand times, yes! I'll stay and I'll protect you and I'll serve you until you're so sick of me, you'll send me away. Never the other way around. On my honor as an American soldier. As a man. Yes. Forever, yes. Words Beckam didn't dare say, but words he nonetheless felt in the deepest hollows of his lonely, empty heart. Instead he whispered sincerely, "Yes, I'll stay, Cam. Forever. If you're sure."

Her lips melted into the most beguiling smile. "I'm sure."

Until Cam had burst into his life with her fire, sass, and her mighty big opinion of herself, he hadn't known how lonely he'd been. Honestly, that one night with her in that tiny tent in the middle of freezing cold Washington, DC, had changed everything. He'd been lost since she'd left The TEAM, unable to think of anything or anyone else. If not for his crazy notion to make the biggest, baddest cat tree ever, he'd have gone nuts. Yet even that had been for her.

So yes. He would stay, and maybe she'd let him hold her all night long. But just on the couch. He wasn't stupid enough to push her for more than she was willing to offer. She'd been through enough crap in her life. He wasn't the kind who bullied and badgered. But to hold her in his arms, and breathe in her sweet feminine scent, and love her—just for tonight—that he could do.

"There must be a God," she whispered. "There has to be."

That certainly came out of the blue. "I know there is," he replied earnestly. "But why do you think so?"

Her shoulders lifted. "Because He's always sending you."

Beckam stared down at the lovely lady in his arms. Man, he loved her. She was beautiful with her hair loose on her shoulders instead of pulled tight into her usual bun. That alone made him smile. But her finally recognizing the possibility of God in her life made him want to crow.

Until Cam's fingertips combed into his hair and the pad of her thumb traced the divot in his eyebrow. "What happened?"

Oh, that. He cocked his head, needing to explain. "A year ago, I was in the Philippines on an operation. We were hunting a couple known Al-Qaeda terrorists. No big deal. My team got the guys, but not before one of them got a shot off and nailed me. It was nothing, just a crease."

"But it must've hurt."

He nodded. "Well, yes, but like I said, it's nothing. I'm still alive and he's not."

Her head canted to one side. "Then why no ER? You still have headaches, don't you? Do you get dizzy? Is there something you're not telling me?"

There was no sense in lying. "Yes, I still have migraines now and then. Not as often as before, but I'm Army, Cam, and proud of it. I know I need to tell Alex the whole truth, but honestly, us guys don't like to share crap like this. I don't want him or you to worry."

"But Alex cares about you, too, and I will worry."

There it was, the sweetest words he'd ever heard. Camilla wanted what was best for him. She loved him. It didn't get any better than that.

He lifted her questing hand to his lips. "I've never blacked out," he told her between kisses to her fingers. "It's no big deal. Alex gets migraines all the time."

"But you're making an appointment to get your head checked, aren't you? Like tomorrow morning?"

God, he loved this woman. She had him there, and she knew it. "Yes, ma'am. For you, I'll do anything," he murmured, closing his eyes as he drew her index finger into his mouth and suckled.

Cam slipped her other hand down his neck to his shoulders, and from there, to his chest. And from there…

His gut tensed. Beckam released her finger as he halted her wandering hands, circling her tiny wrists, to keep her from getting more than she was ready for. He was already on high alert and burning hot. It'd been a long time since he'd been with a woman. Too long. Just the idea of her touching him through his pants sent shockwaves spiraling up his spine. He didn't want to frighten her. She was a tiny thing, and he simply was—not.

Instead of arguing, she smiled up at him. Her eyes were so big and black and sparkling with sincere desire, when she lifted up on her toes and covered his mouth with—ambrosia. Pure. Decadent. Sweetness. And he was powerless under her feminine assault, her lips so lush and tender. Apprehension fled when she rubbed the length of her hot body against his like a cat. Her tongue actively engaged, licking his lips and inside his mouth. She might not know it, but she was breathing life back into him. Damn, things were moving fast.

His hands slipped down to cup her backside, and once he had his hands full, she was off the floor and earnestly resuscitating him. Sucking his lower lip. Nibbling. Moaning.

Panting into his mouth. Writhing her gorgeous body against his, while he gave as good as he was getting. Her ample breasts were so soft and warm on his chest, but… the couch wasn't going to work.

"Bed," he growled around her prehensile tongue, squeezing that wiggling backside and urging her on. "Where's your bed, woman?"

Instead of answering, she cast one arm down the hall, pointing while she made a meal of his mouth.

Of course. The room where she'd taken Lucky. Beck took long strides down the hall, a man on a mission. Intent on his goal. His one goal in life. His wish. But with Cam in his arms, something as simple as walking turned into pushing her against the wall to get a better grip on her ass. She'd shoved his jacket off his shoulders by then, and her hands were busy under his t-shirt, mapping his pecs and his ribs. His throat. She'd turned frantic with lust, and they weren't going to make it to her bed in time.

Another question demanded her answer. "Birth control?" he asked, barely able to think. But this was important. Babies deserved to be made out of love, not lust. "I've got a couple condoms in my wallet, but if you're on birth control—"

"Guess that means you're not a virgin then," she mumbled.

Whatever that meant. "Answer me, Cam. This is important."

"I'm sterile. Botched abortion, remember?"

"Oh, crap." *That. Damn. What a fool I am.* Yet he had to be sure since he couldn't remember her telling him that before. "So your last period—"

"Was when I was sixteen. I've only spotted since then, just like that doctor said. Don't think so hard, Beck. Don't ruin this."

"Don't mean to. Just needed to double-check coordinates before launch."

That made her smile again. "Then get busy. Fire that rocket."

"Yes, ma'am." The wall would have to do, but her hoody had to go. He pushed it off her shoulders. The dress flew over her head next. The moment it was gone, heaven fell into his willing hand.

Beck was a sucker for full breasts, and hers were all he'd imagined, and more. Warm and plush and delightfully fragrant. He ducked his head for a taste of one rigid rosebud, then died and thought he'd gone to heaven once the hot morsel was tucked deep inside his mouth, against his tongue. Suckling her. Tugging ragged moans out of her. Licking and liking and loving every inch he could reach with his teeth and lips.

Cam took over then. She hooked one arm around his neck while her other hand delved between their bellies to parts below. His entire body turned into an active sensor then, alive with the sweetest stimulation a man could ask for. Beg for.

"You're so, so ready," she purred as if she liked what she'd found.

"Yeah, but are you?" he asked, while he palmed one luscious cheek of her ass and fastened her to his hips, needing to be sure. Not breaking eye contact, not for one blink, while he slipped his fingers between her legs and into her quivering folds. Hot damn, yes.

Beck closed his eyes and groaned at the slick anticipation he found there. Every little sound she made urged him onward and upward. Exploring further ensured that this first get together would be hot and fast. But damn. This woman knew her way around male anatomy. With her thumb and index finger, she'd circled him in a noose. Up and down and up and down and...

"No. Stop. Please," he muttered hotly even as his body thrust reflexively forward, searching for bliss. "If you keep going, I'll finish long before you, and that's just not right. You're first. Always. Every time. But I've got to get rid of these pants."

"So drop 'em," she moaned as she arched into him.

His prayers were answered. "Yes, ma'am. Hold onto my neck, Cam. Get a good grip."

For once, she obeyed, but the luscious, soft breasts with diamond hard tips mashed against his chest were distracting as hell. Damn. Unzipping jeans had never been this difficult. Finally! He kicked out of his boots and pants, free at last.

"There, that wasn't so hard," she purred, licking his jawline.

Oh, baby, I'm so hard right now I could pound nails. But instead, I'm going to pound you. More words he would never, ever say. Somehow, the wall proved worthy despite the wiggling, writhing, and banging it was taking, as once more, Beck held the lady of all his dreams. His fingers spread over her backside, cupping her where he most needed her to stay.

Breathing hard, he looked down into her exquisitely exotic face. Her big, bright eyes were wide open and sparkling. She was everything. "I love you, Camilla," he told her sincerely. "I love you so much it kills me."

She had the nerve to say, "I know," in that sexy, saucy way she had. But then she sweetened it with, "But I love you more."

As if that were possible.

Ever so gently, he took her then with slow, steady thrusts. Careful that she didn't slip or bang her head. Needing to please her with every beat of his heart. To make her scream in passion and in love.

Nothing had ever felt better than her thighs spread wide and her legs wrapped around him, her heels digging into his ass, and every feminine muscle in her body actively engaged. This was it. Somehow, she was filling him at the same time he was filling her.

It was difficult to hold back now. He'd been celibate too long, and Mother Nature had not endowed her sons with long enough fuses for a once in a lifetime moment like this. Not now. Not with the woman he loved on the verge of their first climax together. His thighs quivered with his impending release. *Please Cam. Relax. Let go before I do. Fly high. H-hurry.*

As if she'd read his mind, Cam arched her back against the wall, bowed her hips forward, and growled, "Beckam. Beck, Beck, Beck. More, damn it, more."

"Go ahead and scream," he ordered as his hands gripped her backside hard and his body filled hers to the hilt. Again and again. "I've got you. You're safe. I'm never letting you go."

Like clockwork, her body clamped down on his, anchoring his manhood in a viselike grip that soothed as much as it ramped up his excitement. As if he needed more stimulation.

"Beck," she whined. "Oh, oh… Beck!" Her long legs locked around him like a beast, a very sexy beast who'd—thank you, Jesus—just come all over him.

And BOOM! One crazy hot detonation zipped up his spine like det cord on fire, ending in a vivid implosion that rocked

Cam's cozy, little house with pure, unadulterated, sweet-smelling sex. With a burst of reds, blues, and bright, white yellows that all but shattered the wall one last, glorious, damned time.

"Yes!" he growled. Fireworks! Damn! That was a first. He'd never come so hard nor so fast, nor been so pleasantly mashed. This wasn't just lovemaking. This was primal claiming. A man and his woman at their carnal best, as pure and as simple as could be. It was love, life, and procreation all rolled into one supreme act.

"More," she ground out, her mouth open on his chin, then his mouth. "I need more, Beck," she breathed into him. "Do it again."

"Yes-s-s-s-s," he hissed, secretly pleased she'd used his name. More, he could do. Whatever she needed or wanted, he would do.

Beckam dove into Cam. Again. He couldn't stop, and she hadn't let go, her fingernails dug into his shoulder muscles like grappling hooks. Her second climax came on just as fast, but stronger than the first. Damn, those feminine muscles had some grip. She was locked on tight. Urging him with every thrust of her hips. Dragging out every last ounce of all he had to give until…

He swallowed hard and filled her again. With life and love and all that he was. Every last bit of his heart and his soul. Another first. Another gift. He'd become her slave, unable to do anything but what she asked. Whatever she needed.

Finally spent and sweating like a beast, Beckam bowed his forehead to the crook of her neck and rested. It was enough to simply breathe in the scent of her hair while he weighed his chances of getting her safely into bed before his legs collapsed.

To draw every scent molecule of her body into his. His combat conditioned legs were shaking like two sticks in the wind, but he didn't care. For once, he had everything he'd ever wanted. In that second, life was perfect. No regrets. No second guesses. Only the woman of his heart at last in his arms, and their bright shining future ahead.

Cam made it better when she tipped her forehead to his chest and kissed him over where his heart still jackhammered. "Took you long enough."

Ah, Cam. Forever pushing his triggers. He had to smile. "What, was I too slow for you, tiger? Or should I say tigress?"

Her head shook against him. "Tiger's good. But I meant it took you long enough to say you loved me. I've been waiting for those words."

Oh, that. He grinned. Her idea of a long time amounted to little more than a month, but Beckam went for honesty instead of correcting her. "I was afraid to love you, Cam. I'm older. I should know better. I didn't want to hurt you."

"Then don't," she growled, still grinding her core against him as aftershocks rippled up her spine and over her shoulders. "Just love me. Is that so hard?"

There was a day he would have said yes, but that day was gone. "As God is my witness, Cam, no. It's not hard loving you, and I don't lie."

"I know that about you," she murmured. "I think that's what I like best. You're a good guy, and you, umm, love me in spite of myself."

"Not true. I love you because of who you are. You're beautiful, but you're also fierce and not afraid to stand up to people. You're resilient and strong, and you're going to marry me someday." *Okay-y-y-y....* That popped out of his big mouth a little unexpectedly. But once it was out there, he meant it. "I mean, if you want to. Cuz that's the only way we could adopt, and I just figured maybe you'd say… yes?"

"Me?" she asked. "You actually want to—?"

"Yes, ma'am," he told her unequivocally, using his best Army captain voice to set her straight. "Look down, Camilla Lopez Brinkman. What do you see?"

Her gaze trailed down his chest to below his belly, to where they were still very much joined. "I see us," she whispered, a tiny bit of wonder in her tone. "Together."

"That's right. Us, Cam. Not just you. Not just me. We made this decision together. I love you, and you love me, and, well, it took me losing you to realize that I don't want to live without you. We can date if you want, and we don't have to get married right away, but…" *Please say something.*

"Yes, but…" *Here it comes.* "I'd like to get to know you better first, Beckam, and I'd like to visit Oklahoma and meet your parents. I want to meet Corky and Carrie. I know they're growing up, but they sound so sweet. Would that be okay?"

Damn, he loved this woman so damned much. He could barely speak. "You bet. They're going to adore you."

He could see his mom and dad fawning over her, showing her the farm, maybe letting her collect eggs or pet the new spring calves. One minute he was on top of the world, the next he had tears in his eyes. "I love you," he breathed, nearly choking on his heart. "So damned much. Marry me, Cam."

She blinked up at him. "I already said yes." But then she kissed him, and everything was good and right again.

Stiffening his back, Beckam cradled her tender body while, somehow, he managed to open her bedroom door. Lucky looked up with wide yellow eyes and hissed at the sight of Beck holding her naked mistress.

"Move it, Mama," Beck told the testy feline while he pushed back the blankets and set Cam on the side of the bed. "Your bed's in the living room, Miss Kitty. Scram."

Cam giggled. She actually, finally, tipped back her pretty head and giggled like a happy little girl.

Beckam knew it then. This was the mission he was meant for. The mission of a lifetime. His lifetime. This woman.

Chapter Forty

It was morning, and Cam was finally head over heels in love. Her body tingled in all the best ways. Beck seemed to like her up-side-down in her bed, his face tucked between her legs while he made her scream. Course, he liked her in the shower and on the edge of the kitchen counter like that, too. And she liked him in return, every chance she could. He had amazing fingers, but that tongue of his sent her to the stars every time.

For now, they were spooning on her couch, her back to his front, like puzzle pieces while they stared out the window at the winter storm that had finally arrived. The District was shut completely down. Schools were closed, and business on the Hill as well. Life slowed to a crawl on snowy days like this. Even FBI Headquarters had issued a warning for its employees not to come in. As if she would have. Uh uh, not with this man in her arms.

Which he was. She couldn't not hold onto the muscular arms wrapped around her. Didn't want to let him go. Wouldn't dream of it. Her backside fit perfectly warm into the cradle of his hips, and he fit inside her like a key fit a lock. A very nice, velvety-smooth key with ridges.

"What are you thinking?" he asked, his voice a deeper timbre since they'd just finished making love under Lucky's cat tree while the nosey cat looked down, her golden eyes barely visible through half-closed lids. Talk about erotic, making love on the carpet with the curtains open. Not the sheers though. Uh uh. They still covered most of the window glass. Cam might be adventurous with Beckam, but she wasn't that crazy.

Although, she was still naked. So was Beck. They'd covered themselves with a blanket from her bed, but yeah. They were both naked, crazy in love, and they knew it.

She bumped her butt into his cock. Poor thing had to be chapped by now, as much as she'd licked it, and liked it, and licked it again. "I was thinking pizza. How about you? Aren't you hungry?"

He should be. They hadn't eaten at all today. Well, except for each other. But food. She needed actual carbs and proteins in her stomach. Soon.

"Hmmm, pizza," he purred. "Pepperoni, bacon, and sausage. A little cheese. Mushrooms-s-s-s..."

Eww, that sounded like a lot of greasy carbs, but, oh well. Cam was open to most things Beck suggested. He'd been right about the cheesecake, hadn't he? "Do you think anyone will deliver today?"

"Only one way to find out. Call them."

She grinned. Like she had anywhere to hide her cell phone to make that call? "You call. I'll wait. Hurry," she teased.

"Okay, I will," he replied easily. But then he bumped her off the couch and onto the floor and had her bent over the coffee table and...

"Beck," she whimpered, her breasts on full display even pressed to the table like they were. "The drapes are open."

"Shush. Just watch the snow," he whispered as his big, manly hands cupped her hips and his thumbs pressed into her backside. "No one can see you. Promise. Besides, they were already open. It's snowing. Isn't it pretty?"

Well, yes. The view was lovely, and no one was out in this weather, no kids playing, either. Just crystal pure silence and a winter wonderland of swirling flakes and frosted streets.

He started to slowly rock into her. How could he do this, make her want him like she did? Make her willing to do anything for him? She couldn't seem to get enough. A car rolled by, instantly sparking a flood between her legs. Wow. Danger did enhance sex.

"See?" he asked, rocking with deeper, harder strokes. "You just watch the scenery while I do all the work and—"

"Yes-s-s-s-s," hissed out as her body clamped around him. She wasn't seeing snow. Only stars. Bright, brilliant stars. "I'm coming," she warned in case he couldn't tell.

His fingers kneaded her backside as, with another mind-blowing thrust, he growled and came with her. His deep throaty growls were sexy all by themselves. Heath had always whimpered like a woman, and for the life of her, Cam couldn't recall what came out of Hector's lying mouth when he'd climaxed. But that was then, and this was Beckam growling in her ear now, urging her through yet another fierce, clenching orgasm. If they kept this up, they'd starve.

"I'll never look at this table again without smiling," she said, her cheek now flat to the tabletop and the wintery scene forgotten.

He'd leaned back, his thighs against her backside but his warm hands still firmly cupped her ass. "Damn, don't look now, but we've got company. Get up."

"We do?" Of course she looked. A car had parked outside, its headlights still on.

"Some lookout you are." He laughed, his fingers tapping a rhythm on her bare butt cheeks. "Didn't you see that car drive up?"

"No, I was kinda busy, you know, coming."

Beck landed a gentle smack to her rump that didn't hurt at all. "Well, whoever that is, he's headed this way. Come on, sweetheart. Up you go. Take the blanket. I'll grab my pants and see what he wants. If it's important, I'll call for you."

She lifted her head and really looked at her soon to be visitor then, "Oh, God. It's him, Beck. It's him! That guy who took pictures of us that day at the train station. Remember?"

Cam didn't wait for an answer. She grabbed the blanket and ran.

Beck opened the front door, his pants back on and zipped, his holster in place as well. Both pistols were loose in their pockets, one in each chamber and ready to draw. He'd left his shirt off on purpose.

"Can I help you?" he asked the short, squat man standing in the foot of snow accumulated on Camilla's one-step front porch. A good easterly wind pushed incoming snow sideways, pelting the side of this stranger's round head.

"Does Ms. Camilla Brinkman live here?" the guy asked, blinking against Mother Nature's onslaught.

"Who wants to know?"

"Oh, yes, excuse me. My mistake." Danny DeVito's clone reached into his inner suit pocket and pulled out a business card. Extending it forward between two fingers, he said, "Noah

Trudeau, private eye extraordinaire at your service. You want somebody found, anybody, even a body, I'm your man." He rattled that off without blinking once, like he was proud of it.

But it sounded like a cheap commercial come-on to Beck. This guy was dressed too well for a private dick. The business suit he had on rivaled any of Alex Stewart's. His shoes were just as slick and polished. Plus, the car parked at the curb was this year's model Lexus.

"What do you want with Mrs. Brinkman?" Beck asked, staring down at the altitude-challenged fellow blinking up at him.

"Would it be too much for you to ask me in? It's cold and windy, or ain't you noticed?"

Crossing his arms over his chest, Beckam blocked the door. "State your business or take a hike. We're busy."

Trudeau, the dick, huffed a cloud of frozen exasperation, cocked his chin, and glared up at Beck. "It's against client privilege to divulge the nature of my business with Ms. Brinkman, but for your information, buddy, she ain't Missus no more. She divorced Heath Brinkman a year and seven days ago, and this is the house she just bought and moved into. It ain't yours, so maybe you're the one who needs to take a hike. You see where I'm going with this? I got a copy of that broad's divorce decree and the title search she paid for this piece of crap lot to prove it. So it ain't none of your business why I'm here, and I'm only asking nicely one more time. Is *Mizz* Brinkman home or not?" He put an extra zip in her ex's last name that time.

Beck palmed the butt of the pistol under his left arm. "Don't threaten me. I don't give a shit what you've got. You're on private property, Bozo, and you're not big enough to get past me until I know precisely who you work for and what your client wants. You're the toad who took pictures of us without our permission. Why would I let a sleaze bag like you near her?"

A car door slammed and Beck looked over the PI's head at the man shuffling his way through the snow. Looked to be six feet tall, with an extra six inches stacked on top of that. Slim. Older. White-blond. No, make that silver-haired. Dressed in a camel trench coat. No hat. No boots. Spit-and-polish dress shoes like Trudeau's. Not particularly athletic. The closer he came, the sicklier and skinnier he looked. His hair wasn't the only thing that was gray.

"What do you want?" Beck asked as he stepped onto the porch and closed Cam's door behind him. She could watch from behind her sheer curtains if she wanted, but these two jerks either anted up right damned now and spilled their real reasons for being here, or they were history. Beck took a twisted pleasure in crowding Trudeau off the step and back into the snow where he could stand with his buddy. Or go home. That'd work too.

"Sorry, Mr. S," Trudeau muttered as he made room on the snowy walk for the client in question. "I know she's here, but this jerk won't let me in to see her."

"No worries, Noah. I'll take it from here." The stranger extended a long arm past Trudeau to Beck. "Pleased to make your acquaintance, Agent Garner. I'm Carlos Salas, anchor reporter for the *New York Minute*, a local broadcasting station. Maybe you've heard of me."

"Nope." Beck shook his head, refusing the handshake. His crossed arms were shields to protect the woman of this keep. A smart man never led with a close, personal handshake. That was asking for trouble. "How do you know my name?"

"Ah, yes. That." Salas cleared his throat. "Mr. Trudeau has been searching for someone for me for a long time. In the course of that search, he also found you and a few of your associates. Facial recognition led me to the gentleman you work for, a Mr. Alex Stewart. From there, it was easily deduced that, either you and Ms. Brinkman worked together or you're her bodyguard. But now that I find you here together, I suspect both. Am I right?"

Trudeau and Salas had done their homework well. But nothing they said or wanted mattered. Salas wasn't getting past Beckam until he knew precisely what these guys wanted from Cam. She'd had enough crap dumped on her this year, and it was only the end of February. No damned more.

But then Salas made it worse. "That's okay. I'm safe. I'm a friend of Alana Escobar, Camilla's mother. At least, I was a long time ago."

The wrong thing to say. Beck shook his head. "Not interested in whatever you're selling. Alana Escobar's dead, so's Luis. Or should I say Molina Escobar? That's all you need to know."

"You're right. I saw on the police blotter how they'd murdered each other. I'm sorry…" He cleared his throat again, "but I've been searching for Camilla for the good part of twenty years, and I'd very much like to meet her. To speak with her. Just once. You see…" He paused, withdrew a white handkerchief from inside his coat, and coughed a bright red blood blossom into the folded cloth. "I'm dying, and I have something to give her before I go, something I believe she would want to have. Just a minute of her time. That's all I'm asking. Then you can throw us out if we don't leave first."

Trudeau hmphed at that, but damn. Salas did look the part of a man who was dying. His skin was that kind of gray.

"Cancer?" Beck asked.

"Brain tumor," Salas admitted evenly, his eyes gone as gray and colorless as the day. "I'll be a screaming idiot before I'm allowed to die. Serves me right."

But Beck was leery of all things Camilla. "You can give me whatever it is."

Wiping his lips one last time, Salas folded his soiled handkerchief, stuffed it inside his coat pocket, and nodded. "Yes, I could. I suppose that's all I deserve." But when he reached into another inner jacket pocket, Beckam's pistol sprang instantly to his hand.

Both Salas' palms came forward in placation. Trudeau's, too. "Now, hold on," he sputtered. "We ain't—"

"It's okay, Noah. I understand. Agent Garner is perfectly right to put Camilla's welfare over ours," Salas murmured, one palm still forward placating Beckam, the other hand withdrawing an old leather wallet from its hiding place inside his coat, slower now. Carefully. "No gun. No knife. See?" he asked Beck as he displayed the tattered wallet high enough for all to see. Maybe even Cam if she were watching. "I don't like weapons, and I don't carry, though I suppose I should. The world has become a cruel place. I should know. But here…"

The wind kicked up a burst of snowflakes as he held the wallet out for Beck to take, blowing his gray hair hard enough that Beck could see the pale gray pallor of his scalp.

"Would you be so kind as to pass this onto Camilla for me? Tell her it's a gift from her sister's father. That's all I came here for. To meet the brave older sister who was just a child herself the last time I saw her, and to finally know what happened to my precious Acindina."

Oh, damn. This was about Acindina. Beck holstered his piece. "Keep it. She'll want to meet you," he told the unhappy gentleman. "But no more cameras and no lies," he said pointedly to Trudeau. "No damned pictures."

"On my honor," Salas replied wearily as he tucked the wallet back where it came from. "Noah and I will be perfect gentlemen. That is, if you can believe anything reporters say these days. It seems most of us have become brain-dead celebrities instead of seekers of factual truth. More's the pity."

"I don't care what you think or what you want." Beck made that clear. "But know this. Cam is the only one I care about. Not you, and not your sidekick. You guys so much as breathe hard on her and I'll kick your asses back to the curb. Got it? You treat her like the lady she is. With respect. She's had enough bullshit in her life."

Carlos Salas nodded glumly. "Yes, I suppose with Alana for a mother, she surely did."

Chapter Forty-One

Cam scrambled into an old pair of designer jeans, a comfy red sweatshirt, and navy-blue, slip-on boat shoes, so she could hurry back to the front window and eavesdrop. She didn't know either of the guys on her porch, and she hadn't heard their side of the conversation. Only Beckam's. When he declared his staunch protection of her, her heart swelled like a balloon too big for her chest. No one had ever proclaimed his intentions to defend her so fiercely. He'd made it clear that she was his one and only priority. She? Luis and Alana's daughter? She could've cried.

The front door cracked open, and there he was, bare-chested and grim, but filling the room with the beastly presence of an apex predator on high alert. His blond hair was dark and wet with snow. He slicked it back. The black leather holster hanging loose over his broad, muscular shoulders made her heart pound like a hundred hummingbirds had gotten trapped in her rib cage. His blue eyes were as laser-deadly as the night he'd gone after Hector.

Beckam was a lethal Boy Scout today. He would brook no deceit or attempts to harm her. Above all, he would keep her safe—like he'd been saying all along. He'd been born to be her protector. She wouldn't have been surprised if dark angry wings unfurled behind him. He was so much that ruthless archangel in that old New York cathedral, sent to do God's will.

Her usual tough-girl core melted into butter. Everything feminine in her leaped into cheerleader mode with a lust-filled, 'Rah! Rah! Rah! Go, Beckam!' And cartwheels! Which was so not like her. The primal aura that predators exhibited while hunting prey had always been such a turn off. But now… With Beckam… Those wide shoulders… The muscles rippling across his chest… The blazing hero shining forth from his deep blue eyes…

The room shrank under the tsunami of alpha hormones he was transmitting. This man filled her simple, little starter home with strength she'd never witnessed before. He'd gone caveman, and… She liked it.

Cam backed her butt into the nearest chair before her knees failed. Thankfully, he'd left his shirt there. Pulling it onto her lap, she twisted it into her hand. Her throat had gone too dry to even say, 'Hey.' She couldn't summon enough saliva to swallow. Tiny prisms sparkled in the corners of her eyes. Was she crying? She might be. All she could see was this man's ferocious love for her, that love held high, like a fiery brand for the world to see. For people to know that he really would kill for her, but that he'd die for her, too. How had she not seen this in him before now? No wonder people loved him. This man really could save the world.

He jerked his head at the two strangers entering her home. "These guys want to talk with you. Camilla Brinkman…." Beck glared at the taller gentleman. "Meet Carlos Salas. Mr. Trudeau? Remember what I told you."

Carlos Salas? Alana's lover? Oh, God.

Both men stepped forward, but the shorter one paused when Mr. Salas extended his hand and said, "Camilla. Finally. I am so very pleased to meet you."

Cam lifted to her feet. She recognized pain when she saw it. This gentleman was tall and elegant, but his eyes were glittery bright and his gray pallor was frightening. She returned a gentle but firm handshake into a palm that was icy cold, instead of warm like Beck's. Alana's lover was not well. "Please, sit down. May I get you anything to drink? Coffee? Tea?"

"Coffee'd sure be nice," Mr. Trudeau said as he took a seat at the end of the couch.

But Mr. Salas had yet to release her fingers, which he now held in both hands. "My God, you look so much like Alana," he whispered with something akin to worship in his pale blue eyes. Like some prince out of a child's fairytale, he bowed his head and placed an icy cold kiss on her knuckles. "Please forgive me, but I've been waiting a long time to meet you."

Cam shivered at his creepy words and his clammy touch. He looked more like a pale vampire than a man. What was wrong with him?

"You said you've been looking for Camilla for twenty years." Beckam interrupted. He was still standing in the center of the room, his arms crossed over that magnificent chest like these two had better understand who was in charge here. "Explain."

"Please. Sit," Cam told Mr. Salas.

With a deep inhale, he let go and sank into the corner of the couch nearest her. "Coffee would be nice," he murmured, "but not today." Reaching into his coat, he tugged out a well-worn leather wallet. "I came here to give you this. It's not much, but I've kept it safe for you."

Cam looked up to Beckam. "Would you mind making coffee for our guests?" she asked as sweetly as she could.

Beck shot her a glare of disbelief, but turned to the kitchen and said, "Sure. Coffee. Coming right up."

Mr. Salas put a stop to that. "No, stay, Agent Garner. We don't need coffee as much as you two need to hear what I have to say."

Like an obedient sentinel, Beck took his place on the armrest at Cam's right while Mr. Salas sat at her left. "You were saying?" she asked as she accepted the wallet.

Pain glimmered out of Mr. Salas' pale blue eyes as he gently reclaimed her hand. "I'm the man who cheated your father out of his wife. Who ultimately cheated you out of a happy, at least happier, childhood. I'm Acindina's father."

"I already know that." The wallet dropped to her knees. "Why are you really here? What do you want from me?"

His throat muscles flexed as if he had trouble swallowing. "You are right to judge me. I was a scoundrel back then, driven by my success. I've never been proud of what happened between me and Alana. But today I came here to finally beg your forgiveness. Please. Open the wallet."

Cam stared at this skeletal man telling her what to do. In her home. The nerve. Her hackles lifted up her back like armor plates on a stegosaurus. She was no longer willing to play hostess to the liar and cheat who'd had an affair with Alana. Was he the only one? Was that the only time she cheated? Cam had no way to ever know, but it wouldn't surprise her. Alana had run a prostitution ring out of that monstrosity of a house in NYC.

"Keep it," she said, tossing what had to be her mother's wallet back at him. "Alana's been dead to me all my life. Why should I care what she left for me now?"

"The wallet's not important. It wasn't hers, it was mine," Mr. Salas explained kindly. "It's what's inside that matters. It was mine. Now I'm passing it onto you."

Passing. Interesting word choice. Almost made it sound like a torch in a college relay race. Or something rare, like a long-lost family jewel. Yet Salas didn't radiate arrogance, hostility, or deceit. Life had taught her early how to detect the slick tenor of hidden lies. To recognize the breathy hesitation that preceded foul play. The quiet timbre in this man's voice held neither.

Beckam's big hand settled warm and light on her shoulder. She fully expected him to tell her what to do like everyone else had. To settle down. To give Mr. Salas a chance. To forgive and forget.

But Beckam didn't. He just sat there and silently supported her, his fingertip tracing tiny circles of encouragement on her shoulder, telling her he was on her side. That whatever she decided, he would agree with. The loneliness she'd expected to rise up like a wave and crash her back into oblivion never materialized. Because she wasn't alone anymore. Better yet, Beckam believed her.

Cam let a deep, satisfying breath fill her lungs, her belly, and her heart. She didn't owe her parents anything. This guy, either.

Mr. Salas nodded like he recognized her upcoming response, then flipped the trifold wallet open and pulled out a single color photo. Of a baby.

"Oh. Is that…?"

He nodded. "Yes, Camilla. This is all I've ever had of Acindina. This one picture. But you were and will always be her older sister…" He choked through a noisy, wet cough, hurriedly pulling a clean white handkerchief out of his pocket to cover his mouth as he handed the photo to Cam.

Oh, my. The little girl in the picture was just months old. Her light brown hair had been curled into a peak and a tiny pink ribbon stuck there. Wrapped in a pink and white striped blanket, she smiled into the camera with a baby's wonder at life.

"You're sick," she told him as blood darkened the cloth.

He nodded. "I will finally get my just reward, yes. But please, do you remember anything of Acindina, anything at all?"

How sad. He'd lost his infant, too. Cam shook her head as she blinked quick tears away, sorry for all the grieving parents with empty arms in the world. Her heart softened for this poor man. "I'm sorry," she told him, leaning closer toward him now. "I never knew until last month that I had a sister, or that my parents fled Honduras. As I understand it, that was when Acindina was lost. My father told me what happened the night they left their country. How she fell overboard and how he tried to save her."

Mr. Salas nodded sadly. "He did. I was there. I saw everything, even the moment he laid that tiny limp body on the deck. I'd just hoped that she'd…" He shook his head. His brows came together in a V. "…lived, once that fishing boat left port. That she might have had the chance to grow up and play with you. That you'd loved her and watched over her like big sisters did and…" An enormous growl choked out of him. "I was such a coward. I chose wrong that night. Instead of hiding in the shadows, I should have insisted Alana let me keep you and Acindina. I could've easily taken you girls out of the country. But Alana was such a shrew."

That Cam understood.

"When I begged her to allow me to take you and Acindina to America, she laughed in my face. You and Acindina could've had good lives. You would've been loved."

Cam pursed her lips into a tight knot, fingering the photo of the baby sister she never knew. Petting her thumb over the sweet innocent face of a cherub. Stroking that photo as if she could bring Acindina back to life. As if she could turn back time. "I would've liked that."

Mr. Salas leaned into her. "Please. I need to do this. Let me…" He choked again. It took him a moment to catch his breath before he said, "I must make this up to you. I know this is crazy, and highly irregular but… Please. May I adopt you?"

Beckam stiffened beside her. He'd been quiet until now, but Cam could tell he had something to say. She settled her palm on his knee, signaling him that she was capable of speaking for herself. "That's highly unlikely. I'm a divorced woman. An adult. I may look young to you, but adoption is for children who have no one. It's for kids who need someone to love them."

Mr. Salas' pale blue eyes brimmed. The crepey skin at his throat quivered. He licked his lips. "But sometimes…" he said with a tremulous ghost of a voice. "It can be a gift for fathers who've lost their only daughters, and for daughters who've lost their baby sisters. It can be a link between what was, and all that could've been. That's all I want with you, Camilla, that precious link with Acindina. I know you don't remember her, but you will always be her older sister, and now that I've met you, I know you would've loved her as I did, with all your heart. At least think about it. Please. I'm dying. I won't be a burden for long."

Ah, this man! He knew precisely how much she'd lost, how much she'd craved someone like Acindina in her life. All those years stolen. All those sisterly hugs and kisses lost for all eternity. How could any legal document repair the tragedy in both their lives? What could she say to ease his suffering?

Overwhelmed with empathy, Cam leaned forward and rested a hand on his wrist. "If you're looking to make me your heir, please don't. I have everything I need right here," she said as she squeezed Beck's knee. "But would you consider moving in with me and spending your last days here? I have the room, and I may be able to coax my boss into granting me leave for however long you decide to stay. I may not have much, but all I have is yours."

Beckam sighed a deep, breathy sigh. She looked over her shoulder at him and he winked like he approved. Which was nice. Knowing he had her six added to her confidence in this impromptu decision.

Mr. Salas stared as if mulling the idea over. But Mr. Trudeau cleared his throat, fidgeted as if he couldn't sit still. "Umm, boss—"

"I'd like that very much," Mr. Salas interrupted, "but I'm already on hospice. That's what Noah's worried about. You see, he's not only my investigator, he's also my friend. I'm afraid I can't be away from my apartment for long." He pushed back his right sleeve, revealing an intravenous catheter taped to the back of his hand. "The devil already owns my body. Soon, he'll own my soul."

"Then I will come to you," Cam told him with conviction. "Beckam will help me."

"Yes, sir, I will," he said, his hand now on top of her hand on his knee.

"You would do that for someone you don't know?" Mr. Salas asked.

"Maybe, maybe not," she said earnestly. "But I'd do that for my little sister, Mr. Salas. And I'll do it for you."

Chapter Forty-Two

Beckam had never been prouder of Cam. She'd changed so much. Every day she spent nursing the father of a sister she'd never even known, only made him prouder. Not once did she complain, even when Carlos' sheets needed changing, or when he cried out at night in pain. Not even when his disease reduced him to a barely breathing corpse. Once she'd settled into his plush apartment across the Potomac River from the Palisades, she'd forgotten her problems and turned into a modern-day Florence Nightingale. And Beckam fell in love with her all over again.

The end came swiftly, seven days after Beckam and she had moved in. By then Libby Houston, Judy Mortimer, and McKenna Villanueva had become part of Cam's team of expert comforters. Carlos had eaten the tiniest bit of rice pudding that morning. He wanted Cam to sit with him awhile, not in the chair, but at his side on the bed.

While Beckam cleared the breakfast trays from his room, they talked. Carlos was still strong enough to hold her hand. Libby, Judy, and McKenna busied themselves tidying the room and preparing to change his bedding. They were all there when his alarms went off. In less than seconds, Carlos slipped away, and Cam was orphaned again.

It was Judy, not Beckam, Cam turned to in that moment. It was Judy who wrapped her strong, resolute arms around the sad angel who'd nursed Carlos until the end. Not that Beckam hadn't been close by the entire time. Only because Libby, McKenna, and Judy knew from experience how hard losing Carlos was for Cam. They'd stepped in and become the sisters Cam never had. Of course, they'd comforted her like a flock of motherly hens.

But now, the ladies had left Cam and Beckam alone to make their calls home and to the mortuary. Cam stood still and silent over Carlos, her jaw hard, her eyes glimmering, and fighting not to cry. She bit her bottom lip, dragged her top teeth over it, and bit it again. Then she repeated the torture as if she needed to feel the sting of pain.

Beckam gave her a minute alone with Carlos, before he stepped wordlessly behind her and enfolded her back against his chest. She came easily, then turned into him and buried her face in his shirt. Still fighting for composure, she swallowed hard enough he could hear her throat muscles work.

"He was more of a father to me than Papa," she whispered. "Do you believe that? I knew more about Carlos in a week than I did my own father in a lifetime."

Well, yeah. Luis had done plenty *to* Cam, but not enough *for* the daughter he'd claimed to love. He'd been too busy being a bigshot drug lord, gunrunner, and cartel wannabe. Which was okay, because in the end, he didn't deserve Cam anyway.

Carlos, on the other hand, had given her a taste of a loving father-and-daughter relationship. When he'd been well enough, he'd regaled her with his travel exploits across the world. Better yet, he'd never missed telling her how much he loved her. How much he cared for her, and how he wished he'd found her sooner. Compared to the worldly things Luis had left Cam, Carlos simply gave her the last days of his life.

And because Cam would've taken care of her baby sister with all the kindness she'd been storing inside her these long, miserable years, she'd contented herself with taking care of her sister's father. Somehow, the tenderness she served Carlos healed the dissonance in her poor fractured soul. It healed her heart. It made her a better person.

So Beckam said nothing. Just stood there with the lady of his dreams wrapped tight inside his arms while she wept. Words were pretty much worthless anyway.

Poor, broken-hearted Noah peered into the room. Come to find out, Carlos owned the elegant suite, and Noah lived there with him. Much like a man-servant, Noah was Carlos's trusted go-to guy. "Ah, guys? The, umm, mortuary people are here to, umm, take him."

Cam shattered then, sobbing while Beckam walked her into the guest room next door, where she and he had stayed these last few days. The mortuary attendants were kind and gentle people. They wouldn't take long removing Carlos Salas. Noah could handle it.

At last, Beckam said what his mom said on the day Desiree Jones and her tiny murdered baby were buried. "I'm so, so sorry, honey. I wish I could make it stop, but this pain you're feeling is what happens when you give a piece of your heart away. That's what we do when we fall in love. The hurting never goes away, but it's the cost of loving someone more than you love yourself. Cry all you want. Those tears are your last gifts to Carlos, and trust me, he knows. His spirit's still here, and he's gathering those tears like diamonds right this second, before he flies home to heaven. You've given him precisely what he needed. You gave him yourself, and I'm so proud of you."

"But I miss him," she cried. "It makes no sense, but he was… he was my father, too. He would've been. He wanted to be."

Beckam nodded. "As odd as it might sound to you, I still miss Desiree Jones, and I miss that baby of hers, too. I never knew either of them, not really. Never even saw the little girl. But I've come to know Desiree through the cute little tykes she left behind. Corky and Carrie would've loved their baby sister, just like you would've loved Acindina if you'd had the chance."

He ran a hand over her hair, loving the warm, silky tresses in his palm almost as much as he loved the fierce heart beating like a drum inside this gentle woman's chest. "Carlos was right. You'll always be Acindina's older sister. I know you're hurting, but Alex has a saying. *'It's not the load that break you down; it's the way you carry it.'* It'll take time, Camilla, but you'll figure out how to handle this, too. You're fierce. You're a fighter. Best of all, you're a winner."

"I'm tired," she whispered. "Let's go home."

"Good idea. I'll get your things."

But Noah was at the door again, this time with a formal envelope in his hand, the expensive type, embossed with fancy legal script on the face of it. His eyes were red, and he looked like he needed a hug. Beck released Cam and waved him to come in.

"So…" Noah murmured awkwardly, swiping the back of his free hand under his nose. "I got something to give you, Miss Camilla."

"How about you settle for a hug instead of whatever it is?" she asked.

Beck's eyes filled at the anguish on this man's face when Noah agreed and politely leaned into Cam's shoulder and patted her back. "You're going to be okay, kid," he told her. "For the rest of your life. No matter what happens with your parents' estates and holdings and all that messed up crap, you're going to be okay."

She tipped back on her heels, looking down on him like she would a little kid, because, well, Noah was a round, but quite short, gentleman's gentleman. "Why would you say such a thing?"

He handed her the envelope. "Because he left all his upcoming royalties to you. From his books and articles, every piece he ever wrote. It'll all be yours now. He asked me to locate your bank account number, so I did. Direct deposit. You don't have to do a thing. Just sit back and remember the good times you had with him. That's what he'd want you to do. Relax. Be happy. That kind of stuff."

"But I didn't want this," she insisted, even as she pressed Carlos's last written wish to her heart. "I didn't help him because I wanted his money. I just wanted him. A father."

Beckam steeled his heart because it was breaking for the little girl who'd only ever wanted an honest-to-god father in her life. She'd never wanted bogus college degrees or doctorates. Not uppity mansions or cartel money, either. Just one man in her life who would stand up for her against Alana's cruelty.

Carlos could've done that back in Honduras, yet he'd failed Camilla and Acindina the night at the dock. Molina had failed her every day since. The greatest difference between the two was that Carlos had searched for Camilla until he found her. Molina had only, ever, used her.

"He knew that," Noah murmured. "But it's his last request, Miss Camilla. I own't know. Maybe you can sign it over to some charity or something."

She handed it back. "Keep it. Please. You take it."

"Good idea," Beckam said. "You might as well. He loved you like a brother."

But Noah shook his head, both his palms forward. "Nah. I'm going to Jersey. Ma's been keeping the porch light on long enough. It's time I went back home."

"But you knew him better than me. Longer," she insisted tearfully. "Please, Noah. I don't want his money. I never did."

"But he loved you more," Noah said simply, his eyes watery. "I'm just some guy, Miss Camilla. But you were his baby girl's big sister, and that makes you family. You meant a lot to Carlos. He told me every single day."

"Oh, God!" she cried as she wrapped Noah back in her arms and wept. "He told me that, too. I don't know what to say. Beck… What do I do?"

Noah relinquished her to Beckam.

"You take a deep breath and you tell Carlos thank you," he told her gently. "He needed to take care of you, sweetheart. Let's set that envelope aside and sleep on it. You don't have to decide anything right now."

Noah cleared his throat. "Ahem. Yeah. Listen. I got a story to tell you. Me and Carlos were talking a couple weeks ago, you know, before he found you and before the pain got too bad. And he told me to tell you, in case he forgot, which he might've. I own't know for sure. You be the judge, but he says to me, he says, 'You know what Camilla's name means in

Arabic?' And heck I don't know one language from another, so I says, 'No, sir. What's it mean?' And he says, 'It means *the perfect one*, Noah. In ancient times, it was the name of a servant girl some idiots gave the goddess Diana. Well, she loved that girl like her own and trained her to be a warrior maiden.' He says to me, 'I'd give everything to live my life over again and save Acindina and Camilla from her mother. I would. Alana was bitterly rotten from the inside out, but her daughter *is* perfect, Noah. Camilla has been my perfect angel since the moment I laid my eyes on her. Just like that ancient warrior maiden, the spirit of a lioness beats in Camilla's heart.'"

By then Noah was wiping his face and all out bawling. Cam too. Beckam was just as hard pressed.

"Funny thing," Noah sputtered, "then he tells me my name means *comfort*. You believe that? But I guess the shoe fits, you know? I would've done anything for Carlos. He was like a big brother to me. And you know, Miss Camilla? That's enough. I'm glad I got to be with him at the end. But I don't need to be rich. I already got a nice car and a house in the 'burbs. I'm doin' okay."

"Yes, you are," Beckam agreed evenly.

"Did he know what Acindina's name means?" Cam needed to know.

A small, sad smile curled the corners of Noah's mouth. "You ain't gonna believe it, but yeah. He knew. That little baby's name means *safe*. She's safe in heaven, and she's with her father now. So, don't be worrying or making yourself sick about her or Carlos no more. They got each other, just like you and Beck got each other. Now git. Go home with your boyfriend and make your own little babies. Live long and prosper and all that good stuff."

And Noah was gone, but he'd left Cam in tears. Little had he known.

She couldn't have kids.

Or could she?

Chapter Forty-Three

As if Cam didn't have enough on her plate, a little boy with coppery red hair met her at her door with a joyful, "They came! Six of them. You got five tiny boys and one little girl!"

"Kittens," Harley explained over the redheaded Mini-Me who could only be his son. Same hazel eyes. Same big smile. But not his father's sandy-brown hair. "They must've come early this morning, because—"

"Cuz last night me and Georgie came with Daddy to check on Lucky, and there weren't no kitties then!"

Cam couldn't help but smile at this precocious little guy. "And who might you be?" she asked as she hung her coat in the closet behind her front door.

"I'm Daddy's helper," the little guy crowed. "Wanna see 'em? They're so-o-o-o-o cute!"

"But what's your name?" Beckam asked as he snagged the easy chair near the picture window. "If you're not Georgie, you must be—"

"I'm Little Alex. The handsome one. Mom says," he said with a cocky head swagger.

Harley rolled his eyes. "What Mom said is you're both handsome, Little A. Come on. Let's get acquainted."

"Where'd Lucky have her babies?" Cam asked as Harley and his son led the way down the hall to her spare bedroom.

"Not sure. Mama cats are pretty good at cleaning up behind them, and I haven't found a trace of anything anywhere. Hope you don't mind, but I brought Sonic over so she could be here when you got home and…" He palmed the door open. "There they are."

Awww… Sweet, boisterous Sonic was curled inside her crate with the door open, her eyes bright with questions and snuggling three of the tiniest balls of orange fluff. Lazy Lucky meowed from the rocking chair with two more tiger-striped kittens, and one black, gold, and orange fluff-ball.

Cam felt like a little girl, ready to jump up and down with excitement. Her fingers were tingling to touch these babies. All of them. "Can I hold one?"

"Sure you can!" Little Alex declared like the man of the house. "Daddy says the more we handle 'em, the friendlier they'll be when it comes time to give 'em away. Unless you wanna sell 'em. I been saving my 'lowance in case you do, cuz…" His cute little shoulders lifted as he looked tentatively up at Harley, those young hazel eyes glimmering with childish hope. "There's always room for one more, right Dad?"

Camilla fell in love with Little A right then and there. This was what she'd wanted, a tiny child to look at her like that. With trust, mischief, and adoration. With the purest love on earth.

Harley rolled his eyes while Beckam angled past Little A and scooped a tiger baby up from Lucky's nest. "He's got you there, Dad." Then to Cam he said, "Will this one do?"

"Oh, yes," she breathed when that tiny new life nestled inside her fingers. But she'd no more than felt the fragile warm fur in her palm when pain flooded her heart like a living beast. Here she was cradling a newborn kitten, but remembering the tiny lives she hadn't been allowed to keep or hug or hold or—anything. Her own child. Her sister. And what about the babies Ember and Rory had lost?

Beckam closed in around her, his hand under her hair at her neck, pulling her into his side and cradling her. "Didn't mean to make you cry."

"It's okay," she blubbered, ashamed she might be frightening Little Alex. "I'm fine. Really. It's just that…"

"Zack," Harley deadpanned.

"What? Zack?" Beckam asked. "Is he here? What's he got to do with anything?"

Harley cleared his throat and did one of those chin-jerk things at Beckam that guys did. "Little A, you and Camilla sit on the floor while you show her the rest of the kitties, okay? I'll be right back."

Well, that was odd, leaving her with the little boy Cam was sure she'd just traumatized. Little Alex didn't seem to mind when his dad closed the door behind him, though. Nonplussed, he extracted another kitten from its purring mother and told Cam, "Sit down on the floor. We gotta be extra careful, so you don't drop 'em."

Obediently, she did.

"He what?" Now Beck had heard everything.

Harley dragged a hand over his messy hair. "Yeah, I know it sounds like a cockamamie fib, but it's true. Zack's got some kind of gift, is all. He just takes one look at a woman, and he knows. He was right with Kelsey, and he was right again with

Jake's wife. Doesn't matter how far along they are, either. Lacy wasn't even a month when he told her. I'm telling you, Beck. Camilla is pregnant. Call Zack. He'll agree with me. Do it now. That women in there needs to know."

"But how'd you know?"

"Just had a feeling. She's all kinds of sad right now, but there's something different in her eyes."

Beck scrubbed his fist over his chin. She couldn't be pregnant. As much as he wouldn't mind if she were, it just couldn't be. He and Cam had made love for the first time only eight days ago. Yes, it only took once, but...

"I've got to admit, I had a funny feeling, too," he murmured. "Back at Salas' apartment. Just after he died. You know Cam's mother did some dirty things to her daughter, but mostly she lied. And well... Cam's been acting different these days. She cries at the darnedest things. Did you notice she stopped swearing?"

Harley's head bobbed. "She's easier to talk with, too. She's finally asking questions like she really wants to learn."

"She does, but nothing Alana ever did was because she cared anything about Cam. I mean, damn. Why tell your traumatized teenage daughter right after you forced her to have an abortion that she could never have babies?"

Harley blew out a soft whistle. "What a bitch."

"Exactly." Beck nodded, faced with telling Cam about yet another betrayal in her life. *If* Harley was right and Zack really could tell on sight whether women were pregnant or not. Harley seemed like he had that same knack.

"I was going to ask McKenna to talk to her," Beck admitted. "You know, just ask Cam if she'd mind taking a few tests to be sure she was physically okay after the last couple months. Maybe sneak in a pregnancy test. Her life's all but turned to crap. Then Hector… But now…"

He looked at the closed door, behind which six kittens were either breaking or healing Cam's heart. Asking McKenna anything behind Cam's back just seemed wrong. "I don't want to get her hopes up."

"But she needs to know," Harley insisted. "Especially about this. That little mama in there needs a baby in her arms. Can't you see?"

Beck nodded. Yes, he saw Cam every waking moment. In his dreams. In his arms. In his bed. And from the very start, he'd pictured her with a baby. But hurting her so soon after she'd lost Carlos seemed cruel. Unless Harley was right. She'd be ecstatic if she were pregnant, and what would it hurt? Cam already knew Alana had been a walking, talking nightmare. What was one more lie?

"Okay. Yeah, call Zack. But let's not tell her why he suddenly drops by. If he sees what you think you're seeing, then maybe…" But no. Beck just couldn't do that to Cam. "Belay that. She needs medical tests and facts first, not me sneaking behind her back. I won't betray her, too."

"Then get her to make an appointment with a lady doctor," Harley insisted. "Because I'm telling you, Judy cried at the drop of… Hell, at the drop of any and everything back then. A diaper commercial couldn't come on TV without her bawling. She was especially sensitive around other women's babies. Even the puppies in the barn turned her to mush. I used to think it was me, that she couldn't stand the sight of me. But thank God, for once I didn't do anything wrong. It was just—her." He ran his hand back over his head. "Women's hormones go ape-shit crazy when they're pregnant, man. You've got to handle this right, or you know."

Beck shook his head. As the new guy on The TEAM, what else was he supposed to know? "I know what?"

"That you aren't ever getting any again if you piss her off."

Oh, that. Beckam almost laughed at Harley's deadpan expression. Except going without *that* wasn't funny. There was nothing Beck loved more than being deep inside Cam. And talking about *that* with Harley put Beck in a class above most other males on the planet. Almost made him feel like he was already married to the fierce warrior in the other room.

"Trust me," Harley breathed. "You never want to make your lady mad."

Which meant Harley had gone without *that* once or twice. Beckam could see it happening. Judy was a force to be reckoned with. As was Cam.

"Call Zack," he told Harley quietly. "Get him over here while I go sit with Cam and broach the possibility of her getting an appointment. She likes McKenna and Libby. Maybe they know a good gynecologist who can check for scars or damage or… something." Or whatever that witch of a mother paid to have done to Cam.

"Will do." Harley palmed his cell out of his pants pocket and thumb-dialed a number.

Gingerly, Beck reopened the spare bedroom door. Cam looked happy enough sitting there on the floor, but he could see rain clouds in her pretty eyes. She was drained and needed a good long bath, followed by twenty-four hours of shuteye. But maybe she needed the possibility of motherhood more.

Folding his long legs, he sat beside her, his palms on his knees. "Lucky did good. Six little ones and they've all got all their parts."

"They do. I checked," Cam purred at the tiny guy or gal snugged up against her like a human child that needed to burp. "Twenty toes, one tail, two ears, and two eyes each. Not a single troll in the litter."

How did women just know how to be moms? Must be instinct. Either they had it, or, in Alana's case, they didn't.

"But I've been wondering…" Beck let that hang for a second, needing her to buy into the idea of one more lie before Zack Lennox showed up. "Did you always believe everything Alana told you?"

She snorted. "That's a stupid question. You know better."

"Yeah, you know better," Little A mimicked from where he'd spread out on his back with sleeping kittens snuggled under his neck. "All us guys should know better, huh, Uncle Beck?"

Beck grinned at the words Judy had obviously told Harley more than once. "We do, Little A, but sometimes we forget what we know," he told Cam, needing her to understand how much he loved her. "About procedures that are too painful to think about when they're happening to us. About the repercussions of those procedures. You know? What if one was true…?" *Meaning the abortion.* "…but the other wasn't?" *Meaning the error her attending physician had allegedly made which had resulted in Cam being sterile.*

And there he stopped. Beck didn't want to spell it out with Little A nearby.

Cam's eyes filled. "But I'd have a baby if she'd lied."

"Or you'd still be able to," he corrected gently. "Think about it, sweetheart. Brinkman was as big a liar as Alana What if he was just another one of her flunkies? What if Heath knew you weren't sterile? What if he used some kind of protection but never told you?"

"I love babies," Little A crooned softly to his armful of felines. "I'm just as lucky as Lucky, cuz Miss Camilla's got one kitty, and Sonic's got one, but I got all the others."

Her eyes went wide. "You think that's why he cheated on me?" she whispered, glancing over at Little A.

Beck shook his head. He had yet to confront Heath Brinkman over what he'd done to Cam. But that day would come. Brinkman could plan on it. "Honestly? I don't think he cared from the start. He used you. Just like Rojas."

Beckam didn't break eye contact with his lady when her glare zeroed down on him. Anger flashed in those melted chocolates, then pain, the last thing he wanted. The air vibrated between them, but then she asked, "How do you do that, honey?"

Honey. She called me honey. Another first. He closed the distance between them, needing her inside his arms. "Do what? Love you with my whole heart?" he asked as he tipped her into his side.

"Well, yes, that too. But how do you always look at me like I'm not who I am? Like I'm special?"

"Aw, Cam, because you are. But if you don't know that by now, that's on me," he whispered into her ear. "I haven't told you enough. I'll do better, I promise, at making you smile and giving you everything you need. But right now, let's make sure Alana didn't set you up for failure before we give up on the miracle you need. Let's spit in Alana's evil eye. Let's show that witch, once and for all, she's always been wrong about you."

"I don't know…" Cam dragged that last word into a tormented whine. "I almost don't know if I care."

"Yes, sweetheart, oh yes, you do. You're stronger than Alana, and you know it. Ask McKenna or Libby to recommend a good doctor, a real doctor, this time. I'll go with you. Because the truth is…" He cupped her tearful face with both hands and kissed her forehead. "I'll go anywhere with you, Camilla Garner." At last! A name that fit her. "To doctor's appointments or to the stars, to the moon and back. Just ask. We're a team, remember? We work together. Always."

A sigh shuddered over her shoulders.

"But in the meantime…" Beckam picked one of the kittens from Little A's stomach and gave Camilla another handful, so she wouldn't pick up on how his eyes were watering. "You've got to come up with six names for these critters."

"We did!" Little A piped up, totally oblivious to the adult drama around him. "This one's Goldie. That one's Rainbow. There's Lightning McQueen and Bambi and Thumper and…"

"And I think someone watches too much Disney," Cam whispered slyly, her head now tucked under Beck's chin and over his heart, where she belonged.

"And Ringo!"

Damned if Zack didn't poke his big bald head around the corner then. That was fast. "Hey, Little A!" he called out. Camilla got a polite gentlemanly nod from the big guy, then a quick visual once over. Beckam got a genuinely warm smile.

"Miss Camilla. Good to see you again. Six kittens, huh?" Damn, were his dark-brown eyes sparkling? They were!

"Hi, Zack," she answered. "Yes, Lucky's a good mom. Six furry babies, safe and sound."

"Well, congrats. Mind if I bring the girls over later to see them?"

"Sure. I'd love that. Please do."

Beck smiled at the genuine hospitality Cam exuded now that she was in charge of her own life. She was going to make it.

"Hey, Beck?" Zack asked, his bulky body blocking the doorway, one hand hooked on the overhead jamb. "You know that technical question you asked the other day?"

Beckam frowned over Cam's head to signal Zack to keep his big mouth shut. Just in case he really could tell on sight whether she was pregnant or not. "Yeah? What do you think?"

"I don't think. I know." Zack grinned. His teeth were extra white against the rich mocha-latte colored skin of his smile. If that wasn't answer enough, he flashed a hearty thumbs-up. "Harley's right. Better get ready."

"Get ready for what, Uncle Beck?" curious Little A asked when Zack ducked out of view.

"Nothing, A," Beck said, despite the way his face cracked into a smile. Despite how badly he wanted to call his folks and crow like a Neanderthal that Cam and he were going to have a baby. He was going to be a father. Him! Finally!

Better yet, he couldn't wait to tell Cam.

Chapter Forty-Four

Nine months later – To the day…

An Army Ranger's life in service to his country was hard. He could spend days, maybe weeks, hunting his target. Waiting for that designated tango to show. In burning sand. In bitter cold. In jungle rot so deep he might as well have been lying in a cesspool. But knowing one, well-placed round could save American lives, had always made the misery worth it.

Beckam had only ever counted his wins. The loss of any enemy combatant never registered on the internal Richter scale whereby he measured his worth. They were nothing but varmints as far as he was concerned, and he'd shot plenty varmints back on his dad's farm. Rabid dogs after the sheep. Wolves out to steal a newborn calf from its unwitting heifer mother. Foxes and thieving coyotes that dined on brainless stray chickens. Snakes that struck like lightning and poisoned the innocent as easily as the foolish.

But not all days were hard. Some were actually quite spectacular. Like today.

"She's beautiful," blue-eyed Carolyn Garner gushed over the head of her sleeping granddaughter. "She's got her mama's pretty brown eyes."

Yes, Santana Marie definitely had Camilla's dark eyes. So far. Some of the ladies from the office insisted they might change color, that you couldn't be sure just because they were obviously chocolate brown at birth. They could still turn out to be blue.

Beckam knew better. This beautiful baby girl was all Cam, from the tips of her perfect tiny pink toes to the fragrant riot of dark brown curls at the crown of her precious head. Santana Marie even had Cam's lovely coloring. But when she smiled in her sleep… When she burped and passed gas like a boy… He counted himself one damned lucky man.

Why Santana? Blame that on Cam. She'd chosen the Spanish name that meant *holy* for her daughter. Which pretty much summed up the changes in Cam as well. Still engrossed in prayerful study of all the world's religions, she'd wavered between embracing Christianity and Buddhism. Until Beck introduced her to Senior Agent David Tao, who explained patiently how Buddhism wasn't so much an organized religion as a way of life. Like yoga, anyone could do it.

Then enter Kelsey Stewart one bright, spring, Sunday morning and her simple question whether Cam wanted to go to church with her or not. It was no big deal. Kelsey was one of those rare, guileless women. She just wanted to be friends. Yet something happened inside Kelsey's ordinary chapel that day.

Beck didn't know precisely what because he hadn't been there. But he now found himself deep inside the elusive TEAM circle, invited to dinners at the Stewarts with other agents and their wives, and privy to confidential scuttlebutt—all because of his wife's devotion to Mrs. Stewart. Whether she knew it or not, Camilla was now working herself back onto The TEAM. Beck had overheard plenty of negotiations between his boss and FBI Director Chase. It was definitely in the works.

Why Marie? Because of Cam's focus on a teenage mother who'd lived more than two thousand years ago in a land called Galilee. Only Mary's Son had lived long enough to preach about sparrows, and that simple parable resonated with Cam. Once she'd learned that His eye was on the sparrows of the world, somehow, she knew He'd loved, maybe even more than she had, the baby Alana had murdered. Cam knew how much He still loved Acindina and Beau's sister, AJ; Kelsey Stewart's murdered little boys, too. Which truth somehow healed a little more of the brokenness inside Cam. She'd found peace—in a sparrow. Beckam didn't care which church she finally decided on. He only knew that when his wife was happy, so was he.

Things between him and Cam could not be better. Once her parents were both in the ground and she'd divested herself of her father's ill-gotten gains, she'd settled down. Harley turned out to be the recipient of some of the funds the federal government didn't take. Which, unfortunately for Alex, had Harley thinking of expanding his veterinarian business/kennel into a full-time venture. America had an insatiable need for properly trained K-9 officers, service and rescue dogs. Harley bred, trained, and loved some of the best. He hadn't given Alex notice yet, but rumors were flying.

Cute Sonic became the steadfast companion Cam needed throughout her pregnancy. Crazy dog was just like a kid, couldn't let Cam go anywhere, even to the bathroom, alone. Lucky still perched high on her cat tree, watching the world below while her last *neutered* tiger kitten stalked Sonic's fluffy tail.

Harley became one of Cam's dearest friends. He and Judy, Little A and Georgie, were prone to show up unannounced. Beau and McKenna visited often with their daughter and son,

Essie and Diego. Ember, Rory, and Tyler were around so often they might as well move in next door.

It was satisfying to watch the difference love made in a person's life. Camilla Garner was living proof of that. She now had one helluva rock-solid family at her back.

Turned out Alana was the most hateful, lying witch Beck had ever run across. She'd set out to intentionally injure her daughter in any and every way possible. Instead of a surgical mishap during the abortion, she'd paid that lying physician to insert some kind of intrauterine device, an IUD, into Cam while she was still knocked out.

Normally, those devices came with a thread in case the woman in question changed her mind and no longer wanted birth control. She could safely remove the device in the privacy of her home. But that female doctor had clipped the thread where no one could reach it. Since Cam had no motherly intervention, she never suspected she'd been on involuntary birth control for four years. Four long years! Which could've resulted in serious infection, or death, damn Alana—the bitch!—to the deepest pits of hell. If she wasn't there already.

Yes, Beckam swore like a sailor now, but not in front of his wife, and only because he had everything to lose. Or when thoughts of how Alana had hurt her only living child crossed his mind. *How could any woman be so mean?*

But because that IUD had been way past its expiration date, and because Beck had loved Camilla vigorously, to the depths of his good-old-boy-from-Oklahoma soul, he'd gotten her good and pregnant somewhere around the first or second time they'd made love. And he couldn't wait until he could do it again.

"You'll stay?" Cam asked his mom from her hospital bedside.

Their first meeting since Santana's birth yesterday afternoon had been downright chilly. Cam had been tired, uptight, and unwilling to share her newborn daughter with the woman she'd only met once. But when Carolyn rushed Cam and just hefted her and that little baby girl into her arms and cried, well. Cam cried, too. A lot. Guess being hugged by a real mom was the powerful medicine she'd needed all along. Kind of like a tsunami of all the things she'd missed growing up. Unconditional love. A real, no kidding family, with a good mom and dad who'd fallen in love with her on sight. Simple things like that.

Beckam's mom was another one of those powerful forces in nature. She either loved you on the spot and proved it by never losing touch with you, or she hated your guts and wasn't afraid to prove that, either. She'd stood up to a few bullies and gossips back in Horse Hollow in her time. But mostly, she got along with everyone. Including her once-upon-a-time prickly daughter-in-law who now called her Mom.

They'd met before the wedding in Oklahoma, but Cam hadn't jelled with Carolyn back then. She'd been uptight and uncomfortable the entire time. Almost made Beckam wish they'd eloped. She hadn't relaxed until their honeymoon. Of course, by then they both knew she was pregnant, and he'd chalked it up to hormones. But now… Look at her glow.

"I'll stay as long as you need me," Carolyn replied easily. "I'm so proud of you, Camilla. Ten minutes in hard labor? You were made to be a mom, little girl."

Which brought instant tears to Cam's eyes. She turned into a puddle every time his mom called her that. Didn't hurt that Mom also never failed to pronounce her name correctly.

"I'm not going back to work," she told Carolyn, as if that decision were only between the two ladies in the room. Not Beckam. Which would've been a nice touch, her asking her husband how he felt, instead of her telling his mom first. Yet at the same time, he felt honored that Cam trusted Carolyn. She needed a mom, and he didn't mind sharing.

"You do whatever you want," he told the new Mrs. Beckam Garner, you know, in case he had a say in her decision, too. His mom just smiled knowingly.

"And I want twelve kids," Cam blurted.

That was unexpected. "A dozen?" he asked, scraping his thumbnail under his chin. "I don't know. Only need eleven for a decent football team. Five for basketball. Why twelve?"

They'd moved out of her crowded little starter home and into a bigger rambler on a thickly wooded acre situated nearer Harley and Judy's ranch. If Ross and Carolyn wanted to stay for months, they had the room. They could accommodate twelve children, too.

"Because…" Cam breathed. "I want an even number."

She wasn't making sense. Had to be all those pesky hormones, but it didn't matter. Beck loved his lady. So fiercely damaged, but ready to heal and live and finally become the woman she was meant to be. Not a pawn. Not a cast-off child, but his woman and the best mother their baby girl could ask for.

"How about you two decide how many kids you want while us old farts go to dinner?" Ross asked from the doorway. "You ready, Caro? I'm starved."

Carolyn beamed down at her granddaughter. "If I have to, but I'll be back."

Poor tenderhearted Cam's eyes watered when Carolyn placed that newborn baby girl back into her arms. "I love you," she bleated. "Please, umm, Mom. Hurry back."

Which elicited another motherly hug, and damn it. Now Beck's eyes were watering. So were his dad's. And he'd thought childbirth was hard. This sweet little girl was breaking his heart all over again. Turns out watching someone struggling to put themselves back together was just as tough as childbirth. But Cam was doing it. Little by little, and step by step.

"And I adore you, sweetheart," Carolyn told her daughter-in-law. "Now you rest and let Beckam wait on you hand and foot, you hear?"

"Yes," Cam said quickly, again talking only to his mom, her head nodding like an obedient daughter. "I will."

Beck leaned back into his chair, content to be invisible if it helped his wife feel more at home. This was what family was about. Them. Not him.

Ross sank into the chair beside him. "You done good, son. Proud of you."

"Thanks, Dad, but I just cut the cord. She did all the hard work."

"Not true. That little girl's gonna wrap you around her finger, and if you're smart, you'll let her."

"Which little girl? Cam? That's already done."

Ross turned his shoulders to Beck, his wintery blue eyes full of sparkle again. "I mean both of them. It's easier to make a baby than it is to raise one, but that woman you married?

She's the real deal. You done good. Yessirree, you done real good. Whatcha doing for Thanksgiving?"

Beck shrugged. He was officially on two months paid maternity leave. Alex's rule. "Taking my family home. Getting up at night. Walking my little girl. Loving her mom. Learning to be a good dad like you, I guess."

"That'll do it." Ross clapped a hand to Beck's shoulder. "Two months off, huh? Then why don't you kids come back to Oklahoma before the snow sets in? Let us get to know Camilla better. Let her get to know us. The kids are dying to see you two again. Heck, bring that fellow Beau and his family, too. We've got the bunkhouse."

Cam's sudden friendship with Beau Villanueva was another surprise Beckam hadn't seen coming. Come to find out, they'd endured similar life experiences as kids, and those childhood heartaches had turned them into the unlikeliest brother and sister. Go figure. That big bear of a guy now owned two of Lucky's kittens, one tiger-striped and the black, gold, and orange fluff-ball. Big, bad, burly Beau had a soft spot for cats and babies. Who knew?

Until now, Beck hadn't thought of going home for Thanksgiving and Christmas. He hadn't wanted to rush his new wife because of her pregnancy. It had been one helluva year for her, and she'd been emotional and prone to cry at the drop of, well, anything. He'd understood. Camilla had a lifetime of heartbreak to heal from. Like Beau, she suffered post-traumatic stress that most people would never understand. But also like him, she had a good counselor guiding her through it. And she had Beckam, her most faithful protector. Didn't matter how old he was. He adored her, damn it, and love really did cure everything. Every. Thing. Even the difference in their ages.

He straightened in his chair and asked his wife, "Want to visit Horse Hollow for the next two months? Get to know Corky and Carrie better? Cut down our own Christmas tree?" *Maybe make another baby...*

Her eyes lit up. "Can Joslyn and Georgia come, too?"

"Well, sure."

Then Beck had two happy, bawling women on his hands. He shot his dad a grin. "I'm pretty sure that's a yes."

Epilogue

Alex took a knee at the solid steel door, his heart a proverbial rock. Steady. True. His fingers just as reliable. He honored the men and women on his TEAM, almost as much he honored his wife and daughter. Every day. Every night. Even now, on Christmas Eve. Tucker Chase, the official holder of the FBI warrant, stood at his six. From boots to gloves, both were dressed in black. But Tuck was on a mission to bring Heath Brinkman in. Alex had something else in mind.

Tonight's operation marked yet another joint FBI/TEAM effort, and, hopefully, the end of Brinkman's carefree, perverted ways. In the months ahead, the blind, fickle gods of Justice would decide his ultimate fate. But for this pivotal moment in time and eternity, Alex intended Heath to pay for what he'd done to Camilla. No one ever—ever—harmed one of his men or women.

Tucker finally seemed to grasp that Alex held a grudge. That payment for crimes against women, children, animals, and elderly, required finesse and precision timing. At long last, Tuck also understood that Camilla Garner was most definitely returning to TEAM HQ, one way or the other. If she wanted to. Cam certainly wasn't psychic, but she had proven herself worthy of junior agent status, damn it. She was TEAM worthy, through and through. Alex still needed to reach out to her and extend the offer. Seemed like a good Christmas present—for him. He just hoped she'd feel the same way.

Christmas shoppers were home for the night, those young fathers probably assembling last minute trikes or doll houses. Stores were closed, thank God. Ember had already disabled Mr. Brinkman's silent alarm, while her husband Rory stood silent watch a half-block down. Like a stalwart ghost in the streetlight, he'd taken up post there in case the odd coincidence happened. Like the midnight arrival of one of Brinkman's sleazy friends, or perhaps his pedophile father. It was known to happen.

Click. The last tumbler fell into place, nudged expertly by the tiny pick in Alex's gloved hand.

"He's gonna shit bricks," Tucker commented dryly.

As he should, Alex thought as he straightened to his feet. No abuser should feel safe on this hallowed eve. "You got a bead on him yet?"

"You bet. Lower level. In the far east corner of this joint."

It figured.

"Finally know where Molina Escobar got the pistol he killed his wife with," Tucker murmured.

Alex froze, wondering why that detail mattered now. Here. When they were supposed to be breaking in covertly.

Tucker kept yakking. "FBI Special Agent Holloway was there that morning. We had Escobar under surveillance. Guess Hector Rojas thought he could waltz into a gun-free zone if it meant killing Alana. He supplied the pistol that ended Alana."

That actually made sense, Alana, gunned down with a weapon provided by the young man she'd used, her boy-toy. The madam of 5th Avenue, NYC, ended by one of her high-priced prostitutes. There was a certain karma to her death.

Kelsey would've called it poetic justice. Made Alex almost—almost—want to shake Rojas's hand. Only would've been better if Cam had shot the witch.

But tonight, Camilla, Beckam, and their baby were safely tucked away in Horse Hollow, Oklahoma, where they'd spent Thanksgiving and now Christmas with Beck's family. Beck needed a clean alibi for what was about to go down, and Cam needed freedom from having to watch over her shoulder the rest of her life. Heath, on the other hand, needed a lesson in the laws of physics. For every action, there was a reaction. A just reward. Tonight was simply family business. If Alex had his way, Brinkman would pay.

This same night, Senior Agents Mark Houston and Harley Mortimer, along with two of Tucker's most trusted special agents, Ky Winchester and Tate Higgins, were confronting Penn and Spence Brinkman in their lush digs along the Potomac.

The barest hint of a smile quirked the corners of Alex's stern mouth. Yes, Tucker seemed distracted, but Alex was proud that Ky and Tate had once worked for The TEAM. But when it came time to stand up the FBI's first psychic team, it seemed only fair to offer Ky and Tate the career choice of a lifetime. Either continue in the work they already knew, or expand those latent mental skills they'd both denied they owned, but had in aces.

Both men were not only doing better now, but they'd matured into amazingly intuitive investigators. They were crime solvers, profilers, and two of the best former snipers Alex had ever worked with. They made him proud.

"He's not alone," Tucker shared.

Works for me, Alex thought. He knew how to clean house. The more friends with Brinkman, the merrier. "On three," he advised under his breath. "Two. Three."

The door slipped open as easily as if the wind had merely come calling and found its way inside. Which, in a way, it had. Black operators. Ghosts. Wind. One was pretty much the same as the next. Silent. Covert.

"Nice digs." Tucker seemed nervous tonight. Too talkative. *Wonder why.* He'd done this hundreds of times before. Every former Navy SEAL had. Where were his legendary nerves of steel? His big, bad, brash ego? Alex didn't care.

The sight he walked into took his breath, and not in a good way. Heath had decorated the front entry of his palatial home in leather and rosewood, heavy curtains and plush carpeting. Acoustic sound absorbing panels. Metal window blinds. Cork ceiling-tiles. No doubt double-paned windows and extra-thick walls, too. Alex recognized the room for what it was. Brinkman was into soundproofing. He needed to dampen whatever noise came from inside his house. Like screams for help. Or worse.

Alex's earpiece clicked quietly. Just once. A signal from Mark or Harley that the meeting with Brinkman's parents had turned up nothing.

Tucker growled softly. "Damn it, Spence isn't home tonight. Penn, either."

Which meant Ky and Tate had psychically contacted Tuck with an actual Sitrep. The news sickened Alex. "Then they're here. Are they with their son?"

"Yup. Downstairs. A three-fer?" Disgust tinged Tuck's question.

Which made Alex want to puke. In the course of investigating the Brinkman dynasty, Over the past few months, Tuck's elite team of psychic investigators had uncovered evidence of money laundering, gun running, and drugs. Then they hit a disgusting motherlode. Spence owned an island in the western Caribbean, and he liked Spanish girls, the younger the better. Which was why he'd pressured his son into an arranged marriage. Heath had never wanted Camilla. But Spence did.

Call it whatever. In Alex's book, rape in any form and at any age, was torture, pure and simple. Given Camilla's tender years when her parents had all but sold her to the Brinkmans in exchange for political influence, Alex was sure the sweet young thing cornered in Heath's web of lies tonight, needed an assist.

He led the way. Swiftly. Surely. Past open doorways and into a banquet hall with a wide, curved, gilded staircase to the right. Interestingly, the door to more utilitarian stairs leading down to the lower level were located just behind that eye-catching staircase. Glittering chandelier lighting invited the way to the second level, but Alex's gut knew better. Dungeons were always in basements.

Out of the blue, Tucker asked, "You know how your bag lady friend knew Max Bird?" Then answered his untimely question with, "They worked that high-profile case against Navy Seal, Chief Petty Officer Walker Judge, remember? The guy wanted for killing his CO? They're the ones who nailed him to the wall."

Only Alex had never believed the prosecution in that trail. There'd been too many coincidences. Too much ambiguity. Too much jury-rigging, witness tampering, and leaks to the press. But of course, the Navy left their sailor high and dry, refusing to back Walker's version of the story. In effect, they'd disavowed him. When Judge escaped custody not three days after his sentencing, the case grew even murkier. Something stunk, but now was not the Goddamned time!

"I'm going down," Alex growled at Tucker to shut him up, his boots already on the thickly carpeted stair treads, his footfalls muted per Heath's fiendishly clever design.

Tuck didn't argue, just followed like he worked for Alex. Which was odd. Why was he distracted tonight? Talking too much? Again, Alex didn't have time to care. The basement stairs ended at a closed door. But soft feminine, muffled moaning had just come from beyond that door. Then the snap of a whip. Another cry. Another snap.

"Can you kill the lights with your mind?" he asked his partner in crime tersely.

Instantly, the place went dark.

"Anything else?" Tucker asked without a twinge of arrogance. That's what was missing—his ego. He wasn't himself tonight, not by a longshot.

Alex put his head down, gritted his teeth, and asked, "Can you do this mission or not?"

"I'm here, aren't I?"

"No, you're not. Your mind's somewhere else. What the hell's wrong with you?"

"Geez, Alex. Back off, will you? I'm just—"

A woman's frantic scream sounded from beyond the door, and Alex forgot Tuck and his problems. First things first. Whoever she was, Alex meant to save her. Tuck could take care of himself.

Pressing one palm to the door, Alex turned the knob and let himself into a nightmare. Heath was into soundproofing all right. And now Alex knew why. One giant, round, and very red bed stood in the center of the scarlet room. Red sheets. Red pillows. Red carpet on the floor, walls, and ceiling. Hell, everything was red. Including the back and buttocks of the slender naked woman tied face down on the bed, writhing under the sting of the riding crop in Penn Brinkman's right hand.

Dressed in thigh-high leather boots, a leather bustier, leather boy shorts, and black stockings, Penn was a picture of a dominatrix from Hell. The tools of her trade hung from hooks lining the walls. Whips. Paddles. Bamboo sticks. Other things sadists used on willing and unwilling partners. The woman was grinning, damn her.

Spence wasn't wearing anything at the moment. Neither was Heath. That old saying the apple doesn't fall far from the tree? God's honest truth.

It took Alex a split second to take in the scene; another to wish he hadn't. This room wasn't anything new, but the prevailing genre that had breathed new life into another wave of violence against women, sickened him. His sweet wife had survived brutality by her first husband's hand. It hadn't been fun or romantic for Kelsey, and it hadn't been right. Not a day went by that Alex didn't wish he could dig Nick's dead body back up and kill him again. How could anyone find flogging, whipping, and depraved cruelty, erotic or alluring?

While Penn's crop landed on the back of the girl's thighs, Spence's flabby backside obscured another tiny, whimpering thing on her knees in front of him. Two more young women were naked and bound like spread-eagle sacrifices on the beds to the left. With Heath. But none of these women seemed willing, or on the verge of doing anything but screaming for help.

Because he seemed shell-shocked—or something, damn it—Alex signaled Tucker to wake up, do his job, and take Spence and Penn down.

"FBI!" Tuck bellowed as if he hadn't faltered. "On the floor! All of you! Well, except you girls."

One of the women lifted her head and shrieked, "Please! Help me! Help us all!"

Enough said. Alex headed for Heath, who'd just now wiped a hand across his sweaty face and looked up. Guess beating women was hard work for a jerk like him.

"On your knees," Alex snapped, but he thought, *Run, you sick bastard. Better yet, pull a gun on me. Make. My. Day.*

That would make revenge easier and sweeter. But it was not meant to be. Predictably, Heath lifted both hands high over his entitled, pretentious head and sank to his knees. Just like his cowardly folks had done. Just like most bullies did when caught.

There would be no revenge tonight, damn it. Alex rolled his shoulder to get the tension headache blossoming up the back of his neck to back off before he did something rash, like dispense the kind of justice Heath wouldn't get anywhere else.

"Face down," he ordered. Maybe not having to look at the smirk on Richie Rich's arrogant face would keep Alex from kicking it.

While Tucker read the Brinkmans their rights, Heath complied like a smirky wuss. *Damn it.*

The sight of his pasty-white, naked backside should've been enough for Alex. Heath was finally exposed. He would pay—somewhat.

Besides, Alex was here on official business. He couldn't, wouldn't dishonor Tucker or the Bureau, certainly not The TEAM, by taking the law into his own hands. But for the love of God, it was hard not bludgeoning this wimp, his deviant father and mother into oblivion. Instead, Alex flex-cuffed Brinkman Junior with tender care rather than hang him by his testicles to the rafters.

Once Tucker called for EMTs and backup, Alex reached out to his men over his two-way. "Spence and Penn Brinkman are contained. We're mopping up. You can go home now."

"No, Boss. We're upstairs. Coming your way," Harley answered.

"Do not come down here," Alex ordered as he covered the woman nearest him with a discarded blanket, then pulled a blade up from his boot and cut her wrists and ankles free. "I'll come to you."

There was no need to humiliate these women further. All were stripped and bleeding. Hurt, not aroused, Goddamn it. All were also dark-haired, young Hispanics, possibly Latinos. Alex knew the difference. Just because a woman spoke Spanish did not make her Latino. People from South America were Latinos. Not like the distinction mattered now.

The one nearest rubbed her raw wrists, the blanket pulled tightly around her. "Thank you," she said quietly.

"How long have you been here?" he asked.

She lifted her chin, tears dripping down her embarrassed cheeks. "A week, I think. Please, sir. Can I go h-h-home now? It'll be Christmas soon. I think."

"She's lying," Heath called out. "She asked for it!"

Alex stared at the man on his belly, his naked ass still exposed, begging for a boot. "Shut. Up."

"I know who you are. You're Alex Stewart. You own that piece of shit bodyguard business. You can't do this! My lawyer's on his way," he threatened.

"Good. You'll need one," Alex said simply as he took a knee at the side of the bed the woman was now sitting up on. He wasn't close enough to touch her, just close enough to prove that he cared, and that he would defend her. That she was safe from the Brinkmans. But he couldn't promise her anything.

"You can go home soon," he offered. He wanted to know how she'd come to America or if she were American born, but those questions were not his to ask. And what did they matter? Only that Brinkman Senior might also be into the sex-trade, smuggling underage girls into the country. Prostituting them. God, what an ass.

So Alex kept a close eye on the Brinkmans, while he and Tucker listened to one rant after another. How Spence could and would ruin them both. How Alex and Tucker would pay. How the Brinkmans had rights!

Until Tucker bellowed. "Will you shut the fuck up? What part of FBI warrant do you not understand, Spencer Brinkman? You see this body cam I'm wearing? Do you honestly think you can bully, blackmail, or threaten a federal agent after what I've got you and your family doing on film?"

That shut old man Brinkman up.

But it seemed to affect his wife differently. "He made me do it," she murmured, squirming on her belly next to her husband. "Spence is a twisted sicko. You've got to believe me."

Alex turned away then. Spence was sick alright, but Alex had seen the thrill written on her face when she'd used that crop. Mrs. Brinkman was no prize.

It took a while for the EMTs to arrive. By the time Alex followed Tucker out of the basement, it was well after midnight. Penn, Spence, and their spawn from Hell, were headed to FBI Headquarters in downtown DC. The women were being cared for while EMTs transported them to local ERs.

Alex needed to get home before Lexie, his little girl, woke up. He was Santa after all.

"Hey, Boss," Mark called out from where he and Harley waited in the entry. "Good job."

For some reason Alex couldn't explain, tonight's bust didn't feel like a good job. Heath was still alive. The Brinkmans were only on their way to jail. Not prison. Surely not the electric chair. Given their wealth, and connection with the liberal media, they could still go free. It was entirely possible.

But those frightened, damaged women now on their way to the hospital to undergo the indignity of rape kits and intimate questioning? They'd never be free, would they? And that injustice gnawed at Alex.

Tucker's worried voice drifted from where he stood with his back to the room, a finger in one ear, his handset at the other, and his back stiff. Too stiff. Still distracted. "You okay, honey? Now? Oh, God, but… yeah, okay then, Mel. Tell Deuce to hang tight. I'm on my way. Him first, then you. Got it. I love you, babe. Please… please wait for me. At least try."

Mel, aka Melissa McCormack Chase, was Tucker's sweet wife and a good friend of Alex's. Deuce was Tuck's son by his first marriage and his old man's clone. But Alex caught the worry of a husband for his wife in Tuck's tone.

Ky's whispered explanation solved the mystery. "Melissa's been in the hospital most of today."

Tate, another surly man who'd changed after he'd married, grinned. "Boss is gonna have a Christmas baby."

That explained Tuck's lack of attention to detail. But finally. There was something to smile about. Alex beelined to the former SEAL who'd lately become one helluva friend. "Congratulations!"

"Thanks. It's going to be a little girl, but—"

"Then why the hell are you here?" Alex barked. "You should be with Mel."

"I know but…" Tuck blew out a huff. "I'm here."

"Is she having trouble?" Harley asked.

Tuck shook his head. "No, Mel's a rock, but damn it. I'm not there." The angst in his tone rang out like a bell.

"We can fix that, Boss. Where are we going? Which hospital?" Ky asked, his bright blue eyes alive with understanding. "I've got a siren, and I know how to use it."

"How about we clear the way, you guys follow?" Mark, the father of five girls, asked. "Come on, Harley. You haven't had a speeding ticket in that new red Jeep yet, have you?"

"Me?" Harley guffawed. "I've never had a speeding ticket."

Mark's brows arched. "And you drive like Alex!"

"Thanks, guys." Tucker's voice cracked. "Shit. You make it sound like we're all one big team."

Alex slung an elbow around the FBI director's neck. "We're better than a team, Chase. We're family."

Wasn't that the truth?

The End

Thank you for reading Beckam's story!

You are the key to this book's success

Please tell other readers why you liked BECKAM by leaving an honest review at the retail site where you purchased it.

Recommend it to your friends. Lend it. Most of all, enjoy it!

Other Irish Winters' best-selling books/series

In the Company of Snipers

Alex
Mark
Zack
Harley
Connor
Rory
Taylor
Gabe
Maverick
Cassidy
Adam
Lee
Ky
Hunter
Eric
Jake
Seth
Beau
Renner

Coming soon:
Walker's story

Deuces Wild
King of Hearts
Joker Joker
One-Eyed Jack
Ace

Hearts and Ashes
Smoke
Ash

SOBs Novels
Angel
Assassin

Coming soon:
Julio's story

The best way to keep up with my new releases, giveaways, and actionable intel is to sign up for my spam-free newsletter at IrishWinters.com.

Preview of CONNOR

In the Company of Snipers, #5

"Damn it."

USMC Sergeant Isabella Ramos cursed as her ammo clip hit the dirt on the other side of the wall. Sergeant Connor Maher could not help but notice. He didn't write the rules of nature. A real man's always gonna look, and this particular gal's derrière, albeit camouflaged in the uniform of the day and plenty of dust, made for a choice view. What red-blooded, all-American male wouldn't?

One minute she was seated all nice and comfortable on that three-foot wall. The next, she was bent over it, damn near ass over teakettles with her boots, legs and butt on display. He glanced away, not wanting to be caught looking—at least not by her.

He and his buddy, Jamie, were part of the United States military response to the increased violence of the Iraqi insurgency in Fallujah. Both short-timers and counting the days, this was their final tour together unless Jamie got another brilliant idea to re-up. With home only a couple months away, Connor was antsy. All he had to do was stay alive. In Iraq. During one of the hottest USMC campaigns of the war. Stolen commercial breaks like this show with Ramos made the grind endurable.

She'd gotten the short end of the stick when their commanding officer decided someone ought to show the two newly arrived non-commissioned officers the lay of the land, and voilà. Just like that, they got a snappy tour of U.S. Camp Baharia, and along with it, a floorshow that couldn't be beat.

The good thing about the predominantly USMC camp was the large clear water lake in the center of it. The bad thing was it was still in Iraq. The once-upon-a-time desert resort town was now filled with hard-core military men and women who sometimes forgot how to behave. Like Lance Corporal Jamie Ramos, who by sheer coincidence shared the sergeant's last name, but obviously, not her dedication to the Corps.

Already passed over once for promotion, Jamie was headed for trouble with his CO. He didn't seem to have a problem with his rifle qualification or combat fitness, but his true talents lay in another direction—entertainment. Jamie was a tease to the mathematical power of a gazillion, and that innate need for attention would land him in the brig one of these days.

"You know you want to." He elbowed Connor again, urging him to do the unthinkable. "Just one little smack. It's easy. I've done it a million times. No one else will see you. Just walk over, lay one on her ass and run like hell. She's short. She'll never catch you. Go on. Do it."

"Shut up," Connor muttered out of the corner of his mouth, glancing again at the ass in question and doubting the 'I've done it a million times' line. "You know better than to treat women like that. Knock it off."

"What's she gonna do? You're both the same rank," Jamie persisted. "It'll be fun."

"Cut the crap. She's a lady."

"No, she ain't. She's a jarhead just like us. She's GI. Loosen up, Maher. Walk on the wild side for once in your geeky life."

Connor glanced at the ass in question again. Damn. It was spank-a-licious and hard to keep his eyes off of. This dark-haired and olive-skinned beauty had potential in his book. Lots of potential. He didn't want Jamie's crazy antics to blow his chances before he knew if he had any.

Raised in a house filled with six younger brothers and no sisters, women still perplexed Connor. Sometimes they loved a guy who only two seconds earlier they'd hated. He couldn't keep up. Besides, his mother had taught him early what Jamie's education must have missed. A real man does not disrespect women, even when they cussed like sailors. He'd grown to appreciate Bridgette Maher's wise sayings more now that he was out of her house. *Treat a woman like a lady and she'll never turn into a nag.*

With a twinkle in his eye, Jamie edged closer to the irritated sergeant's backside, a big cheesy smirk on his trouble-making face. She tipped farther over the wall, the toes of her boots nearly off the ground and still cussing a blue streak. No way was Connor getting close to that action. He shook his head and mouthed a definite, *No. Don't do it.*

Jamie's eyes brightened with, *Are you daring me, man?*

Connor didn't know whether to nod or shake his head. Either way spelled trouble.

Jamie's left eyebrow spiked into an incredibly wicked, *Here goes.* His arm lifted higher.

Connor shook his head, disgusted at himself for letting Jamie take a prank this far. He stepped forward to halt the wise guy before things got more out of hand. Retrieving the clip in question would solve the Sergeant's problem and torpedo Jamie's stand-up comedy once and for all.

"Excuse me, ma'am—"

Jamie's perfectly white teeth flashed a big shitty grin. His flattened hand lifted over the rump in question.

Apparently, Ramos hadn't heard Connor yet, leaning over the wall like she was. He was nearly behind her. "Ma'am, let me get that for—"

The sergeant tipped one booted foot to the sky and exclaimed, "Finally. Got the damned thing."

SMACK!

Crap. Sergeant Ramos came off that wall so fast she landed in Connor's arms. The deadly scopes of a deadly sniper skewered her one-man viewing audience.

Oh, sweet Mother Mary and Joseph.

He gulped and caught a peripheral of his trouble-making buddy. Jamie was on his knees. At the end of wall. Out of sight. Clear out of sight.

Ramos could only see—him.

Those sizzling brown windows to a she-devil's soul were pointed straight up at—him.

Crap. I'll be busted back to private first class.

He should've pushed off. He should've been a gentleman and apologized for the inappropriate contact. He should've done anything, but no. Generations of hopeless romantics from the Emerald Isle had led him to this pivotal moment. His fingers refused to unclench from her biceps. Looking down into two dark pools of what felt like the strongest, bitterest, sweetest coffee, Connor was doing good just to keep breathing.

Hot damn. If I'm dying, it's gonna hurt, but I'm going to heaven.

Equal rank or not, something about this diminutive spitfire had stomped the hell out of his ego from the first moment he'd seen her. With the meanest reputation in the squad, she could teach the drill sergeant's *How to Be an SOB* class all by herself. Ramos was a cherry bomb with a short fuse and right now, he was cannon fodder. Nothing but.

"You want to die right here and now, Boston?" she hissed, her shoulders rolling along with her swagger. How could a gal with such sexy brown eyes be so mean and sound so tough? His eyes refused to move off of her, even though her top lip was curled over a wicked Devil Dog bite.

And here he was holding her. Not just holding her, but chest to breast kind of holding her, and either she didn't mind the contact or he was in for one helluva lesson in smack down, hand-to-hand combat. The woman was pure muscle, her biceps as hard as her eyes. Contempt glittered there, and just maybe something else. Mischief?

"Ahh, no, sir – I mean—no, ma'am—I mean—" He dropped his hands and took a full step back to get out of her personal space, stuttering like an idiot.

Jamie was still crouched with his hand clamped over his big fat mouth he was laughing so hard. Right then and there, Connor should've handed his buddy over, but real men don't do that either.

Ramos stomped right back under Connor's chin, her eyes dark and deadly, full of the promise of nothing but pain. Maybe death. "You think hitting another soldier's ass is funny, do you?"

"No, ma'am, I do not."

God, she was so damned gorgeous. Yeah, she radiated a certain amount of radioactive hostility, and he was pretty sure he glowed already, but damn. What a package. His nose filled with the lovely whiff of roses and incense. How fitting. The sweetness of flowers mingled with the unmistakable hint of burning ash. He'd been an altar boy. He ought to know.

That drab green T-shirt peeking up from her uniform didn't conceal the rounded landscape beneath from a man of his height, either. Six-foot-three should be the one doing the intimidating instead of peering down a woman's shirt like he was. The thought of peeling her out of those desert cammies tweaked what was left of his common sense. He wanted to touch. Hell, he wanted to fondle, pet, and a whole lot more.

Should I pour on the Maher charm?

Sizzling death glowered up at him, not even blinking once and full on daring him to keep breathing.

Ah, maybe not.

The verbal assault commenced. "I'm gonna make you wish you died during boot camp, you pig-faced, camel-lipped, piece of..."

On and on she went. He took it like a man. Almost. His jaw kept moving, but sound had ceased coming out. Article 128 of the United States Code of Military Justice flashed through his blood-deprived brain. *Question: Is a slap on the butt considered sexual battery?*

Answer: Damn straight. Don't touch. Don't tell. And all that stuff.

Jamie howled, at last overcome by his own hysterics.

Ramos shot a scorching look over her shoulder. "You!"

The instant she looked way, the magic faded. Connor was half-inclined to cup her chin and direct her gaze back to him. Just him. Not Jamie. But he was afraid to touch her. She might be too hot for him to handle.

"Why don't you grow up?" Kicking a boot scrape of sand in Jamie's face, she stalked off, which only made him laugh harder. The dumb ass looked like he was having a heart attack the way his face was all screwed up.

Oddly, Connor felt a chill when Sergeant Ramos left. A chill in Iraq? How'd that work? He watched her walk away, her dark brown ponytail twitching side to side in time with her butt, both sassy as hell. Taking one step forward to follow and apologize, he came to his senses and stopped short. Not now. Let her cool off. Mad women were unpredictable.

"You shoulda... You shoulda...." Still laughing his guts out, tears streamed over Jamie's cheeks. "I mean it. You shoulda seen the look on your face!"

"You could get me court-martialed," Connor ground out, even as his gaze returned to the command tent where Ramos had gone. He wasn't so much scared as interested. Maybe it was all those blond brothers he'd grown up with, but dark-eyed girls always caught his attention. Hers seemed darker than most, full of sparks, promise, and a whopping dose of cayenne. The moment he'd seen her, he knew. They would spend time together.

"Oh, hell." Jamie pulled himself onto the wall, dusting his pants off. "Don't worry. She won't do anything. You're safe."

"Yeah, right." Connor huffed out an aggravated sigh. "You ever heard of friendly fire? She was an MP sniper, jerk-off. Now I gotta watch my back the rest of my rotation."

Jamie guffawed through another laughing attack. Connor had half a mind to kick his friend's ass if it would douse the hysterics, but he doubted it would. Jamie was a fun-loving, risk-taking Hispanic who could charm the socks off most ladies. Didn't seem to have any effect on the sergeant, though.

Finally, he turned semi-serious. "Don't worry. I've got your six. You know that, Bro."

"Bullshit, you do," Connor shot back at him. "You've got nothing."

"No, really. I've seen how you look at her." Jamie almost sounded sincere. "Listen, Connor. Remember how I told you I'd never seen her before in my life, how lots of us Hispanics got the same last names only it don't mean we're related? You know, like Martinez, Gonzales, Sanchez, Moreno, Garcia?"

"So what?" Connor could feel it coming. The joke wasn't over yet.

Jamie winked. "I lied. That's Izza. My sister."

About the Author

Irish Winters

...is a best-selling author of military romance who, when she isn't writing, dabbles in poetry, grandchildren, and rarely—as in extremely rarely—the kitchen. More prone to be outdoors than in, she grew up the quintessential tomboy on a dairy farm in rural Wisconsin, spent her teenage years in the Pacific Northwest, but calls the Wasatch Mountains of Northern Utah, home. For now. She believes in making every day count for something, and follows the wise admonition of her mother to, "Look out the window and see something!"

Connect with Irish online:
On Facebook: https:/www.facebook.com/author.irishwinters
On Twitter: https://twitter.com/irishwinters1
Or at http://www. IrishWinters.com

www.ingramcontent.com/pod-product-compliance
Lightning Source LLC
Chambersburg PA
CBHW060940190726
48286CB00005B/1359